NanoMorphosis

MARLA L. ANDERSON

Published by

Wolfheart Press
Alpine, CA 91901

www.wolfheartpress.com

TO MY SONS,

TRAVIS AND RYAN,

WHO ALWAYS INSPIRE ME

PART 1

Chapter 1

Earth Year 2183, Houston, North Americas

The Houston Olympic Dome enclosed four levels of rotating grandstands. Above the stands, giant holoscreens provided three-dimensional close-ups of the on-field action. Built to withstand the worst inclement weather, the stadium kept the 80,000 spectators filling its seats and the playing field below dry even while an immense tropical storm raged outside—a common occurrence in the gulf region these days.

Usually, people came here to watch tech-enhanced football players go head-to-head, but today an austere stage sat in centerfield, with a dozen chairs facing a podium. This was the Annual Commemoration Ceremony; the first Daniel Walker had ever attended. It had taken fifteen years to get him here, a wait that had fueled the public's hunger to hear from him to a near frantic state. Every time the camera sent a live image of Daniel to the holoscreens, the crowd grew louder. Hundreds, if not thousands, pointed, whistled or waved at him.

Sitting onstage, Daniel stared at his knees, struggling to breathe under the weight of all that attention. He rubbed his damp palms across his slacks, trying to remember his opening line.

In the seat beside him, his uncle, Dr. McCormack, whispered, "Nervous?"

Daniel shrugged, avoiding eye contact.

As usual, his uncle wore a rumpled plaid jacket with mismatched pants. Daniel remembered asking him years ago if the

International Medical Research Center appreciated having their chief of surgery look like he pulled his clothes out of a dumpster. The snarky remark earned him a lecture on the perils of judging others by appearance, including quotes by Thomas Paine and other philosophers on the subject of superficiality. Daniel learned to curb his tongue after that.

"You've drawn quite a crowd," McCormack said, looking up and around.

Daniel followed his gaze. The holoscreens zoomed in on spectators in the stands and VIP's on the stage. When he saw his own face displayed again, he grimaced, then forced himself to smile and wave at the crowd. Nearly everyone wore scarlet and gold, the official ceremonial colors. People tooted golden horns and waved cold-fire flags alive with harmless red flames. Daniel had chosen a dark suit, white shirt, no tie. The only red and gold on him was the commemorative pin on his lapel.

"Must be billions more watching at home—all dying to hear what 'little Danny' is finally going to say."

"It's not all about me," Daniel countered. He looked back down at his knees and blew out a breath to unwind the knot in his stomach.

McCormack snorted. "You just keep telling yourself that."

"Are you trying to rattle me?"

"No, I—course not. I'm just trying to understand why you signed up for this."

"Maybe it's time to put an end to all this 'poor little Danny' crap."

"Okay, but why now after all these years? It's not like anything's changed, has it?" McCormack raised an eyebrow, waiting.

Daniel squirmed. He needed to give him an answer but wasn't ready to reveal the whole truth of it just yet. "I wanted to impress someone."

McCormack choked back a laugh. "So this is about a girl?"

"No," Daniel snapped. "Don't be stupid. It's about finally getting an interstellar ship."

McCormack's amusement vanished. "What? How?"

Daniel sighed. "I didn't want to say anything yet. Nothing's for certain, but I'm on the short list for ACES' new director."

"ACES? *The* ACES—the Allied Coalition for Exploration of Space? Good Lord, Danny. You really think you're ready for that?"

"Yes. Absolutely." Daniel felt his ire rise. "And those therapy sessions you keep ordering for me need to stop."

McCormack glowered and looked away.

Seeing the worry lines in his uncle's face, Daniel softened his tone. "Look, I know you just want to help, but try to remember that I spent two years in the military, running through battle simulations."

"Yes, I know but—"

"And earned four advanced degrees in the sciences after that. Think I've proven myself."

McCormack sighed deeply and nodded. He covered the back of Daniel's hand with his weathered one. "You're right. You're a grown man. A very successful one and you don't need me meddling in your life." He paused to smile and look around. "You're also right that this isn't all about you. It's about them." He pointed to the crowd. "What they need to hear."

Daniel glanced up, feeling more pressure than ever.

"I may not say it often, but your parents would be proud of you—as proud as I am."

Daniel's throat tightened. "Thanks." His vocal cords constricted further as he noted the deep lines in his uncle's face—evidence of old age creeping up on the only living person he still thought of as family. Ironic, since they weren't related. This generous, kind-hearted man had been his father's best friend. Daniel knew something more needed to be said, but just then a hand landed on his shoulder.

Senator Nelson Bromberg posed for the floating cameras aimed in their direction.

Daniel wanted to punch him.

"Looking forward to your speech, my boy. Remember, keep it short and sweet."

Daniel watched Bromberg walk away to take a seat between a stately blonde and a severe-looking man in a gray suit.

"Asshole," Daniel said under his breath.

"Speaking of . . . do you recognize the one he's sitting with?" McCormack asked, keeping his voice low.

"Holly LaCroix?" The therapy sessions his uncle sent to him usually included her old news report.

"No, not her—him."

Daniel stared at the profile of the man conversing with Bromberg—long thin nose, pointed chin—no one he recognized. He shook his head.

"The New York Archbishop for the Unified Church of Earth. Word is he's in line to replace the UCE's Supreme Father."

Daniel narrowed his eyes. "What's he doing here?"

Before McCormack could answer, the holoscreens darkened to black and the crowd hushed. Daniel braced himself for what was coming next—one of the many reasons he avoided these ceremonies. In bright orange letters 'BREAKING NEWS!' zipped across the circled screens, then were replaced by a neatly coiffed blonde, news anchor Holly LaCroix. Some questioned the propriety of playing the original broadcast of the attack at these ceremonies, but those in charge insisted on refreshing people's memories. Stoking continued fear of an alien invasion had proved the most effective tool ever for distracting the masses from the shenanigans of the governing class.

Aloft, Holly's multiple images spoke in unison. "We interrupt this program to bring you breaking news. We have just learned that the science team on Enyo may have been attacked while broadcasting their dedication ceremony for the installation of Luna University's new stationary deep-space telescope. We do not know yet who is responsible but are working to obtain a recording of the live broadcast and will share that with you shortly."

"The Cannon Long View telescope," she explained during the interim, "was named after Annie Jump Cannon, a pioneering woman astronomer who—we have it?" Holly glanced to the side. "All right, here is that broadcast now. Keep in mind there is a ten-hour delay. These images were recorded by an automated video robot, which I'm told is still transmitting. Along with you, I will be seeing this video for the first time, but I will offer what commentary I can."

Daniel didn't need her commentary. His memory was as real and unforgiving as the cold-steel floor under his feet.

The screen image split, the left side showing Holly, the right, Enyo's black star-filled sky, where a tall man in a spacesuit stood on a dark rocky surface. Behind him, a gigantic mirrored dish tilted on a reticulated robotic platform that seemed to grow from the bare rock. Off in the distance stood their tall egg-shaped vessel.

"You're looking at the team's leader, Dr. Benjamin Walker, standing in front of the Cannon telescope. His team consists of nine other scientists including his wife, Charlotte Walker. I'm told their ten-year-old son, Daniel, also accompanied the team." Holly gestured at the image. "You can see their transport in the background."

The camera swiveled to show space-suited people gathered together, all of them rendered anonymous by their helmets, and similar height until a much shorter version squeezed to the front. Wearing an oversized spacesuit, the smaller figure moved awkwardly until another reached out to steady him.

"That must be little Danny there." Holly smiled.

Hearing his boyhood nickname tightened Daniel's stomach.

The camera refocused on his father, Dr. Walker, who began to deliver a well-rehearsed speech—stirring words about the value of space exploration for mankind's future—but then a rumbling sound drowned him out and the recorded image shook violently. Dr. Walker turned aside, and the confused voices of those with him rose in the background. He waved for silence. "Everyone wait here, until I find out what it is." The camera remained focused on the telescope as Walker strode out of view. Moments later, a man screamed, and the murmuring voices cried out in alarm. The camera jostled and went sideways, showing the legs of fleeing scientists. A pair of oversized, wedge-shaped boots much too large for any human flashed by in pursuit.

Holly gasped. "What was that?"

Amid the screams, Daniel's young voice called for help.

The automated camera righted itself, then focused on a creature striding away on two backward-bending legs. The thing had a large head, and a pair of overlong arms, one of which carried a suited human less than a third its size. The creature's head swiveled ninety degrees, revealing a protruding profile that curved out and downward like the beak of a predatory bird.

Holly, shocked into silence now, offered no comment.

The transmission showed more giant beaked creatures moving in the distance, their legs bending in reverse like stalking ostriches.

Wide-eyed Holly turned aside to speak to someone off-camera. "Has—has any of this been verified?" Shaking her head, she looked back and continued her commentary. "It's hard to see what exactly is going on from this distance, but it appears that these—these creatures are piling things into a net of some sort."

Not things . . . people! Daniel thought angrily.

In the transmission, a boy's voice called out, "Mom! Dad!"

"That must be poor little Danny," Holly said.

The transmission zoomed in on the source of the sound, focusing on a small figure caught in the grip of one of the creatures.

"But we didn't do anything," the boy yelled, and took a swing at his captor.

As Daniel watched, hate and fury rose in his chest like bile.

More beaked creatures approached. The one holding the boy lifted him high for inspection. He thrashed wildly, fell loose from the creature's grip and scrambled away. The creature went after him, but the boy threw himself inside one of the science team's storage tubes and closed the lid. The creature bent over the long tube, spun and rolled it about in an apparent attempt to find an opening.

Breathe, Daniel reminded himself. He never thought he would need to use his survival training, not back then in that tube, and certainly not here now, fifteen years later.

The right side of the screens went black.

"It appears we've lost the feed." Holly turned back to her audience. "These are disturbing images, but keep in mind, none of this has been confirmed and it's quite possible someone is playing an elaborate hoax. You history buffs may recall the first, back in the 1940's, when a radio show created widespread panic. Pure fiction, and this may be as well." She paused and smiled. "Giant bird-headed aliens, a child in danger—does seem a bit melodramatic."

Idiot! Daniel shook his head, still annoyed by her old comment.

It turned out the news station cut the feed to spare viewers the worst of it, images of bloody human body parts. Danny had also been spared seeing that part of the carnage, as he was already trapped in a pitch-dark cargo tube. He remembered screaming as he tumbled about. When the movement finally stopped, his helmet light was broken, and he was left in absolute dark and silence to imagine what terrible things the monsters would do once they got the tube open.

The video feed returned, showing an empty alien landscape, the creatures gone from view. Only the closed storage tube remained visible. Daniel stared at it, claustrophobic fear closing in on him. He struggled against it, but when the image shuddered and the stadium sound system rumbled, shaking his heart as it had then, he was back in that tube.

***

It's like before, when the monster's ship landed. They must be taking off.

Emotions rushed through him—first relief—*They're not going to eat me*—then terror—*They're leaving me here!*

He pushed hard on the tube's lid, unable to budge it. He felt for a release, a button, a lever, something, but these things were never meant to be opened from the inside. He knew the combination for the tube's exterior panel, but that did him little good now. The silence in his helmet turned to an empty roar.

Wait, maybe my headset's broken, like the helmet light. That's why I can't hear anyone. Dad and the others must be out there, waiting until it's safe.

Forgetting for a moment that there was no air for sound to travel through, he pounded on the inner wall inches above his head, his only thought to alert Dad to his plight.

He'll come get me and everything will be okay, like before, when we were all together, happy and excited.

He remembered his father's proud words, his mother's big smile; then his mind switched to screams, to her dark hair floating above a crushed helmet and monsters making a pile of limp human bodies, one onto another.

No one's coming. They're dead. They're all dead.

***

"No!" Daniel said aloud.

McCormack grabbed Daniel's clenched fist. "You're okay, Danny."

Daniel flattened his hand and nodded, hoping no one else had heard him. "Sorry."

The feed on the screens above were dead silent now, but the image of the closed storage tube remained. The stadium crowd watched in reverent silence as a full eleven seconds ticked off on the display—as per tradition—one to mark each day poor little Danny spent trapped and alone inside that tube.

As the seconds counted down, the silence grew into that same empty roar Daniel experienced in that tube, pulling him into the past. He fought to remain grounded in the present. It didn't work.

**

Panicked, Danny clawed at the tube's round metal walls, screaming for help until his throat burned and he gasped for breath. Time passed immeasurably in the dark silence as he went in and out of consciousness, each time waking to the same nightmare. The vicious cycle of screaming and fainting continued until finally, in an act of pure self-preservation, his mind tricked him.

"Danny!" his father's disembodied voice called out.

He stopped crying.

"Come on, use your head."

He took a long slow breath.

"You know the drill—follow protocol, plan for the worst."

"Right," he answered, and took stock of his situation. He already knew what crowded around him—hand-sized canisters of condensed oxygen. He counted and did the math. Twenty-eight days' worth— *probably longer since I'm small and can't do anything but lie here.* He made emergency adjustments to his suit controls, moving them to their lowest settings.

"Fully charged, an ECS can recycle fluids and keep you alive for a week, even longer with minimal activity," he recited from memory, or did his father remind him?

"True, but I shouldn't need that long. Lunar City, from where we launched, is a ten-day journey, but the Kuiper Belt outposts are only two."

"You can do two, easy."

"Sure. Easy."

Time ticked by achingly slow. The blackness took on a living quality, undulating, thickening, as if alive. His skin itched beyond his reach. Despite knowing it impossible, he pictured bugs crawling inside his suit—

***

"Ugh!" Daniel shuddered.

"You okay?" McCormack asked.

Daniel snapped back to the ceremony in progress and nodded. On the holoscreens above, Holly LaCroix talked about messages coming in from concerned viewers.

The locked cargo tube abandoned on the surface of Enyo still remained visible to her right.

Dammit!

Daniel closed his eyes against the image but couldn't stop falling into the past again.

***

No one to talk to, nothing to see, nothing to do. During his training, his parents had warned him isolation was the biggest enemy. In the void, people go crazy imagining things—like bugs in your suit.

"Keep yourself mentally occupied. Practice your math, tell yourself stories, make plans, lots of plans," his Dad's voice told him.

"Okay," he replied, lost in the hallucination, and started to think about plans, his and theirs, especially his parents' search for an Earth twin—his anger growing because they'd never see it, never know if they'd been right.

"It's not fair!" he yelled into the dark. That's when it occurred to him that 'crazy' might also mean talking to dead people. "No, you can't be dead. You have to finish what you started."

"I'm sorry, Danny; we can't, but you can," his mother answered. "Picture what an interstellar ship like that would be like. Make it real in your mind."

The more he visualized an interstellar ship, the more real it became. His tiny prison vanished as he walked through the corridors of a huge multi-leveled vessel. Rooms and equipment surrounded him. He felt the floors under his feet, the walls with his hands, and smelled cool clean air pumping through the vents. He saw powerful fusion reactors, talked to scientists on board, and marched beside soldiers armed with terrifying weapons ready to lay waste to the monsters. He imagined traveling to a new world and taking people there to build settlements. While a part of him knew this imagined future existed only in his mind, the waking dream felt more solid than anything truly happening to him and he became convinced his life depended on making it so.

And if those bug-eyed, beak-faced monsters get in my way . . .

***

"I'll kill them all."

"Pardon?" McCormack inquired beside him.

Daniel startled back to the present, fearing he'd spoken the old vow aloud, hoping he hadn't. "Nothing. Never mind."

Maybe crazy is reliving the same thing over and over.

His uncle's eyebrows formed a deep 'V' above the bridge of his nose.

Daniel looked away and focused on the holoscreens again, where Holly LaCroix stared into the camera, skepticism showing in her forced neutral expression.

"Those of you calling for a rescue mission to Enyo, please keep in mind this attack is as yet unconfirmed. As we all know, images can be edited, even created from whole cloth. Our experts are analyzing the recording and we will bring you updates as they—"

She paused in mid-breath to touch her ear, and her eyes widened.

"We have verification. I—I'm being told all communication has been lost with our manned outposts in the Kuiper Belt including Pluto, Eris and Sedna. UN Armed Forces are launching as we speak."

She took a deep breath and looked at the camera with a raw new intensity.

"For anyone just tuning in, our Kuiper Belt outposts are under attack. We have experienced first contact, and it was an act of war."

The playback ended there, and the screens went dark. The stadium remained hushed and expectant. From her seat next to Senator Bromberg, the present-day Holly LaCroix rose and approached the podium. The screens lit up again to show her face. She looked almost the same as she did in her history-making report fifteen years ago, right down to her same signature swept-back hairstyle, heavy gold necklace, and scarlet red dress.

"That was a day none of us will ever forget." Her voice echoed throughout the stadium. "Nor will we forget the fearful days that followed as we all waited to learn who, if anyone, had survived. It took eleven days to reach Enyo, but oh, what joy we shared when poor little Danny was found alive." She smiled in Daniel's direction and clapped, instigating a roar of approval from the crowd. When it died down, she no longer smiled. "Sadly, he was the only one."

The cameras zeroed in to catch Daniel's expected emotional breakdown. Instead, he set his jaw tight and nodded as the cameras projected him on the screens above. Whether he liked it or not, 'Little Danny,' as everyone thought of him still, remained a symbol of perseverance against the alien threat.

"We named them Garuda after the birdlike Hindu demi-god," Holly stated.

That fact still infuriated him. *They're not that big and there's nothing god-like about them.*

"And concluded little Danny was spared because of his youth, left as a warning to never explore the heavens again," she continued.

Daniel never bought into that theory, but the world took it to heart, and the search for new planets died of fright. Each commemoration put the attacks a year further back in history, but Earth remained on high alert, its deep-space program frozen in time.

As someone who'd met the enemy and lived to tell about it, Daniel had the gravitas to sway people. That's why he was here today. He'd polished his speech until certain it would have the desired effect—if only he could remember his opening line. He blinked in dismay at the blankness in his mind.

Holly LaCroix finished her speech and introduced him all too soon. Static reverberated in Daniel's head as he took his place at the podium. Looking out at the sea of people waiting for him to speak, he nearly panicked before remembering what his uncle had said.

It's not about you. It's about them, what they need to hear.

He took a deep breath, smiled, and began.

"A great man once said, 'We have nothing to fear but fear it-self.' I have looked in the eyes of the enemy and it frightened me far less than what's coming out of the mouths of our leaders today. The greatest threat to the human race isn't out there. It's right here among us, taking over our lives, our government, our future—impris-oning us on a doomed planet.

"Earth's habitable land is shrinking—miles of coastline gone, forests turned to ash, with what's left pummeled by raging storms like the one outside this stadium here today—driving us under-ground, or beneath sealed domes like this one. If people are to have any quality of life, perhaps even survive at all, we must conquer our fears and find a new world. Not just for ourselves, but for our chil-dren and grandchildren.

"Sadly, the only ventures beyond our solar system are those of the privately run Extra-Terrestrial Trade Association which continues to raid Nereus for exotic pets. This trade is nothing I applaud but does prove that we can still travel into deep space and return suc-cessfully. Yes, some ships fail to return, but it hasn't stopped the ETTA from going. Why do we allow ships to travel to distant worlds for mere profit, yet deny those who would do so for the betterment of mankind?"

"The answer, of course, is money and politics. The trade is profitable. Exploration is expensive. And by continually reminding us about the existence of an extra-terrestrial threat, our government has cemented its rule. Some of it is good—border disputes have ceased, and national pride's gone out of fashion. There hasn't been an organized war on Earth since, but peace at home has come at a high price—fear. That fear has fueled the belief that space explora-tion is a dangerous evil. This is perilous thinking, people, and it is being exploited by a pseudo-religion. Its leaders would take us on a path to annihilation.

"The time has come to stop listening to cowards who preach surrender!"

He paused for dramatic effect, then went on to condemn the fear mongers, naming names, including Bromberg's and leaders of the Unified Church of Earth. When Daniel exclaimed that it was time to stand up for humanity, the crowd jumped to its feet and roared in approval.

The ceremony's organizers expected him to introduce Bromberg as his good friend and the next speaker. He did neither, leaving the podium amidst thunderous applause. The Senator glared and clenched his hands as if he wanted to strangle Daniel.

Daniel strode past Bromberg, jostling the Senator's shoulder. His uncle stood to join him and together they exited the stage. Daniel waved to the crowd still on its feet and kept moving. McCormack trotted his far shorter legs to keep up. Once they entered the tunnels beneath the stadium, the noise lessened.

"Holy crap, Danny," his uncle said. "You insulted the wrong people just now."

"I'm only worried about impressing the right ones," Daniel replied.

"The wrong ones in positions of power can make your life miserable. Senator Bromberg is not a forgiving man."

Daniel glanced at him without slowing. "What he can't forgive is that I didn't die in that cargo tube."

"I'm sure that's not true. Even so, why antagonize him?"

"Because he's an unrepentant asshole. He denies exploration of space, but takes money from ETTA, and passes laws protecting them. Some say he even keeps Nereids himself."

"Seems unlikely. He's a card-carrying member of the UCE. I've heard him denounce the Nereid pet trade on numerous occasions."

"It's what he does behind closed doors I worry about."

A message alert vibrated on Daniel's wrist. He stopped to see what his strict privacy settings allowed through.

"Terrific speech." The message was from Cedric Peterson, Chairman Overseer of the Allied Coalition for Exploration of Space.

Daniel punched a fist in the air. "Yes!" He showed his uncle the message. "Said I wanted to impress the right people—looks like I just did."

McCormack frowned at him. "You don't really intend to do this ... to go to Tau Medea?"

"Augh!" Daniel threw his hands into the air. "How can you even ask me that? I've only been talking about it … forever. I don't know why no one takes me seriously—especially you."

"I do, of course, I do, but—" McCormack ran a hand over the top of his gray head and let out a breath. "I just didn't see it ever happening."

"It will if I can get support. ACES is a big step in the right direction, but the main thing is to swing public opinion. To do that, I need people with influence, people like you, Uncle Charlie."

McCormack let out an incredulous laugh. "You're talking about a major campaign—speeches, press conferences, media interviews."

"I understand that."

"Do you?" McCormack held his hands out palms up in a pleading gesture. "Do you really? You'll have to come out of your scientific cocoon, get down in the mud with the very people you despise. Play politics."

"I'll do whatever it takes. I just need back up."

For a moment, Daniel thought he was in for another lecture.

Instead, McCormack nodded. "Fine. I'll twist arms and empty the wallets of everyone I know. But only on one condition. If you pull this off, you take me with you. I want to be your chief of medicine."

Daniel stared in mute surprise.

"I'm one hell of a doctor, you know." McCormack glared at him.

"I know. Just never thought you'd consider it—but the answer is yes, hell yes." Daniel stuck out his hand to shake his uncle's. "You got yourself a deal."

Chapter 2

A week after his speech at the commemoration, Daniel stood outside a soaring obelisk of a building in downtown Houston. People in evening attire passed by him to walk up the entryway's wide concrete stairs. This building housed the headquarters of ACES, and inside, there was a party going on. With offices spread from one end of the solar system to the other, the ACES Annual Convention provided an opportunity for networking in the flesh. On this occasion, it would also evaluate the social skills of the remaining candidates for its next Director. After months of interviews, the pool had been winnowed down to three.

Daniel checked the time display on his wrist. He didn't want to be either too early or too late. Neither made a good impression. He smoothed his dark hair back, straightened his tux, and trotted up the stairs to the twelve-foot-tall, star-laden glass doors which slid apart at his approach. The lobby opened to a soaring expanse extending from the roof-high ceiling down to an open ballroom below. Above, suspended in mid-air, twinkling lights mapped out the Milky Way. From this vantage point, the building's many floors appeared as railed balconies narrowing upward to form an isosceles triangle. A glass wall across from him displayed breathtaking three-dimensional images of galaxies and star clusters which morphed one into the next.

The ballroom below was decked out in a metallic-themed décor filled with equally decked-out people who crowded around tables of food and drink. Interspersed with the tables were lit cages exhibiting extraterrestrial lifeforms. An orchestra provided background music for the conversational hubbub.

Shimmering movement pulled his gaze to a large display in the room's center. Inside, hundreds of iridescent jellies from Jupiter's helium rich atmosphere spiraled like self-contained rainbows in a slow-moving current. *Wow. They figured out a way to keep them pressurized.* He pulled his attention back. *You're not here to gawk, buddy. Time to convince them you're the right man for the job.*

He watched the crowd for a moment— chatting in tightly circled groups, clinking glasses, and sampling hors d'oeuvres. Everyone here was connected to ACES in some way or other—suppliers, private donors, political supporters, high-ranking employees, or prospective ones like himself. Despite the social atmosphere, plenty of business was being conducted.

He searched for the faces he needed to approach. Number one priority was to talk to Cedric Peterson. As head of the ACES Overseer Committee, Peterson would make the final selection for the next director. The man's portly shape took up a lot of physical space, so he wasn't hard to spot. Daniel trotted down the curved stairs and made his way over.

Peterson's face lit up in recognition and they greeted each other with a handshake. A self-propelled serving tray carrying champagne-filled flutes floated over and Peterson replaced his empty flute with a full one. Though not a fan of the stuff, Daniel followed suit and snatched a glass before the tray drifted away.

"Enjoyed your speech at the commemoration. Very inspiring. Fifteen years." Peterson frowned and shook his head. "Hard to believe it's been that long." Peterson lifted his glass. "To survival."

"Survival," Daniel echoed and concentrated on not making a face when he took a sip, uncertain if he'd succeeded when Peterson squinted at him.

"Mind if I ask you a question?"

"No, of course not," Daniel answered, already guessing where the conversation was going.

"When that Garuda had you in its grip, could you see its eyes?"

"I'm afraid so."

"And even then, you tried to punch it. Ha. Brave, brave boy." Peterson looked around and waved a hand in the air. "Amanda! Amanda, over here."

In a moment, a silver-gowned woman, as tall and slender as her husband was short and rotund, wound through the party-goers to reach them. Peterson slipped an arm around her waist. She smiled, but Daniel thought she looked bored and mildly unhappy.

"This is Daniel Walker, dear. Little Danny. You said you wanted to meet him."

"Oh," she said, and her blue eyes widened. She grabbed Daniel's hand with both of hers and held it. "Yes, I so wanted to meet you. I can't stop thinking about everything you went through and I can't believe you're willing to risk another encounter."

"Space is where our future lies," he said, though sick of his well-worn catch phrase.

"Absolutely," Cedric Peterson said. "Couldn't agree more. Too bad not everyone sees it our way, but we'll bring them around, won't we, son?"

"Yes, sir." Daniel smiled genuinely at the words 'we' and 'son' coming from Peterson. It had to be a good sign.

When the Petersons released him from their attention, he told himself to get his butt in gear—mingle, press some flesh. Schmoozing did not come to him easily, but after years of post-traumatic stress therapy and one-on-one coaching, he could make a good show of it. Buoyed by his exchange with Cedric Peterson, he moved through the crowd, trading introductions, light banter, and humorous remarks, all the while keeping a wary eye out for the competition. He'd earned his way here with advanced degrees in astronomy, physics, astro-metrics, and bio-chemistry, but his rivals, Serena Covington and Cadmon Dhyre, owned degrees and accomplishments every bit as impressive.

He still had one thing going for him no one else could claim. He'd met a Garuda face-to-face, which made him a continuing source of morbid fascination. People responded to him like a traffic acci-dent, relieved not to have been the victim, but still wanting to absorb the impact second-hand. The harder he hit them with it, the more satisfied they seemed to feel. He could turn the coldest, most aloof stranger into a bosom buddy within the space of one mesmerizing blood-soaked tale of terror.

Get their sympathy, then get their support. He sighed in resig-nation to it. *Whatever it takes.*

He made a point to meet every member of the ACES Overseer Committee and located the last one listening to Serena Covington. He recalled meeting Serena during a behind-the-scenes tour of an ACES research facility back when he was still working on his doctor-ate in astrophysics. At the time, she was dressed in a loose blue lab coat with her hair pulled back, bug-eyed behind thick magnifying safety glasses. She'd shooed him away. He remembered her as annoying and plain. Seeing her now, with her lightly-freckled face revealed and long wavy brown hair swinging loose as she gestured, his impression flipped one-eighty. True, her short stature and button nose might take her out of classical beauty category, but that clingy formal gown curved in all the right places.

Idiot, that's the last thing you should be thinking about. It's not her looks that matter, it's the letters following her name and the long list of accolades under it. Stop staring at her rack and make sure the Overseers don't pick her.

A group clustered around, riveted. He moved closer to listen.

"There's no question the Mars Project will eventually prove successful," she was saying. "We've already achieved a point two percent increase in freed oxygen levels in the atmosphere since melting the ice caps. We just have to keep working at it."

"Right," Daniel interjected over the heads in front of him, "and in a couple more centuries, our great-grandchildren's grandchildren might live long enough to witness the first blade of Martian grass."

Serena turned to see her heckler. "Nevertheless, it's our best hope."

"No, Tau Medea IV is our best hope," he countered. "We need a world that's ready now."

"Unless your planet turns out to be another disappointment," said a severely thin woman beside Serena. The last Overseer Daniel needed to impress looked as stiff and unbendable as a titanium rod. She pointed with a red fingernail toward a glass case nearby displaying a preserved Nereid with staring yellow eyes—female, of course—they all were—about five feet tall and covered in blue seal-like fur. "We learned on Nereus, the presence of liquid water is no guarantee of a planet suitable for human habitation. The only ones who profited are exotic pet traders. And we all know how you feel about that, don't we, Doctor Walker?" She watched him with dark, discerning eyes, waiting for his reaction.

He stopped himself from fingering the long scar on his cheek, a testament to his dispute with exploiting defenseless Nereids. He decided to steer the conversation to safer ground.

"True, but it's an unfair comparison. Analysis of extra-solar planetary atmospheres has improved since then. We know for a fact that TM IV contains large landmasses and a complete carbon-based eco-system. Humans should have little difficulty adapting."

Serena Covington spoke up. "Even if you're right, deep-space colonization is an enormous undertaking. Terraforming Mars may not be as glamorous as sailing off to a new world, but it's certainly safer and more cost effective in the long run."

"Perhaps, but while you're playing it safe and saving rich people money, millions are already suffering. Predictions are for even worse environmental catastrophes. There's a real chance humans won't be around long enough to benefit."

Serena looked away, and he feared that he had shamed her, which he immediately regretted.

"But what about the Garuda?" a man in the circle asked, sounding agitated. "Isn't an interstellar voyage just asking for trouble?"

Daniel narrowed his eyes. "Nothing we can't handle. Trust me, if they show up again, we'll be ready."

"Perhaps that's what you're hoping for." Serena cocked her head and focused her cool grey eyes on him again.

He saw that he'd been wrong. There was no shame there, and for a moment, he was taken aback. "I . . . of course not. I'm just saying we can defend ourselves. And really, it's pointless to speculate about what they may or may not do when they had no reason to attack us in the first place."

"Just because we don't understand their motive, doesn't mean they don't have one," Serena replied.

"I don't care what their motivation was. We have as much right to explore this universe as anyone," he snapped, feeling righteous.

"Here, here," a voice responded, and someone clapped him on the back, but all he could see was Serena's half-smile as if he stood before her naked and transparent. Uncomfortable now, he looked for a way to excuse himself.

"But I've interrupted," he said, in hopes of a graceful exit. "Please continue. You were discussing terraforming Mars, a worthy goal. It just shouldn't be our only one."

He lifted his glass to her and moved on. He felt guilty for poaching her audience, but it didn't change the fact that humans needed an alternative for this depleted world now, not in some distant future.

After his interaction with Serena, he realized he needed to confront his other rival as well. Cadmon Dhyre supported inhabiting Mars, too, but he promoted genetic engineering to adapt humans to hostile environments. Cadmon had excelled in such research at the Tokyo Institute of Nanotechnology, but recently suffered a falling out there. As to the nature of that dispute, Daniel could only speculate, but it seemed not to deter the Overseers from considering him a candidate. The man's expertise in nano-based bioengineering could be a deciding factor.

In contrast, Daniel had no desire to work with anything smaller than he could see with the naked eye. The idea of tiny machines infiltrating one's flesh made his skin crawl. While he recognized the potential benefits, the dangers were equally apparent. One had only to look at the mutilated face of Cadmon Dhyre to be reminded.

Daniel moved about the crowd, searching until he located the man off to the side of the room. No one was talking to him, despite the man's lofty professional reputation and his numerous awards for breakthrough patents. As Daniel watched him standing alone, something about the man's stance and separateness pulled at him— maybe because he too felt set apart. Maybe they could find common ground in that. He approached and extended his hand.

"Doctor Cadmon Dhyre? I'm Doctor Daniel Walker. I've been looking forward to meeting you."

Cadmon turned toward him and Daniel got his first up-close look at someone suffering a full-blown T-nanogen infection. The man's face was a pale paste, carved with painful-looking ribbons of red. Daniel did his best not to grimace in sympathy. He kept his outstretched hand steady, reminding himself that nano-genetic interfacers could only be transmitted through the intimate exchange of bodily fluids. Cadmon's gaze lifted from the proffered hand to look him in the eye. Daniel froze in that ice-blue stare, sensing the man's keen intelligence and quick assessment of him.

"It's an honor to meet you," he said, and felt the stupider for it. His empty hand hung in the air.

After a long pause, Cadmon raised a hand to take his. Daniel tensed, assuming the hand would be a mirror image of the ravaged face, but when it touched his own, he felt fabric, not flesh. He glanced down.

"You wear gloves," he said, and immediately wished he hadn't.

"Yes. They protect my tender flesh. And yours," Cadmon added with the merest twitch of his lips as he let go.

Daniel got the impression that Cadmon's face would crack and bleed if he allowed himself to smile. The windy, reed-like quality of the man's voice sounded as if his vocal cords had been hollowed out. As they stood there face-to-face, it hit Daniel that here was someone whose personal tragedy exceeded his own.

As did the man's accomplishments. How could he compete with that kind of suffering and determination? If he lost the Director position to Cadmon Dhyre, maybe his back-up plan should be to work for him.

"I've long been an admirer of your work. In my opinion, the Tokyo Institute lost its greatest asset," Daniel said.

"In that case, I wish your opinion mattered, Mr. Walker," Cadmon said.

Daniel laughed, ignoring that he'd just been stripped of his doctorates. "Call me, Daniel, please."

"Of course," Cadmon replied, but didn't say the name.

"I know we're both vying for the same job, but why let that get in the way, right?" He was blathering and knew it. Silence fell between them. *Time to leave.* "Well. Good luck to you. Guess we'd better go mingle."

"As you say." Cadmon gestured toward the crowd mere feet away, but which somehow seemed to occupy a completely separate space.

Overwhelmed by a vague guilt, Daniel nodded goodbye and stepped back into the crowd as if passing through an invisible barrier. *Toads and normals don't mix*, he thought, then mentally scolded himself for using the 'T' word. Cadmon Dhyre traveled at-large, but that was rare for his kind. Though no longer legally required, the vast majority of carriers still lived in the camps set up when the T-nanogen first began spreading on Earth.

He glanced back at Cadmon, noting how everyone kept their distance, faces turned tactfully aside, and realized how unlikely it was that Cadmon would get the job. Cadmon might be more qualified, even the better man, but his presence here was for show, a demonstration of how open-minded everyone was—in word, if not in deed.

Daniel looked over to where Serena still held court. In all honesty, she was also better qualified, but he doubted she would get the position either. Bright and experienced, but unimposing, she had no tragic history to trade on. If ACES wanted a front man, a crowd-pleaser, substance might be a secondary consideration. Daniel desperately wanted this job and was more than willing to snatch it from anyone, no matter how hard they might have worked for it or how deserving they might be. The need for a new world took precedence over all else.

When his gaze crossed Cedric Peterson's on the far side of the room, he raised his eyebrows in question to the man who would decide his fate. In answer, Peterson nodded and gave him a furtive thumbs-up. Daniel smiled and nodded back. Elation ran through him in a thrilled rush, but at the same time he recognized a certain injustice to it.

I'll make it up to them, ask them to come work for me—assuming they aren't too proud to accept.

Tomorrow, the selection would be announced, and the losers would go home. Convinced he would be the one staying, Daniel took a celebratory swallow of champagne to mark the moment. The taste of victory was bitter.

Chapter 3

Earth Year 2186, Los Angeles, North Americas

Three years after losing his bid to become ACES' Director, a cloaked and hooded Doctor Cadmon Dhyre limped through the back alleys of Los Angeles, taking refuge in shadows. Black watermarks on the building walls twenty-feet up documented the last time rising tides and storm-driven seas combined to overwhelm the city levies. Despite the ever-present risk of flooding, even the bottom floors of these soaring skyscrapers were prime real estate, and prices went up from there. Though he had the money, Cadmon would never be permitted to rent here, not even a moldy basement. 'No Carriers Allowed.'

Cadmon kept going until he found the corner he sought, not far from the main boulevard. A cacophony of buzzing voices and trampling footsteps emanated from dense pedestrian traffic ahead. Colorful advertising lights cut between the buildings, reflecting rainbow hues onto the wet pavement. He stayed back far enough for the colors to melt to black before reaching his feet.

High on the building, an observation cam for this corner lay frozen and pointed in the opposite direction. It wasn't due for repair until morning. His hack into the city's maintenance log today informed him of this gap in the system—a dead zone within walking distance of the hotel where he was staying. He had to travel on foot, since he couldn't risk leaving a transport trail. No one ever forgot having him as a passenger. Here he could transition to normalcy unobserved before continuing on to his destination. He checked the time on his wrist display.

Lester's always late. Maybe I should start docking his pay to teach him a lesson.

Impatience pushed Cadmon to lean around the corner to look toward the busy boulevard where he eventually wanted to go. Filled with vehicles and pedestrians, the sounds of voices, feet and machinery echoed up the alley gorge. Under the floating ads the crowd looked like a sea of multicolored heads, arms, and legs. He marveled at the sight, more taken by their sheer numbers than their psychedelic hues. Vibration from the foot and auto travel on the boulevard ahead flowed through the old asphalt under the soles of his shoes. The stink here assailed his nose, a combination of stale urine and rotting trash carelessly thrown aside. The grimy bricks of the wall he leaned against looked ancient in comparison to the colorful high-tech world beyond.

The passing crowd seemed intent on their destinations, moving fast, few looking about. The locals here were known to be self-absorbed and distracted, making it the perfect place to try this stunt. Cadmon noticed a man and woman strolling by, slower in the human current than the rest, their faces turned to each other, arms lovingly entwined. A deep, familiar longing yawned open within him, pulling him down toward its emptiness. With sudden bitter awareness, he slammed it shut again. He frowned at their backsides, until the unexpected sideways glance of a stranger froze him in mid-breath. He quickly pulled back. The face turned away and kept going. Shaken by the near discovery, he retreated from the building's edge and hid between a pair of tall recycler units.

How appropriate, hiding where society disposes of its garbage.

His pulse quickened at the thought, and his breathing came in angry hisses. The struggle to force his lungs back into a slow, even rhythm reminded him once more he was in the declining stages of his disease.

Footfalls crunched toward him down the rough alley. A dimly lit silhouette paused and looked about.

Finally.

Cadmon hissed at him. "Over here."

"This is disgusting," Lester Merritt grumbled and picked his way forward.

"My deepest apologies. These were the best accommodations I could find," Cadmon said sarcastically. "Do you have it?"

Lester produced a vial, small enough to fit in his fist.

Cadmon stared at the tiny container in dismay. "That isn't nearly enough."

"It's plenty, believe me."

"I tell you it's not. I know my own formula."

"Marketing had the production techs concentrate it. They say it'll sell better this way."

"Did they? And what else did they change?"

"Nothing, I swear. They told me otherwise it's the same stuff."

Cadmon wasn't sure whether to believe him. He considered calling things off, but it took months to get this far and he didn't know when he'd have another chance. "Are you absolutely certain?"

"I told you exactly what they told me." Lester sighed in exasperation. "For Mother's sake, stop worrying, will you?"

Cadmon still hesitated.

"Look, are we doing this or not? Because I'm not going through all this again if you—"

"All right, all right. Get on with it then."

Lester pulled out a palm-sized glowpad and set it on the ground. Blue-green light puddled at Cadmon's feet.

"Do you really need that?"

"Gotta see what I'm doing, don't I?"

Cadmon frowned but made no further objection. He slipped off his cloak, shoes and socks, and undid his pants, while Lester snapped on a pair of heavy-duty surgical gloves. Cadmon soon stood naked and shivering in the night air. Lester double-clicked the vial open, took a step forward and froze in place.

Cadmon nearly bit himself keeping his anger in check. He'd suffered through three hours of self-inflicted torture cauterizing the dark lumps of necrotic tissue from his face and body for the sole purpose of providing Lester with a smooth, if blotchy, canvas to work on.

"Hurry up. Please," he added with controlled politeness. "It's cold out here."

Lester's lips tightened, but he closed the gap between them and began dabbing thick liquid from the vial onto Cadmon's scarred flesh, moving down and around as Cadmon turned. Having to rely on anyone else, especially Lester Merritt, galled Cadmon, but Lester had a reputation for taking risks, and most importantly, he was a normal, which meant he enjoyed a freedom Cadmon lacked.

"I may not have much longer," he'd told Lester. That much was true, then he'd added a lie, "I'd like to experience a little of life's pleasures before the end."

If caught, the worst fate Lester might suffer was a change in employment. The consequence to himself would be a bit more drastic—execution.

"Wouldn't you be taking an awful big risk?" Lester had asked, then went on to answer his own question, "but what's a toad's—sorry—a carrier's life expectancy these days? Thirty-three? Thirty-five max?" Cadmon was already thirty-two. "Guess you don't have that much to lose, do you?"

"No." Not much to lose, but far too precious to waste. "So, will you do it?" Cadmon waited while Lester mulled it over, eyes twitching from one side of the room to the other considering the ramifications. When they stopped moving and focused back on him, Cadmon expected the answer would be no.

"Yeah sure. You've been good guy to work for, so why not?" Lester replied with shrug.

It took a moment for the yes to register. As it did, suspicion kicked in. "I must say your generosity surprises me."

"Never said it would be free, did I?"

Hearing that caveat, Cadmon relaxed. Kindness was suspect, but greed could be relied on. With his low opinion of Lester Merritt confirmed, Cadmon agreed to a price and made the deal. So far, Lester was keeping his end of the bargain.

Lester took a step back and held out the vial. "I'll just let you finish up there."

Cadmon looked down at his belly to see skin-colored splotches thinning and spreading—the wonder of nanotech engineering—self-replicating, carbon-based molecules multiplying themselves exponentially as they consumed and restructured the dead cells of his epidermis, reforming them into a tightly woven permeable layer of unblemished human skin. There was just the slightest stinging sensation. Only his genitals remained visibly red and blistered. He grabbed the vial from Lester's outstretched hand and emptied its last drops onto the exposed area. Slowly, the liquid connected, completing the illusion.

"See? Told you there was enough," Lester said.

Cadmon ran his fingers over the amazing smoothness of his face and neck on down. Part of him hadn't really believed it would work until now. The elation was quickly replaced by a wave of apprehension threatening his resolve. He had survived in the world of normals only by exercising the utmost caution, painstakingly following their rules, or at least appearing to. This undertaking went against well-honed instincts, but life for him was nearing the end, and all his caution wouldn't buy him one more day. Cadmon pushed the rising fear back down.

"How do I look?" He pirouetted slowly, arms extended.

"Healthy." Lester smiled. His teeth glowed green in the pale light. "Covers up everything, just like you said it would. You look a little stiff, though. Try to relax. Smile."

Cadmon tried. Lester's expression shifted uneasily. Cadmon tried harder.

"Eh, not bad. You'll pass." Lester folded the light pad, plunging them back into shadow.

"And my doppelganger's in place, back at the hotel?"

"Yep, all tucked in for the night. No one will ever know you were gone."

"And you received confirmation from the tech dealers that they're meeting us there?"

"Yeah, yeah, I already told you," Lester said, his impatience evident. "Though why you're determined to conduct business tonight beats me."

"I just want to be sure you haven't any more surprises in store."

"Look, if you want to blend in out there, you gotta loosen up a little. Go with the flow. Got it?"

Cadmon nodded but didn't move.

"You just going to stand there in your brand-new birthday suit all night?"

Cadmon frowned at his underling's insolence but turned aside to dress. He folded the hooded cloak and placed it along with his ID into the small security pouch he'd brought along, then attached the pouch to the bottom of one of the recyclers and armed it. Unlikely anyone would find his pouch there, but if so, they would receive one hell of a shock for their trouble.

Rising, he patted his back pocket, checking for his counterfeit ID. He'd already reprogrammed the encoded tag implanted in his upper left arm to match it. His other back pocket held plenty of cash. As long as he stayed away from skin-scanners, he should be fine. Lester handed him a fistful of small tightly wrapped packages.

Cadmon squinted to make out the labels in the dim light. "Slick Jim Condoms?"

"You never know—you might get lucky."

Cadmon dismissed the idea, but since it fit the story he'd fed Lester—the last hurrah of a dying man—he deposited them into his other pocket.

"If you keep hunched over like that, this isn't going to work," Lester said.

"Noted." Clenching his teeth in preparation, he stood tall, squaring his shoulders, feeling the burn of tender flesh pulled taut under the faux skin. Grimacing, he maintained the normal-looking posture by taking slow deep breaths.

"You sure you're gonna be okay?" Lester's mouth twisted in doubt.

"Yes." He forced the pain into the background and made his face relax. He'd felt worse, far worse. "I'll be fine. Let's do this."

Taking one more deep breath, Cadmon stepped out of the shadows.

Chapter 4

The Moon

While Cadmon Dhyre was maneuvering through the back alleys of Los Angeles, Daniel Walker was walking alone on the Sea of Serenity, leaving a long trail of boot prints in the ancient lunar dust. After three years in the limelight as Director of ACES, he hungered for rare solitary moments like this. He paused to look up, searching the sky. It took a moment to find it, that faint white circle pasted against black, the shipyard where his interstellar vessel awaited. Just one last hurdle to negotiate—a press conference, of all things. He sighed, unhappy he would have to deal with reporters again, something he never enjoyed. That's why he'd come out here for some alone time.

Although inherently dangerous, nothing worked better to calm his nerves than exploring empty moonscape. Serena wouldn't be pleased. He'd heard more than one angry lecture from her about the lack of oxygen, extreme temperatures, and low gravity which invited risky moves, but he valued the solitude more than personal safety, or even her blessing. Besides, this might be his last opportunity to be alone for a long time. Most importantly, it did the job. He felt relaxed now, ready to field even the most ridiculous questions. He was even ready for Serena.

He smiled thinking how far they'd come these last few years. After getting the Director position, he'd sent word to both Serena Covington and Cadmon Dhyre, inviting them to come work for him. Cadmon never replied—perhaps thinking the offer an insult, but Serena had said yes. It occurred to him now that she was probably pacing the Lunar City Convention Hall, worrying about where he was. He tapped the com on his sleeve and dictated a text.

"On my way. Try not to wear out the floor."

He sent the message, then cut communications again to enjoy his last few minutes of isolation as he waited for the train to the underground city. Soon, the long, bullet-shaped maglev train slid over the crest and snaked toward him, coming to a stop when it detected his presence. As soon as he boarded, it accelerated again. Heads swiveled to stare at the crazy man who'd been walking around outside by himself. He decided to keep his helmet on even after he found an open seat. When the train dove into the underground tunnels, he felt his Earth equivalent weight return, courtesy of the gravity wells buried beneath the city. The transition felt like bottoming out on a rollercoaster. Bouncing around on the Moon like a balloon was fun, but extended exposure to it deteriorated bones and muscles and eventually barred one from ever returning to Earth. Those who lived in low-G too long paid the price of permanent exile.

Still anonymous in his helmet, he disembarked at the convention center and worked his way backstage to his assigned dressing room. He removed his helmet and began taking apart his suit when Serena stormed in.

"I can't believe you went outside again." She yanked the back of his suit down throwing him off balance. The physical strength and forceful personality contained in her petite package took people by surprise, him included.

"Easy there," he cautioned.

"What were you thinking? I should never have let you out of my sight." She tugged the suit's legs down making him hop on one foot. "Will you hurry up?"

"Will you calm down?"

"How am I supposed to be calm when you act like a lunatic?"

"You worry too much. I'm fine." He wrapped her in his arms and gave her a kiss. "Besides, it did me good. I'm ready now to deal with all those idiots out there."

She scowled up at him. "They're not idiots. They're reporters. They have a job to do, just like you. And in less than ten minutes you need to be dressed and ready for them, with your head on straight."

"It's on straight and we have plenty of time—enough to fool around, if we're quick about it."

She shoved him back. "Not enough for me. You also knew I wanted to go over your opening statement." She grabbed his dress pants, wadded them up and threw them at him.

He caught the pants and snapped them flat before stepping into the legs. "Don't worry. I know it backwards and forward." He fastened his pants and slipped into his shirt. "I'm ready, really." He took the pair of socks from her hands.

She folded her arms across her chest, watching him. "Is that so? And just how ready are you to deal with a couple dozen Unified Church of Earth reps lobbing questions at you?"

"What?" He froze with a half-socked foot in the air.

"They talked the conservative networks into letting the UCE represent them. Nobody knew. Surprise!"

He lowered his foot, but still felt off-balance. Inside, he cursed. On the outside, he shrugged. "Doesn't matter. I can handle them."

"You can, *if* you keep your cool." She stuck a tiny receiver into his ear hard enough to make him wince. She spun him around, tucking and adjusting, and finally stepped back to take a look. "You'll do." She pecked him on the lips. "Go get 'em, Tiger."

Daniel reached to grab onto her for more, but she was already on the move. He shook his head and smiled, watching her trot away. *She's right, I need to focus.* As he walked backstage toward the main hall, he could hear the rumbling voices of the assembled crowd and press corps. When he entered, the volume rose in response. The technicians scurried faster, trying to complete last minute visual and sound checks as Daniel took his seat at the speakers' table onstage.

Facing him were eight long rows of chairs filled with those cleared to ask questions on behalf of the news media, and behind them were hundreds of observers standing in the back. Through the dome beyond, the Moon's stark white landscape was visible and a crescent of Earth waxed a bright blue and white in the black sky. He loved looking at his home world like this, a quarter of a million miles away, comfortable mother-in-law distance.

As he waited to begin, he studied the great hall with its signature piece, a ten-meter-tall statue of an astronaut standing beside a replica of the old United States' flag. The oft-debated words uttered by Neil Armstrong were etched across the base. "That's one small step for [a] man, one giant leap for mankind." The hall had been constructed over the original 1969 lunar landing site. Items left behind by the six successful Apollo landing missions (the original flag, discarded boots, cameras, backpacks and assorted equipment) were displayed in transparent cabinets along the walls. Looking at the statue, Daniel wondered what might one day be erected on Tau Medea IV.

A technician flashed a two-minute warning with a pair of raised fingers just as Captain Devon C. Kowalski strode in with his hat in his right hand and his shorn steel gray hair revealed. He gave a curt nod to Daniel, sat in the chair on Daniel's left and placed his hat in his lap. Built like a tank, Kowalski cut a formidable figure in his crisp navy-blue United Nations Armed Forces uniform with its rows of glittering holographic insignia. By comparison, Daniel felt decidedly plain in his tan civvies.

Under the terms dictated by the United Nations, Kowalski would command the ship, while Daniel headed the mission. It still rankled Daniel, but Bromberg and his kind insisted the Garuda threat demanded a large military presence. Refusal meant no mission at all. The exact division of responsibilities were spelled out in black and white, line item after line item. How it would work in real life remained to be seen.

Kowalski nodded to him, then faced the reporters with the grim determination of a condemned soldier staring down an execution squad. Daniel sympathized. Although he'd learned to handle fame, he'd never learned to like it. A roving camera bug zoomed in a little too close and he batted it away.

Multicolored lights on the display panel at his fingertips twinkled on and off as the technicians finished their tests. Daniel wished he knew which light corresponded to which person, noting with displeasure the number of them dressed in the gray suits of the Unified Church of Earth leaders and the green robes of their die-hard followers. Unfortunately, the lights were left purposely anonymous to prevent any bias in selection.

Serena's voice whispered in his ear, "Testing, testing?" He raised a finger in confirmation and looked across the crowd searching until he spotted her. As usual, Serena positioned herself near the back, observing everyone. From there, she would offer advice and pertinent information into his earpiece. In doing so, she'd saved him from many a public relations disaster.

"There's Bromberg, conferring with the reporters. Notice how he's fawning over the UCE reps," she said into his earpiece.

He nodded subtly, recognizing the middle-aged man going from chair to chair, undoubtedly poisoning minds against him.

Senator Nelson Bromberg, an avid proponent of the Church, had nearly swung the vote of the United Nations against allowing this mission at all. By the slimmest of margins, Daniel gained UN approval and funding, but it could still all be swept away should opinion turn against him. Until his ship escaped safely beyond Earth's influence, he couldn't afford any mistakes.

"Relax, smile," Serena reminded him. "They'll try to embarrass you, so keep it together. Don't question their beliefs or trade insults."

"I know, I know," he said under his breath, though he knew she couldn't hear him. The lights on the panel flashed once in unison — the signal for all clear. He raised a hand and the technicians activated the sound-dampening field, quieting the restless crowd in the back to a murmur. He put on his best smile.

"Good morning, everyone, and welcome. Our mission to Tau Medea is proceeding as planned, preparations are in progress, and we have a launch date . . ."

Chapter 5

Los Angeles, North Americas

The Wrec-U Club in downtown Los Angeles advertised itself as 'The Most Intoxicating Place on Earth." The ads seemed to be working. Sensation seekers crowded the bar, tables, and dance floors, parading their bodies in various stages of undress and glittering skin-tight outfits. Some glowed or displayed moving pictures encircling the torsos of their wearers. Underfoot, the floor vibrated with heart-pounding music synchronized to tiny holovid dancers skimming across the bar, floor, walls and ceiling. At first, only their size and luminescence distinguished them from living patrons, but a closer look revealed that only the living wore vividly designed stim patches stuck to pulse-points on necks and wrists. Cadmon sported a patch as well, but his was inert to keep his wits intact, worn only to discourage the roving pushers.

As far as his employer Fabri-Tech, knew, he and Lester Merritt were in LA for the sole purpose of attending a Nano-Engineering Conference—part of the company's outreach program. This night on the town was unauthorized and risky as hell. If caught, getting fired would be the least of his worries. Lester suggested the Wrec-U Club, based on its reputation of being a discreet gathering spot for those seeking certain services. Cadmon's own research confirmed the club drew both the elite and fringe elements of society, either looking for a good time, or to do business in an atmosphere where illegal transactions were lost in the noise and the crowd with no camera eyes recording the terms. For black market deals, this was the place.

Cadmon stood at the polished brass-trimmed bar waiting to pay for Lester's order of three Wrec-U's, the alcohol-based house special. It appeared he was expected to foot the bill. The wide mirror behind the bar sparkled in refracted light and movement, while his steady reflection centered in the middle of the chaotic distortions. He wondered if everyone saw themselves framed in it so. He checked his face to make sure the simskin remained smooth and even. He fought the urge to test it with his fingers. He looked fine, he decided, better than fine. He looked normal.

Relax, he told himself, and consciously forced the stiff expression in the mirror to soften. He glanced around for anyone who might be taking interest in him, and locked on the steady gaze of a peach-haired beauty with a holographic tattoo of an amorous couple wrestling across her left breast. She flashed him a seductive smile. Probably just a club hostess looking for a customer, but if she were undercover, she could be trouble. He looked away and to his relief, she aimed her smile in another direction. A hostess, he concluded. No threat, but he would never consider employing her services. She was a complete unknown. That wasn't quite true, however, in the case of Lester's friend, Katie.

He looked over his shoulder and she looked back, fluttering long-nailed fingers in his direction. She sat next to Lester, who smiled and winked. Lester's title might be Fabri-Tech Production Sanitations Engineer, but he had the soul of a pimp. No doubt, Katie's attentions came at a price, but wouldn't be offered to him of course. Then he remembered the Slick Jims in his pocket. No, Lester was scum, but even he wouldn't allow that. He put the idea from his mind.

It was rumored Lester had been slipped into his job at Fabri-Tech through the sleight-of-hand of an influential relative. Cadmon concluded it was probably true. The man's only real expertise seemed to be playing guinea pig for every cosmetic enhancement in development. The man's dedicated pursuit of skin-deep perfection appeared daily on his face. Tonight, Lester sported an over-thick coif of raven hair, metallic blue eyes, impossibly smooth bronzed skin, and a rakish smile too dazzling to have been a gift from Mother Nature.

Lester's conniving ways of gaining inside access to products still in development irritated Cadmon, enough to fire him until he realized such connections might prove useful. Still, this was hardly the route he would have preferred. If only Fabri-Tech's Board hadn't been so pigheaded. CEO Cedric Peterson had rejected his proposal, and the Board followed his lead like sheep, a unanimous no.

He imagined sinking his teeth into their stupid complacent faces. How he'd love to inject a torrent of his tormentors into them to consume their flesh and bones until reduced to pale, rake-scarred wraiths like himself. Instead, he had thanked them for still allowing him to attend the L.A. Conference. *Idiots.*

A hand dropped on his arm, waking him to the raucous club around him. The peach-haired hostess had sidled up to him.

"You okay, sweetie?" she asked.

"What? Yes, I'm fine. Go away."

She made a sound of disgust and drifted back into the crowd.

"Here you go."

Cadmon spun back to see the three drinks and a credit registry plate sliding toward him.

"I'm paying cash," he told the bartender and laid down a stack of bills.

The big man squinted at them. "Don't see cash much anymore. Need change?"

"Keep it." Cadmon twitched a smile and grabbed his drinks. Threading back to the table, he kept his back straight and prayed the stiffness in his gait wouldn't give him away. He sat down and presented one glass to the lovely Katie, and another to Lester. The third he kept for himself. He could barely keep his muscles from cramping and hoped a judicious bit of alcohol would help. He sipped his drink and watched Katie as she fiddled with the controls of the mask Lester had bought for her—something to do with the club's 'Hollywood Legends' theme for the night.

"Hey, Katie," Lester said loud enough to be heard over the music. "Did I mention Caddy's a top nano-engineer? Supervises our whole lab. A real genius, this guy. Comes up with some great stuff."

"Wow. Maybe you can make something for me," she said and leaned forward, revealing a clear view down her low-cut dress. He couldn't help but stare. "How about it, Caddy?"

The detestable nickname jarred him—as if he were some lackey for golfers. He looked up at her face again. "Cadmon," he corrected her. "It's Cadmon."

Lester tapped him on the arm. "Tell her how you won that award for eye implants."

"I think you just did," he replied taking no pleasure in the fact. It was just another example of how his employer squandered his talents. Katie was still smiling at him. He tried to smile back but wasn't sure his facial muscles were cooperating.

Lester saved him, getting Katie's attention again, pointing to his own sparkling irises. "I'm wearing a pair, right now. Great, huh?"

Katie nodded approvingly. Lester glanced at the floating time display, then looked up at the 3-D monitor above their heads showing a football game in progress. Just as a huge bio-enhanced defensive tackle mowed down the opposing team's quarterback, Lester switched channels with a snap of his fingers. A clamor of voices rose in objection.

"Hey, this is important," he yelled back. "Educate yourselves."

Cadmon thought Lester would have preferred the inanity of full-contact sports, so he was surprised to see the image of a distant star system revolving in the air with a news logo under it. The scene switched to a handsome dark-haired man. Cadmon tensed, recognizing Daniel Walker, the one who edged him out for Director of ACES. Although never particularly interested in deep-space exploration, it would have given him access to hundreds of privately owned labs.

"He's the real deal, I hear. No enhancements," Katie said pointedly to Lester.

Lester snorted a laugh. "Yeah sure, Danny's real all right. A real bore."

The tone of familiarity caught Cadmon's attention. "You speak as if you know him."

"I should. He's my cousin."

That gave Cadmon pause. Could this be the rumored influential relative? "I don't recall you ever mentioning him."

Lester shrugged. "Yeah, well, it's not like we got a whole lot in common."

"Understandable," he said, not quite able to resist. "Walker's highly intelligent."

Lester's eyes narrowed. "Book smart's not street smart. Believe me. Back when we were kids, I was the one in charge."

Cadmon recognized a sore point and wondered how it might be turned to good advantage. He pushed a little harder. "That's a bit difficult to believe."

"Oh, yeah?" Lester pointed at the image. "See that scar on his face? I'm the one who gave it to him."

Cadmon chuckled, amused, though not entirely convinced. Katie, apparently even less so, barked a laugh.

"Get off! I bet you don't even know him. You're jealous is all. He's famous and nobody knows you from dirt. Here he's going off to save the world and you can't even save enough to pay your bar tab, let alone what you owe me for—"

Lester shushed her.

Smirking, Katie directed her attention to Cadmon. "Hey, you're a real brainy guy, right? Think Doctor Dan will find us a new world without getting himself killed?"

"Let's just say odds are not in his favor," Cadmon said, vastly understating his opinion.

"Yeah, I worry about him, too," Lester said, misconstruing his words. "This mission thing's been an obsession. The Holy Father says it's stupid and dangerous. Says mankind's highest calling is here on Earth." The other two stared at him. "Well, it's true. Says so right here." He whipped out a small card. Cadmon took it for closer examination. The card displayed the quote and bore Lester's name in raised gold and green script, identifying him as an 'Initiate of The Unified Church of Earth.' The title did not impress him; the card did. It was paper. Not the smooth paper-like plastic of the bills he'd given the bartender, but genuine organic tree-birthed paper with all its imperfections. Lester snatched the card back and tucked it in his pocket.

"No way. You? In the UCE?" Katie barely stifled her laughter.

"Just covering my bases," Lester said. "Way things look, the Church could be running the whole show before long."

"Looks like they already are." Cadmon tipped his chin at the televised image, and sighed. "Not that it matters. Church, government, corporate interests—there's no real difference. All they ever do is bicker over trivialities ultimately irrelevant to the human equation."

Katie blinked at him. Clearly, she had no idea what he was talking about. He didn't bother explaining it to her.

She nudged Lester. "Turn it up, I can't hear."

Lester obliged, and Walker's voice rose over the club noise. Cadmon sighed, resentful at being forced to pay tribute to such absurdity. Walker might be credited with a formidable intellect, but on this issue he was hopelessly misdirected. Until the basic nature of humanity was addressed, humans would take their weaknesses with them wherever they went.

Cadmon wanted to get on with his business and leave. His goal here tonight was to purchase restricted lab equipment to set up a hole-in-the-wall nanotech production facility, somewhere beyond the prying eyes of Fabri-Tech. He'd told Lester he needed it for making more of this simskin. It wasn't a lie, per se. It just wasn't the whole truth.

"So where are these friends of yours?" he asked.

"Don't worry. They'll be here." Lester waved a hand and continued staring at the holo projection.

With no choice but to wait, Cadmon turned to the cold drink in his hand. The icy liquid bubbled hot on his tongue, and a slow dizzy warmth rose in his head. He relaxed into it, feeling lighter, almost as if he weren't quite touching the hard surface beneath him. His usual irritation with outright stupidity softened. The more he drank, the more the room's hubbub faded into the background of his awareness, and voices proclaiming Walker's merits turned to a meaningless buzz. Cadmon focused on the perfect smoothness of Katie's skin flowing down her neck and chest into the curving shadows below. Unattainable, he knew, but he wanted her nonetheless. Well, not her exactly, but the feel of her, the look of her.

Lester tapped his arm, then bobbed his eyebrows and tilted his head at Katie. Cadmon looked higher and realized she was staring at him through the eyes of the mask Lester had purchased from the bartender for her. The mask adjusted to her facial contours, forming an attractive but unfamiliar countenance. Cadmon sat there, stonelike, unsure what was expected of him.

"I'm sorry, did you say something?" he asked.

"I said I vant to be alone," she said huskily, "with you, darling."

Slowly his brain processed what she was suggesting. Acting on his desire was something he'd only considered in the abstract. He looked at Lester, certain he would put a stop to it. Instead, Lester shrugged. Katie was fair game. The choice was his. He felt a fire ignite inside him. But this wasn't what he'd come for.

"What about the people we're supposed to meet?" he asked.

"Probably won't show for another hour or two. Go on, have a little fun." Lester leaned back and grinned. "What have you got to lose?"

Cadmon felt Katie's hand on his thigh, sliding upward, and his breath shortened. Her moist tongue licked the screen star lips. "Vell, darling?"

He had no idea who she was impersonating, not that it mattered. This was an opportunity unlikely to ever come again. He gulped the remainder of his drink. "Let's go." He took her hand and pulled her from the table. "Where to?"

She pointed to an old-fashioned stairway on the other side of the club.

As he followed Katie cutting through the crowd, the room seemed to sway and pulse around him, surreal in a rhythmic flow of glittering bodies and projected images. More than slightly drunk, he hung onto the railing to climb the stairs. They passed life-sized holovids on the steps playing out the club's theme for the evening. A man in a top hat and tails tapped and twirled from bottom to top. Katie steered them around a real flesh-and-blood man in a psychedelic jester hat dangling mind-buzzers at them, then directly through holos of a man facing a tearful woman in a long velvet dress. Deep, male-pitched words, "Frankly, my Dear . . ." hummed in Cadmon's ears. A curvaceous blonde projection at the top of the landing squealed as her white, pleated skirt fluttered up to reveal lush thighs, a teasing imitation of the womanly promise he hungered for.

They entered a long hallway dotted with locked doors. Katie stopped and gestured at a control panel to one of them. He started to raise his hand to it, then pulled back, realizing his near error. "You open it."

Seeing her annoyed look, he changed his tone. "If you wouldn't mind, I'd prefer to keep my employer in the dark about my visit here."

She rolled her eyes, but said, "Fine," and pressed her hand against the plate. "I'll just add it to Lester's tab."

The door slid aside. Other than a bright pink color scheme and wall-to-wall ceiling mirrors, the room itself was unremarkable. There was a round bed between a pair of night-stands, an Insta-Shop vending machine covering one wall, and a recycler beside the door to a bathroom. Katie removed her mask and propped it on one of the nightstands, so that its empty eyes stared at the bed.

Her face looks much younger without the mask "Exactly how old are you?" he asked.

Her saucy expression faltered for just a moment. "Old enough. I'll be right back. Why don't you get undressed." She disappeared into the bathroom.

Things were moving fast. The thrill of anticipation, an elixir even more potent than the one he'd downed, stirred Cadmon into action. He dumped his pocketful of Slick Jims onto the end table next to the mask, dimmed the lights, and took off his clothes. Naked now, he stood by the bed, running his hands over his unfamiliar smoothness, trying to calm the raw excitement within.

The bathroom door opened and out stepped the living image of his fantasies—beautiful, naked, healthy female flesh—backlit in the bathroom light like an old movie-house projection. He reached out a beckoning hand. Her gaze crawled up the length of his body and froze.

"Oh, my god!" she gasped, recoiling. "What's happened to your face?"

"What?" He pulled his outstretched hand back to touch his cheek and felt the simskin slide like thick goo under his fingers. "Oh no. No, no, no!"

She screamed and ran for the door.

"Wait!" He threw himself in front of her and she skidded to a halt.

"Don't you dare put your sick hands on me." She backed away, arms up.

"Please. You'll be fine. See?" He pointed at the condoms. "I have Slick Jims."

"Are you insane? You're a toad."

The t-word stripped away the alcoholic blur in his brain. "I'm not a toad. I'm a man."

"You're a stinking, rotting toad!" She opened her mouth wide and screamed at higher decibels than he thought possible for a human.

"Son of a bitch!" He slapped a hand over her mouth. She fought back, hitting and kicking at him. He forced her onto the bed, sat on top of her and pushed a pillow over her face. Gradually, her muffled cries faded, and she stopped fighting him. He pulled the pillow away. She lay unconscious, but still alive. Good. Murder wasn't what he'd planned. He turned to look at the door. The lock-light remained red. No alarms went off, no police burst through the door.

Looking about, he scanned the walls, floor and furniture for reflections, the mirrored ceiling for any tell-tale blemish. He saw none—no camera eyes. The absence of surveillance gave him a strange liberated feeling. He could hardly remember a time when he hadn't been watched. Lester promised this club was private, very private. He was safe, for now.

When Katie moaned, he pressed the artery on her neck until she passed out again to give himself time to think. He focused on the satin sheets—twisted, one could serve as makeshift rope. Her blouse would do for a gag. He improvised with what he had, binding her hands and feet together behind her back, then stepped away to flex away his cramping muscles.

Now, how am I going to get out of here without alerting the authorities?

Perhaps in that rowdy, intoxicated crowd, he could pass unnoticed. He checked the bathroom mirror to evaluate the extent of the damage. A ghostly white face carved with the signature blood-red sores of a carrier stared back beneath dripping cosmetic skin. No, he wouldn't go unnoticed. He looked over at the mask on the table. A man's body, a woman's face? Considering the bizarre scene he'd witnessed below, the combination shouldn't raise any eyebrows. But the mask would only cover his face, and he could feel the simskin sagging down the back of his neck. He needed more coverage. He considered the second pink satin sheet envisioning how he would look wrapped in it. Odd, at best.

He groaned in frustration. He'd been so close to realizing a long cherished fantasy. His lingering desire, and the adrenaline still rushing through his body combined to infuse him with an unfamiliar heat. He walked back over to the bed and stared. Unable to resist, he ran the back of his hand along her cheek.

Her eyelids fluttered, and she snapped awake. Finding herself bound and gagged, she screamed a muffled cry, and squirmed to free herself. He reached down to hang on to the sheet rope so that she couldn't worm her way off the bed.

"Calm down," he said, but she only struggled harder. He watched her naked gyrations with growing interest. *Oh, what a fine couple we make—the woman of my dreams, the man of her night-mares*, he thought, and chuckled bitterly.

She stiffened and glared at him.

He recognized the loathing in her eyes, but kept his voice soft. "I assure you there's no need to be frightened as long as you cooperate."

She lay still then, staring up at him and he thought perhaps she could be reasoned with now. He sat beside her and gently removed the gag from her mouth.

She spat at him.

In that moment—spittle dripping from his nose—his mind constricted into a single concentrated point of rage shooting up from the depths like an air-starved beast. Roaring, he yanked her off the bed and slammed her to the floor. She cried out. He no longer saw loathing in her eyes, only fear.

A violent trembling gripped her and she sobbed, "I'm sorry, I'm sorry, don't hurt me, please, this is all Lester's fault, please, I'm only sixteen."

Cadmon thought of his own sixteenth year of life—already a full-fledged toad and thoroughly despised.

"Just let me go. I won't tell anyone, I swear." Her wide eyes promised him anything, everything.

His rage cooled as he found himself experiencing a strange new pleasure.

So this is what power feels like, tastes like—hot and sweet. He wanted more. And why not? He'd already done enough to earn the death penalty. *If I have to pay the ultimate price, I may as well make it worthwhile.*

Ignoring her pleas, he freed one of her arms and dragged her over to the vending wall where he forced her fingers against the In-sta-Shop's buttons. Drawers lit up and rolled out one-by-one, displaying every sex toy ever imagined by well-balanced minds and the hopelessly demented, plus a pharmaceutical cornucopia. He pressed her right palm against the credit registry plate, then jabbed her fingers on the selection screen, choosing the items he found intriguing.

With one arm full of loot, and the other dragging Katie, he returned to the bed. He dumped his toys and flung her alongside. She screamed and bucked but he easily pinned her with his weight. He slapped an orange tag on one wrist and three blue on the other. Within seconds her body slumped, and her pupils dilated to empty black circles. He'd used a powerful hallucinogen and a triple dose of muscle relaxant. Her mental anguish would increase exponentially while her body became as pliable as a rag—the perfect combination for an evening's entertainment.

He waited for the drugs to take full effect then untied her, positioning her limbs as it pleased him. She lay there staring upward. Seeing her unblinking terror froze him for a moment, teetering on the brink. He could still turn back. But to what? The best he could ever hope for were a few more years of misery before succumbing to an agonized death, empty of meaning, devoid of pleasure, bowing and scraping to the end, to insipid idiots like this insufferable girl, this snip of womanhood, all of them thinking themselves better than he, simply because of their sweet, soft skins.

He deserved better, he was better. The world denied him everything that made life worth living. It was time to take what he wanted—what he deserved. That mental step off the edge felt like being launched into flight, winging like a dark predatory bird to avenge the indignities he'd suffered. Time to balance the scales, and he knew exactly where to begin.

His first act was to check for a vaginal insert protecting her against transmission of venereal disease, something he understood prostitutes employed as a matter of course. He probed with his fingers until he found it and pulled it free—a thin, clear flexible shield. Though tiny in comparison, it reminded him of the medical barriers he was required to sit behind in public transports. He made a show of combining her shield with the condoms and tossing them all aside. He saw her pupils track them as they flew, and heard a strangled whimper.

"There, there," he clucked. "We can't have anything coming between us. That would spoil my surprise. I have my own present for you, a very special mask—far more impressive than the one that idiot waiting for us downstairs gave you. This one's a guaranteed show stopper."

He leaned over and kissed her mouth gently with his ragged lips.

"And the best part is . . . you'll get to wear it forever."

Chapter 6

The Moon

After finishing his prepared statement, Daniel opened the floor to questions. With no idea which light on his panel matched which reporter, he punched the colored lights at random. It was pure luck that he'd avoided any UCE reps so far. When a statuesque blonde stood—dangerous curves in a snug black pantsuit—his eyes lingered appreciatively.

"Focus," Serena hissed into his ear.

"Doctor Walker, I know you said your ship's name won't be revealed until launch—something about tradition and bad luck?" The woman smiled as if embarrassed for him. "But after all the not-so-flattering names being tossed about, wouldn't you prefer to put the topic to rest?"

Daniel sighed, his brief attraction already forgotten. "The name will be revealed at the ship's christening."

A grumbling protest arose. Someone from the standing crowd of observers shouted, "Come on, Doctor Dan, give us the name!" Others joined in. "Yeah, we want the name. Give us the name!"

He raised his hand to quiet them, but the gesture had little effect. More and more voices joined in until an organized chant coalesced.

Serena spoke in his ear, "You're making too big a deal of this. Defuse it, now."

"Very well," he said. The crowd hushed and waited. He had opposed the presumptuous moniker from the start, but was overruled. "We've named her the Niña."

Voices murmured in response. He jabbed another light.

Oh no, he thought, seeing a narrow-faced woman rise. Her hair was tied back so tightly it nearly disappeared, and she wore a gray suit buttoned to the neck in green-and-gold Earth symbols—signature dress for administrative members of the Unified Church of Earth.

"The Niña?" Her words snapped. "Are you suggesting we equate you with Columbus?"

"I hope not. I know exactly how long the voyage will take and won't be mistaking the new world for India." Polite chuckles followed.

He selected another light. A man stood wearing the green robe of Nature's True Children, an extremist offshoot of the Unified Church of Earth. Looked like his run of luck had run out.

"It is our duty to protect our God-given home," the man said. "The Garuda attack was a clear message to attend to matters on Earth. We mustn't put our future at risk by—"

"This is a press conference, not a pulpit," Daniel cut him off. Serena clucked a warning and he softened his response. "I understand your concerns. Any voyage of exploration involves inherent risk, but it also expands our knowledge. Humanity's greatest achievements have come about when someone was willing to take a leap of faith—"

"Don't play their game," Serena warned.

Was he waxing too philosophical? Treading on dangerous dogma? Either way, he got the message.

"But now I'm the one preaching," he apologized. "Suffice it to say that this endeavor is based on years of solid research and careful planning."

He punched another light. To Daniel's relief, an older man in non-sectarian clothing stood.

"Could you describe what you expect to find on Tau Medea IV in terms the layman can understand?" he asked.

"I'd be happy to. We believe the planet's stage of development may be comparable to Earth's late Cretaceous Period, which—"

"You talking dinosaurs?" someone in the crowd yelled. A few whoops followed.

Daniel's smile relaxed into real humor. "That would be something, but no. More likely we'll find primitive sea life, amphibians, insects, and plants. We don't anticipate any large land animals."

"The Ferrigan rats weren't large," the man in the green robe commented out of turn.

A moment of wretched silence followed. The graphic images of half-eaten bodies at the Ferrigan Station were still fresh in people's minds.

"Those were mutated descendants of earth-born lab rats," Daniel reminded everyone.

"A mutation caused by the influence of an off-world environment," the robed man added.

Daniel ignored him and poked another light. Now a middle-aged woman also wearing a green robe had the floor. He fought against his mouth wanting to twist. He wished he could magically turn back the clock to a time when the UCE was a little known cult, when faster-than-light travel still fired people's imaginations, and no one had ever heard of the Garuda.

"You say your purpose is scientific exploration, but you're operating under the auspices of the UN Armed Forces. Does that mean you're planning to engage the enemy?"

He sighed, his patience almost depleted. "No, we're not *planning* on it. I believe I already explained that—" He stopped himself and glanced sideways at the uniformed man next to him. "Perhaps Captain Kowalski can shed light on the subject."

Caught off guard after being ignored for so long, Kowalski hesitated. "Uh, yes. Yes, Ma'am." He pinned his hat under his left arm and popped up to his full six feet, his solid block body ramrod straight.

Daniel watched his actions in surprise, wondering if the captain did all that simply because he was addressing a woman.

"UN Armed Forces presence is required on all interstellar vessels. It's mandated," Kowalski stated, then abruptly thumped back down into his chair.

"Yes, I know," the woman said, "but only in an advisory capacity. Your crew includes over one hundred combat-ready troops, with you, a military officer, in command of them."

Daniel leaned back to look at the reseated captain. Kowalski stood again, in the same stiff pose. "We consider it a precautionary presence." He nodded and sat down again.

The woman opened her mouth again, but Daniel took pity on Kowalski and intervened. "Let me add that we need the military's support for staffing purposes. Trained volunteers for deep space are hard to come by."

He punched another light, but the woman refused to relinquish the floor, saying, "They're hard to come by for a reason, Doctor Walker. People have the good sense to be afraid, while you, on the other hand—"

"Don't let her take control," Serena cautioned in his earpiece.

"If you'll please—" he began, but the woman talked over him.

"—You personally witnessed the Garuda massacre and equate the sale of Nereids to 'slave trade,' yet would take us to the very source of these horrors."

"None of that has any bearing on . . . " He raised his voice as the crowd's jeers increased. ". . . on this mission."

"You don't know that." The green-robed man yelled. "The Garuda could be out there right now, just waiting to attack at any sign we're venturing back into their territory."

"And what territory would that be?" Daniel asked. "We know nothing about them. Not why they attacked, where they came from, or where they've gone. It's time to stop letting fear rule us."

"We are children of Earth and Earth alone. That is indisputable," a dark-haired woman wearing the official charcoal gray of the Church elite called out and rose to her feet. The dozens of UCE reps in gray and green stood in unison.

He heard Serena's voice. "Tell them to sit down. They're out of order."

"If you will please take your seats—" he began.

The woman in gray shouted over him, "We will not sit; we will not be silenced! This mission is your personal vendetta and will bring ruin on us all."

"She's baiting you," Serena said in his ear. "Don't—"

He bit. "All you people preach is stagnation. My father discovered a world habitable without terraforming. We can't afford not to investigate."

"Your father didn't know about the Garuda, and it cost him his life and the lives of everyone who followed him."

"You hardly need remind me," he said, hoping to shame her. "I was there."

The woman lowered her eyes, but not in shame he realized, as she pressed a finger to one ear. She was wearing a hearing-piece like his own. A premonition of what was coming next hit him a moment too late.

"His High Holiness, the Supreme Father of the Unified Church of Earth, will address you," she announced.

A twenty-foot tall holo of the wizened UCE leader appeared in the air, glowing as if lit by angelic fire. Special effects, obviously, but people's instinctive awe response kicked in, and they sucked in their breath as one.

Damn it! There's no way I can side-step this now.

Father Pompilio's voice rang out, amplified to a soul-pounding resonance.

"Hear me, my son. You are a child of Earth, as are we all. Consider wisely lest personal ambition blind you to God's will. Many more may die should you fail to heed His warning that His children do not belong among the stars, a message you yourself delivered to us. If you will not listen to your Heavenly Father, then learn from your earthly one. Surely, the late Doctor Benjamin Walker would not want his only child to repeat his mistake."

"Mistake?" Outrage filled Daniel's vision like a field of red. Serena was saying something in his earpiece, but he wasn't listening. "That was no mistake. The long-term survival of humanity depends on off-world expansion. He knew it, I know it, and so do they." Daniel waved his hand to take in the assembled crowd. "If you were half as concerned about securing the future for mankind as in securing power for yourself, we wouldn't be having this discussion, but I suppose there's no point in arguing with someone who has the arrogance to speak for God."

Serena gasped in his ear. He looked past the shocked face of the Supreme Father to the hushed crowd beyond. He'd gone too far, but there was no taking it back now, even if he wanted to . . . which he didn't. *Time to end this.*

"Ten years from now when we return from Tau Medea we will have the answers you seek. I look forward to that day. This press conference is now concluded. Thank you for coming."

He tugged the tiny speaker from his ear and slashed the air for the technicians to cut power. With the sound dampener off, the crowd exploded in a bedlam of applause, whoops, whistles, and shouts, drowning out the reporters' objections. Above them, the furious face of the Supreme Father winked out.

Kowalski turned to stare at Daniel, as if the latter were some new form of species yet to be identified. Daniel shrugged in response. The captain smirked and shook his head, leaving Daniel confused as to his meaning. In contrast, Daniel had no doubt about Serena's state of mind. She stood across the hall with her arms crossed, glaring at him. Knowing she would corner him first chance she got, he jumped up and headed for the exit. He didn't want a lecture, not now. He didn't need her to tell him he'd offended people—something he seemed to make a habit of—that was the price of honesty. He just hoped he hadn't risked everything for a parting shot.

Chapter 7

Los Angeles, North Americas

Lester snorted a laugh watching his cousin's press conference come to an abrupt end. Nobody in his right mind would insult the Supreme Father in public, especially during a live event.

Ha, nobody but Danny.

The scene cut to local news reporters—three-dimensional heads analyzing the impact of Walker's statements. When someone at another table snapped the channel back to the game, Lester made no objection. His curiosity was satisfied, and he had more pressing business to deal with—the scheme he'd set into motion. As arranged, Katie had lured Cadmon Dhyre upstairs, and the camera eye hidden in her mask should be recording it all.

Pleased with himself, Lester turned to watch the action on the dance floor where men, women, and sexes undefined writhed to the club's music and their own drug-induced demons. Atop floating platforms, gyrating strippers with metallic ribbons wrapped strategically around their bodies, peeled the ribbons away and flung them into the crowd. A thin gilded stream sailed toward Lester. Snatching it from the air, he chuckled and wrapped the ribbon around his forefinger where it solidified into a gold ring.

***

Katie lay with her eyes squeezed tight, the only part of her body over which she had regained control since Cadmon drugged her. Thin red lines wormed from her pelvis, making her groan and twitch as the virus ate its way along. Mesmerized, Cadmon sat cross-legged on the bed beside her. With each growth spurt, a tangible thrill ran through him. Since the T-nanogen in his body was fully mature, it raced to duplicate the same level of infestation in its new-found organism. Cadmon felt as awed as if he were witnessing the birth of his own child.

As the damage progressed, his emotions boomeranged between elation and terror. He had never felt more powerful, yet knew the peril of discovery. This little snot would soon be so deformed no one would recognize her, but she still knew her name—and his. Even if she were brain dead, her flesh would identify the one who did this to her.

Playtime's over.

He scooted off the mattress and retreated into the bathroom. Normally, he kept the shower temperature and pressure low to protect his delicate skin, but now he set both on high. The steaming water burned like a cleansing flame, seeping under the torn simskin, working it loose. Bits and pieces swirled down the drain at his feet, but parts of it refused to come off. He gave up, dried in the air jets, then returned to gather his clothing from the floor. He forced his thoughts into order. By the time he finished dressing, his emotions had flat-lined and cold logic took over. There was only one possible course of action.

I need to get rid of the evidence. All of it.

He thought something in the Insta-Shop might work, but a search through the display proved fruitless. Items sharp enough were too small to be of use, and those of sufficient length, too dull and fat. What he needed wasn't in this room. He needed help.

Damn it, I need Lester. But maybe that's not all bad. I'll have to deal with him sooner or later anyway, and the more involved Lester is in this, the better.

Using his knuckle, Cadmon tapped the room's com-panel. "Call Lester Merritt, send audio only." Within moments, Lester's blazing white smile appeared on the small screen.

"Having a good time?" Lester asked.

"More than I ever imagined." Cadmon kept his tone casual. "I'm not late for the meeting yet, am I?"

"Um, no, I, uh—just got a message from them. They won't be here for another hour or two—at least."

"I see." Cadmon doubted now there'd been any meeting scheduled at all. "In that case, why don't you join us?"

"Huh. Okay. You're kinkier than I thought. On my way." The image winked out.

Cadmon picked the cleanest of the sheets from the floor, covered the girl, and waited. When Lester buzzed the door, Cadmon slid it open, grabbed him by the collar, and yanked him inside.

"Hey!" Lester objected. His eyes flared wide at Cadmon's ruined face. "Holy Mother, what happened?"

"Exactly what you expected. I can't believe I trusted you."

"Hey, you're the one who designed the stuff, so don't blame me." Lester pulled away and grimaced. "What a mess."

Cadmon grabbed him back. "Which you're going to clean up or—"

"Okay, okay." Lester again extricated himself from Cadmon's grip. "Relax. I'll get you out of here, don't worry." Straightening his rumpled shirt, he stepped into the room and his gaze fell on the bed where a still figure lay covered head-to-toe with a sheet. He froze in place.

"She wasn't pleased when my face collapsed."

Lester stared, unable to move closer. "You didn't. I mean, she's not—is she?"

"No, but she needs medical attention. There should be a physician's emergency kit around here somewhere. Find it."

Lester exhaled in relief, "Oh, okay."

"Don't say anything to anyone."

"I'm not stupid," Lester said, and slipped out the door.

Cadmon hoped Lester was more stupid than he realized. In minutes, Lester returned, emergency kit in hand. Cadmon rummaged through the bag until his hand closed over a thick rod—a cauterizing laser—exactly what he'd hoped for. He re-calibrated the instrument, putting the width and depth on maximum. Reaching back into the bag, he pulled out two sets of surgical gloves. He donned one pair, and handed the other to Lester. "Put these on, then take the cover off that." He gestured toward the disposal chute with a gloved hand. "Hurry, we don't have much time."

Lester nodded and did as he was told, pulling off the lid. "Good thing you got a medical degree," Lester said. "What's she got, a concussion or something?"

"Or something," Cadmon said under his breath as he approached the bed. He pulled the sheet down just low enough to expose her head and neck. A jagged red line peeked out, crawling up her throat. Lester's arm whipped around him and snatched the sheet away. Katie's body oozed in red ribbon paths—the deep twisting sores of a T-nanogen carrier.

"Holy Mother!" Lester dropped the sheet. "What have you done?"

"What you arranged, obviously."

"No, no, I gave you condoms."

"They must have been defective, like this simskin. Seems you have a problem with quality control."

Lester's eyes were wide with panic. "What are you going to do? You can't leave her like this."

"No, of course, not." Cadmon tried to sound sympathetic. "That's why I sent you for this medical kit. Now calm down, and do exactly as I say."

Lester nodded, but his face was slack.

Cadmon knew he needed to work fast before Lester's wits returned—and before Katie's pumping heart could overwhelm cauterized flesh. Turning his back to Lester, he grabbed her by the hair. Her eyes opened wide, but the paralysis had yet to wear off. Cadmon brought the laser down like a guillotine, severing her head from her torso. Before Lester had a chance to react, he tossed the head into the open chute. The unit hummed on as Lester gaped, open-mouthed. Cadmon sliced again and thrust a severed arm at him.

"Take it!" Cadmon ordered. His fate teetered on this moment. Only the force of his personality would save him.

Lester stared at the appendage as if he couldn't fathom what it was, but then slowly reached out, and dropped it into the chute.

Cadmon kept his external expression unchanged, but inside he celebrated. Working quickly, he handed each severed body part over for disposal. Lester, pale as milk glass, performed like an automaton. In short order, the bed was empty.

***

Lester fought the rebellion in his stomach, a bitter taste bubbling in the back of his throat. He fought even harder to keep his mind-numbing haze intact. Part of him couldn't grasp what was happening, and he preferred it that way. Just minutes ago, he'd been in charge, ready to have a little three-way fun, then blackmail the hell out of Cadmon. Now it had all gone horribly wrong.

His unfocused gaze swept the room, taking in the soiled sheets, the emptied bed, the discarded shield, and unopened condoms, along with a scattering of red-stained objects of debatable function. He lost the battle with his gut, starting to retch. Cadmon grabbed him by the back of his neck and bent him over the open disposal chute.

Coughing and spitting, Lester opened his eyes and saw whirling disassemblers below his face. "Shit! Let me up, let me up!"

Cadmon pulled him back. "Don't do that again."

"I won't, I promise." Appalled, he watched Cadmon gather the damning evidence into the remaining sheet, turn back and thrust it at his chest. Fear of exposure to the virus-filled fluids overcame his revulsion and he shoved the bundle into the chute.

"That's the last of it, except for these." Cadmon tugged off his gloves and gestured at Lester's. "Put your gloves in then replace the safety cover using your sleeve."

Dazed and spent, Lester followed orders. The room looked clean now, as if he had dreamed the entire nightmare. Cadmon stared at him intently. Somehow Lester found his voice again, but it seemed to be coming from a great distance. "You never said—I just thought—"

"Never mind what you thought. It's done now."

"But they'll find out."

"How? There's nothing here to find, and you and I are the only witnesses. There's no one else involved, is there?"

Lester heard the cold sharpness of Cadmon's tone. He'd clearly misjudged his target. All he'd wanted was a little something to hold over the head of Fabri-Tech's Nano-Engineering Research and Development Department, but not this, definitely not this. The predatory look in Cadmon's eyes cut through Lester's mental fog, and his mind up-shifted.

If I'm Cadmon's only remaining liability, what's to stop this freak from disposing of me as well?

Cadmon looked emaciated, but exercised fanatically, something Lester never bothered to do. Under that shattered-toad flesh was pure muscle; and Cadmon still had that surgical laser in his hand. Lester's instinct for self-preservation kicked in. *Stick with the original plan.*

"Of course, there are others," he lied. Unlike his emotionally transparent cousin, Lester knew how to work a con.

Cadmon continued to stare at him, clearly skeptical, but waiting for more information.

"I told you I had to make arrangements for all of this." Lester went on, layering credibility on the fabrication. "It takes deep connections to set these things up, believe me, but don't worry, I always plan for contingencies. Here, you're going to need this."

He slipped out of his jacket and swung it across Cadmon's shoulders, arranging the hood. Grabbing the mask from the nightstand, he palmed the hidden camera, then shoved the mask at Cadmon. "Put this on and go out the back. Lay low until first light, then head for our transport. I'll meet you there."

Cadmon looked at the mask, then back at Lester. "And what do you plan to do?"

"I gotta clean up this mess, like you asked. You've seriously complicated things here. I'll have to grease a few more palms and it won't be cheap, believe me—but don't worry about that now—we can settle up later. Better get going while it's still dark out." Lester spoke rapid fire and tried to steer Cadmon to the door. "I'll take care of everything. All you got to do is act like nothing happened."

Cadmon donned the mask and moved toward the door.

Lester almost exhaled in relief, but then the masked face turned back, the eyes behind it boring into him.

Cadmon enunciated his next words with deadly precision. "Should any of this come to light, I promise you'll regret it."

"Come on, it's me, your buddy, Les." Lester put on his most sincere smile. "I got you. Believe me."

Cadmon stood immobile between Lester and the exit, gripping the laser, and staring hard through the mask. Lester froze in that icy blue gaze, feeling the cold sweat of terror trickle down his armpits, mustering the last of his self-control to meet that stare without flinching. The mask nodded once, the door swished open, and Cadmon disappeared into the hallway. Lester slapped the lock back on.

The air held tight in his lungs gushed out and he leaned his forehead against the locked door.

What should I do? I have to report this, right? How can I report it? I helped.

Katie's healthy alluring image came unbidden into his mind, followed by the vision of her severed head sailing into the bin. *Oh, dear Mother!* Flipping around, he fell back against the door and squeezed his eyes shut, digging fingers into his scalp to push the image away.

No, no, no, it wasn't me, it was him. She was already ruined when I got here. I would never have hurt her. Yeah, but you didn't help her either.

The images tumbled in his mind, vivid and unrelenting. Another wave of nausea threatened. He swallowed it back down, taking deep steadying breaths. Crossing himself, he whispered half-remembered prayers—some for Katie, some for himself.

Okay, okay. Pull it together. You can't stay here.

The room looked clean, but evidence lay in things far too small for the human eye to see. Cadmon Dhyre, master of the atom, was well aware of that. Lester looked down at his hands.

What did I touch?

He stood away from the door. His skin cells must be floating in the air settling over the room's surfaces. Every breath he took in here could damn him, but only if someone bothered to look. An investigation might track her to this room, but for that to happen, someone needed to report her missing.

The girl was a runaway—no family, few friends—none who would seek out the authorities. Katie would be just one more fringe element fallen off the edge—among the missing, but unmissed. He doubted anyone would come looking, but on the off-chance someone did, he wanted to make sure the right person took the fall.

Poor Katie wouldn't blame me for that.

He pulled out the camera he'd retrieved from the mask, and played the time-and-date-stamped recording back. It began with Cadman removing his clothes. Naked, he moved toward Katie as she came out of the bathroom. Lester shut it off. He didn't need or want to see more. It was already enough to put Cadmon in his pocket as planned. Problem was, what he originally envisioned was a mouse, not a viper.

I'm going to have to be careful, very careful.

Chapter 8

Los Angeles, North Americas

Leaving Lester behind to tie up any loose ends, Cadmon slipped away through the club crowd and returned to the same dark alley where he'd met Lester. He peeled off the over tight jacket Lester gave him and removed Katie's movie idol mask. Though he doubted anyone would look close enough to discern the presence of deteriorating simskin mixed with his own distorted flesh, he methodically plucked the bits and pieces away. He dropped them into one of the recycler bins along with his fake ID and the cauterizer he'd hung onto until now. Lester was probably expecting him to return the jacket, but he flung it in as well. He looked at the mask, wanting to keep it as a souvenir, but knew better, so he tossed it in with the rest.

Listening to the hum of the recycler dismantling his deposits, he thought about how ridiculously easy it became to destroy incriminating evidence after nano-manufacturers like his employer won a campaign for wide distribution of these energy efficient recyclers. The bins converted waste into free raw material for the use of Fabri-Tech and others. He smiled, wondering if he himself might turn Katie's molecular content into some useful new product. *One has to appreciate the irony.*

Retrieving his pouch from under the bin, he pulled out his Carrier ID badge and waved it over his upper right arm to make his implanted tag revert to its original coding. He tucked the badge in his hip pocket, pulled out the cloak and swung it around his shoulders. The pouch folded itself into a palm-sized square which he slipped into the cloak's inside pocket.

There, back to my former self, far as anyone else will know. He checked his wrist display. Nearly an hour until sunrise, time enough to make it to the transport station.

He set off, a full-fledged toad once more. As before, he kept to the back alleys, working his way through the early morning shadows like a dark ghost. Recognizing his cloak of deformity, people stayed out of his way, letting him pass by untouched and untouchable. Still, he kept a wary eye out for any roving street gangs who might relish the opportunity for a little toad-bashing.

By first light, he reached the transport station and the relative safety of its small quarantine area. For a long while, no one joined him behind the medic shields. He wasn't surprised. Not many of his kind ventured outside the Carrier Camps. Even fewer owned passes for off-world travel. As he waited alone, the far larger area on the other side of the medic shield filled with passengers. He soon spotted Lester walking into the terminal. Several yards behind Lester hitched a stooped man in a cloak similar to his own—this had to be the carrier who'd slept in Cadmon's hotel room last night. One benefit of their disease was that it made it difficult for normals to tell them apart, especially since normals seldom looked any carrier in the face. Cadmon's doppelganger joined him in the quarantine section. They pretended to ignore each other.

"Thank you," Cadmon whispered without looking at him.

"It was my honor," the man whispered back, and their conversation ended.

As he waited for his designated transport, Cadmon kept an eye on Lester. He wondered if the promised black-market traders were mere fiction or if they'd actually shown up. He'd been too busy running for his life to find out. If the traders met him there at the start as Lester had promised, he never would have had that drink, and succumbed to Katie's charms. She shouldn't have been there either, but it seemed Lester had his own agenda last night. Still, if the simskin formula had been unchanged as Lester also had promised, it would have held up and she wouldn't have rebuffed him, and he wouldn't have had to kill her. Any way he looked at it, the blame came back to Lester.

He remembered now how all that rage he'd suppressed for a lifetime simply exploded. Letting it out had been a relief, but in the cool light of morning he despised his lack of self-control. He'd put everything in jeopardy, and for what? The momentary pleasure of taking his need for revenge out on one silly young woman who hadn't brains enough not to insult him. He'd taken a stupid risk, but appeared to have gotten away with it, so far. The only loose thread remaining was Lester.

He studied the man's movements for anything out of character. As his assigned escort, Lester would be held accountable as well.
Unlike Cadmon, Lester wouldn't be executed, but he could end up in
rehab fitted with behavioral control implants—a normal's worst
nightmare. The rehabilitated were easily identified by their glazed
expressions interspersed with grimaces of pain.

No, Lester wouldn't risk that. He'll keep quiet.

A booming automated voice announced the Fabri-Tech
transport ready for boarding. Cadmon left his look-alike behind with
a subtle nod. He had no concern for his silence either. The man was a
loyal fan and well-paid for the honor of serving him. Cadmon entered
through the ship's open rear door and took a seat in its hermetically
sealed section. He and his fellow passengers were all Fabri-Tech employees traveling to the same destination, a carrier camp in Death
Valley. This trip was a company-sponsored humanitarian visit and
Cadmon was its featured speaker. His underlings glanced back at him
through the hermetic seal and he nodded permission to depart. Over
the years, Cadmon had gained a certain notoriety. Among his professional peers he enjoyed a grudging respect, while the carrier
population cited his achievements for inspiration.

*I wonder what they would think of my latest conquest. Equally
inspiring?* He was certain some would.

The transport ascended to its assigned elevation, spun forty-
five degrees, and accelerated. G forces pressed him back, then faded
when they reached their designated travel speed. This would be a
short trip. Thirty minutes later, Cadmon spotted the camp. Sunlight
reflected off a clear glass dome enclosing a long, rectangular building
with a flat, metal rooftop. He'd never been to this particular camp
before but it looked like all the others, including the one in which
he'd spent his childhood. There were six hundred carrier camps in total, all built within months of each other from the same set of
architectural plans.

Their transport hovered over the landing area, a wide donut of
concrete. When they touched down, his restraints automatically released and the exit door opened. He stepped out into a blazing dry
heat that sucked the breath and last bit of moisture out of him.
Within seconds, his exposed flesh started to prickle and sting.

Already perspiring, he limped forward, hurrying with the others to get inside quickly. Like all these camps, this one was built in a place no one would choose to live. Doors ahead opened for them. The cool moist air inside was a welcome relief. A greeting committee awaited them—four uniformed normals and one toad. Cadmon didn't need to wonder which was assigned to him. The deformed woman rushed toward him with a hitching gait similar to his own.

"Dr. Dhyre, it's such a pleasure to meet you. I'm Naomi. I'll be your assistant today," she announced breathlessly. "If there is any-thing I can do to—" she stopped and grimaced. Her wide smile had split her bottom lip open. "Excuse me." She dabbed at the blood with a dark handkerchief. "I'm so sorry."

"Don't apologize," he told her, feeling a rush of anger. "Never apologize."

She nodded, looking embarrassed. "No, of course not. Please, come this way. Everyone is so excited you're here."

He fell into step with her as she led him to the camp's interior rail system. A large group of the camp's residents applauded at his approach. He nodded and said thank you repeatedly until finally the train arrived and their clapping ceased. Everyone parted to let him board. As he walked past, hands shyly reached out to touch the fab-ric of his cloak. Naomi pointed him toward the luxury seats at the front of the train and informed him they were going to camp's main auditorium, which he already knew, of course. He didn't really need a guide. These camps were all the same. So were the people—all of them scarred, deformed, and pain-ridden like himself—except he had escaped, and they hadn't. He knew they admired and envied him for that, but it was an envy born of ignorance. They had no idea what it was like among normals, to live one's life as a pariah.

At the auditorium, Naomi showed him to a chair on stage alongside leaders of the camp's community. They, too, treated with him with great deference. He sat and waited for his introduction. Scanning the audience, he saw none of the other Fabri-Tech employ-ees he had flown in with, nor any normals for that matter, except for the camp guards stationed in the hall, who had no choice. Appar-ently only carriers were interested in anything he had to say. No surprise there. No doubt, Lester and the other Fabri-Tech employees were being given a VIP tour of the now emptied facility. That way they wouldn't have to look at the suffering faces of the people who lived in it. The community mayor beside him stood and approached the podium.

"Welcome, everyone. I know you're all eager to hear from our esteemed guest today, one of our own, who has enjoyed great success in the outside world. Not only has he succeeded, he has excelled by any measure. Before accepting his current position supervising a state-of the art orbiting lab for Fabrication Technologies, he was a tenured professor at the Tokyo Institute of Nanotechnology, where he developed the nano-suppressants many of us here rely on to make our lives more manageable. The list of inventions and medicines he has authored is so long it would test your patience just for me to list them, so instead, I will allow him to speak for himself. Please welcome Dr. Cadmon Dhyre."

Cadmon rose to more applause and approached the podium, where he thanked the mayor and took his place. He looked out at the sea of scarred faces before him as they fell respectfully silent and looked up at him, waiting expectantly. For a brief moment, he closed his eyes against the sight. He'd delivered his memorized speech so many times before, with its formulaic words of encouragement, but now the idea of praising these people for their courage and perseverance sickened him. He wanted to tell them the truth. He needed to tell them the truth. What he'd experienced last night—that was truth. He couldn't pretend it wasn't anymore.

"I'm a monster," he said, surprising himself and them. "You're looking at a sideshow, a freak genius, an unnatural curiosity valued by normals because I happen to know more tricks than they do. Sadly, like you, I will be gone far sooner than I would wish. My talents might be missed, but not me. Nor will any of you. Our early deaths are expected, welcomed. Anyone outside of these walls would say the sooner the better. They hope we will all die out—finally ridding the world of the ineptly programmed nanogen infecting us. I hate them for that, but I can understand it. This tiny beast is a sadistic killer that tortures its victim to the last breath.

What I can't understand is why the world blames us for its existence. You didn't create it. You didn't choose it. Yet here you are locked up and despised for your affliction, and worse, denied all hope for a cure."

He paused to look at their shocked expressions. This wasn't what they expected to hear, nor what he'd planned to say. He kept going.

"How many of you here even know its origin?"

He looked around the room as hands lifted tentatively. He shook his head, seeing how few there were. He pointed to a man near the front. "You there. What were you told?"

"It was made for settlers on the Moon and Mars."

"Yes, and who designed it?" The man's hand went down. No one else raised theirs. "Who tested it? Who distributed it?" Still no hands. "You don't know, because no one knows, or no one's telling. The military, probably. A government sponsored experiment, I suspect, but all we know for certain is that after what was thought to be a routine inoculation of off-world settlers, they began to change. Their pores tightened to combat water loss, their subcutaneous fat diminished, while muscle and bone density increased. They were ethereal looking—tall, slender, with skin as smooth as glass, and perfectly suited to thrive in parched, low-gravity environments." He paused to let that sink in, watching people exchange looks. "And then it made its way to Earth. How did that happen?"

"Visitors caught it from them," the earlier man volunteered.

"A few, perhaps, but the real culprits were drug dealers who harvested body fluids to smuggle through customs to sell as beauty and weight loss treatments. Early users turned into unblemished angels. Not surprisingly, their love lives improved dramatically and their intimate partners evolved too. More and more wanted the same, and wasn't everyone so happy to share, when all it took was a little screwing around?"

A few nervous titters followed.

"Trouble was, the T-nanogen was designed to create a specific ratio of bone and muscle to body mass. Earthbound, it faced a challenge. To compensate for the increased gravity, it gradually modified its rate of tissue consumption, turning its human host into the scarred, emaciated wraith you see in your mirror. That's when people went into panic mode and the Plague Riots ensued. Ignorance, fear, and prejudice—the three go hand-in-hand-in-hand."

No one was smiling now.

"Since you're here, it means your parents or grandparents survived long enough to be relocated. No doubt, they lost everything in the process and probably died before you ever knew them."

Heads nodded in solemn agreement.

"The healthy think of themselves as normal and call us toads—insulting, but memorable. Even now there are those who call for mass sterilization, or worse. And yet here you sit, second and third generation carriers, proof that the will to procreate won't be quashed even under the worst of circumstances. I see a few women here ready to give birth. I wish I could congratulate you, but I remember what it's like to grow up in a camp like this. You wouldn't know it to look at me now, but even among carrier children, I was exceptionally striking. I come from good Nordic stock—a blessing in the normal world, a curse in here. With my parents dead and no one to protect me, I was used often and badly, and nearly always for the profit of others. I wonder how many of you have suffered the same? Did any guards come to your rescue, or did they pay for the privilege of abusing you as well?"

People turned their heads to stare at the armed guards, who shifted uncomfortably.

"I finally sought out the meanest, strongest, camp monster I could find, and offered myself up in return for his protection. You mothers will soon be dead, and that's what awaits your child. So no, I can't congratulate you."

A woman in the front row, whose belly was near term, burst into tears.

"I was luckier than most. I had a formidable intellect and gained access to a computer. I zeroed in on the two areas that gave birth to our damnation—medicine and nanotechnology—and bought myself a ticket out."

They looked at him eagerly now. This was the part they wanted to hear, the part that gave them hope. He decided to crush it.

"Don't for a moment believe you're likely to do the same. I'm unusually gifted. Offers came rolling in: scholarships, employment opportunities, research grants for the taking, but, of course, none who offered realized that their online expert was a twelve-year-old tadpole on the brink of turning into a full-sized toad. Not until Professor Natan Hyaku at the Tokyo Institute figured it out." He paused, remembering the man who'd mentored him.

"It could have ended his career, but Hyaku campaigned relentlessly until he obtained permission for me to study with him. For years I was grateful, until he discovered I was using my access to the University labs to alter the T-nanogen to find some way to stop it without killing the host in the process. I thought Hyaku was a great humanitarian, but he turned out to be like all the rest, willing to let our kind die rather than risk his career.

"The only way to combat a self-replicating nanogen is to build a better one. One that can recognize that its own fate depends on the fate of its host. In other words, intelligent—and that makes it illegal. I have the knowledge and the will, but not the way. I'm not allowed to create a cure, and neither is anyone else. In short, my advice is to disabuse yourselves of hope. Maybe then you'll stop procreating and die out the way normals want you to."

He looked at their stunned expressions and thought about walking away right now, but he needed to make himself clear.

"What my parents did to me in ignorance, you continue to do in knowledge. I'm not looking for sympathy, I'm offering blame. I understand the short-lived beauty of your children reminds you of your lost humanity, but it's selfish, and I can't help but wonder what's happening to them this very moment as you sit here listening to me. If you can't protect them, don't have them. If you can't do either, then end yourself."

He saw his anger reflected in their eyes now, ready to explode back at him. Before it did, he walked off the stage. Voices erupted, and Naomi went running after him. He exited through the nearest door, turned left down the hallway and out another door on the right. He knew these backrooms as if carved into his bones. Apparently, Naomi knew them too.

"Dr. Dhyre, Dr. Dhyre," she called behind him.

He ignored her and exited through another door, then another.

"Dr. Dhyre, please. Don't give up on us!" she yelled.

That stopped him. He turned around and she ran up to him.

"You're right," she said, and had to pause to catch her breath. "Many of us are selfish and afraid, but you're not."

"I'm not sure that's true."

"I don't believe that, or you wouldn't have said those things. You have the knowledge and the will. We're need you to find the way."

He wanted to laugh, but she was too sincere. "It's impossible. I'm watched round the clock. I'd have to be Houdini."

"You're smarter than any magician."

He couldn't argue with that, but his superior intellect hadn't proven enough so far. "I appreciate your faith in me, but it's not like I haven't tried. No one will listen."

"I'm listening. We all were. We'll do anything to help."

"There's nothing any of you can do. Not in here. Change must come from outside."

"You're on the outside."

"Yes, and I'm reviled and defied at every turn."

"You think we have it easier in here?" Her face hardened, and he saw she was not the innocent he'd assumed her to be.

"No, of course not, but what you ask simply isn't possible. I'm sorry." He turned and walked away.

She didn't follow, but he heard her speak again and her voice took on a deep bitter note. "If you can't make them listen, then make them pay."

He paused and nodded. "That I can do."

He made his way through the familiar hallways toward the exit, remembering the unrelenting determination of his youth to find a way out, and reflecting on all that he'd experienced since. His peers at Tokyo U. had accepted that he was interested in a variety of topics: genetic research, human medicine, artificial intelligence, and nano-engineering. As long as he'd appeared to be working on disconnected projects, the disparity in his interests caused no alarm. As a further precaution, he'd professed to using only non-human DNA in his research. Relying on deception and distraction, he'd kept everyone in the dark for years, but finally someone caught on. A pre-cocious student perhaps or maybe a jealous colleague recognized the patterns, connected the dots and filed an anonymous complaint. When called before the Board of Trustees, he'd denied everything, but his tenure at the Institute had been pulled with the blessing of his mentor Hyaku.

Left without an employer to sponsor him, the threat of camp re-internment loomed large. But then he'd learned ACES was looking for a new Director. Cadmon felt confident of his qualifications, until he saw Daniel Walker at the ACES gathering. Ten years his junior, Walker stood a broad-shouldered six foot two with clean classical features, a rakish cheek scar he made no effort to disguise, and the muscles of a man accustomed to physical exertion. Walker smiled and laughed in an easy manner and carried himself with a casual grace that said he was comfortable in his own skin. Cadmon despised him on sight.

When Walker strode toward him with his hand outstretched, Cadmon stared at it in disbelief. People seldom shook hands any-more and never with him. His hopes sank abruptly. Who better to be an icon for ACES than the sole survivor of the Garuda massacre? When the selection was made, it came as a bitter disappointment, but no surprise. It wasn't a question of good science, but of good PR. Walker made an excellent front man, something Cadmon could never be.

He recalled how the following day, Walker had sent him an of-fer for a subordinate research position at ACES, but before he could accept, the offer was withdrawn, and Cedric Peterson offered him a consolation prize, head of research and development at his own pri-vately held company, Fabri-Tech. Cadmon assumed Walker must have regretted making the original offer and had Peterson cover for him. Left no other option, Cadmon accepted the Fabri-Tech position.

It took him over a year to find the loopholes in Fabri-Tech's se-curity so that he could hide programs within programs and continue his real work in secret. Each design came a bit closer to success until finally he had a prototype that worked...or at least appeared to in mock-ups. In his excitement over finding what could be a cure, he allowed himself to think Fabri-Tech's Board might sanction his work. He recalled Peterson's horrified reaction.

"Are you insane? We shouldn't even be listening to this."

Thankfully, he hadn't been foolish enough to reveal that his AI-nanogen was anything more than a theoretical hypothesis, and he'd already had it in mind to use his simskin to strike out on his own. It had all seemed so doable then, but now his back-up plan had failed, all because he'd relied on someone else, someone named Lester Merritt. He wouldn't make that mistake again. Unfortunately, he still had to deal with the man. He reached the camp entrance and waited for Lester and the rest of their group. His fellow travelers trickled into the area, clustering together some distance away. When Lester arrived, Cadmon waved him over.

"I'm canceling the rest of the tour," Cadmon told him.

"But we have two more camps to visit and everyone's expecting to be wined and dined on the company tab for another three days."

"And I care because …?"

"Okay, I get that, but don't you think changing our schedule might bring unwanted attention?"

"I'm sick, remember? No one will question it. We're going back, now."

"Fine," Lester agreed sullenly, and left to go inform his co-workers.

Cadmon could tell by the expressions on their faces and the angry way they glanced over at him that they were disappointed, which gave him a momentary pleasure.

Soon after their transport's departure, the company's orbiting lab came into view through his portal, revolving slowly against the backdrop of space. The silvery-gray structure looked like a giant, spoked wheel from an old-fashioned bicycle, but it held a state-of-the-art nanotech manufacturing facility employing more than five hundred technicians and support personnel, all working under Cadmon's supervision. His plan to set up his own lab had only been a way to do what he should be allowed to do in there. Constructing a nanogen in the Fabri-Tech lab wasn't the real problem. He'd done it many times. The problem lay in extricating it. He recognized now that it wasn't his circumstances stopping him, but his own timidity. Each time he birthed his nanogen into existence, he'd dismantled it, certain of being caught. Now he realized that instead of dismantling his nanogen, he needed to dismantle Fabri-Tech.

Chapter 9

The Moon

Immediately after the press conference, Daniel met up with his uncle and together they headed for the train terminal.

"Is Serena joining us?" McCormack asked. He glanced over at Daniel. "You did let her know you were leaving?"

"Um … yeah, she had some stuff to do first. We'll meet up later, on board," Daniel said. When McCormack looked away, he messaged Serena. "See you onboard."

There, now he hadn't lied, and she wouldn't waste time looking for him. Conscience clear, he checked the time. "We can still make the 4:15." He trotted forward, his uncle grumbling, but keeping up. They wound through the underground tunnels following the arrows labeled Magtrain Terminal 3.

A car was pulling away just as they entered the station.

"Come on." Daniel sprinted ahead.

"Oh, for pity sake!" McCormack protested, but broke into a run.

The side door opened, letting Daniel hop on. He grabbed his uncle by the arm and pulled him inside. Heads swiveled at their risky last second entrance and followed their search for open seats until they dropped into an empty pair in front of the cargo hold. Leaning back into the seat padding, Daniel sighed.

"God, I'm glad that's over. No more press conferences."

Pursing his lips, McCormack said, "No, not until we get back at least. A year for us, ten for them. It's a strange thing. Turns you into a time traveler of sorts. Those two ship years your father and I did cost us over twenty on Earth."

Daniel nodded. He'd heard the story many times. The two of them met aboard a deep-space research vessel. His father was injured by a piece of heavy equipment and was rushed to surgery, saved by the ship's doctor, and 'voila,' a lifelong friendship began.

"Stasis makes it seem like no time passes, but the world leaves you behind," McCormack added, then looked at Daniel. "Hope you're prepared for that."

Stasis. Daniel kept his expression neutral, but grimaced internally, envisioning those small pods.

"I've been preparing for this my entire life," he said, and broke eye contact to look out the window as the train climbed to the surface, revealing the Moon's flat landscape, a harsh white under the sun even through the darkly tinted windows. He stared at the lunar rocks sliding past until he heard soft snoring. His uncle had nodded off. *Good idea.* Daniel closed his eyes, hoping to get a few winks as well, but almost beneath his hearing, a soft mewling worked into his awareness, making him open his eyes again to peer through the mesh divider into the cargo hold behind them. Round yellow eyes in a furry blue face looked back.

"Sonofabitch!" Daniel hissed.

McCormack startled awake and turned to see what Daniel was looking at—a five-foot tall, ultra-thin Nereid. She blinked forlornly at them, clinging to the bars of her cage with webbed hands and feet. Her dirty, seal-like blue fur was matted from neglect.

Daniel half-lifted from his seat to look around. His search stopped on a bulky man two rows ahead wearing a shoulder patch with the swirled blue and gold letters ETTA—the logo of the Extra-Terrestrial Trade Association. He thought about shoving the man off the train and setting the caged Nereid free.

"Don't be stupid," his uncle warned, pulling him down into his seat.

Daniel glowered, the desire to act burning inside him. *He's right; don't even think about it.* He could imagine tomorrow's lead story: "Walker on Rampage. Mission to Tau Medea Canceled." *You can't afford to get involved, not this time.* Still, the impulse was hard to put aside. Especially since he'd done it so many times before.

The first time he'd set a Nereid free had been in self-defense when he was only twelve years old, a few months after the Garuda attack. When released from the hospital, he'd been placed into the custody of his father's sister, Aunt Emily, whose family included his then seventeen-year-old cousin, Les. On that particular day, the adults went out, leaving him in the care of his teenaged cousin. Les interpreted it as an opportunity to sneak six of his buddies into his father's off-limits basement. When Daniel tried to follow them, Les stopped him at the door.

"You wouldn't like this party, Danny, believe me. Besides, I need you to keep watch."

"But we're supposed to stay together—that's what your parents said."

"You're better off out here." His cousin locked the door in his face.

Daniel waited outside, unhappy to be ostracized, but keeping watch. As the muffled whoops of laughter on the other side of the door grew louder and more enticing, the injustice of being excluded grew in proportion. The door lock was a simple five-digit combo. *Probably the same one Les always uses.* Daniel's fingers went to work and soon the door slid open. What he saw froze him in place. Les and his friends cavorted in various stages of undress around a Blue Fuzzy leashed to the bed. Daniel's mind screamed, *Shut the door!* but his body just stood there, mouth agape.

The biggest teen saw him and yanked him inside. "Hey, guys, look who wants a piece of the action."

Daniel tried to pull free, but the older teenager was a lot bigger and wasn't letting go. Daniel looked over to Les for help.

"Take it easy, Greg," Les said. "Anything happens to him, I get blamed."

"I'm not gonna hurt him. Just educate him," Greg replied and seemed to be in charge.

"Where—where'd you guys get a Nereid?" Daniel asked, partly from sheer amazement and partly to act like he had no problem with it. "Don't they cost a fortune?"

"She's his dad's," Greg said, and pointed at Les, who took a deep breath and looked aside. That the Nereid belonged to Lester's father shocked Daniel as much as the scene in front of him.

"What do you care?" Greg asked.

Daniel tried to cover his surprise. "Just . . . just wondering."

"Yeah? Well, what we're wondering is whether you know what to do with one? Right, guys?" The boys all laughed. Daniel knew he was in trouble. "People say you faced down a Garuda. If you're such a bad ass—let's see you prove it."

Greg tugged him toward the bed. The others followed, chanting, "Danny, Danny . . ." Les wasn't joining in, but he wasn't stopping them either.

Daniel didn't know what they expected of him, but he wanted no part of it. "Let go of me!"

The teens threw him forward and he fell on top of the Nereid. It felt like a furry blue, stuffed toy, except that it was alive and as big as he was. Her yellow eyes blinked wide in a terror that matched his own. He tried to push away from her but was shoved back down. Someone tugged on his pants, upending him, and his nose pressed against the locked leash tying her to the bed—a lock with Les' initials. His cousin might be bigger and worldlier, but he wasn't overly bright. No doubt, Les used the same code on the lock as for the door. Daniel struggled to open it, his felt fingers thick and clumsy in his panic, but the lock popped open. The Nereid scrambled from beneath him, screeching in high decibels as she leaped for the tilted cellar window and shot through its narrow opening.

For a moment, the boys stood staring at the open window with their mouths ajar. Then they turned on him with their fists clenched. Daniel curled into a ball crying out as they pummeled him until his cousin jumped into the fray with a wicked nine-inch blade, swinging it like a wild man. The pummeling ended with blood on the floor— Daniel's as it turned out—but it got everyone running out the door, Daniel included. He ran and ran, and hid in the dark streets and back alleys, blending in with the unwanted, and managed to survive among them on those mean streets for months until someone turned him in for the reward. Without medical treatment, it had taken a long time for the knife wound to heal.

Remembering, Daniel lifted a hand to the deep indentation in his cheek.

"I don't know why you won't get that fixed," McCormack commented. "You wear it like it's a badge of honor."

"More of a reminder." He could forgive Les for wounding him, but not for the rest. There was no excuse for abusing such docile creatures.

McCormack sighed. "Just let it go, Danny. It isn't your battle."

Maybe not, but Daniel still felt responsible. Uncle Charles and his father had been involved in the discovery of Nereus. It was supposed to have been the Earth twin humanity needed. Instead, it turned out to be an endless salt-water ocean sparsely dotted with volcanic rock—great for fish, not so much for humans. Few would have ventured back if not for the discovery of a native lifeform that looked like a cross between a human and a blue seal. Following the tradition of naming worlds after figures in Greek mythology, the planet was named Nereus, the old man of the sea, and its creatures became known as Nereids, his sea-nymph daughters. No one could figure out how these warm-blooded, four-limbed, air-breathing, ocean-going mammals ended up living on a watery world with nothing else more evolved than amoeba and seaweed. Even stranger, Nereids all appeared to be female. Their nature and true origin was a subject of continual debate, but one thing about them was indisputable. They were ill-equipped to deal with humans.

Accidentally freeing that first Nereid when he was twelve inspired Daniel to become a vigilante rescuing Nereids, something he pursued through his early teen years until caught. Back in the limelight again, his fate became a hotly debated topic. That's when Uncle Charlie stepped in, saving him from being turned over by his blood relatives for rehabilitation.

Daniel wondered whatever happened to all those Nereids he'd set free. Runaways were common, even without help from self-appointed activists like himself. Ads offering rewards for lost Nereids filled the Web. He supposed people probably found the escapees and quietly took possession. He also suspected some covered up the deaths of their exotic pets by claiming they'd run away.

Uncle Charlie made him promise to stop breaking into people's homes to release Nereids, but he still did everything possible to discourage the trade. It saddened him that despite protests against the trade, and the risk of encountering the Garuda, the ETTA continued making hit-and-run raids on Nereus. For every ship that didn't make it back, the demand and profit rose higher. Daniel doubted the Garuda had anything to do with the missing ships, but if so, he almost felt like rooting for the enemy. The thought brought him up short and horrific memories threatened to flood back. Like dark phantoms, the bird-like figures always loomed at the edges of his mind. He shuddered internally and pushed them into the blackest recesses. No, he didn't wish the Garuda on anyone.

The caged Nereid mewled again, the sound scraping at his nerves. He longed to see this one fly through an open window too, but of course that wasn't an option. This was the Moon.

Don't be a moron. Running around setting Nereids free would make you look like a lunatic. He sighed and shifted in his seat, unable to get comfortable.

"Maybe you should find somewhere else to sit," McCormack said.

"Fine." Daniel got up and walked back through the cars, putting distance between himself and the caged Nereid. No open seat presented itself, so he hung on to a pole until the train reached the Central Station. Peering through the window as the train slowed, his heart skipped a beat. The Niña shuttle was already there waiting, parked on the tarmac.

As he and his uncle approached, the pilot jumped down to greet them. "Lt. Taggatt, Sir. You can relax in the back, or, if you like, one of you can take the co-pilot seat."

Daniel grinned and climbed into the cockpit. McCormack rolled his eyes.

"Don't let him crash us, please," McCormack said and headed into the back.

Although his hands itched, Daniel kept them in his lap and watched Taggatt go about the business of take-off, running through the safety check list, and communicating with the control tower. The shuttle soon lifted, aimed toward the curved lunar horizon, and took off, skimming over the Moon landscape of brightly lit crater ridges and dark glassy inclines. In the harsh light, phosphorescent minerals (fools' diamonds) sparkled in the regolith, soaking up the sun's energy. When night fell again, they would glow like fireflies trapped in the rock. Daniel listened to Taggatt speaking in that slow drawl test pilots had made standard since Chuck Yeager in the mid-twentieth century.

"This is Niña Shuttle Four Niner to Shipyard Lunar One, re-questing clearance for approach." Taggatt said then paused. "Roger that."

The shuttle aimed steeply upward. When the orbiting shipyard filled the view screen, he maneuvered around its circumference until the Niña came into view.

"There she is," Taggatt said. "Ain't she a beaut?"

"Yes, she is," Daniel agreed, grinning wide. He'd waited so long for this moment. His long-imagined ship was far from the modest vessel his parents once envisioned, but very close to the one he'd created in his mind when trapped in that cargo tube.

Never intended to enter an atmosphere or touch down on soil, the impressive interstellar voyager looked like a triple-decked flat-tened moon. The top deck housed cargo holds, docking bays, crew quarters, mess halls, and a recreation center. Middeck, the protected heart, contained the command center, the research labs, sickbay, and the stasis chamber where the crew, and anything else with a beating heart, would be ensconced for the duration of the intra-stellar flight. The bottom level held storage areas, the brig, and the engine room. The last was the most expensive part of the ship's con-struction as it housed a diamond fusion reactor to power the ship's Hawking Drive, and the zero-point-energy gravity well. Corridors, lifts, and emergency stairwells linked everything together. Daniel had taken a long-range view, designing the ship not only for this first ex-ploratory mission, but for many more to come transporting settlers and supplies.

Taggatt skipped them over the top of the Niña, where a circle of robotic satellites bristled like a spiked crown. The satellites would be launched upon arrival at Tau Medea to scatter reconnaissance probes over its surface. Assuming the results were as favorable as Daniel expected, they would follow up with manned survey teams.

A long line of dark gray shuttles like this one were wrapped nose-to-tail around the Niña's broad equator forming a fat metal belt. One link was missing—this one. Taggatt dropped level to fill the gap and a metallic clang echoed through the hull. Daniel had ex-plored the Niña in an interactive holo many times during its construction, but never in the flesh until now. When the airlock opened, he stepped into a cargo bay bustling with activity. Magnetic cranes hummed, crisscrossing each other's paths as they moved crates under the watchful eyes of their human operators. A lanky young officer wearing the insignia of a lieutenant walked toward him with a grin on his face.

"Dr. Walker, welcome aboard. Lieutenant Riley, Communications and Navigation, at your service, ready to answer any and all questions," he said as they shook hands.

"Ah," Daniel replied, uncertain why he would come greet him in the cargo bay. "Well, I was going to ask about the status of our fusion reactor."

"Still in production, sir. Fabri-Tech promised it will be shipped along with the probes by the end of the week."

Daniel nodded, remembering that it hadn't taken him long to figure out why Cedric Peterson was such an enthusiastic supporter of the space program: he wanted his privately-owned nano-tech company to get the manufacturing contracts.

"Anything else I can answer for you?" Riley asked, lifting his wispy brown eyebrows.

"No, not that I can think of."

"Then allow me to show you around."

"I designed this ship. I think I know my way."

"Yes, of course, but as this is your first time aboard, Captain Kowalski thought you might appreciate a guide."

"Did he now? Let the captain know that I prefer to explore on my own. Please, don't let me keep you."

"Yes, sir." Riley's smile faded. He looked down and walked away.

"Another broken heart left in your wake," McCormack said ruefully. "Speaking of which, call Serena. Then come by sickbay first chance you get. I need to complete your medical exam."

McCormack turned and called out to Riley, "Hold on there, Lieutenant. I, for one, could use your assistance."

As Daniel watched his uncle leaving with the lieutenant, he thought about his appointments with Serena and sickbay. In the first, he was destined to get an earful about his performance at the press conference, while the second promised a different sort of unpleasantness. *This is my first day on board. I should get to enjoy it.* Decision made, Daniel set off to explore his ship without interference, poking his head into every room and compartment, and only introducing himself to posted crewmembers long enough to gain access before moving on.

He relished his self-led tour for hours, until he ran into Uncle Charlie in one of the corridors.

"There you are. Figured you were avoiding me. Come on. Into my exam room. Let's get you cleared."

Daniel groaned. "We'll do it tomorrow."

"No, we'll do it now. It should have been done already as you well know. Now don't you give me any more trouble, or I'll sic the captain on you."

Daniel chuckled at his uncle's empty threat. "Fine, long as you make it quick."

"I promise. Quick and painless—well, mostly."

Daniel followed him through the hall to sickbay, which looked exactly as he expected. Hospital-white floors and walls, with chrome-framed beds, tables and chairs. McCormack gathered his tools as Daniel sat on an exam table. He began probing Daniel here and there with this and that. Some of it smarted and made Daniel grimace.

"What did Serena say about your abrupt departure after the press conference this morning?"

Daniel looked aside. "We haven't exactly had a chance to talk yet."

"Running away from her too, then, are we?"

"No, there's no running. I have a lot of responsibilities. I am in charge of this mission, remember?"

"Oh yes. Yes, you are. Terribly impressive." McCormack jabbed him in the neck with hypo spray.

"Ouch!"

"There, that's the last one. Still sticking to your regimen? Daily workouts? Supplements?"

Daniel nodded yes to each.

"Good. Your stats look fine. Keep it up. Remember, the better shape you're in, the better you'll do with stasis."

"I know, I know. You don't have to keep telling me."

McCormack regarded him for a long moment. "All right. I'm done with you for now. Better get going. I'm certain someone else is waiting for you . . . and has been for quite some time, I'd guess."

Daniel sighed in response. As he exited sickbay, he noticed the ship's automated lighting had darkened to twilight. His uncle's comments about avoiding Serena irritated him but he couldn't deny the truth of it and now he felt guilty. He checked his wrist-link and saw four missed messages. Instead of reading them, he sent one of his own.

"Sorry I missed your calls, my love, but I'm on my way now. Time to celebrate!"

There, that should be mushy enough to earn a pass.

He swung by the mess hall to grab a bottle of champagne and a pair of stemmed flutes.

Spirits high, Daniel stepped through the door to his quarters. As his foot went down, an ear-piercing screech coincided with a stabbing pain in his right ankle. He yelled and jumped sideways. Serena's cat hissed and fled across the room.

"Stupid cat!" Daniel snarled and hobbled over to his desk. He set down the champagne and glasses to rub his ankle.

Serena rushed in through their adjoining door. "What did you do to Sugar?"

"Stepped on its tail, I think. What's it doing lying in front of my door?"

"Oh, poor little thing." Serena pulled the fluffy white feline into her arms to deposit a flurry of kisses on the flat of its head. "Did he hurt you?"

"What about me?" He gestured at his injured ankle as he experienced a stab of jealousy and felt all the more absurd for it.

"Pick on somebody your own size." She kissed the cat again.

"Keep it out of here, or it'll be more than a tail that gets squished."

"Shame on you," she scolded, but wore an amused look.

Despite his objections, Serena had been adamant about bringing her cat. At least her parents hadn't insisted on coming along, too. He watched her set the animal down in the middle of his floor, then stand to look at him with her arms crossed. Seeing her cool stare, he thought better of complaining again. Instead, he turned his attention to the room itself.

Next to the roll-out bed, built-in shelving and drawers stretched the length of the room. His executive flowchair faced a work station of blond wood polished to a high shine that reflected the champagne bottle and glasses sitting atop. On the other side of the station, a pair of smaller chairs stood ready to accommodate guests. The room's hard surfaces, fabric-covered furniture, and tiled floor were all done in muted beige tones. An interior door on one side of the room connected his quarters to Serena's, while a door on the other side led to his *en suite* bathroom. All as expected.

The personnel areas had been designed in cooperation with psychological consultants to be compact, comfortable, and esthetically pleasing enough for long-term use. All the senior staff had been accorded similar accommodations. Even the crew quarters were roomy by ship standards. Some of his critics called it decadent, but Daniel knew every additional square centimeter meant improved morale.

He noted his father's hardbound books in a recessed bookcase lined up by author's name. The antique collection was rare enough to be valuable, but Daniel kept them for sentimental reasons. He felt a small tingle of pleasure seeing his new dark blue uniform laid out on the bed, with his name and title, Mission Commander. He was about to thank Serena for that, when her cat leaped up and curled into a ball on top of it.

"Hey!" he objected and started forward. The green-eyed cat laid back its ears and flicked its long white tail in warning. Serena stepped between them and pressed her palms against his chest. "He's not going to hurt your precious new outfit. Besides, you're not going anywhere, are you?"

He glared past her at the cat. "Well, no, not right now, but—"

"I wouldn't think so. It's been a long day for you," Serena said as she pushed him back and down into the desk chair, "exploring the entire ship, hands-on inspection, and the whole time, you had to be so careful to avoid me. You must be exhausted."

"What? No, I was just excited to see everything."

"Come on, admit it," she said, and moved behind him to knead his shoulders. "You didn't want me lecturing you about your temper tantrum at the press conference this morning."

"That wasn't a temper tantrum. I meant every word."

"I'm sure you did. I'm also sure you've been wondering how much it cost you ever since."

He rolled his eyes annoyed that she knew him so well, but gave in to the truth under the pressure of her strong fingers. "Okay, you're right, but it looks like no harm's done."

"That's because I smoothed things over for you."

"What does that mean?"

"I sent an open letter of apology to the Supreme Father."

"What?" Daniel's voice rose an octave, and he twisted to look at her. "Please, tell me you're joking."

"I explained that you were overtired and being reminded of your past was more than you could handle."

Daniel blinked in shocked silence, his mouth opening and closing.

"Fortunately, his high holiness was in a generous mood," she continued, and twisted him back into position. "He expressed sympathy for your deep-seated emotional issues and stated that although he cannot agree with your position, as for your unfortunate choice of words, he forgives you."

"Forgives me? Augh. That insufferable demagogue. I can't believe you did that. Really, Serena, you had no business—"

Serena dug her fingers in.

"Ow! Take it easy."

"Admit it, I did you a favor."

"By making me sound unstable?"

"No, you did that for yourself. I made it sound like you'd come to your senses." She kept him pinned in place.

"This is a matter of principle," he objected.

"Enough to sacrifice the mission?"

Daniel stopped short at that. "No, of course not, but—"

"You offended people today . . . people in power. It would have blown up in your face if I hadn't stepped in. And it may not be over yet." She still held him in check with her hands.

"Come on. It wasn't that bad."

"Yes, it was. Fortunately, my abject apology worked, so as you said, no harm done . . . I hope." She went back to working his neck and shoulders.

He sighed in resignation, though still annoyed. "I don't see why I'm the one who has to dance around their super-inflated egos. It's preposterous."

"And necessary."

Daniel sighed again. "Okay, I know you're better at this stuff than I am, but still, you need to clear things with me first. I suppose there's no way to undo that apology now."

"No, nor should you. Anyway, we'll soon be long gone from here so what does a little dent in your pride matter?"

He sulked and didn't answer.

Serena went about kneading his neck in a more pleasant manner and he let his eyes close.

"New topic," she said after a bit. "Our quarters here—it's like we're still on the road, staying in connected hotel rooms. I was thinking we should we turn one side into a bedroom and the other into a dedicated work space."

His eyes popped open. He knew he'd better be tactful about this. "Well, that's an interesting idea, but of course you know we'd have to unbolt everything, and it would mess with the premise that all the quarters be identical, so no one could complain. We want everybody happy, right?"

The massage stopped. "In other words, you want me on one side and you on the other."

"That's not what I meant. You can come in here whenever you like, but I'm sure there will be times when we'll each want some privacy. It's nothing personal."

"Nothing personal? That about sums it up, doesn't it? Nothing personal."

"Don't get all melodramatic on me. This isn't a honeymoon. I'm going to need my own work space, especially since you insisted on bringing that stupid cat along."

"This isn't about my cat or your work space and you know it." She spun his chair around and turned that penetrating gaze on him that always made him feel squeezed into a corner. "Relationships are built on trust, Daniel."

He had a hard time looking back at her. "This has nothing to do with trust. It's about work."

"So, you think sharing quarters with me would undermine your work?"

"Yes, no, I . . . stop twisting my words. The point is that I'm going to need to concentrate. I have a huge responsibility here. This mission bears my name. It's always me they're attacking. In the end the responsibility will be mine."

"Me, my, mine," Serena mimicked. "Your mission, your ship, your quarters. I thought we were a team."

"We are. But let's not overdo it."

Her expression tightened. "I hardly think rearranging the furniture is overdoing it."

"I'm sorry, but—it's better the way it is."

"I should have known. Even after all that therapy, you're still scared to let anyone get close."

"Don't go there. I'm just talking about separate rooms."

"Fine, if that's the way you want it." She stepped away and scooped up the cat.

He watched dismayed as she headed for their common interior door. He still wasn't sure what she was so worked up about. He had a right to some privacy, didn't he? Not that he wanted it right now.

"Come on, don't make a big deal out of this." He tried to think of something to save the moment. "We should be celebrating. Look, I brought champagne."

"Hoping for a little action, were you?"

He smiled lopsidedly and shrugged. "You know me so well."

"I'd rather sleep with my cat." With that green-eyed fur ball tucked under one arm, she disappeared through their adjoining door.

"Pervert!" he sang out, hoping humor might break the mood. He waited for the closed door to reopen. Instead, the lock clicked on.

Should he run after her? If he didn't go begging immediately, there was no way he was getting any tonight. And as much as he resented that unauthorized apology on his behalf, he recognized she was probably shrewd to have done it. Her diplomacy had saved him more than once after he'd stuck a foot in his mouth and chewed thoroughly. And it was Serena's mega publicity campaign that turned his personal obsession into a global vision. If not for her, he might still be begging handouts from small time corporations and private investors.

Still, it's my dream. I'm the one carrying the load. If anything goes wrong, it's on me, not her. She should appreciate the pressure I'm under.

He knew if he made the first move, she'd assume she was in the right. "Dammit!" he cursed as he chose pride over lust.

Daniel turned his back to their common door and punched up the ship's roster—a long list of forty-six engineering technicians, one hundred ten civilian specialists and one hundred twenty combat-ready troops from the UN Armed Forces. He needed to review each profile to assess abilities and personalities for assigning them to teams for the on-ground manned surveys he planned to do on Tau Medea IV.

Initially, he read and reread the words, trying to focus, until the drumming of the ship's engines worked into his brain, enabling his concentration. Before long, his irritation with the cat, the argument with Serena, and the final disappointment of sleeping alone faded into the background hum and there was nothing left but the work.

Chapter 10

Fabrication Technologies, Inc. Orbiting Lab Station

Outwardly, Cadmon went about managing the Fabri-Tech facility as if nothing had changed. Inwardly, his mind focused on devising a new exit strategy. Or rather it would be focused if not for a pestering distraction creeping about in his peripheral vision—Lester Merritt, lurking around corners, stalking him like some half-starved predator. Within a few days following the night at the Wrec-U, Lester came into his office to ask a favor, a small one, a trifle, an extra day off.

Cadmon said, "Fine," just to get rid of him.

The next day Lester returned slipping into Cadmon's office unannounced.

"Now what?" Cadmon asked, looking up from the graphic display of a fusion reactor lighting up his desktop.

Lester rolled the edge of his jacket back to reveal a sound dampener in his inside pocket. He tipped his chin down as he spoke, hiding his mouth from prying camera eyes in the ceiling.

"With this on, we can talk freely,' he said. "Just don't let them read your lips. Sweet, huh?"

Cadmon sighed. "And why is that important?"

"Need another favor. A sample of that fabric you're testing for subzero temps."

"That's proprietary information."

"Yeah. I know. That's why I brought the sound dampener. Duh."

Duh? Cadmon's jaw clenched and his eyes narrowed. He wanted to throttle Lester and might have, if he didn't have so much at stake. As it was, he couldn't afford to bring attention to himself.

Just go along. Do whatever it takes to get him to go away. Besides, that fabric's already old tech, not worth fighting over.

"I suppose this was your plan all along," Cadmon said as he rose from his chair and went to the wall of cabinets to get a sample of the cloth.

"Just a little *quid pro quo* between friends, right?"

Friends, ha! Discreetly handing over a palm-sized square of the cloth, Cadmon noted the guileless smile on the face of his black-mailer. Amazing how Lester could look so innocent—a well-practiced performance.

"Thanks, Caddy," Lester said, flashing that artificial smile again. He flicked off the sound dampener. "Yes, sir, Dr. Dhyre, I'll get right on that."

As Lester went out the door, Cadmon imagined knives flying into his back—*snick, snick, snick.*

The next day, Cadmon looked up from his desk at yet another unannounced entry.

"Okay, got the dampener on," Lester said. "This time I need the plans for that hand-held medical scanner you're working on."

"Absolutely not," Cadmon covered his mouth to shield it from the camera. "You idiot, that scanner's still pending patent approval. Fabri-Tech expects it to be a big money maker. Security's tight."

Lester leaned forward onto Cadmon's desktop, tipping his chin down. "I just need the specs, not the unit itself."

"To sell to the highest bidder, I assume?"

"Got a few people interested, yeah."

"And you think Fabri-Tech won't get wind of it? Are you really that naïve? I'm not about to let your stupidity put me in jeopardy."

"I'm the stupid one? You couldn't even figure out how to use condom. I saved your ass, remember? You owe me, big time."

"Do I? It's my word against yours and we both know which carries more weight. Now get out." Cadmon uncovered his mouth and pointed to the door.

"Remember who you're talking to." Lester kept his hands flat on top of Cadmon's desk. "You don't want to cross me."

Cadmon rose to his feet, too angry to restrain himself even for the sake of the cameras. "Get the hell out of my office!"

Lester pulled back in surprise, but then he nodded and smiled. "You're gonna change your tune. Believe me."

"Doubtful."

"You'll see, you'll see." Lester chuckled as he back-walked out the door.

It took a long time for Cadmon to stop envisioning ways to eviscerate Lester Merritt.

That night locked away in his cramped quarters, Cadmon lay on his bed with his tablet propped on his chest. He angled it to make the screen invisible to the cameras in the ceiling, so he could study the lab station's blueprints without anyone asking why. Swiping silently from one page to the next, he committed each section to memory, until the images wavered. He tapped the screen in frustration, then stopped when an unsolicited scene overwrote the display. Cadmon sat up and angled the screen further downward. A carefully edited recording showed a horror of a man with melting skin methodically torturing a helpless young woman, then single-handedly disposing of her corpse. At the end, a silent message scrolled across the darkened screen: "A copy is safely under the control of a third party, who's been instructed to forward it to the authorities if anything happens to me."

Cadmon cursed and slammed the tablet onto his nightstand, wishing it were Lester's face. "First chance I get, I'm shoving that worthless parasite out an airlock." He pictured Lester's blood boiling in the vacuum of space, taking pleasure in the fantasy, but as satisfying as that thought was, he had a far more important goal, which meant dealing with Lester would have to wait. Besides, he could still have the pleasure of seeing Lester die in the vacuum of space if he went forward with the one foolproof plan he had come up with so far. Cadmon ran it over in his mind again. He'd been hoping to come up with a less drastic solution but kept circling back to the same conclusion. There weren't any. The losses would be regrettable—there were talented people on this station—but with Lester blackmailing him now, he couldn't afford to wait any longer. Having made up his mind, Cadmon ordered lights out, closed his eyes, and slept the dreamless sleep of the resolute.

At exactly 4:00 a.m., the overhead lights flicked on and woke him. Cadmon rose from bed and inserted himself into his body-stretcher, a form-fitting exercise machine which pulled every joint and muscle to its maximum extreme—a necessary evil he endured daily to combat the debilitating effects of the T-nanogen infecting him. The painful ritual seemed pointless under the circumstances, but any deviation from his daily regimen might trigger alarm. As always, Cadmon methodically performed each step of his well-rehearsed morning ritual: a quick medicinal-based shower, followed by a pharmaceutical cocktail of mega-vitamins, immunity boosters, and the nanogen replication suppressants he himself had designed.

Dressed and ready, Cadmon stepped out into the exterior hallway at exactly 4:30 am. He had set this work schedule for himself long ago to have a few hours free of his underlings' looks of revulsion. An added bonus was never running into Lester at this hour. Deep shades of lavender simulated twilight in the curved outer hallway, and safety stripes in the corporate colors of blue and orange glowed softly along the sides of the gray carpeting.

Cadmon went straight to Central Replications, the manufacturing portion of the station. He waited beneath the flashing 'Authorized Personnel Only' sign, while a curved security panel circled him to scan the chip in his bicep, confirm his voice ID, read his iris pattern, and check his palm print. He kept his breathing regular and heartbeat steady, knowing any undue physical excitement might also trigger an alarm. The doors opened to double sterilization locks which sent cleansing air swirling around him, before at last allowing him entry into the lab.

The cavernous space of Central Replications still impressed him. Shaped like a crescent moon, the lab's metal walls soared high above hundreds of deeply stacked stainless steel cylinders graduating in size from no taller than himself, to ones that could give birth to a Tyrannosaurus Rex. The latter always came to mind because a life-size robotic version of one had been created to illustrate this lab's capabilities. He remembered seeing the animated beast growling and rearing outside of Fabri-Tech's corporate headquarters.

At his designated work station, Cadmon lowered into a pumpkin-colored flowchair which spontaneously conformed to his contours and weight. When he placed his right palm on the darkened desktop panel, the controls came online, and a grid-marked globe of brilliant orange and blue light appeared, revolving in the air before him. Inside the hollow orb floated the words Fabrication Technologies, Inc. Cadmon frowned at the familiar corporate logo, recalling his last meeting with its Board of Directors.

"Redundancy—redundancy is the key," he had told them. "I will create a nanogen with heavily redundant self-policing programs using old WORM technology: write once, read many. Once encoded by the host's DNA, it will interface with that host alone." He had been so clear in his presentation, explaining that unlike the T-nanogen, his creation would understand never to harm its host or allow itself to be accidentally transmitted. But all his safety precautions fell on deaf ears.

Cedric Peterson had answered for the entire board, "You know very well that combining artificial intelligence with nanogens is banned. This discussion ends now. There will be no such research conducted at Fabri-Tech."

Thinking of Peterson's response, Cadmon felt a rush of anger. *Normals want protection from the toad plague, not a cure for it. Why bother when they have the camps?*

He had to take even breaths to quiet himself enough to concentrate again.

He checked the main production board, then ordered the exterior platform to bring one of the largest cylinders level with him. This T-Rex sized vat was currently manufacturing a diamond fiber fusion reactor. The magnified view window on its side revealed multi-faceted crystals taking form within a milky fluid of bacteria-sized assemblers. Fusion reactors like this one provided unlimited clean energy for Earth's cities. Maybe if they'd been invented sooner, Earth wouldn't be in so much trouble now. Unfortunately, the greenhouse effect had already reached its tipping point, the very reason this engine was destined to power an interstellar ship in the search of another world humans could destroy.

Cadmon shook his head, thinking of mankind's folly. He tapped the control panel to open the reactor's assembly program to make the one small adjustment he needed, but just then the skin on the back of his neck prickled. He turned to see Lester Merritt taking a seat at the work station next to him. *What the hell?*

"This is a restricted area," Cadmon said, frozen in tightly-controlled panic.

"I'm the janitor, remember?" Lester rested his elbows on the seat's arms and pressed his fingers together in a steeple. "Clean-up goes everywhere, and you know just how good I am at cleaning up, don't you?"

"What do you want?" Cadmon glanced back at his panel and darkened it so Lester couldn't see what he was working on.

"Same thing I wanted yesterday. After the little show I sent you last night, I expected you to come crawling to me first thing. Instead, you came here, which means you must be up to something, or you wouldn't be ignoring me like this."

"The only thing I'm 'up to' is performing my duties. You should be doing the same."

"Don't play dumb." Lester leaned forward and peered at the darkened panel. "What are you working on?"

"You can read the production list as well as I can—a diamond fiber engine, some surgical equipment, and a large order of reconnaissance probes—no new cosmetic enhancements at the moment—sorry to disappoint you."

"I'm more interested in what's not on the list. Like maybe something to do with why you met with the Board last month."

Cadmon managed not to flinch.

"Did you think they'd say, 'Why sure, Caddy, go right ahead, violate the treaty, put our entire operation at risk, we've got your back'?"

Cadmon eyed Lester's weasel-like expression, and decided he was just fishing for information. At most, Lester could know only what had been said aloud.

"No, of course, I didn't. It was an intellectual exercise. Nothing more."

"An exercise, huh?" Lester said, smirking. "Maybe, or maybe you got something in the works I should know about."

"Trust me, there is nothing you should know about. Now, if you don't mind, I need to get these orders ready for delivery, and you need to staff the clean-up crew." Cadmon turned away, hoping Lester would leave.

"I know my job. I also know when somebody's trying to change the subject."

"I haven't time for this, and you should know better than to pester me here. Unless you want us both to come under scrutiny, I suggest you get back to work. We have a deadline to meet, remember?"

"Yeah, I remember just fine, and you better remember who's in charge now. We'll talk again after the shipment's launched." Lester stood and started to walk away, then turned back. "And how come you're on the list for clean-up? Isn't that a little outside your job description?"

"No, it is not. My duties require filing performance evaluations of our waste management procedures. I can't evaluate them without witnessing them."

Lester stared at him for a long moment. "Yeah, sure, if you say so."

Cadmon watched him depart, hoping it would be for the last time. Assuming all went as planned, it would be. He turned back to view the fusion reactor under construction, now well past the point where he had intended to alter its program. *Goddamn Lester . . . look what he made me do. Suppose I could unwind it—no, better not. Rewinds are immediately recorded and closely scrutinized.* With a discreet finger movement, he made a single errant entry creating a fundamental weakness in the crystalline structure. *Not exactly what I'd planned, but good enough. Failure will be long delayed, but the catastrophic result will end up the same.* He felt a sense of relief. Destroying the Niña would ensure no loose ends.

He exited the program and sent the cylinder back to its original location, then called up another vat, this one set to construct the self-propelled reconnaissance probes ordered for Walker's ship. The ACES contract called for one hundred thousand of the ant-sized machines. Along with the fusion reactor, the probes were scheduled for shipment this afternoon. The outer platform whisked around, bringing the vat's window level with him. At his command, a swirling soup of organic matter shot into the cylinder and the assemblers inside went to work. That was the authorized portion of the program. *Now for the unauthorized part.*

A series of eye flicks revealed a subroutine visible solely on the lens of the contact in his right eye. There, for his view alone, appeared a complex combination of atoms forged into a spider-like molecular machine—an artificially intelligent, self-replicating genetic-interfacer that violated every restriction set forth in the International Nanotech Treaty. A slow blink made his creation revolve, allowing a final look before signaling the assemblers in the vat to birth it into reality. All he needed to do now was say the word.

The barest hint of a smile played across his cracked lips and he whispered, "The word."

A hidden program went into action taking control of the assemblers in the cylinder. Along with the hundred thousand reconnaissance probes, ten AI-nanogen bots were also being created, each one attached to a probe of its own. Under the direction of Cadmon's subroutine, those ten probes would exit their shipping container and enter the tube's exhaust pipe to be expelled into space upon launch. While the rest of the shipment continued to the Niña, these ten errant drilling probes would assemble at coordinates Cadmon designated, waiting for retrieval. In this way, Cadmon would circumvent the lab's security. Any attempt to smuggle his nanogen out on or within his person would have set off an alarm and accompanying disintegrator. Cadmon's creation would do him little good if he ended up molecularly disassembled. But out there floating in space, they would be free for the taking.

He'd checked earlier to make sure his name was still listed on clean-up duty. Cadmon would recover his couriers by piloting a one-man 'Poop-Scoop,' officially called a Waste Management Vehicle. He was giving himself ten chances, but in truth he only needed one, just one. As he had told the Board, redundancy was key. When at last he had one of his AI-nanogens in hand, he would be free to end his long-suffering affiliation with Fabri-Tech, and end it he would. He again thought of the many people on this station, but when he thought of the dead and dying from the carrier camps, the number paled in comparison. The world had condemned his kind to an early death, without trial or appeal. In the eyes of normals, he and those like him were abominations best forgotten. Well, they would not forget him.

More eye flicks initiated the construction of another closely regulated nanobot: molecular disassemblers, the same as those in recycler units like the one he'd used to dispose of Katie's body. These disassemblers would also attach themselves to probes and be expelled into space in the launch sequence, but instead of waiting for collection, their probes would deliver them back to this station and upon contact, the disassemblers would take it apart, molecule by molecule, atom by atom. While this lab was equipped with a magnetic plasma containment system for keeping nanobots trapped inside, the station's designers never contemplated the necessity of keeping them out. The consequence for that lack of foresight would prove fatal.

Cadmon congratulated himself for his resourcefulness and determination. Ah, but he should give credit where due. Lester's blackmail scheme had provided the momentum, a debt Cadmon intended to repay in full.

***

Six hours later, Cadmon sat at the controls of a Waste Management Vehicle, staring at its curved 180-degree digital recreation of the view beyond. The panorama showed the slowly revolving lab station which lay between his tiny ship and the wide expanse of the blue and white mottled Earth below.

He thought of Walker on the far side, orbiting the Moon in his new toy. Being repeatedly upstaged by Walker rankled him. He took comfort in thinking about the flaw in the Niña's engine. He didn't even mind that it would take a while to work. That might give the Garuda a chance to terrorize the boy-wonder again. Wouldn't that be sweet justice?

It was certainly possible, likely even, considering the fact that months ago, he'd added a little something to the warnings that Earth continuously broadcasted into space from its perimeter buoys—an image of Walker's new interstellar ship. If anything could stir the Garuda into action, that should do it. Another attack would serve him on two fronts: ruin Walker's credibility and scare the hell out of everyone else. A demoralized and frightened populace was more easily manipulated, especially by someone offering salvation. Still, the Garuda were a long shot and he knew better than to rely on anyone else, which was why he'd taken the precaution of sabotaging the ship's engine. The Nina's failure to return would demoralize the public and stir debate, and by then he intended to be the one ready with the answers.

He tapped his console, magnifying the view of the Fabri-Tech station, his first target. There should be little, if anything, left. Not that it would stop the authorities from investigating, of course, probably tying up the corporation for years. A sudden inspiration hit him.

I can sue! A joint civil action for the unlawful death of every employee on the station would not only compensate these people's families, it would be the sweetest revenge. What special pleasure I'll take escorting Cedric Peterson down the road to financial ruin, while in turn bankrolling my own future.

He was amazed he hadn't thought of it before. It was a solid plan, a brilliant plan, but only if he kept his wits about him and took nothing for granted.

He checked his straps, making sure he was held in tight, then double checked his coordinates. He calculated this position offered adequate distance for safety, but not so far away as to appear suspicious, which meant the shock wave would still be considerable. He could see the other four Poop-Scoops jetting about, checking for debris from the launch of the shipment to the Niña. He had stopped looking; he had what he needed, more than he needed. He'd recovered nine of his tiny emissaries at the prescribed coordinates as planned. Admittedly, it worried him to have lost even one, probably still stuck in the shipment headed for the Niña, but it was of no consequence. He'd designed the defect in the fusion engine to cover that very contingency. He was certain he'd addressed every possible outcome. Now that his vessel was in position and the clock was ticking, he silently counted down: *four, three, two, one . . .*

The flat circular center of the station where the power core lay puffed outward, undulating as if there were some desperate creature trying to tear through the metal skin, then the hull split, bursting forth fiery flashes of yellow, white, and blue. The flames zipped up the spokes of the outer wheel and the entire structure collapsed inward like a hollow toy, melting and shrinking into a chunk of charred revolving metal. It had all happened in a soundless instant.

He saw now that two of the Poop-Scoops had vanished, disintegrated in the explosion, but two more floated in the distance, one nearly as far from the destroyed lab as he. He braced for the oncoming wave. Though invisible and silent, it would be felt. He saw the two remaining ships flip as the wave hit them, then his too pitched and rolled wildly. The metal hull groaned and whatever wasn't strapped down bounced, pinged and smacked against the walls and him. He cursed when a hand-held radiation monitor whacked him on the head. He struggled to stop the sickening roll and stabilize his vessel. When he regained control, he rubbed his forehead, reminding himself that bruises would only add to his credibility.

He saw that one of the surviving Poop Scoops had lost its nose section. Its occupant hung half-in, half-out, arms floating up and down as if waving for help. Clearly that person was no longer a concern, but the other vessel was still intact. Cadmon sucked on his teeth thinking it through. He had prepared for this possibility but hadn't quite decided whether another survivor would prove an unfortunate complication or a fortuitous one. On the plus side, it would take half the attention away from him. Suspicion would be halved as well. And now that he had decided a lawsuit should be undertaken, an additional living claimant might be an even more valuable asset. He opened communications.

"Waste Management Vehicle 3. Do you read?" Cadmon waited, listening to static. He repeated the call. "WMV 3, come in."

"Holy Mother of Earth, Caddy. What have you done?"

Cadmon listened, not wanting to believe the voice he was hearing—the one person he had so looked forward to being rid of. He opened the channel again, letting sarcasm drip heavily in his voice. "Lester Merritt, how delightful. I take it you are uninjured?"

"No thanks to you. I knew you were up to something."

Cadmon paused and considered the pros and cons again. Having another survivor would reduce suspicion against him, and with his new idea of suing for wrongful damages, he could use the help. Oh, but why did it have to be Lester? He hated letting him live, yet despite his personal loathing, he had to admit that Lester might be the perfect con man for the job. He opened communications again.

"Listen to me carefully. If you value your life, you will do precisely as I say."

"Is that so? Aren't you forgetting that recording I've got? Once the authorities see that, they'll know what kind of person you are, and they'll believe me when I tell them you destroyed the lab, too."

"Threatening me is pointless. I'm already near the end of my projected lifespan and have little to lose. You have no power over me, whereas I have a great deal of power over you." Cadmon tapped his panel, initiating override for the controls of Lester's vessel. "I suggest you take note of your current trajectory."

A flurry of curses followed and Cadmon smiled, picturing the man's frantic attempts to correct his course. Lester's tiny unprotected ship was headed for the atmosphere where it would burn up on entry.

"I've lost helm control!"

"That's because I'm the one controlling it." Cadmon whipsawed the vessel to make his point. "Do I have your attention?"

"Yes, yes! Stop this!"

Cadmon corrected the ship's course, bringing it level again.

There was a long pause before Lester's shaken voice came again. "Okay, Caddy, what do you want?"

"To begin with, stop calling me that. The name is Cadmon."

"Fine, Cadmon then. Is that all?

"Hardly. Your first task will be to file a lawsuit."

"A lawsuit? Why would I do that?"

"Because you're one greedy son-of-a-bitch, Lester, and I'm going to make you rich. You'll have more wealth than anything you could ever have made with your petty blackmail schemes. Are you listening to me now?"

"Yeah, I'm listening."

Chapter 11

Mars

A silvery shower of metallic hail pelted the cold rocky landscape of a deserted Martian plain, sending up clouds of rust-colored dust. As the dirt settled, the hail mobilized into an army of insect-sized machines. The tiny invaders sprouted drills, and dove into the soil, tunneling underground to gather soil samples, all the while reporting their findings to the orbiting satellite that had expelled them. All except one. One probe sat immobile, paralyzed by contradictory instructions, searching in vain for coordinates that did not exist in its present location.

Its hitchhiking nanobot waited. Time passed without resolution. Finally, the nanobot communicated with its transport to determine the source of delay. A check on current coordinates with the orbiting satellite revealed that the probe's original instructions were no longer applicable. The nanobot had no experience for addressing this situation, but it could think for itself. Its exaflop of artificial intelligence analyzed its options and devised new operating parameters. Deciding the probe was still its best available mode of transportation, it rewrote the probe's programming to complement its own. The probe sprouted its drill and dove into the Martian soil.

Initially, no one noticed this single errant machine out of the hundreds of dutiful ones, even as it passed up precious minerals and ignored rare trapped gasses, reporting nothing, saving its energy for what its tiny master sought. When it drilled into ice, the nanobot analyzed the content. Hydrogen in the ice provided a fuel source, but no blueprint. The probe drilled deeper. The thin frozen thread led to a sizable deposit, where it encountered a complex protein chain. This registered with the nanobot as a significant discovery, which in turn kicked the probe's original programming into action. The probe reported the finding and its coordinates to the orbiting satellite.

The nanobot noted the probe's communication, but since it neither interfered with nor fulfilled its own mission, it concentrated instead on the protein chain. The deteriorated bits of information formed no coherent whole. *Data insufficient, format unrecognized;*

retain for future reference. With fuel available and evidence that carbon-based material was to be found within the ice, the nanobot moved to the next logical step. *Replicate and expand search.*

Soon, instead of one probe under the nanobot's control, there were two sifting through the ice, evaluating and conferring. When that proved insufficient, the matched pair made two more, the four became eight, the eight became sixteen, and within a short time, thousands upon thousands, all doing the nanobot's bidding.

***

Daniel read the incoming order again, but no matter how hard he looked at it, the message didn't change.

"*High Priority. Proceed to Mars to recover subterranean ice. Coordinates and detailed instructions attached. Signed: Senator Nelson Bromberg of the United Nations.*"

"This can't be right. Are we intercepting someone else's communication?" Daniel asked.

Lt. Riley shook his head. "No, sir. The message bears our signature code."

"Patch me through to Bromberg. There must be some mistake."

Riley went to work and in short order, the senator's face floated in the air before them in real-time communication, which meant about a three-second delay—just enough to be irritating.

"Senator, I think there's been some mistake. We just received a message with your signature, rerouting us to Mars for an ice recovery operation."

After a frozen moment, Bromberg nodded. "There's no mistake. Tau Medea will have to wait."

"I don't understand. Since when is Martian ice a high priority?"

"We've received some unusual readings. It's all explained in the reports. Our people want the ice removed intact for analysis."

"Okay, but why us? Why not send one of Mars' dedicated mining ships already on site?" Daniel asked.

"Their equipment is antiquated compared to the Nina's, and the probes that reported the find came from Serena Covington. They were made to your specs, which makes you an even more logical choice."

"Senator, we've been ready to launch to Tau Medea for nearly two weeks now and you're sidelining us to look at bacteria? This makes no sense."

Bromberg's eyes squinted, and his voice hardened. "Let me remind you that the Niña is under UN jurisdiction."

Daniel bit his lips together, not daring to speak his mind.

Bromberg's expression softened again to a patronizing 'I know what's best for you' face. "I understand your disappointment, but rest assured that your government wouldn't ask this of you if we didn't feel it of utmost importance. Also, just between the two of us, some of my colleagues have expressed doubts as to whether someone of your youth and inexperience is qualified to lead a full-blown mission into deep space. Think of this as an opportunity to prove yourself. Good luck."

The monitor blinked to solid blue.

Daniel clenched his fist, and felt like putting it through the screen. Serena had been right about his outburst at that last press conference. Bromberg and his cohorts had been delaying them ever since and now they'd come up with this ridiculous Martian project, probably hoping he'd screw it up. He didn't dare refuse, but at least he could make sure he disappointed them. He realized Riley was staring at him. He opened his fist.

"You didn't hear any of that," he told Riley.

"No, sir, not a word."

Daniel sighed in resignation. "All right. Forward this communique with the attached reports to the senior staff, and tell them to assemble in the conference room at—" he hesitated, deciding how much time they would need to review the material. "Fifteen-hundred hours."

Riley sped the information on, and Daniel turned to leave.

"Uh, sir? What about this message from your cousin? It came with an attached video file. Should I delete it?" Riley asked.

"No, it shouldn't be a security issue. Just leave it in my inbox. Lester's annoying, but harmless." His cousin was always asking for favors, or trying to pull him in on some money-making scheme. He'd read the message later, when he had time. Right now, he had more pressing concerns, the first of which was to figure out what was so damned important about Martian ice.

After reviewing the reports in his quarters, he still didn't know. In contrast to Bromberg's claims, the findings appeared unsurprising. A malfunctioning probe had gone off course and inadvertently located a patch of frozen subterranean water with bacteria in it. Bits of Martian bacterial microbes were a rare, but well-documented phenomena—a fascinating source of endless speculation and experimentation, but nothing new. Either Bromberg was hiding something, or this really was just another delay tactic.

Daniel checked the time and headed out for the meeting he'd called. He could ride the lift or take the stairwells. He opted for the second, deciding he needed the exercise. He trotted down the corrugated metal steps to reach mid-level then turned left, heading forward. He had to smile at thinking in such terms, since the Niña in fact had no forward or aft, being a round shape that spun in flight. Such references were a mere convenience for reckoning within the ship's interior.

The command center was located deep in the ship's belly next to the stasis chamber where the crew would spend the majority of their journey to the Tau Medea system. He passed by the entrance to the chamber where the empty stasis pods waited to be filled. A quick trip to Mars was a disappointing maiden voyage, but at least it didn't require stasis. As he entered the command center, he glanced at the people on duty, dozens of military personnel sitting at their stations, monitoring control panels. The ceiling display showed the dark starlit sky above, the walls displays sweeping around the room provided a 360-degree view of the surrounding shipyard, and the floor looked like an open window to the pockmarked surface of the Moon below. There was no harm walking across its stomach-dropping display, but he preferred not to. Instead, he maneuvered between the work stations to enter the command conference room. The long oval table was already surrounded by staff, and the annoyed look on Captain Kowalski's face told Daniel he was last to arrive.

Kowalski sat at the head of the table with his military personnel arrayed to his right—all but Chief of Security, Manuel Sanchez, who stood at the back. Sanchez met Daniel's gaze, then averted his eyes. Daniel had the distinct impression Sanchez disliked him. The feeling was mutual based merely on the fact that Sanchez had come with the strong personal recommendation of Senator Bromberg. That alone made Daniel want to reject him, but it wasn't smart to oppose a UN senator. Battles of that magnitude should be saved for bigger issues.

Daniel nodded to everyone as he entered and didn't apologize for being late. He noted the open seat saved for him. Military on one side, civilian on the other. He hoped this wasn't a line of demarcation. Lt. Riley, sitting next to Sanchez's empty chair, smiled at him as he sat down. Serving double duty as both Communications and Navigation officer, Riley seemed young, but full of enthusiasm. Between Riley and Kowalski was the captain's second-in-command, Michael Drummond. The thin, middle-aged career man had yet to offer an opinion without clearing it with his captain first. Nondescript in Daniel's view, but reliable and dedicated.

As for the captain himself, Daniel knew Kowalski had worked his way up through the ranks, propelled by a combination of self-discipline and dogged determination. Kowalski demonstrated a no-nonsense approach Daniel appreciated, and most importantly, shared his enthusiasm for deep-space exploration.

On Daniel's side was his top civilian staff members: First Assistant Serena Covington, Alien Lifeforms Specialist Lauren Chambers, Planetary Research Analyst Steven Nakiro, and Director of Medicine Dr. Charles McCormack. Despite the doctor's advanced age, Daniel insisted he be assigned to this mission. McCormack was renowned for his medical expertise and keen diagnostic abilities, so it was easy to claim that the doctor's sterling reputation motivated his choice and had nothing to do with personal loyalty. In other words, he'd lied.

Lauren and Nakiro's heads were bent together in whispered conversation. The two seemed to have hit it off. Daniel shared a longstanding working relationship with Nakiro, a part-Asian, part-African, self-described historian who was top in his field of planetary evolution. Daniel had never worked with Lauren Chambers before, but she too came with high recommendations. Unfortunately, the tall statuesque redhead appeared to annoy Serena. He hoped it wouldn't be a problem. He noticed how different they looked even though dressed in identical uniforms. Lauren wore make-up and let her red hair hang loose, while freckled Serena was barefaced with her brown locks tied back, ready to get to work.

At Kowalski's nod, Daniel summarized the probe reports and their revised orders, then opened the floor for discussion.

The captain said, "We'll launch for Mars in four hours, set up a base upon arrival and then your people can get to work recovering the ice.

"This mission isn't about Martian ice. It's politics, pure and simple," Serena said.

"Not my jurisdiction," Kowalski replied. "My people here need to attend to business, but please, stay and discuss politics as long as you like."

Kowalski stood, and his fellow officers pushed to their feet. Daniel and his side of the table watched the captain and his entourage exit.

"Ah, for the simple military mind . . . just do as you're told," Nakiro said when the conference door closed. He winked at Serena. "Too bad we science types aren't so easily satisfied. I've gone over these reports and I also fail to understand what requires an interstellar ship's attention. Unless, of course, there's something in those reports that I missed?"

"You didn't miss anything," Serena said, "because there's nothing there."

"It's hardly nothing," Lauren objected. "The probes discovered Martian DNA."

"We've got test-tubes full of the stuff." Serena frowned at Lauren.

"I pointed that out, but the order stands." Daniel leaned forward, blocking the women's mutual glare. "What's vital now is that we give our detractors zero ammunition."

"Until they come up with something else to delay us," Serena said.

"Don't you think you're being a bit paranoid, dear?" Lauren asked, peering around Daniel.

Serena tilted her head and pursed her mouth in a sarcastic twist. "No, dear, I do not. This is a repeating pattern. Someone should tell them exactly where they to put their Martian ice."

"Careful, or *someone* might think you're serious." Lauren laughed.

Serena shot back. "I am serious. They're wasting our time."

"This discussion is the waste," Lauren replied, and coolly tucked her red hair behind her ear with a long-nailed finger. "Obviously, we have to follow orders."

Daniel suspected Serena's ire had more to do with Lauren than with their new orders, so he moved forward to block Serena's view of the other woman. "Yes, we do."

Lauren smiled at Daniel. "I'm glad someone's making sense. Instead of getting all worked up, we should think of this as an opportunity to learn more about Martian bacteria. There were multiple DNA sources reported. We may identify ones never recorded before."

Daniel half-smiled. "I suppose that would be something." His gaze turned from Lauren's pleasant smile to Serena's narrowed glare, which now focused on him.

"Well, no point in beating this into the ground," McCormack interjected. "Time to let our Mission Commander and his second sort out the details." He stood and swept his arm toward the exit as he looked at Nakiro and Lauren. "Shall we?"

Nakiro got to his feet, but Lauren looked as if she still wanted to argue, until her eyes focused back on Daniel. "Of course. Whatever you decide, you know you can count on me."

"Yes, I'm sure I can. Thank you, Lauren," Daniel said and watched her leave with the others, unable to shift his gaze from her backside. When he turned back to Serena, her glare had intensified. "What?" When she didn't answer, he decided it was time to fess up to his error. "Okay, you were right. I insulted his high holiness and now we're paying the price, but what am I supposed to do about it now?"

"Well, at least you're thinking with the big head again."

He pretended not to understand. "Am I missing something?"

"Not yet."

He laughed in self-defense and tried to steer the conversation to safer ground. "You weren't seriously suggesting that we ignore our orders?"

Her expression softened. "No, though you have to admit, it's tempting."

"Not with a meathead like Kowalski and a hundred soldiers on board."

"I know," she sighed, but then smiled, "but I sure did enjoy goading Lauren just now."

"So I noticed." Again, he wanted to get back on topic. "Anyway, this looks like a simple recovery operation. Shouldn't take long or be much of a challenge."

"I hope not, because you know Bromberg is dying for us to make a mistake."

"Then we'll just have to disappoint him, won't we?" As she smiled in reply, an idea he'd been toying with solidified. "I've been thinking about doing something else that should annoy him. I want you to be first on the ground at Tau Medea."

"Me? Well, yes, that would do it, I suppose. Pretty sure he likes me even less than you." She laughed, then paused. "But no, it's not appropriate. It should be you. You're the one who—"

"No, I've thought about this. We've never had a woman take that first step before. Plus, we're going to need a memorable quote—definitely your strong suit." When Serena said nothing, he chose to push harder, adding, "Unless you'd rather I ask Lauren."

The glare returned. "You do and I'll cut your balls off. I'm your second, and a proponent of both terraforming and exploration, so it actually makes sense. If for any reason I can't, don't you dare put Lauren or any other random woman in front of those cameras or it'll look exactly like what it is, a cheap publicity stunt based on gender alone."

"Okay, good, then it's you for sure."

"Assuming we ever get there."

"Trust me, I'll get you there I swear. One way or another, you're going to be the first human on Tau Medea IV."

***

Although it galled him to admit, Daniel had to agree with Senator Bromberg on one point. This Martian project would allow him to demonstrate his readiness to lead a large-scale science expedition. Even after passing the required psychological evaluations, not everyone believed he had beaten his childhood demons. No one blamed him for the trauma he'd experienced, but proving the resulting claustrophobia and anti-social behaviors of his youth were no longer a hindrance was another matter. Now everyone would see that he was in full control.

Under Daniel's supervision, Nakiro whipped together concise summaries of the incoming geological data, Lauren readied her lab personnel to analyze the bacteria in the ice, and Serena used her experience with the Martian environment to guide the recovery process on the ground. Meanwhile, Dr. McCormack kept his medical personnel in a state of readiness to deal with any injuries that might occur. As for ship operations, Captain Kowalski handled all with clock-like precision, contributing the expertise and strong arms of his crew to move heavy equipment down onto the Martian surface. Working in low-G in a near airless environment carried inherent dangers, but everyone performed their duties without hesitation. Daniel had no complaints and couldn't see how anyone else could either.

The ice in question turned out to be 156 metric tons of permafrost buried four hundred meters below the surface. They set up a small work base near the find, and the recovery effort began. The job required that the slab remain insulated from the thin water-starved atmosphere or the pressurized ice could literally explode. They drilled three man-sized tunnels, one above the recovery site, and two which dead-ended on opposite sides of the deposit for purposes of triangulation and taking core samples. The center tunnel opened to a cavern carved out to accommodate their work party and equipment. They sealed off the cavern and pressurized it to protect the ice. Once it was freed from the sedimentary rock, they would encase the ice securely and transport it to the Niña, intact, as ordered.

Things were going smoothly, although Serena grumbled through the entire operation. To her, Martian ice was old news, encountered and analyzed hundreds of times. In contrast, Lauren remained relentlessly enthusiastic, insisting the ice might reveal new information for origin of life studies.

"She's just hoping to name a microbe after herself," Serena said aside to Daniel. "Chamberyliad or some such nonsense."

Daniel agreed with Serena, but since it was vital he promote morale and provide no room for criticism, he made a show of sharing Lauren's scientific curiosity. When the two women butted heads, he found himself more than once overruling Serena's time-cutting suggestions in favor of Lauren's more methodical approach. Despite his attempts to explain his reasoning, Serena took it personally. The friction bothered him, but he felt sure that once this operation was over, all would be forgiven. Meanwhile, the work went forward.

Daniel preferred a hands-on approach, but followed protocol, staying onboard to supervise the operation. By the end of the fourth week, an irregular-shaped ice deposit measuring nearly 170 cubic meters had been freed from the surrounding rock in the cavern. Daniel sat with Nakiro at the ship-to-base communication station in the command center, monitoring the recovery team.

"How much longer is this going to take?" Captain Kowalski asked.

Daniel looked up. "Nearly done. Once the ice is hermetically sealed, we can blow the cavern open and transport the ice up to the ship. Another day, day and a half at most." Daniel was equally eager to finish the job, but not about to rush it.

Kowalski nodded and sighed. "Not exactly what we signed up for, is it?"

"Captain," the woman on radar called out. "I'm detecting an incoming vessel."

"Hail them," Capt. Kowalski ordered.

Lt. Riley was already on it, sending repeated demands. "No answer, sir."

"Do we have visual?"

Someone zoomed in the large view screen and a small black dot appeared in the distance. Daniel stared as the dot grew larger taking on a distinct elongated shape.

"Dear God," he whispered.

"All hands battle stations!" Kowalski's voice boomed. "I want it shot down as soon as it's in range."

The man on fire control responded. "I can't get a fix on it. There's some sort of defensive shield fracturing the signal. My readings show hundreds of incoming."

The visual display still showed one lone ebony ship skimming low over the surface in the direction of their domed structures below.

"We could set up a spray pattern," the man on fire control suggested.

"No," Daniel said. "We'd hit our own base."

Kowalski looked back at the visual display. "That's where it's headed. Abandon the base. Now!"

Riley slid in front of Daniel, taking over communications to the surface. "All personnel abandon base. This is not a drill. Incoming Garuda ship. Abandon base. This is not a drill. Abandon, abandon. Repeat, this not a drill."

Daniel listened in horror, knowing enough to stay out of the way.

Nakiro leaned next to him, keeping his voice low. "What about our extra people on the ground?"

Kowalski spun around. "What did you say?"

"Six additional personnel," Nakiro said, straightening to face him. "Maybe they can squeeze in?"

"Squeezing in is not an option. Exceed a shuttle's payload, and it can't reach escape velocity. Drummond!" he called to his first officer. "Send a rescue detail—ten troops, heavy armament. Looks like we're going put those new suits of ours to the test."

Drummond went into action and Kowalski pointed at Nakiro threateningly. "Who gave you the right to authorize extra personnel?"

"I did," Daniel said, meeting Kowalski's glare. "We were moving the drilling equipment off the surface and I let the technicians stay behind to package the ice . . ." Daniel trailed off, appalled. His decision, so carefully considered then, sounded incredibly stupid now.

Kowalski frowned and turned away, giving orders again. The communication channels flooded with alarmed voices from the planet below. Kowalski picked out one: Serena's.

"What's your status, Covington?"

"Both shuttles are loaded and departing now." Her voice sounded tightly controlled. "Any recommendations for the rest of us?"

"You've got ten minutes max. Get below. We're coming for you. Maintain radio silence until all clear."

"Understood."

"Good luck." Kowalski cut off communications and spun around. "Damn it, Walker, why the hell—?" but Walker was gone. "Where is he?"

"I—I'm not sure," Nakiro said.

"Find him."

"Yes, sir." Nakiro sprinted out the door. Kowalski turned back to deal with the crisis.

"Planet-side shuttles have departed," Drummond reported. "If they aren't intercepted, they'll dock with us in eleven minutes. Our rescue detail is launching now."

"Is the Garuda ship altering course to intercept?"

"No, sir. Looks like it's still headed for the base."

"Just the one, then? Are we certain?"

"Radar still can't tell us much, but visual shows only the one," Drummond confirmed. "ETA minus six."

At the one-minute mark, the shipboard computer began an automatic countdown in its emotionless monotone. "Sixty seconds, fifty-nine seconds . . ."

Nakiro reappeared, out of breath. "Walker joined the rescue detail."

Kowalski shook his head but said nothing.

The computer continued, ". . . forty-three seconds, forty-two seconds, . . ,".

Chapter 12

Ice Recovery Base, Mars

Ignoring the soldiers' exchanged looks as he jumped aboard the shuttle, Daniel strapped himself in only seconds before it shot away. He knew the layout of the base and its tunnels first hand—they didn't. More importantly, Serena was down there. When he was a boy, the Garuda killed the ones he loved—no remorse, no explanation. He couldn't let it happen again.

At the helm, Lieutenant Taggatt, the pilot who'd first brought him aboard the Niña, refused to look at him. The ten soldiers did the same, staring at the forward display, watching the Martian surface grow closer.

He recognized their leader. "Chief Sanchez. Good of you to volunteer."

The big man turned and narrowed his black eyes. "Captain's orders."

Daniel nodded and shut up, recognizing conversation was a transparent attempt at self-distraction. He didn't want to think about what might be happening to Serena, or whether he or any of these people with him would survive.

They're back.

Countless hours spent in digital simulations battling the Garuda didn't lessen that heart-stopping realization, but he hoped it would at least prevent him from freezing up.

"There's our base. What's left of it," Taggatt said.

Smoking black dots came into view. A tall black slender winged ship stood on end towering over the leveled structures. The ship looked exactly like the one he remembered seeing on that asteroid as a boy.

Sanchez signaled a silent command to his men. Their flexible, form-fitting suits flashed, rippled and blended into the background, leaving what looked like abandoned boots lined up with ten human heads floating in midair. Reverse Background Imaging Combat Suits—the latest in military camouflage. The men lifted their still-visible feet up to allow their armor to seal under their boots with metallic clicks. When the suits hissed over their heads, the men disappeared, all except Sanchez, who watched him, a challenging sneer on his floating head. Daniel's fabric suit sealed in the needed temperature and air supply, but offered no camouflage or protection from weapons' fire.

Their pilot glanced back, struggling to remain silent.

"Spit it out, Taggatt," Daniel said.

"Sir, when we land, these men are going fast and hard. They won't be watching your back. I strongly recommend you remain on board with me."

"I'm not looking for babysitters."

Daniel pulled the hood of his suit down over his head, locking it shut. He reached for the heavy resonator rifle he'd grabbed before jumping on board. He'd trained with one in boot camp and knew it used pulse detonation technology to funnel an explosion through its barrel at high-velocity. On low, the waves were strong enough to knock down and deafen targets a hundred feet away. On high, it caused gruesome, painful tissue damage. He looked at its controls and saw that they had changed. "New model."

"Yep. Better let me take a look at those settings," Sanchez said, snatching the rifle away.

"Hey," Daniel objected, unable to see Sanchez's hands as the rifle spun in the air, accompanied by some clicks. "I need to see what you're doing."

"Sorry. You'll have to go back to basic training when we have more time." The floating rifle thrust back at Daniel. "There. You're good to go." Sanchez sealed his armor over his head and feet and vanished from view.

Daniel frowned at the seemingly empty space where Sanchez sat, but said nothing more. He was the interloper here, and it was his own fault that he hadn't updated his training.

"Initiating landing sequence," Taggatt announced and shifted them into a steep dive, headed for the opposite side of the base which would put a dirt hill and the blackened structures between the shuttle and the Garuda's ship. Daniel's stomach climbed into his throat as the rocky, red-streaked ground rushed to meet them. At the last possible second, Taggatt pulled up and leveled out, bringing the shuttle to an abrupt parallel with the ground and set it down with a bone jarring jolt.

The side hatch sprang open. Puffs of red dust already showed the invisible soldiers' sprinting path toward the burned buildings. Daniel jumped out behind them and ran hard, relying on his weighted boots to move him forward without gaining too much altitude in the low gravity. On reaching the torched building, he took up a crouched firing position assuming his invisible companions were doing the same. Behind him their fat gray transport ship had sealed itself tight again. Taggatt would wait there until they returned, or he was attacked, whichever came first.

"Clear," someone said.

Daniel entered what was left of their base. Most of the roof was gone letting in sunlight. Red dust on the exposed gray flooring showed footprints—both human and Garuda. An invisible hand grabbed his arm.

"Remember who's in charge here," Sanchez's voice came through.

"I won't get in the way."

"And don't talk."

Daniel nodded.

"Taggatt," Sanchez said. "Our sensors show six targets total, five went in, one still on board, so watch yourself."

"Acknowledged."

Sanchez released Daniel's arm with a shove. "Move out."

Invisible soldiers pushed past. A hand on his back pressed Daniel forward. Moments later, another hand against his chest stopped him.

Ahead were three bodies—two humans, one alien. The humans lay sprawled at odd angles, their throats and chests slashed open, red blood frozen in crystallized shards over their helmets and white suits. Daniel recognized the technician nearest him. The man's blue eyes stared up in sharp surprise. The other body faced away. He forced himself to walk around. The faceplate was smashed, the features crushed and unrecognizable, but the straight dark hair told him it was not the person he feared it might be.

The Garuda jerked sideways, and Daniel jumped back before realizing someone had kicked it, testing for signs of life. Garuda were notoriously hard to kill. Only one body had been recovered from the attack fifteen years ago, an injured Garuda that ended up dying by its own hand when cornered, but there seemed little concern this one still posed a threat. The thing had walked into a booby-trap—a strategically balanced, meter-wide, stone-cutting blade—which had sliced its thick torso nearly in half.

Daniel wondered if Serena came up with that.

Frozen copper-colored blood trailed the Garuda to the wall, where it had crawled to prop itself up and rip off its helmet. *Another self-imposed death?*

"One down, four to go," Sanchez barked.

They moved past the stained blade and its victim. Daniel looked to see if this alien matched what he remembered seeing as a boy. Though brown overall, its elongated head was crowned with orange-speckled feathers, the paired frontal eyes, now dull and glazed, bulged from their blue rims like yellow tennis balls on the edge of exploding and below those eyes, a dark, curved beak hung ajar with a swollen purple tongue lolling from the black interior. Close enough. He shuddered involuntarily and looked away.

"Halt," Sanchez ordered.

Three tunnel openings yawned into the dark ahead—human and Garuda footprints going into each.

"The sides are dead ends," Daniel said, gesturing. "The center one leads to the main cavern."

"I told you not to talk. We have schematics and heat imaging— if you think you're helping, you're even more of an idiot than I thought. Now shut it," Sanchez said. "Okay. Looks like we got one on each side, two straight ahead. Johnson, Schmidt, take the right. Caruthers and Silva, the left. Get them birds when they double back."

An unseen hand pressed Daniel forward again. Instinctively putting up his own, his gloved palm fell against someone's back. He felt like stuffing in the middle of a six-soldier sandwich. The ground angled down and the pale sunlight streaming in through the wrecked roof ended at the edge of an inky black well.

"One way in, one way out," Sanchez said. "We'll wait here and hit them when they come back up."

"What? We can't just wait," Daniel said. "Our people are down there. What kind of rescue is this?"

"The kind we survive. That's a dead end, emphasis on *dead*—get it?"

"You've got weapons and fancy suits to protect you. Our people down there have nothing. We need to go now."

"This is my team."

"And I outrank you. We're going in. That's an order."

Sanchez snorted. "Yes, sir. By all means. Lead the way."

"Go dark," Daniel ordered, switching off his helmet light. At least in the dark, he too would be invisible. Going by feel alone, he held onto the railings of the ladder's self-repairing rope and stepped down the rungs that dived into the shaft to the excavated cavern below. As he descended into the depths, the narrow passage seemed to go on and on, the walls closing in, tighter and tighter. Blood rushed in his ears with a familiar panic.

Stop it! Focus! Keep going! One more rung, one more . . .

At last Daniel reached the bottom where the shaft opened into a larger tunnel. He waited a moment for the others but could only assume they had followed. If not, he was on his own. He moved forward and felt his suit shift as he passed through the membrane sealing in the pressurized air of the cavern ahead.

Without warning, weapons' fire lit up the tunnel and human screams tore through his headset. He crashed against the wall when someone shoved him aside. A pillar of orange flame illuminated two soldiers on the ground burnt to black despite their so-called impenetrable armor. The flames died in the oxygen-poor air, revealing a looming alien figure glowing like dying coal. The massive charcoaled form ended at the shoulders—its bird-like head blown away. It crashed backward.

"One left!" Sanchez's voice rang in his ears.

The soldiers' breathing turned to primal war cries and the trapped air reverberated with resonator shots. Daniel ran forward into the cavern, spilling into what looked like Hades itself. Thick black

clouds roiled against a flame-lit background. He stumbled over something, fell, and rolled away from another charred body.

Down on his belly, Daniel aimed his rifle, searching for a target.
Through a thin spot in the smoke, he glimpsed two struggling figures.
The far larger one held a soot-blackened soldier aloft while two more
lay charred at its feet. Daniel aimed, trying to get a clear shot at the
Garuda, but before he found it, a short person in a white-hooded suit
dashed forward and clobbered the gigantic bird on the back with a
metal canister. The Garuda turned to confront its new antagonist
and the pinned soldier twisted aside, creating the opening Daniel
needed.

He took the shot.

The energy blast hit the Garuda just below the helmet line, a
known weak spot. It staggered and dropped the soldier, its long forearms flailing. Daniel pressed the trigger again for the kill. Nothing
happened. He kept pressing, but the rifle wouldn't fire. Fortunately,
his first seemed to have done the job. The Garuda fell back and lay
still.

Unable to fire his weapon again, Daniel approached with caution. The cavern's overhead lights flickered and flashed to life, and he
saw the small white-suited person at the control panel.

"Serena!" Daniel ran over and their eyes met in recognition.

She gestured and her mouth moved. He reached over and adjusted her com until her voice came through.

"—you doing here? Have you lost your mind?"

He hugged her—and over her shoulder saw three more ground
personnel crawling out from hiding places. Daniel heard a string of
deep curses and the Garuda he'd shot flipped over. He scrambled
back, dragging Serena with him until he realized it was Sanchez
emerging from beneath the fallen Garuda.

The battered security officer clambered to his feet, minus his
resonator, and kicked the prone alien repeatedly until satisfied it
wasn't coming back to life.

"Report!" Sanchez demanded.

One of the four men Sanchez had ordered into the side tunnels
responded, "Enemy down, but we lost Schmidt." The three remaining soldiers emerged in the entrance, their camouflaging armor

made visible by the smoke as indistinct sooty shapes. The imaging mechanisms of their suits shimmered then revealed the men beneath.

"It's over?" Daniel asked.

"Looks like. Still have the one Garuda on their ship to deal with," Sanchez said, "but yeah, we got 'em all down here."

One of the soldiers whooped and threw a fist in the air. Their heavy new resonators had proven effective. His own heart beat wild and Daniel raised a fist as well. This was a moment he'd waited for all his life—to stand triumphant with Garuda dead at his feet. The shared elation soon ebbed. Six of their fellow soldiers had fallen, burned beyond recognition.

"What went wrong with the suits?" Daniel asked. "I thought they were supposed to protect you."

"Yeah, nobody counted on those things." Sanchez pointed ahead.

The restored ventilation had cleared away the smoke, but flames still sprouted from a fist-sized metallic object embedded in the drill shaft.

"What is it?" asked Serena.

"Some sort of small-caliber plasma missile, metal-seeking I'm guessing. Went right through our armor." Sanchez looked over at Daniel in his fabric suit and shook his head.

"It's melting the ice," Serena said.

Water gushed from beneath the still burning missile, forming a steaming pool on the cave floor. The rising mist crystallized in the freezing air, forming refracting rainbows on the smoke and walls, before raining back down through the flames to melt and turn to steam again, setting up a continuous cycle. The pool was growing, the rainbows multiplying. The beauty was incongruous in the midst of such destruction.

"I suppose we better try to save the ice." Serena looked around the ground. "Did anyone see where that fire extinguisher went?"

"Seriously?" Sanchez asked. "That's your main concern?" He turned aside and tried to contact their shuttle. "Dammit, I can't get a signal. We're down too deep." He pointed at one of the soldiers. "Go up, check on Taggatt, and report in. Go!"

Daniel agreed the recovery operation felt trivial now, but deep down he knew better. They would be judged by the success of their assignment, Garuda attack or not. He looked around and saw the dropped metal fire extinguisher behind him. "Got it."

"Oh my god. Daniel, look!" Serena exclaimed.

He spun back and saw the water rising upward. Like someone trapped beneath a crystalline blanket, it rose into a rounded crest, rainbows dancing inside it. Daniel stared in confusion. *What the hell is happening?* His peripheral vision caught another movement to his right. The Garuda they'd thought dead was on its feet. He yelled, "Serena!" and jumped to shield her, but it slung her into the flames with one arm and threw him into the rock wall with its other. Daniel felt his spine crunch and lights flashed before his eyes.

The three armed-soldiers crouched and fired at the Garuda as it dove sideways. Unarmed, Sanchez scrambled clear.

Through a haze of pain, Daniel saw Serena splashing in the water trying to douse the flames on her suit from the missile's plasma. He desperately wanted to help her, but couldn't move. The unnatural crested water turned toward her like a living thing and swept over her. Her screams reached a crescendo, then cut off.

One of the soldiers ran to her aid, entering the water, then cried out, fell and disappeared into it with her. The water rose again, turned and rushed toward the one remaining soldier, who sprinted away. Cornered, he turned back to fire at the oncoming wave as the water shot forward in an aimed attack. Daniel couldn't believe what he was seeing. The man's screams died abruptly.

"Walker!" Sanchez's frantic voice yelled out. He was balanced on a narrow ledge, trapped in the far corner, pointing to Daniel's right. "Get the extinguisher!"

There, a foot away, lay the metal canister. Daniel stretched, crying out when pain sliced through his back. His fingers clasped onto the hose and pulled. The extinguisher rolled toward him. The water seemed to detect his movement and changed direction. He got his hand on the trigger just as the water reached his boots. A thousand sharp needles shot through the soles of his feet. He screamed and blackness swirled before him, but someone else screamed even louder.

"Shoot it, Walker! Shoot it, damn you!"

Daniel squeezed. The pain dissipated, replaced by an icy cold and the blackness lifted. He saw ice covering his legs and feet, and his fingers locked convulsively on the spewing extinguisher. He aimed the freezing spray farther out, at the center of the watery mound where the missile still burned. He sprayed until the last flame died, the rainbows shattered, and all of the living water sheeted over, forming strange curved shapes, and kept on spraying until the canister sputtered to empty and all before him lay covered in ice.

Then he saw the Garuda warrior. It was still alive, standing near the cavern's exit—its upper chest and throat dark with blood, and its weirdly angled legs and huge booted feet were trapped within the ice like Daniel's. On the Martian surface, the rips in its suit would have spelled instant death, but here in this pressurized cavern, it hung on.

Sanchez dropped from the ledge onto all fours, reached forward and tugged on a rifle half-buried in the ice between him and the Garuda.

The Garuda leaned forward and lunged for Sanchez with its long arms, nearly grabbing hold before Sanchez scrambled back to stand next to Daniel. The Garuda stared at them, apparently unable to follow, but it stood there blocking the exit. No one was getting past that ten-foot wingspan.

"Maybe we'll get lucky, and it'll bleed to death," Sanchez said.

Daniel hoped he was right, but the monstrous alien stood strong. It looked downward at the ice entrapping its feet for a long while then finally lifted its head again. Daniel tensed, expecting the Garuda to pull itself free, cross the ice in one long stride, and rip them apart. Instead, it patted its helmet and opened and closed its beak inside.

"What's it doing?" Daniel asked.

"I don't know. Calling for help, maybe?" Sanchez replied.

In seeming confirmation, the ground trembled in the distance. Daniel thought of Taggatt, wondering if he was still alive.

The Garuda leaned over, and grabbed hold of the rifle Sanchez had tried to pull from the ice. Almost effortlessly, it wrenched the weapon free, and leveled it at them.

"Oh shit," Sanchez whispered the curse like a prayer.

Bracing himself, Daniel looked into the face of his enemy again, waiting for it to complete the job its kind had started so many years ago. For an uncanny instant, he thought he saw his own fear and loss mirrored in those huge golden eyes.

To his shock, the Garuda spun the weapon about and fired point blank into its own chest. The great bird fell back and dropped the rifle.

The two men watched the gun skid across the ice until it came to a stop, then stared at it in stunned silence. Finally, Sanchez picked his way across the ice to grab the rifle and look down at their dead enemy.

"Well, I'll be damned," he said, but Daniel didn't hear him. He was out cold.

Chapter 13

Daniel woke to a room of white walls, lying submerged up to his neck in a tank of warm pink liquid with a breather over his mouth. A control panel beside him blinked with lights and digital read-outs. Disoriented, it took a few moments to recognize where he was—sick-bay.

"Hey!" His voice came out a whispered croak, activating the room's automated monitor.

"Your attending physician has been alerted," it said.

Moments later, his uncle arrived, wearing that patented doctor smile of his—the one that said, 'There, there, everything's going to be fine.'

The hell it is.

"Ah, you're awake. Good." McCormack checked the numbers on the panel, then removed the mask over Daniel's face. "Should be able to breathe on your own now."

Daniel gasped his first independent breaths.

"Easy there. Nice and slow. We'll get you out of this tank to-morrow and start physical therapy. Your back's still knitting together, so don't worry if you can't feel much in your lower extremities yet—just as well—your legs were a mess; had to rebuild them from the knees down. You shouldn't notice any difference except for the baby smooth skin. Your hair growth will return to normal after a few weeks. When the nerves come alive, it'll be a bit rough, but you'll be good as new in a week or two."

"Serena?" Daniel asked, barely listening.

The reassuring smile left his uncle's face and he shook his head. "I'm so sorry."

Daniel squeezed his eyes closed. "It's my fault."

"No, Danny, no. You're not to blame. No one could have fore-seen this."

"I wouldn't listen. I had to have this ship. Now the Garuda are back and she's dead. It should have been me, not her."

"Oh good, just in time for the pity party," Kowalski's voice in-terrupted. "Figured you'd wake up whining."

Daniel looked over to see the captain walking toward him.

Kowalski planted his feet in a wide stance and ran his gaze across the medical rejuvenation tank. "Sorry about Covington. I liked her. I really did, but she's not the only one we lost down there, and I don't want to lose anyone else, so you'd better pull it together fast. I need answers."

"Talk to Sanchez. He saw what happened."

"Yes, he told me what happened, but not *why* it happened."

"You expect me to explain why the Garuda want to kill us? Nobody knows, least of all me."

"No, not the Garuda. The probes, the probes in the ice."

"Probes?" Daniel asked, not understanding.

"He just woke up," McCormack protested. "I haven't had a chance to explain—"

"Reconnaissance probes." Kowalski talked over the doctor. "There were thousands of them in that block of ice. That Garuda warrior didn't kill Serena. The damned probes did that. Same kind as the ones we're supposed to use at Tau Medea. You need to figure out what the hell made them go haywire before it happens again."

***

Over the next few days, Daniel filled in the gaps with Lauren's assistance. She visited him frequently during his recovery in sickbay, answering his questions and providing him with updates. The distant vibration he'd felt after the Garuda seemed to contact his ship, turned out to be not an attack on their shuttle, but the Garuda ship self-destructing. Besides him and Sanchez, the only survivors were the soldier that left to check on Taggatt and two of the ground crew, who like Sanchez, had managed to find safety by climbing atop of equipment or clinging to rocky outcroppings along the cavern's walls to avoid the water. Those who were touched by the water had been riddled with monsters of Earth's own making—Fabri-Tech reconnaissance probes. Their origin was known, but how they had become so numerous and aggressive remained a mystery. The next obvious step would have been to question their maker, Fabri-Tech. Unfortunately, the orbiting lab where they had been manufactured and the personnel working there no longer existed. The very day the probes were shipped, the station had blown to hell.

This morning during Lauren's visit, Daniel hung supported in a robotic harness, his personal torture machine, trying to relearn the talent of walking. Lauren winced along with him even though she was clearly trying not to react.

"Unfortunately, there's nothing left of the lab but a charred hulk, and the shipment records were all destroyed," Lauren reported. "The lab synced its data with Fabri-Tech's mainframe daily so they're using that to run simulations, trying to figure out what went wrong."

Daniel thought of his cousin who worked at the lab, dead now, he assumed. Was that his fault too? After all, he was the one who convinced Fabri-Tech's CEO, Cedric Peterson, to give Lester a job, despite his own misgivings. His cousin might even have been the idiot who triggered the explosion. Something else to feel guilty about.

"Two employees survived, so there's hope they might know something. One is . . ." She pushed her red hair back to read her tablet display, "a Lester Merritt, and the other—"

"Wait. Lester's alive?" Daniel paused mid-step.

"Yes, do you know him?"

He nodded. "Who's the other?"

"The lab's supervisor, Dr. Cadmon Dhyre."

"Huh." He blinked at her. *What are the odds?* "Have they been questioned?"

"Oh yes. They're being held by the authorities until the investigation's complete."

"Good. Keep me informed." He forced himself to take another step, grunting with the effort. Pins and needles in his feet sparked up through his ankles and shins, the joy of nerves regenerating. "Anything else?"

"I have the lab report on the ice." She grimaced watching Daniel struggle, then looked away. "Other than the probes, the only unusual finding was the water's purity—minerals, but no bacteria, just water—pure, plain water as if it were run through a high-grade filtration system."

"So where's all that damned Martian DNA we were supposed to find?" He dragged another foot forward.

"We think it might have been inside the probes, but we'll never know for sure. We had to irradiate them to shut them down, so anything biological would have been destroyed, too."

"But reconnaissance probes aren't supposed to take samples. Just report."

"I know." Lauren shrugged. "It's a mystery. The only thing we can conclude is that their programming was altered by someone unknown, for some purpose unknown."

Daniel shook his head, took a deep breath and another step.

***

The official cause of Serena's death was ruled as massive tissue injury. The Fabri-Tech probes had done what they were designed to do—drilled. By freezing his legs, Daniel slowed them down long enough to save himself. Medical science had repaired the damage to his flesh, but could do nothing to alleviate his self-blame.

Serena wanted me to refuse the Mars assignment, or at least speed up the work, but no, I had to do it all by the book. Why didn't I listen? People warned me about stirring up the Garuda again, but this is almost as if they'd been given a written invitation. And why send only one ship when it would take dozens to bring her down? He had no answers. Only one thing still made any sense—the mission to Tau Medea. Believing in that had given him the strength to go on after the first attack, and now was his sole reason to keep going after surviving a second one. *I was meant to finish this—and I will.*

The UN ordered the Niña to remain in orbit around Mars, while the situation was being assessed. A gag order had been issued and for that much, Daniel was grateful. The last thing he needed was to deal with the press. His automated mental health assessment listed him as marginal, and his uncle advised him to accept the normal grieving process. For Daniel, that meant one thing—work.

Grimly, he pushed ahead on the clean-up at the base, and he and Kowalski ran one practice drill after another. After weeks of repeated exercises, he felt sure the Niña's crew was ready for anything. All they needed now was the UN's blessing to go forward with the original mission. Daniel hoped they would get it, but didn't expect to—either way, his plan was the same. When the blessing didn't come, he put his own plan into action.

Responding to Kowalski's summons, Daniel stepped into the conference room next to the command center and saw him pacing the room. "You wanted to see me?"

Kowalski spun around, strode over, and thrust a transmission pad in his face. "Just what are you trying to pull? This communiqué was sent hours ago." Kowalski snatched the pad back and read aloud, "Mission to Tau Medea terminated. Return to Lunar One immediately.'" He looked at Daniel. "Just when were you planning on telling me?"

"I hoped it would be after we reached Tau Medea."

Kowalski's scowl widened to incredulity. "Now look here, I know you've suffered a personal loss, and these orders are a disappointment, but—"

"This isn't about me. We can't let one Garuda ship panic us into abandoning this mission."

"It's not the one, it's the hundreds that could follow. We may be needed for defense." Kowalski pounded a forefinger down onto the conference room table in emphasis.

"If the Garuda could launch a force like that, I think they would have already. I'm betting that one ship was the best they could do."

"And if you're wrong?"

"Then we need human expansion beyond this solar system more than ever. Besides, this ship was designed for exploration, not a pitched battle. Earth has plenty of dedicated fighter-ships and troops to man them. They don't need us."

"I'm not the one who needs convincing—it's the people I answer to."

"Politicians and religious zealots. You don't agree with them any more than I do."

"Doesn't matter what I think—we have orders to return to Lunar One."

"Orders they have no way of enforcing."

Kowalski stared at Daniel as if he'd grown another head. "You're talking mutiny."

"No, I'm talking about not wasting the thirty years of research, manpower, and money that went into making this mission possible. I'm talking about doing what's in humanity's best interest, politics be damned. If we blindly follow that order, everything goes down the drain—a complete waste. All those people will have died for nothing and not because of that one alien ship, but because the ones giving us these orders see it as a way to solidify their personal power. I say to hell with them, and so should you."

"Walker, I have a crew of almost three hundred people here to consider."

"All of whom signed up to see a new world. I say, let's not disappoint them."

Kowalski scoffed, but then he grew silent, and his eyes narrowed. "There's only one reason I haven't already thrown you in the brig. It's because I'm pretty sure someone set us up."

Daniel smiled in surprise. "I've been thinking the same, but I thought you'd tell me I was nuts."

"No. Well, not about this, anyway. It fits—things said to me before I took command, all the delays and excuses, then getting rerouted to Mars on some half-assed assignment just in time for the Garuda to show up."

"You think someone's actually communicating with them? They've never acknowledged any of our attempts to establish a dialogue."

"Who needs dialogue? All someone would have to do is broadcast pictures of the Niña, and send coordinates. The whole argument against a renewed deep-space program is that it could bring the Garuda down on us again. Maybe someone wanted to make sure it happened."

"Hard to believe anyone would take things that far." Daniel lowered himself into one of the chairs surrounding the conference table. "You think Bromberg and his kind would risk a war just to stop us?"

"To stay in power, you mean, exactly as you said." Kowalski sat down in the chair across from him. "And you can bet, now that the Garuda are back, Bromberg and his cronies will be looking for someone to blame."

"And we'll be the scapegoats," Daniel finished.

Kowalski nodded. "Your mission's over, that's for certain, and there's a good chance I'll lose command."

"And so we both end up in disgrace. Not exactly how I planned to end my career. How about you?"

Kowalski blew air. He tilted back and ran his hands over his bristled gray hair, staring at the ceiling. He sat forward again, looking Daniel in eye. "We need a plan."

"The mission is the plan. If we come back with proof of a habitable world, we'll have a groundswell of public support. They won't dare come after us."

"I'm not sure even that would stop them."

"Well, one thing's for sure, we'd buy ourselves some time. In the ten years we'd be gone, a lot could change on the political front, maybe enough to get us off the hook."

"That's a big maybe. The worst they would do to me now is give me a desk job. Convicted of mutiny, I could be executed."

Daniel knew what he had to say next. "I'll take full responsibility, absolve you of any knowledge. You never saw that order. I doctored it, tricked Riley, whatever you think will hold up."

Kowalski stared at him.

"You know, you really don't strike me as the desk job type," Daniel said, hoping to drive the nail in deeper.

"You must be pretty damned sure about this planet of yours."

"I am."

The captain pursed his lips in thought for a moment then nodded. "I'll want your full confession on the record, time-stamped after I enter stasis, so there's no possibility I could have seen it. I'll set up the launch sequence so that if your confession's not in my file, the launch will abort. Understood?"

He's actually going for it. "You'll have it," Daniel promised, and smiled.

"Wipe that grin off your face." Kowalski looked at the displayed communiqué then held it toward Daniel. "Here. Enter your security code and delete the message."

Daniel did as instructed.

"Come with me."

Together, they headed out to the command center, where Kowalski leaned down and quietly addressed his communications officer. "Send the following to Station Alpha Three."

"Three, sir?" Riley looked confused.

"You heard me. Relay as follows: 'Transmission from Station Alpha Two garbled. Request communications check.'"

"Did you say garbled, sir?"

"Do you need your ears examined? It made no sense; therefore, it must have been garbled. Continue as follows: 'Ice recovery and base clean-up complete. Niña readying for launch to the Tau Medea system as ordered.' Make sure you use Ceti-Omega encoding."

"Sir, previous transmissions ordered us to follow the Delta-Phi coding switch sequence. This being the third day would put us on Ceti-Theta."

"Now would that be Earth days, Lunar days, or Martian? There's a lot of room for misinterpretation there, wouldn't you say?"

Riley blinked at his captain.

"After you send that, shut down. We won't be sending or receiving any more communications before launch."

"We won't?"

"No, Lieutenant, we won't. Do we understand each other?"

Riley's puzzled expression evolved into a wide smile. "Yes, sir, we understand each other perfectly, sir." He saluted and went to work.

Daniel breathed a sigh of relief and shared a conspiratorial wink with the young officer, thinking the failed communications ploy just might work. Maybe his recorded confession wouldn't need to come into play after all.

"Activate the ship's address system," Kowalski ordered. His subsequent words echoed through the corridors. "This is the captain. All hands prepare for departure. Launch sequence to Tau Medea will begin at o-eight hundred hours. May our journey be safe and our mission meet with success."

Daniel could have sworn he heard cheers.

***

With but an hour left before launch, Daniel headed for his quarters. The monitor on his desk blinked at him with a message from the captain.

"Display," he said.

Words zinged across the screen. "Launch sequence set, pending completion as agreed."

Despite the ruse about garbled transmissions, Kowalski was taking no chances. "Has the captain entered stasis?" Daniel asked.

"Affirmative."

So if I don't comply, we don't launch. Daniel sighed and sat down to record the damning confession, as promised. He had it witnessed and time stamped by the ship's central processor, marked the file "For Captain Kowalski's Eyes Only," and punched the transmission. *There, it's done. I'm fully committed—and probably should be.*

He was about to shut down his terminal when the screen blinked again, reminding him of unread personal messages that made it through his privacy settings. He scanned the list, mostly from professional peers. The early ones offered congratulations, the later ones, condolences. He was glad to see nothing from Serena's parents. They weren't speaking to him. He could hardly blame them. He deleted the messages without opening them, until he came across one from Lester—dated weeks before the lab explosion, which meant it probably had nothing to do with it, but he opened message anyway. Lester's smooth artificially enhanced features came on screen.

"Hey, Danny! Congrats on the ship. Got a little something I need you to hang onto for me. Be sure to keep it in a safe place. My life might depend on it. Got it password protected so don't try opening it. What you don't know won't hurt you and you wouldn't like watching it anyway. So don't." The image blinked out, and the monitor stated, 'Message complete,' and gave him his options: 'Forward? Save? Delete?'

The attachment was entitled, 'Caddy'—*as in Cadmon?* Despite Lester's warning, he circumvented his cousin's passcode and accessed the file. A horrifying scene unfolded. His stomach turned and he slapped it off half-way through. He didn't want to see anymore and was certain now what Lester was up to—blackmail. The distorted face of the man in the recording was not easily recognized under dripping cosmetic skin, but between the name on the file and the fact that there was only one carrier who worked with Lester, it had to be Cadmon Dhyre, the only other survivor of the lab explosion.

Could Lester have used this to force Dhyre into orchestrating the lab's destruction? He frowned and shook his head at the idea. *No, Lester's no murderer. More of an opportunist. Even so, it's a disgusting web he's woven. I need to send this to the authorities and let them deal with it.* Immediately, he realized he couldn't. All communication with Earth was cut off. *Damn it. Should never have opened it. This has to be the first time I've been sorry for not following Lester's advice.*

His panel buzzed, and McCormack's voice came over his intercom.

"Better be getting yourself down here. Time's a-runnin', Laddie."

"Okay, Uncle Charlie," he replied, dropping into his youthful habit. "Be there in a minute."

There was no option but to put the recording and whatever Lester planned to do with it from his mind. Considering what he'd just witnessed, he could hardly feel sorry for Cadmon Dhyre. The two deserved each other. Resolved, Daniel chose 'save' and shut down his terminal. He started for the exit, then stopped midstride, snapping his fingers. The cat!

An automated robot had been feeding and watering it for him, so he wouldn't need to enter Serena's quarters. Unfortunately, catching and transporting a cat wasn't something the robot was equipped to handle. Daniel looked at the adjoining door. He blew out a breath and went in.

Sugar lay on the floor. The cat took one look at him and shot under the bed. Seeing Serena's abandoned nightgown and rumpled bedcovers, he had an impulse to wrap himself up in them. Instead, he snatched the blanket, and hit the retract button. The bed slid into the wall, clothing and all, exposing a hissing feline. He lunged for the cat and wrestled it into the blanket. He tucked the squirming bundle under his arm, and paused to suck on a finger the cat managed to claw.

Standing there with his blanket-bound captive, he felt a sick sense of déjà vu. What he had just done bore a disturbing resemblance to the way the girl in the video had been restrained. He shook the correlation from his mind.

My intention is as opposite from that as day from night. This is to ensure Serena's cat survives. I owe her that. I owe her much more than that. He took a deep breath, willing away the dark cloud hovering in his mind. *Come on, you're running out of time.* He headed for the stasis chamber with his meowing bundle.

The ship's engines thrummed in the background, gearing up for departure, a steady backbeat to his footfalls. He moved through the low-lit corridor and down the stairwell, the only means of transport between decks now that power was redirected to the main engines. Hearing their rising hum, he quickened his pace.

The stasis chamber, a huge multilayered room, opened before him with rows upon rows of stacked white pods filled with human cargo. His assigned pod yawned open at the forefront waiting for him to fill it. The device would lower his body temperature suspending all bodily functions, and protect him from the G-forces of rapid acceleration. He accepted its necessity, but his stomach knotted. He chided himself knowing he'd done this before during his service in the military, multiple times and with no ill effects, but the dread remained. He stared at the pod with hate as if it were a living thing waiting to swallow him alive. Within its suffocating jaws he would fall into a dark, dreamless sleep where time incongruously seemed both endless and nonexistent. Considering the blackness of his soul at the moment, he should welcome that oblivion. Instead, he felt only loathing.

McCormack walked up. As Chief of Medicine, his duty was to oversee "interring" everyone into their cocoons for the flight. He paused in front of Daniel and offered a sympathetic smile. "Still hard for you, isn't it?"

Daniel shrugged, feeling uncomfortably transparent.

"You'll be fine. Unless, of course, you believe the latest nonsense from the Unified Church of Earth. In which case, you and I are among the walking dead."

"The what?"

"Oh, you haven't heard? UCE fundamentalists now allege that one dies in the icy grip of stasis only to be revived as an impostor of one's previous self. They're comparing it to recent advances in short-term-death resurrection—you know, the nano-reconstruction of damaged but still viable tissues of the recently deceased. They claim nano-resurrection renders one soulless."

Daniel snorted. "That's absurd. Anyway, it's not loss of my soul I'm worried about, it's—" He stopped short of admitting it was his sanity. Once that lid closed, he would experience a panic so hot and violent that, if permitted to last more than a few seconds, would result in uncontrolled screaming. The diagnosis was severe claustrophobia, a legacy of his time in that storage pod as a boy.

The cat squirmed and yowled inside the blanket again, stirring him. He realized then that a technician was standing next to him wearing an impatient look on her face.

"Sorry," he said and handed over the wrapped cat.

The tech scurried away to ensconce it in an animal specimen pod.

McCormack raised a questioning eyebrow and tipped his head at the waiting pod.

Taking a deep breath, Daniel turned around and stepped back, sinking into the thick suffocating goo. The pod's lid snapped shut over him, and tiny sensors slipped beneath his clothing, crawling across his bare skin, attaching themselves everywhere. Already hyperventilating, Daniel squeezed his eyes shut. To stop himself from screaming, he concentrated on how he planned to fulfill his promise to Serena.

It would be another violation—but only a 'one' on the transgression scale compared to the 'ten' to which he had just confessed. Operating guidelines dictated that all human dead be immolated, and their ashes shot into space. They had followed the rules for everyone except Serena. He'd kept her remains in the morgue, determined to fulfill his promise to her that she would be the first person on Tau Medea IV.

"One way or another," he'd told her, and remembered making her laugh. The sound of it echoed in his memory, keeping him sane as he swirled into oblivion.

PART 2

Chapter 14

The investigation of the lab explosion went on for weeks. Although the news quickly moved on to report the Nina's unauthorized departure, and many events since, Cadmon and Lester continued to protest their innocence and display their bruises to the authorities. Meanwhile, eager attorneys flocked to represent them and found cause to have them released from custody. Their attorneys soon filed a lawsuit against Fabri-Tech for their pain and suffering as part of a class action for the wrongful deaths of everyone on the station, hundreds of lives suddenly terminated.

This afternoon, following another meeting with their lawyers, the two survivors stopped for lunch at a nearby deli.

"Looks like we're going to get the families compensated," Lester said. "I suppose that kinda makes up for it."

"Whatever helps you sleep," Cadmon replied. He glanced up at the waitress pouring his coffee. She wouldn't look at him and hurried away. "We should have gone to an automat."

"Stop bitching. At least they're willing to serve you." Lester took a bite of his sandwich and nodded in appreciation. "Mmmm, this new sim-avocado's not bad. Not that I can remember what a real one tasted like." He chewed and swallowed. "And I'll have you know I sleep just fine, thank you very much, but then I'm not the one who ended them, am I?"

"No, you're just profiting from it, so don't pretend to hold higher moral standards." Cadmon set down his coffee. "I'm leaving soon. You'll have to handle things in my absence."

"For how long?"

"As long as it takes."

Lester looked around and lowered his voice. "This about those experiments of yours?"

Cadmon nodded. "My health is failing. If I'm going to do this, I need to do it now."

"Where you gonna try this stunt?"

"Somewhere no one will interfere."

"How do I get in touch with you?"

"You don't. When proceeds from the lawsuit come in, invest my share. I'll send detailed instructions. And I promise you will be held accountable, so try not to screw it up. I'll either claim the money or my heir will."

Lester choked on his food. "You have an heir?"

"Hopefully," Cadmon said with no trace of humor.

Over the next few days, Cadmon registered his impending death with the authorities, put his legal affairs in order, cashed out his savings, packed up his essentials, and sold the rest. He made his own funeral arrangements and left the woman he'd met at the Death Valley carrier camp in charge of implementing them. He even set the date. And then he went underground—literally.

His destination, purchased with cash under an assumed name, was a small bunker buried twenty feet beneath the earth in a desolate region west of the Urals, one of many underground shelters scattered throughout the northern plains of Eastern Europe inhabited by hardy souls who thumbed their noses at posted signs to vacate the poisoned lands. The government took no interest in the land or its inhabitants, writing them off as lost causes. The bunker's stark isolation promised little chance of anyone interrupting his experiment or stumbling across his bones should it go wrong.

He traveled on public transports with a fake ID, stopped in a small town where he purchased an all-terrain vehicle with cash, and then stayed on little-used back roads, until he reached his new home. Access to the bunker was through a tunnel hidden from above. He drove down and parked beside the bunker's trap door entrance. The place was hooked up to solar power and a well, and he'd brought weeks' worth of food with him. The nearest place to purchase supplies was a four-hour drive back the way he'd come. This was the middle of nowhere, exactly where he needed to be. To prevent anyone from homing in on his location, he'd brought no web-linked electronics.

When he lifted the trap door, a musty odor greeted him. The dark below matched his foreboding. The place had been left unoccupied and unsold for years, which was why he could afford to pay cash. He took in a deep breath of outside air, aimed his flashlight down the steep metal stairs, and went in. The interior looked like the rusty insides of a giant soup can, furnished with a bunk, metal shelves, a toilet-shower-tub combo and a small efficiency kitchen, all covered in layers of dirt and rodent droppings. He sighed seeing the work it would take to make it livable.

The next week he spent cleaning. Once the musty odor was replaced by that of disinfectant, and blankets and portable heaters were set in place, the bunker became reasonably comfortable. He brought in his supplies and arranged them all on the shelves with meticulous precision to ensure that he could find what he needed blind. He fussed and fussed, memorizing everything's location until finally he had to recognize he was simply procrastinating. There was nothing left to do but move forward and deal with the results, good or bad. On the one hand, he trusted his genius. On the other, no one had ever tried this before.

He sat on the narrow bunk and took out the syringe he had prepared. The salt-solution inside it held his last AI-nanogen—the other eight used up in testing on lab rats he'd previously infected with the Toad nanogen. Although his nanogen was programmed to search for human DNA, the genetically engineered rats were a close second. Half of them had survived, the others died in twisted agony. He looked over at the cage holding the four survivors. His odds were fifty-fifty. It could save him or destroy him.

"It's time," he told himself aloud, but his hand didn't move. What Lester Merritt said to him not so long ago came to mind. *Not much to lose, is there?* Trying this might well kill him; not trying it most certainly would.

Taking a deep breath, he lifted the bottom of his shirt and pressed the delivery end of the syringe against his bare stomach. The contents released with a soft hiss and mild sting. He assumed he wouldn't have long to wait. The rats had reacted within minutes.

An hour went by with nothing discernable happening. He tried distracting himself with reading material, but couldn't concentrate. He didn't know exactly what to expect, but nothing was definitely not it. A day went by, then a night, another day—still nothing.

I gambled everything on this. There's nothing left for me now, but a slow demise. I should have considered this possibility and brought some poison with me. Maybe I could extract something toxic from the plants in these contaminated soils. Except I have no lab equipment. I do have rope, however. He looked up at the decaying rafters focusing on the thickest one. *Yes, that should work.*

He prepared a noose, vowing to use it soon, certainly before his food ran out.

In the middle of the sixth night after injecting himself, Cadmon woke in agony. His stomach twisted on itself, hot knives stabbed through his head, and his entire body burned as if his veins were filled with lava. Unable to eat, sleep, or control his bodily functions, paralyzing pain became his entire existence. Gradually, the pain receded, and rational thought returned, but he remained immobile lying on the cold metal floor with no idea how much time had passed. His AI-nanogen's prime directive was to protect the host, which in his case meant destroying the nanobots operating under the old T-nanogen programming, but now all that remained of him was a pile of wrecked flesh.

Seems the war is over, Cadmon thought. *The question is, who won?*

For a long while Cadmon lay numb and paralyzed, then a new pain arose, but of a different sort. This was a victorious sort of pain—the sting and itch of healing. It grew in intensity until he writhed and cried out, surprised to find he had a voice again. Slowly the burning and itching faded and he regained control of his limbs enough that he was able to roll over onto his stomach and crawl toward the full-length mirror on the wall.

His vision was blurry, but he saw his face in it well enough—so monstrously deformed he hardly looked human. Horrified, Cadmon cried out and rolled away to sob in despair. With sudden rage and self-loathing, he tore at his flesh—his twisted fingers strong enough to dig bloody trenches, until the pain of it stopped him and brought him to his senses.

Idiot, you already devised an exit strategy. Use it.

He got to what could barely be described as feet, and with his malformed hands retrieved the coiled rope with the hangman's noose. He dragged a ladder beneath the center rafter, climbed up onto it and secured the rope's end. Sitting atop, Cadmon tightened the noose around his neck and looked down at the sad rusty room that would be his unmarked tomb. *So be it.* He kicked the ladder away and jumped.

The noose snapped his neck as planned, leaving a lifeless body twisting several feet above the floor.

***

Hours later Cadmon woke, hanging by his neck. The noose dug painfully into his flesh, but he was breathing just fine.

"Shit!"

He hauled himself up the rope, hand over hand, until he sat on the rafter again. He pulled the noose free from his neck, leaving an inch-deep groove. As he rubbed at it, the indentation smoothed beneath his hand. The bloody furrows he'd made on his arms and chest were healed as well.

"So that's how it's going to be, is it? You made me a monster, but won't let me die."

The thought of being cursed to live in a body even more repulsive than his former one made him want to sob again.

Stop sniveling. Did you really think this was going to be easy?

Cadmon laughed at himself, because he really had thought that. He'd believed his nanogen would be a magic cure, freeing him from all pain and deformity. Instead, it made him uglier than ever. *At least nothing hurts.* That's when he realized that the ever-present ache in his muscles and stinging of his skin were gone, neither of which he'd noticed until now. He'd been too overwhelmed by the horror in the mirror.

My creation has no concept of esthetics, but it knows how to heal.

He'd programmed the nanogen to operate on a rule-based system for capturing expert knowledge and compiling a translation of it while relying on a library of generic archetypes to create specific roles for its nanobot swarm. He needed to find a way to communicate with his nanogen and explain what he wanted that swarm to do. As Cadmon sat on top of the rafter, he turned his thoughts inward, envisioning his AI-nanogen, the leader of that swarm. He looked at his strong but perfectly horrid maw of a hand and closed his eyes to project an image of the crooked fingers straightening, the fleshy lumps smoothing out, the skin's mottled discoloration transforming to a uniform tan. He opened his eyes to look again and saw no change. *Well, what the hell did you expect?* But as he stared at it, something actually did seem a bit different about the blob where his thumb belonged. He focused harder, picturing a nail bed, a joint. He found that he could flex it a bit more, and a shadow formed where the nail belonged.

It's working.

From that point forward, suicide was the furthest thing from his mind. *The key is intentional communication.* And so he began to experiment on himself—weeks of trial and error—envisioning bones, muscles, skin and hair, testing the resulting levels of strength and dexterity. His medical background helped enormously, but he wished he'd thought to bring along anatomy guides for precise images to reference. If he were ever to leave this bunker, creating a body and face acceptable to others was an absolute necessity. Considering the distorted shape he continued to see in the mirror, that was proving to be a challenge.

He had little appetite, while being continually thirsty. He had known the nanobots would run on hydrogen freed from water, so had made sure to have a near endless supply available. Still, the amount he consumed came as a surprise. He drank gallons and finally took to submerging himself in the old shower-tub in the corner. He marveled how the liquid disappeared into his pores, leaving him surrounded in a bubble of oxygen-enriched air.

Could be hazardous living inside a flammable cloud, he mused, and pictured going up in flames. He felt a sharp heat prickling his scalp and realized he'd accidentally ignited his hair. He dunked under the water to douse the flames. From then on, he was more careful about what he envisioned.

Visualization by itself is dangerous. The subconscious mind is simply too unpredictable. I need the precision of language.

He knew how to set up programs and hack into them, but he wasn't used to thinking in binary. He started teaching the nanobots to communicate in standard English. While he worked on language, and experimented with his physical appearance, he also directed his nanobots to explore his immediate environment. The surviving test rats had nanobots inside them too, and he tried communicating with them on the same frequency. The results were mixed. Three of the rats went into cardiac arrest and died. Now only one remained, but he had a firm link with this rat's nanobots and was having some success in affecting her behavior and appearance as well.

That success led him to try other wireless communication. At first only disconnected images, bits and pieces of information flashed into his mind—the Solar Wide Web, he was certain of it. Since he bore no IP address, he would be untraceable. *Oh, the potential.* If he could learn how to invisibly influence financial markets, distribute information, monitor human activity . . . he began to see just how far his new-found abilities might take him. But before he could leave this place, he needed sufficient control over the nanobots infesting him to trust his face not to melt of its own accord.

Finally, after nearly a year of trial and error experimentation, he was ready.

He packed up, set fire to the bunker, and left in the same vehicle that brought him there.

***

Weeks later, standing nude before a mirrored half circle in a hotel room, the late Cadmon Dhyre took stock of his assets. He checked himself thoroughly, front, back and side.

"Lordy, aren't we in love with ourselves?" The comment came from one of the two naked women lolling on the bed behind him. He wasn't sure which one and didn't care, anyway.

"Time to go home, ladies."

With some grumbling, they gathered their things and left. Cadmon turned back to the mirror and practiced a dazzling smile.

Who could resist me now? Certainly not those women. It's as if I've unbottled a magic genie inside myself. I still need to rely on my wits and powers of persuasion, but things have never come so easily before. Everyone who looks at my face instantly trusts me. And why not? I'm magnificent.

The nanobots inside him had thickened his thin, dry hair into a golden mane, replaced his pale, scarred flesh with smooth tan skin, and padded his gaunt, skeletal frame with firm muscle. He had to stare deep into the unchanged color of his ice-blue eyes to recognize himself there. He imagined this might have been the healthy adult version of his angelic pre-adolescent self. His new body was more attractive than any of Lester Merritt's manufactured illusions, and far more convincing. He didn't look augmented, just naturally handsome and fit. *If only my fellow carriers could see me now.*

Thinking of the number of memorial services at the carrier camps held in honor of his passing, Cadmon wondered if they still mourned. He'd watched a recording of the ceremonies upon returning to civilization and found the eulogies quite touching. His death and rebirth had taken more than a year, but now, he was ready to make his debut.

***

"Mr. Morden Chayd is here," the receptionist announced over a tiny silver intercom chip stuck to her lower lip. She paused, listening to a response audible only to herself. "Sure, Hon, I'll let him know." She lifted her gaze to the fine-looking man standing before her. "Mr. Merritt will be with you in a moment. You can have a seat if you like—unless, of course, you'd rather stay here and talk to me?"

He chose to stay put.

She smiled coyly. "Such a shame about Cadmon Dhyre. So how were you two related?"

"A second cousin, on my mother's side," he replied.

"And you're his only heir—good for you." Her smile and tone turned even more flirtatious. "So, is there anything I can get for you while you're waiting, or . . . maybe later?"

He appraised her—blonde hair, round face, bordering on plump, but attractive enough in a tawdry sort of way. Exactly the sort he'd expect Lester to hire.

"Perhaps," he said, offering hope without commitment.

"Well, you know where to find me." A buzz interrupted her. "He can see you now."

He picked up his briefcase and strolled toward the inner office. Feeling her eyes follow, he rewarded her with a slow look before closing the door between them.

Lester Merritt stood to greet him from behind an ornate Louis IVX style desk. Lester wore a dark gold suit, with a multicolored cravat held in place with a large blue lapis stone set in a thick gold bezel. His eyes were a bright blue encircled with gold to match the jeweled pin.

"Mr. Chayd, so good to finally meet you," Lester said, as they shook hands, bare palm meeting bare palm. "You have my condolences—Cadmon Dhyre was a great man."

"Cut the crap, Lester. We both know you hated my guts."

Lester whipped his hand back, his eyes widening. "Caddy?"

"It's Chayd now. Morden Chayd."

"Holy Mother. I can't believe it. You said you were working on a cure, but—this is incredible. You look fantastic!"

"Don't I, though?" Cadmon moved around the office, frowning at the flocked golden walls, gilded desk and matching cabinetry. "I've come to settle accounts."

"Sure, sure. Well, your estate goes to your sole living heir, but since that's you, it's all good, right?" Lester laughed short and uneasy. "The attorneys did the best they could, but your share wasn't all that much due to the lack of serious injury and your shortened life-span expectancy. I invested it like you asked and it's done pretty good." Lester paused, watching him prowl the room. "When I stopped hearing from you, and the death certificate came, I just naturally assumed—"

"You assumed wrong." Cadmon dropped into one of the oversized cherry-red leather visitors' chairs. Running a hand over the rolled brass-studded armrest, he looked about and shook his head. "This won't do. This won't do at all. Your taste is appalling. It needs to be subtle, sophisticated, unpretentious, yet discernibly expensive. We'll need it all done over."

Standing behind the desk, Lester scowled down at him. "What's this 'we' stuff? You nearly got me killed, and then up and died on me. There's no 'we' anymore."

Cadmon leaned back, clasping his hands in his lap. "How disappointing, and after all I've done for you."

"What you did was scare the shit out of me—probably took ten years off my life—but what's done is done. I'm willing to let bygones be bygones. You go your way and I'll go mine."

Cadmon smiled. "You always were the master of the cliché."

"Point is, I'm not one to hold grudges." Lester sighed and then came around to sit on his desk in front of Cadmon. "Look, I don't want any hard feelings. I've made out fine with the money we got from the lawsuit and set up my own investment firm here. I'll even continue handling your money, if you like. Turns out, I'm pretty good at it."

"The only thing you're good at is self-deception. I'm the one who made sure your investments paid off."

Lester made a rude noise. "I don't know what you're on, Caddy, but—"

"Don't call me that!" Cadmon stood from the chair, forcing Lester to back away. "You are never to use that name again, ever, do you understand? From this point forward, you shall address me as Brother Morden Chayd."

Lester barked a surprised laugh. "Brother? Since when?"

"Since I had the both of us voted into full membership in the Unified Church of Earth." Cadmon pointed to a plaque on the wall from the UCE. "You can thank me for your newfound respectability."

"Ha. I was an initiate long before I met you."

"And without my intervention that's as far as you ever would have gotten."

Lester's disbelieving smirk remained. "I'm supposed to believe you've got some secret pull with the Church?"

"Some, but not nearly enough. Not yet, anyway. That's why I'll need your assistance."

"Oh yeah, sure thing. I'm just dying to help out a murdering rapist, who enjoys blowing shit up. I already told you, we go our separate ways."

"So you did." Choosing to play the game a little longer, Cadmon moved away to study the UCE plaque with Lester's name scrolled across it. "Tell me, are you enjoying being a respected Church member?"

"Sure, I guess. Helps me get my foot in the door sometimes. You gotta have connections."

"Agreed, which is precisely why I chose the UCE. I considered a number of possible affiliations, but decided the Church's high public profile combined with its rigid hierarchical structure provided the most direct route to political and social influence. Its doctrine's a bit backward, sadly, but I'm confident I can deal with that over time." He looked back at Lester's colorful attire and engineered facial make-up. "I take it you haven't studied the Church's philosophies in any depth. You're hardly up to its standards."

"I know them well enough. Besides, I got a special dispensation."

"Yes, a precaution I took to ensure that your vanity wouldn't take precedence over your greed." Cadmon paused and smiled. "You know, Lester, I really do owe you a great deal."

"Glad you finally recognize it."

"Oh, yes, very much so. I often think back on that fateful evening you so deftly arranged in that low-life club . . . what was the name? Oh yes, the Wrec-U. Nothing was ever quite the same for me after that."

"That was your doing, not mine. Try putting any of that on me, I can prove otherwise. I still got that recording, remember? And there's more than one copy, believe me."

"Oh, I'm confidant you've taken every precaution. As I recall, it showed the heinous act of a man suffering from a terrible affliction— who is now deceased. Seeing as you were his co-conspirator, I can see how it might pose a serious problem for you, but what does any of that have to do with me?"

"I know who you really are."

"Who I am is Morden Chayd whose records go back decade upon decade—birthplace, education, employment, ancestral lineage. His pedigree is impeccable and his credentials airtight, as are these." Cadmon drew out a stack of hard copies from his briefcase and laid them onto the desk. "Better check to see who's listed as owner of this building, your business, and investments. It's not you."

Lester grabbed the papers. As he studied them, turning page after page, his scowl gave way to alarm. "This isn't right. How could you—?"

"I have my own contacts now. A whole army of them. Accept it, Lester, I own you. I believe the cliché you want is, lock, stock, and barrel."

"You can't get away with this." Lester threw the papers, scattering them. "I'll tell the authorities who you are, what you are."

"No. You won't." Cadmon turned his attention inward, concentrating. His nanobots should be in place by now. He'd done this before with stray cats, and knew it worked, but Lester would be his first human subject. He struggled for a moment, then found it again—that radio-linked mental connection. His specialized nanobots delivered in that skin-to-skin handshake went into action.

Lester grunted and clutched at his stomach.

"Something wrong?" Cadmon asked. He commanded his nanobots to twist the lining of Lester's intestines.

Lester cried out and dropped to all fours.

"As I said, I have an army at my disposal. These documents are all perfectly legal, recording your poor business decisions right up until the moment you signed over your remaining assets to me in a plea for continued employment, which I have graciously chosen to grant, provided, of course, that you remain in my good graces."

He concentrated again. Lester convulsed, sobbing, and curled into a fetal position. Cadmon let up a bit, allowing Lester to find his voice again.

Lester lay gasping. "What . . . what have you done to me?"

"I've given you a present—a few of my nanobots. They do as I ask, and you had better do so as well." He made Lester convulse again. "Do we have an understanding?"

"Augh! Yes, yes, stop it, please. I'll do whatever you say."

"I thought you might." He allowed the nanobots to go dormant again, then waited while Lester pushed himself to a sitting position. "Now pay attention. Are you listening?"

Lester nodded.

"Good. You shall begin by introducing me in the most glowing terms possible to your friends at the UCE here in Los Angeles. Once I, as Morden Chayd, reach the rank of Bishop, we'll move on to the headquarters in New York where I shall be promoted to Cardinal. Rejoice and give thanks, Lester. You have the honor of serving the next Supreme Father."

Lester stared up at him in dismay. "You're not serious."

"Oh, but I am, quite. The discomfort you've experienced is a mere taste of what I can do. If I find your cooperation and support anything less than unbridled enthusiasm, the consequences for you will be tragic. Not only will I leave you financially destitute, I'll turn you into the social pariah I used to be."

Lester grimaced. "Didn't know I was your type."

Cadmon chuckled at Lester's attempt at bravado. "Trust me, you're not. Thankfully, sexual intimacy isn't necessary." He held his arms wide. "What you see before you is a self-contained nanotech manufacturing facility. I can create messengers of pain, deformity, or even death." He squatted and poised one finger of his perfectly formed hand in front of the other man's nose. "And all it takes is a touch," he said, then watched with great satisfaction as Lester turned every bit as pale as the late Cadmon Dhyre.

Chapter 15

The Niña, day 11 in orbit around Tau Medea IV

Reports from their reconnaissance probes confirmed the planet was in a warm evolutionary stage similar to the Paleocene Epoch of Earth's Tertiary Period, with ice at the poles, deep oceans, lush valleys, vast deserts, and a wide tropical belt. Soil analyses proved the planet could support Earth-born plants, and most of the native ones weren't toxic. Even more encouraging, temperature ranges were all within human tolerance, but after eleven days here, Daniel was no closer to getting his people on the ground, and he was losing patience.

He buzzed at the door of Captain Kowalski's quarters, then strode in without waiting for permission.

Kowalski looked up from his desk. "Come in?"

"Why are you dragging your feet? We're ready to go. Been ready for days. We need to get down there." Daniel stopped in the middle of the room and looked about. He'd never been in the captain's quarters before. The set-up was like his own, but so immaculate it looked as if no one lived here. His own quarters resembled the after-effects of a hurricane.

"I'm still not convinced we should trust the data," Kowalski said, leaning back in his chair. "Your people never pinpointed the source of the problem with the probes that malfunctioned on Mars, and ours are the same design and manufacture date. It worries me."

"It shouldn't. We may not know the who and why of it, but we do know someone had to have changed the programming of the ones we found in the ice. We've tested ours. They haven't been tampered with. It's not an issue."

"But you admit the atmosphere's a problem," Kowalski stated, "high carbon-dioxide, low oxygen. It doesn't have the 19.5 percent oxygen humans need."

"We've already talked about this. I explained that it's temporary, due to volcanic outgassing, which will dissipate, and we can set up automated oxygenators to speed up the process. By the time any colonists arrive, oxygen levels should be up to speed." Daniel plopped into one of the swiveling flowchairs in front of the captain's desk and leaned back mirroring the other man's pose. "Plus, the low oxygen's actually a good thing. It inhibited the size of the native wild-life. No large predators to worry about. We've got the data, and Doctor McCormack has inoculated everyone, so now we need to get down there, video things close-up and gather specimens."

"Or better yet, do it all remotely with robots."

Daniel leaned forward. "Devon, you're missing the point. We have to demonstrate that people can safely interact with this world. Seeing humans exploring it hands-on is the only way to convince those sonsabitches back on Earth that this planet's worth colo-nizing—and isn't that the whole point of coming here?"

"You want boots on the ground."

"Absolutely. There's no substitute."

Kowalski sighed. "All right, send down your teams. Keep in mind, we launch on Day 30."

"Any possibility we can extend our stay?"

"No, we budgeted for thirty days total. You've got eighteen left and that's it."

"But—"

"You want to make it all the way back to Earth? Or just almost make it?"

That stopped him. "Got it." Daniel frowned, but knew the time-table was non-negotiable. "I'm flying down this afternoon . . . alone." Seeing the alarm on Kowalski's face, he added one word. "Serena."

The captain closed his mouth and nodded.

***

The ceremony was brief, attended by one, with the assistance of a robot to dig the grave and inter the remains. Daniel stood at the gravesite. He'd selected a peaceful valley that looked up at blue-pur-ple hills to the north and was flanked with thick green vegetation that thickened into forest to the south. Multi-colored ferns grew low amid yellow grass under tall scattered trees with trunks spotted in orange as if carelessly splashed with paint. It looked like a Cézanne landscape. He knew Serena would have appreciated it.

Staring down into the open grave at the white biodegradable wrappings that held the remains of the woman he once knew and loved, he felt only a flat emptiness, combined with a determination to fulfill his final promise. Still, he knew he should say something. "Ashes to ashes, dust to dust," he said, when no other words came to mind. "I'll always love you." He bent down, picked up a handful of the deep red earth and dropped it over her body. He stepped back and walked away not wanting to watch the robot fill in the grave. A polished brass plaque was already in place: "Serena Covington of Earth, the First Human on Tau Medea IV."

Chapter 16

On day twelve, thirty-five Land Survey Robots shaped like spiders the size of buffalos landed on the sunlit side of the planet and began to clear paths for the four-person teams following in their wake. The LSRs also recorded three-dimensional images of their surroundings, while documenting ambient sounds and odors. Their wide bellies carried emergency supplies for their team, and cages to hold native specimens.

Every team member had been inoculated against the native bacteria and viruses infecting the wildlife, so Daniel had his people out of their helmets breathing the natural atmosphere, supplemented only with oxygen blown in under their noses. Naked smiling faces in the videos would be convincing evidence that this world was hospitable to humans.

The section of the planet Daniel chose for his own team was near the equator, not far from Serena's burial site, where temperatures and humidity were at their highest and the native flora and fauna most dense. Each day on the ground, Daniel and his team encountered an astounding variety of creatures, and he made sure the recordings showed them interacting safely in the environment as they collected specimens along the way. Day after day, everything went as planned and they continued to add more samples to the ship's hold without incident. Still, it was hard work and Daniel started to look forward to returning to Earth with their spoils.

***

Only eight days left, Daniel reminded himself this morning, as the LSR hitched ahead of him on its spidery legs, its whirling propeller blades cutting a swath through head-high yellow grass of a savannah. To Daniel, the robot looked like an overgrown tarantula. Grass cuttings flew to the sides along with native creatures jumping and flying from harm's way. Some reminded him of grasshoppers, dragonflies or lizards, while others looked like nothing he could categorize. Nakiro walked at Daniel's heels while Sanchez and Baker trailed yards behind. For a long while, Daniel enjoyed the relative silence, listening to the whir of the robot, the wind in the trees, and the buzzing of insects.

"We're friends, right?" Nakiro asked without forewarning.

Daniel rolled his eyes. He had met Nakiro in college and they had worked on a number of projects together over the years, but he'd never thought of him as a friend. Then again, he didn't think of anyone as a friend. Colleagues, definitely, friends? —not really. "Sure."

"Well, being your friend, I thought I should warn you that Captain Kowalski isn't happy that you're down here. Every time I see him, he looks ready to explode."

Daniel glanced back. "And why is that a problem for you?"

"It's not. I mean, not for me, but . . . well, he is the captain, and you two have to get along, right? Especially since you two share command."

"We get along fine," Daniel said, unwilling to discuss the matter. He stepped over a pile of cut grass and kept walking, but now he could only think about the ongoing issue of who was in charge of what and which of them had final say.

The grassy meadow fell behind, and the scattered trees condensed into forest. Their path darkened as the trees thickened into a heavy canopy that filtered the hot yellow sun into dappled light. The insect life thickened as well. Shadows of winged things flitted before them and scurrying beetles moved underfoot and over hairy red tree trunks. Daniel barely noticed—his thoughts were stuck on Kowalski's continued objections to his being part of their hands-on exploration teams.

"This is my mission," Daniel said of a sudden. "I didn't come all this way just to look at it on a viewscreen. It's bad enough we only have thirty days here, twelve of them wasted debating the probe reports."

There was a long pause before Nakiro responded. "I understand how you must feel, but Captain Kowalski's caution about the probes is understandable too, don't you think? I mean after what happened on—"

"You don't need to remind me."

"Sorry."

The vine-covered terrain angled upward, steep and slick.

"They're falling behind again," Nakiro said, and pointed a thumb over his shoulder at the empty path sloping away.

"LSR, hold," Daniel ordered, and the robot paused with two legs in mid-air. He activated his comlink and heard ragged breathing. "You all right, Baker?"

"Yes sir," came the panted response. "It's just . . . just a bit steep here, sir."

"Take your time." He knew the man wasn't much of an athlete.

Baker was plump, a lab botanist designated for on-board duty—and even for that, he wouldn't have been Daniel's first choice—but they'd been hard put to find qualified people willing to be absent from Earth for ten years. And now he'd had to call on Baker to replace his regular field botanist who'd come down with "space-traveler's flu." The occasional delayed reaction to stasis wasn't contagious, but its symptoms were disabling. Baker was also probably sleep deprived, like most everyone else. Since taking up orbit here, they had gradually adjusted the ship's days to the same length as the planet's—25.61 standard hours per rotation—not much longer than what they were used to, but it still played havoc with their circadian rhythms. Daniel took advantage of the moment to close his eyes and put his back to the sun. Though smaller in this world's sky than Sol appeared from Earth, its heat was no less intense.

"And how are you doing?" Nakiro asked him.

"I'm fine," Daniel replied.

Nakiro cleared his throat. "You can talk to me, you know. This strong silent act only goes so far. You've still got people who care about you. We're all sympathetic, of course, but—"

"O-kay." Daniel turned to face Nakiro, and waved his arm at the alien jungle. "Do you see where we are? I'm right where I've always wanted to be, doing exactly what I've always wanted to do. So stop analyzing me and let me enjoy it."

"Sorry," Nakiro said again, but his worried look remained.

Daniel frowned and turned his back again to Nakiro and the sun. After a minute, Nolan Baker appeared around the bend and struggled up the hill. Baker had insisted on wearing a full helmet, and behind its faceplate his forehead dripped sweat, his face a hot pink.

"Contamination's still a reasonable concern," Baker had insisted. Daniel hadn't argued, even though they were all immunized, and based on the data, he believed humans were a far bigger threat to this world than it was to them.

Chief of Security Manual Sanchez, a beefy mountain of a man in prime physical condition, stomped at Baker's heels, but seemed only to make the other more uncertain in his climb. Daniel thought it ironic that Baker's positive attitude stood in sharp contrast to Sanchez's negative one. To Baker's credit, he hadn't uttered a single complaint so far, in spite of being pushed to his physical limits. In contrast, this walk presented no physical challenge for Sanchez, but he still grumbled about everything.

One might assume that the experience he'd shared with Sanchez in that Martian cave would foster a battle-born camaraderie, but the truth was, Daniel didn't trust him and felt certain Sanchez had no love for him either. He hadn't forgotten how his gun jammed after Sanchez 'checked' it. He wouldn't have selected Sanchez for his team, but for some reason Kowalski insisted on it. Maybe Kowalski thought they were 'buds' now. Maybe it was time he set the captain straight.

Once the gap closed, Daniel continued on at a slower pace. As they went deeper into the forest, their boots sank into the thick, mushy covering and a pungent odor rose up.

"What's that stink?" Sanchez asked.

"Rotting vegetation under the leaf mold," Nakiro replied, having taken it upon himself to deflect Sanchez's irritability. "Reduced oxygen levels make decay a slow, noisome process."

"Noise? I was talking about the smell."

"So was I," Nakiro said.

"You better not be makin' fun of me, egghead. Eggs crack real easy."

"We're being recorded," Daniel reminded them.

"Right, I forgot you only want people back home to see happy . . . whatever it is we are . . . doing whatever the hell it is we're doing here," Sanchez said.

"Star-Sailors," Nakiro offered.

Sanchez snorted. "Give me a break."

"That is the root meaning of the word astronaut," Nakiro replied, "Astro-, originally derived from the ancient Greek word *astronomein,* which translates literally as 'watch the stars,' and then, of course, -naut, from the ancient Greek word *naus,* meaning 'ship.'"

"Gee whiz, thanks for the lesson, professor," Sanchez said. "I'm sure we're all real impressed."

"Cut it out," Daniel snapped at them. He'd have to do some judicious editing so their squabbling wouldn't taint the recordings. As Serena had taught him, image meant everything. Without her publicity campaign promoting "the man with a mission," he would never have gotten his ship built, let alone launched. *And Serena would still be alive.* The thought kicked him in the gut. At least he'd kept his promise that she would be the first human on the planet's surface. It was the only thing left he could do for her.

BAM! The sharp retort of a gun shattered the air and he spun to see Sanchez kicking at some charred, lizard-like thing on the ground.

"If that weapon goes off again, I'm confiscating it. This is your final warning."

"Damned thing tried to crawl up my leg." Sanchez pointed the muzzle of his sidearm at its blackened victim.

"I don't care if it crawls down your throat. No more shooting."

Sanchez narrowed his eyes, but holstered the weapon.

Daniel shook his head . . . *more editing.* He looked around and noticed the terrain here was level and open. *Maybe a short rest will improve morale.*

"Take five, everyone."

Finding a chair-sized rock, he sat and sucked in a mouthful of a concentrated liquid nutrient solution from the nipple in his suit. Baker shuffled about, then made for a tree to lean against. Daniel saw movement behind him and opened his mouth just as Baker leaned back and something squeaked in protest. Baker jumped away and luminous blue eyes popped open on the tree. The two beings stared at each other in equal amazement. The reddish-brown creature resembled a miniature sloth, and lay nearly invisible against the furry bark.

"It's an H-342, an herbivore," Nakiro stated, checking the catalog display on his suit's arm. "We don't have a specimen yet."

"Should I bag it?" Baker asked.

"Looks kinda like one of those Ferrigan rats," Sanchez said. "Big as cats, they were, chewed through the ventilation system and got into where everyone was sleeping. Nothing left of them poor bastards but blood 'n bones." Sanchez chuckled darkly.

Baker backed away and the animal closed its eyes again, trying to blend in.

"Don't listen to him," Nakiro said. "It's just an herbivore. We've catalogued every lifeform on the planet. There shouldn't be any surprises."

"Yeah, sure, just like on Mars," Sanchez said under his breath, but not below Daniel's hearing.

"Just shut the fuck up, Sanchez. I've about had it with you," Daniel told him. He grabbed a bag from the LSR and tossed it over the tree impersonator. The sack automatically encased the animal, and anesthetized it. Daniel handed the filled sack over to Baker who took it gingerly and deposited it into the belly of the LSR.

"Let's go. And no more talk," Daniel ordered and waved the LSR to lead them on.

Seeing the time, he picked up the pace to be sure they reached their rendezvous point on schedule. Like all the ground teams, they had standing orders to return to the mother ship before dark, a time which varied according to location, putting the teams on a rotating schedule. They came to the wide clearing designated as their pick-up point, then watched the sky. Within a few minutes, a shuttle appeared and lowered into the clearing. Their LSR opened its belly and waited as another smaller robot rolled down the shuttle's ramp toward it to remove the LSR's caged specimens and load them into the shuttle. Once emptied, the LSR spun about on its eight legs and clambered toward Daniel to obtain new instructions. It was all Daniel could do to stand his ground as the giant metal spider came toward him. He held his breath until it stopped in front of him.

I'm never going to get used to these things.

To speed up getting through the thick jungle-like growth in the morning, Daniel told the LSR to clear a path during the night, then return to its starting point to meet them back here in the clearing at sunrise. He watched it move ahead, cutting a green tunnel through the thick growth until it disappeared from view.

On their shuttle's return flight to the Niña, Daniel relaxed into his seat, tired from the long day of hiking through alien terrain. After check-in and clean up, he looked forward to comparing his team's findings with those of the other ground teams, something he did each day before retiring for the night. Together, they had covered over seven hundred square miles of wildly varied terrain and all without any serious injury or unhappy surprises. Each team would be back at it in the morning, when sunlight returned to wherever they'd left off their previous day—after hot showers, food, and a good night's sleep. The last of those frequently eluded Daniel. His bed was too empty, his mind too full. He wondered how much that lack of sleep showed. Losing his temper like he had with Sanchez today was probably a dead give-away.

Doesn't matter—we're almost done and everything's gone fine. Just keep doing the work. The rest will take care of itself.

Chapter 17

Early the next morning, a shuttle off-loaded Daniel and his team back in the same clearing, then took off again. The path their LSR had created the previous night dove darkly into the forest ahead, but of the robot itself, there was no sign.

"Let's check the clearing for specimens and give our LSR some more time to show up," Daniel told the others.

There were plenty of creatures to be found and since none had ever seen humans before, the animals were easy to catch.

"Look at this one," Nakiro called out. "It's so bizarre, it's cute." He walked toward Daniel cradling his prize. The animal was fur-covered in a mottled combination of green and brown, with the body shape of a frog and face of a squirrel. "An H-463. It jumped six feet in the air before I caught it." He rubbed the top of its head and it made a chittering noise. "Seems quite happy now. Could have pet potential."

"I found some eggs," Baker announced and held up a nest of six yellow orbs speckled with red. He waited for Nakiro to cage his furry squirrel-faced frog, then handed him the nest to identify. "Didn't see any birds around though."

"That's because there aren't any," Nakiro replied. "Just insects, reptiles, small mammals, and fish." Nakiro placed the nest in a cage and scanned for a match on his list.

Baker turned to look across the meadow, revealing a long snake-like creature clinging to the back of his suit.

Nakiro inhaled sharply and took a step back. "Think I found who these eggs belong to."

"What? Where?" Baker spun round making the creature swing in the air behind him like a tail. Nakiro scrambled away. Seeing the thing attached to himself now, Baker yelled, "Get it off me!"

Sanchez pulled his pistol.

"Stop!" Daniel yelled at them all, freezing them in place, and pointed at Sanchez. "Put that away."

Sanchez slid the pistol back into its holster, and lifted his hands in mock surrender.

"Don't move," Daniel told Baker, then crouched several feet away to look at the creature hanging from Baker's backside. The long thing had a bulbous black head and a long tube-shaped body striped in black and yellow. Its red-lined mouth was locked on a fold of Baker's bright orange suit. It resembled a snake except for the addition of six short legs, and the fact that its black-slit yellow eyes sat on stalks which bent and swiveled in Daniel's direction.

Daniel stood again, walked over to Nakiro and whispered below Baker's hearing. "Venomous, right?"

"Extremely," Nakiro whispered back, showing the information on his display, "and those are definitely its eggs."

"Okay, Mr. Baker," Daniel said. "Everything's going to be fine; I just need you to remain still, please." He slowly picked up the cage holding the nest of eggs, opened its door and walked toward the animal. A few feet away, he set the cage on the ground and backed up. For a moment, nothing happened.

Damn it—now what do I—?

In a blur of motion, the thing flipped sideways, and shot into the cage, where it curled into a ball atop its nest. The cage locked itself shut.

Daniel let himself breathe again. "Nice catch, Mr. Baker. You found one of the very few poisonous creatures out here. Thanks to you, now Dr. McCormack gets to make an antidote."

Baker looked pale and wavered on his feet. "I'm not sure I'm cut out for this."

Daniel grabbed his arm to steady him. "You're doing fine. Could have happened to anyone." Daniel checked the time. "It appears our LSR isn't coming back on its own. We'll have to go get it."

"Well, that's just great," Sanchez grumbled.

Technically, they weren't supposed to go anywhere without their robotic companion, but since it had already cleared a path for them, it made sense to follow it. Daniel led the way, watching for anything unusual among the overwhelming variety of strangeness. The path cleared by the LSR formed a dark leafy tunnel, its dense green ceiling only half a meter above their heads. Hordes of fat hairy black beetles skittered over the rotting leaves on the ground, trying to dodge his boots. The beetles' resemblance to Sanchez's eyebrows encouraged Daniel to smash a few. He heard Sanchez stomping at the rear with equal gusto and stopped himself.

Their passage resulted in the hoots and screeches of unseen animals cutting through the thick humid air. He didn't like this dim narrow tunnel with its clouds of flitting, hopping, crawling things. He liked even less the things he couldn't see. The dark green shadows seemed to draw in on him ever more closely. *Steady now. It's not getting any smaller.* He took deep even breaths. Despite the poisonous snake thing just encountered, he reminded himself there was practically nothing on this planet to worry about. As far as land creatures went, the probes found no predators bigger than a fat house cat. Serena's Sugar would be king of the beasts around here.

Out of loyalty, or perhaps guilt, he'd pulled the fluffy white cat out of stasis and was doing his best to befriend the green-eyed fur ball. He tried to tempt it with tasty morsels, but scratches on his hands testified to their uneasy relationship.

Rounding a bend, Daniel came upon a mud slick beside a small pool of water. He skirted it, pointing the area out to the men following him. With an uncharacteristic burst of energy, Baker jumped the muddy puddle and ran toward Daniel. Caught by surprise, Sanchez sprinted after him.

"I—I thought I saw something," Baker said. "Something big, like you and me big."

"Come on. You imagined it," Sanchez sneered.

Daniel objected to Sanchez' insulting tone, but agreed with him. The probes hadn't found anything of the sort. "I wouldn't worry. Probably just a trick of the shadows in here," he said, and started forward again.

Ten steps later, something came crashing down through the foliage barely missing him and hit the ground hard. To Daniel's left, a brown-speckled nut the size of a basketball lay rocking. His heart raced, but he told himself that things falling from trees were common enough. Then he noticed the forest was eerily silent.

"Something's off," Sanchez said, pulling his weapon as he looked up and around.

Walker nodded, and drew his own weapon. He lifted his wrist and spoke into his comlink in hushed tones. "Walker to Niña, come in."

Captain Kowalski came online. "Problem?"

"Possibly. Our LSR is missing, Baker thinks he saw something bigger than anything catalogued, I almost got beaned by a coconut, and this jungle's gone strangely quiet all of a sudden. Doesn't feel right."

"Return to your landing site," Kowalski ordered. "I'll send down a shuttle for you and do a detailed scan in the area."

"Acknowledged." Daniel motioned Sanchez to turn around and take point.

Baker and Nakiro followed and Daniel brought up the rear. He kept looking behind as they went, and then he saw it. Heavy-leafed branches in the tunnel's ceiling dipped and swayed, flowing in their direction.

"There's something behind us," he told the others. "Pick it up."

The men moved to a trot. The high leafy wave flowed faster, keeping pace.

"Go!" he yelled.

They broke into a run—Sanchez in the lead, followed by Baker pushed from behind by Nakiro. Daniel ran sideways trying to see what was driving the undulating foliage. With no visible target, he turned and ran hard, hairs on end—certain something was almost upon him.

Baker tumbled to the ground, tripping Nakiro. The two fell into a heap and Daniel skidded just short of adding himself to the pile. He spun back, and aimed at the oncoming wave. The foliage crashed into the trees above him, followed by a high-pitched trill that sounded eerily like laughter. He pointed his pistol and braced for something to leap down on their heads.

Instead, all went deathly still again.

Baker and Nakiro got to their feet, and the three of them backed down the path, while Daniel kept his weapon aimed. When they reached the clearing, they found Sanchez waiting.

"Thought you were right behind me," he said.

Daniel opened his mouth to deliver a tongue-lashing, but Nakiro interrupted. "We're all a bit on edge after that incident with the eggs. I'm thinking our imaginations may have gotten the better of us just now."

"Imagination doesn't move trees," Daniel countered.

"True," Nakiro admitted, "but a narrow opening through vegetation that dense could have generated a wind tunnel effect."

Daniel's gut told him otherwise. "No, something was following us, watching us. I could feel it."

"You could *feel* it?" Nakiro raised his eyebrows.

Daniel twisted his mouth and looked over at Sanchez who still had his weapon aimed at the tunnel's opening. *Ironic that Sanchez would be the one to agree with me.*

Within minutes, a satellite resembling a spiked silver ball appeared in the sky, circling high overhead. It swooped over the canopy of trees to drop reconnaissance probes to search for lifeforms in the area. The spiked silver ball sailed toward them and descended, clicking in warning like an old-fashioned Geiger counter. A floating holo appeared above it, displaying the blurred outline of something bigger than anything documented to date.

"Not the wind then," Nakiro said.

"No." Daniel puzzled at the blurred image. "Why aren't we getting a clear picture?"

Sanchez grabbed the ball out of the air and shook it violently. The holo wavered and sputtered.

"What are you doing?" Nakiro demanded. "That's a delicate precision instrument."

"That's not working worth a damn." Sanchez let go and the ball floated again, its displayed image unchanged.

Daniel sputtered a laugh at Sanchez's brutal repair effort, but came to a decision. "We'll shelter in place and set a trap for it."

He chose to ignore the exchanged looks of the others. They'd be safe enough. Emergency Shelter Units were extremely durable. Once anchored, an ESU was just about impossible to dislodge, short of a nuclear explosion. When the shuttle the captain sent for them landed, Daniel sent Baker and Nakiro in to retrieve an ESU and animal trap. As the shuttle lifted off again, Daniel reported in.

"Walker here. Something chased us back to our landing site The new scan detected a large, warm-blooded lifeform, approximately human-sized, but we can't get a visual on it, and it wasn't previously catalogued."

"What do you mean it wasn't catalogued?" Lauren's voice came on. "How can that be?"

"No idea. I figure our best option is to capture it. We're setting up a trap and will shelter in an ESU."

"The hell you will," Kowalski cut in. "Return to the ship. I'll send down a security team to deal with it."

"No. We're already here—we can handle it."

"You shouldn't even be planet-side."

"Not your call."

"As captain of this ship, I think it is."

"And as head of this mission, I say it's not."

A long pause followed. Daniel pictured steam sizzling from the top of Kowalski's shorn head. When his voice came back, it sounded as if it were being pushed through clenched teeth.

"Report in every half hour."

"Understood." Daniel signed off.

What he really understood was Kowalski's fear of losing the one person who had agreed to shoulder the blame for whatever went wrong with this mission. But that was Kowalski's problem, not his. *My problem is to catalog every lifeform on this planet, a list which appears incomplete, and that shouldn't be possible.*

Looking back at the darkly shadowed tunnel into the forest, he thought of their Land Surveyor Robot out there somewhere. He tried signaling it again. Still no response. Just in case it was receiving, he sent a simple command to return to its starting point. Something orange moved in his peripheral vision, one of his men. With a long-range rifle at the ready, Sanchez was creeping along the edge of the clearing. Daniel called to him.

"That better be set on low. I want whatever's out there taken alive."

Sanchez gave him a thumbs-up.

"And don't shoot our LSR either, if it ever decides to show up."

Sanchez straightened and gave a mock salute.

Daniel shook his head and turned back to watch Baker and Nakiro set the compacted ESU in the center of the clearing. It looked like a square metal box until they activated it and backed away. The shelter unfolded repeatedly, extending itself into a circle. Slender metal rods shot up, forming an exterior framework, while more rods drilled into the ground. Finally, a silvery skin slid up over the frame. Though initially flexible, once stretched, the covering turned diamond-steel hard. The structure now resembled a gleaming, metallic igloo large enough to house eight people—not luxurious, but strong enough to withstand firestorms, thousand-mile-per-hour winds, or the onslaught of an enraged beast the size of a tank.

"Make sure you calibrate the trap to match the size of this lifeform," Daniel reminded them. "We don't want it set off by any of the smaller animals around here."

"What makes you think it'll come this close?" Baker asked.

"Curiosity. It was following us."

Once the shelter was ready and the trap was set, there was little to do but wait. The golden sun sank lower, and twilight came on in brilliant shades of yellows, pinks and purples. Daniel stood outside listening to the screeches, clicks and hoots of the indigenous wildlife. The bio-sensor on the hovering probe continued to click in warning reporting that whatever had followed them was still out there. Heavy footsteps sounded behind him.

Daniel turned to see Baker carrying a caged specimen into the shelter. "What are you doing?"

Baker spun about like a guilty child. "I, uh, was going to run some tests."

"Can't you do that out here in the open?"

"I thought it would safer inside," Baker said, nervously looking about.

Realizing the man was scared silly, Daniel relented. "All right. Just make sure you leave room in there for us."

"I'll stack them off to the side. They won't be in the way."
Baker gave him a fleeting look of gratitude and disappeared inside.

Daniel didn't see him emerge again. Nakiro, wearing a pained expression, made a number of trips to and from on Baker's behalf, bringing him more specimens. The hour grew late, and the pitch-dark night of a primitive world closed in. Their cell lantern, supported by a soaring tripod, lit up the clearing in a bright white circle that ended at the forest's edge.

"I'll take first watch," Sanchez volunteered.

Daniel didn't like the Security Chief's trigger-happy ways, but he was a trained soldier, and wide awake, while Daniel ached for rest. Glancing at Nakiro, he saw him stifling yawns—no help there. And as for Baker—well, Baker was simply out of the question.

"All right. Wake me in two hours. Remember, we want this thing in one piece."

Daniel followed Nakiro inside and closed the shelter's door. The electronic lock activated with a metallic *thunk*.

***

Left alone in the clearing, Sanchez balanced his long-range rifle in his hands and kept his gaze sweeping along the forest. He knew this creature was sizable, and the way it had dogged them through the trees hinted at a predatory intelligence. *Has to be a carnivore.* He thought of his basement back home filled with bizarre specimens. The only ones there now were stuffed and mounted. The live ones he'd had to sell before leaving.

He remembered with fondness a pair of well-trained Nereids. Someone else owned them now, but he could train new ones. Hell, training them was half the fun. It also made them more valuable. Keeping his side business as a Nereid trader secret from the military was a juggling act. Not that he was ashamed of it.

Don't matter what Walker and his kind say. Probably wants one on the sly, anyway. They all do.

Some of the most vocally opposed to the trade paid top dollar for a well-trained pet. The hunts were fun, but training them was an art. He smiled, remembering those sessions until Walker's scowl kept popping up in his mind to annoy him. As always, his thoughts buzzed back and forth like erratic bees. Too many jumps through hyper-space, the headshrinkers said.

Hell, what do those quacks know? I'm as good as I ever was.

To stop the last psych report from grounding him, he'd put in a call to one of his best customers, Senator Bromberg, and the report mysteriously disappeared. Problem was, it also put him deep in Bromberg's debt, and the Senator had been quick to collect.

"I want you on the Niña," Bromberg told him. "The last thing I need is for Walker to come home a hero. Make sure he doesn't."

Letting Walker join the rescue team on Mars should have taken care of the problem for him. His mind switched to the memory of that Garuda in the Martian cave and how it nearly ripped off his head. He pictured things the other way around, with him doing the strangling, but it wasn't a Garuda in his grip; it was Walker. *That's how it shoulda been.* The images twisted, mixing together.

He shook his head and focused on his rifle. Its setting glowed blue, on low as Walker ordered, which would deliver a mild bone-jarring vibration to knock the target out. At full power, its concentrated beam ripped through steel and blew apart flesh and bone.

Not lettin' that son-of-a-bitch risk my life again. Sanchez switched the setting to full. *Oh dear, did I blow a hole in it? Oops.* He chuckled to himself, imagining the look on Walker's face.

As if sensing his wish, the rifle's built-in heat-and-motion sensor hummed to life.

He looked up to see a shadow, darker than the rest, just past the lighting's edge. Sanchez raised his rifle and peered through its seeker. The shadow melted away, and a huge spider-shaped silhouette took its place. He nearly fired before recognizing their LSR. For some reason, the robot's lights were off. Sanchez lowered his weapon and waited for it to approach, but instead it stopped at the opening of the tunnel and sat there blocking his view.

Leave it to Walker to tell the stupid thing to return to its starting point.

The robot looked dead now, completely powered down. Maybe he should wake up Walker to tend to it. *Serve him right. But then he'll take over, and there'll go my chance to bag this thing.* He shut down the perimeter trap and walked over to the LSR to reboot it himself.

The snapping of a twig startled him. He jumped back, leveling his rifle. Its sensor hummed, rising in intensity. Every cell in his body vibrated in tune as adrenaline surged through him, and the floating pieces of his mind fell into place. There, just ahead, a rustling. He waited for it, still as stone. The rustling came again, closer. He tensed, fingers poised to unleash a torrent of destruction. A thick, half-meter-long lizard poked out from behind a tree, raised its thorny, spine-crested head, and hissed at him.

Sanchez cursed, releasing the breath he'd been holding. He'd seen dozens of these things, and although this one was bigger than most, it wasn't the trophy he sought. He toyed with the idea of blasting it anyway, but that might bring Walker running. He settled for hissing back at it and the lizard slithered away. He watched and listened until certain there was nothing else there before turning back to deal with the robot.

Just as he reached to open the LSR's front panel, a steel-hard grip clamped over his mouth, jerking his head back. He grabbed for what held him and twisted to break free, but a sharp pain bit into the back of his neck, and everything went black.

***

The electronic bolt on the shelter door clicked off and the door inched open, letting light from the cell lantern outside stream in. Asleep on his cot, Daniel breathed his oxygenated air in a slow rhythm, his eyes closed and body turned away from the door, unaware of the light or the shadows that crossed it—until something landed hard on his side and scrambled across him. He jumped up with a surprised yelp.

Seeing the cages open, he threw himself at them, crashing a table filled with vials to the floor before slamming the cages shut to trap what specimens remained. Baker and Nakiro leaped from their cots in confusion. Seeing what was happening, they tried grabbing at their escaping animals. Daniel saw one run outside, only then realizing their shelter door stood open as well. He raced outside to give chase, then remembered the trap and skidded to a halt just in time to avoid setting it off. He watched their escapees scamper for the trees, all of them too small to activate the trap. A tall shadow at the forest's edge took form and one of the specimen animals jumped into its arms, then both disappeared.

"What the hell?" For a moment, Daniel thought he must have seen Sanchez standing there, until a loud snort turned his attention around. Sanchez lay slumped in a folding chair leaned against the outer wall of the ESU. He was snoring, with his rifle balanced precariously across his knees. Angry, Daniel walked over and shook Sanchez by the shoulder. "Wake up!"

"Wha . . . ?" Sanchez rubbed the back of his neck, nearly dumping the rifle. Daniel caught it before it hit the ground. Just as swiftly, Sanchez snatched the rifle back and was on his feet, aiming the weapon's long barrel toward the trees. His face was a mask of rage.

"Explain yourself," Daniel demanded.

Sanchez kept his gun and eyes trained on the forest as if he hadn't heard.

Daniel's anger quickened. "I found our door open, our specimens escaping and you asleep at your post."

"I wasn't asleep. I was attacked."

That stopped Daniel cold. "It got past the perimeter trap?"

"No, I shut the trap down to go reboot our LSR over there, and it attacked me."

Only then did Daniel see the Land Surveyor Robot frozen at the tunnel's opening, a huge dark shape without its stand-by lights. His gaze went to the deactivated black box in the center of the clearing and he grew angry again. "Your job was to remain at your post."

"I know my job a hell of a lot better than—"

"Look at the ground," Baker interrupted, pointing to a wide swath in the dirt extending from Sanchez's chair to the edge of the clearing where the LSR stood.

"Must've dragged myself back here," Sanchez said, but scowled.

"Or something else did," Nakiro said.

"Cover me," Daniel ordered, and walked over to the LSR. When he punched in its manual override, it immediately whooped in alarm and pointed a thin blue locator beam to a spot high in the trees.

Sanchez swung his rifle up.

"Hold your fire!" Daniel commanded and hurried back. "It didn't hurt you and it obviously could have. You're not to fire without a direct order from me." Daniel reactivated the trap and backed away, waving the others toward the ESU. "Everyone inside."

Once in the shelter, they bolted the door again. Together they righted the table, and cleared away the mess left by the spilled vials.

"Sorry," Baker apologized. "I shouldn't have brought so much in here."

"It's okay. At least now we know what it wants," Daniel said.

"We do?" Baker asked.

"Our specimens."

"How do you know that?" Nakiro looked over at the few animals that remained.

"It was out there waiting for them. I saw it." He also saw the looks on their faces. "No, it wasn't a Garuda."

"Must be as big as one," Sanchez said, and rubbed his neck again.

"Should we inform the captain? He may want to send reinforcements," Nakiro said.

"No, we just need to let the trap do its work, like we were supposed to," Daniel replied, looking pointedly at Sanchez. "We're safe enough in here."

"Are you certain?" Baker questioned. "That door was open."

"Yeah, how do you explain that?" Sanchez asked.

"You were the one standing guard, so why don't you tell me?"

Sanchez's eyes narrowed, and Daniel thought for a moment he was about to be in a fistfight. It wouldn't be his first, but it had been a long time and he wasn't sure of the outcome. To his relief, Sanchez just sneered and planted himself in front of one of the viewing scopes in the shelter's walls. The others followed suit and kept watch. Time crept by.

Sanchez fidgeted, growing restless. "How long do you expect us to wait?"

"As long as it takes." Daniel kept his voice even.

"We oughta be out there hunting it down, not hiding in here like little girls."

"Your hunting skills didn't seem so successful the last time around," Daniel replied.

Nakiro intervened. "If it truly wants our specimens, as you believe, maybe there's something we could do to hurry things up."

"Maybe." Daniel's gaze came to rest on a pair of electronic animal prods sitting on the bench. "Hand me one of those." He reset the prod on stimulate instead of sedate, and touched it to the rump of a piggy-looking thing. The animal squealed mightily. Sanchez barked a laugh.

Daniel frowned at what he'd done, but thought it just might work. He reprogrammed the other rod as well, and then handed the rods to Baker and Nakiro. "Make some noise. Let's see what happens." The two men looked unhappy, but dutifully pressed the rods to the animals. which let out high-pitched screeches.

Daniel and Sanchez kept watch on the forest.

"Hey, think I see something," Sanchez announced.

Daniel turned the angle of his viewscope to match Sanchez's and saw a shadow moving at the edge of the light. "I see it."

Baker and Nakiro stopped harassing the specimens and went to their viewscopes to peer out.

A baseball-sized nut rolled across the ground and clunked against the small box at the heart of the trap. Moments later, a fat, gray lizard-like thing crawled out from the dark, nudged the box, then dragged itself back into the forest. Another animal, possibly one of their escapees, appeared in the clearing next. It looked like a fat guinea pig with a pair of hind legs better suited for a kangaroo. The thing hopped toward the trap, circled it then hopped on top. When nothing happened, it bounded back into the dark woods.

Almost immediately after the guinea pig-aroo disappeared, thin triangular winged creatures sailed out of the dark like black leather kites, skimming inches above the trap. One landed on top and grabbed an edge with its curved claws, flapping hard as if trying to lift it into the air. To no avail, of course. The trap was anchored as securely as their shelter.

"They're testing it," Nakiro said.

Daniel nodded, disturbed by the implication.

"Don't matter," Sanchez said. "They can't set it off—they're all too small."

The others exchanged looks of understanding—Sanchez was missing the point. These creatures appeared to be working together.

The black-kite things gave up and flew away, circling higher and higher until they disappeared into the night. Moments later, dozens more of them swooped back in and dive-bombed the tall cell lantern that lit the clearing. Its tripod tipped and the light smashed onto the ground, plunging everything into darkness. The men inside stood back and pulled their weapons, no longer convinced the shelter's walls offered sufficient protection.

Seconds later, the trap alarm sounded, and above its pulsing wail, a feral roar.

"I think we got it," Nakiro said, with a nervous laugh.

Daniel nodded, and let go of the air in his lungs. "Lights off," he ordered, and the shelter went dark inside.

They tapped on their suits' night-vision lights, which cast distorted, red-hued shadows onto the floor and walls. Daniel nodded to Sanchez who slammed the bolt off and kicked open the shelter's door. The roar sounded again, then changed to high-pitched shrieks. Something banged loudly inside the trap. Daniel focused his light ahead, revealing a four-limbed something, desperately flipping and crashing against the trap's electronic bars.

"Pin it," Daniel ordered the trap and its barred walls closed in, stopping just short of crushing its contents. Held in place now, the thing inside snarled at them.

Daniel and the others moved closer until they could see what the trap had caught. What they saw was a skinny, four-limbed, simian-like creature, not more than five feet in length, hanging upside down. Its thin body was covered in dark fur, with a thatch of shimmering white on its head. Its round face had a wide mouth, a slight bulge for a nose, and two large frontal eyes, which at the moment were squeezed tightly shut.

Realizing this frightened little thing was responsible for their panicked retreat, Daniel nearly laughed, but his amusement faded as the real mystery of it all came home to him. A creature of this type shouldn't be here.

"It looks scared," Baker said.

At the sound, the squeezed eyes popped open, revealing reflective orbs with dark vertical pupils. Daniel couldn't determine their color, but they reminded him of Serena's cat.

"So this is the monster that attacked you?" he asked Sanchez dryly.

Sanchez bent down to look at its face. The creature hissed, baring two sharp white fangs. He rubbed the back of his neck, and backed away.

Daniel activated his comlink and waited for Captain Kowalski to come online. "We've captured the uncatalogued lifeform," he said. "Sending you the data now." He nodded Nakiro to transmit. "We'll need to reset the probes to do a specific search for more of them."

"Acknowledged." Kowalski's level response didn't reveal the surprise he must be experiencing. "But I don't see how they could have missed something like that."

"Neither do I."

Daniel summoned the shuttle back, this time to return to the Niña. He and his team dismantled their shelter and loaded it into the shuttle, along with their remaining specimens. Meanwhile the captain sent down an automated recovery unit for their malfunctioning LSR. The hovering unit lifted the robot into the air and flew away just as Nakiro and Baker were carrying in their newest captive, now heavily sedated. Both Sanchez and Daniel kept their eyes on it during the return flight, but it never moved.

Back onboard the Niña, a team of bio-suited techs took over, unloading their specimens and sending Daniel's team off to decontamination. Inside the sealed chamber, sterilizing mists hissed around them. When the blue light came on, they stripped off their suits and deposited them in a receptacle chute. Another tech cornered them to initiate the necessary, albeit humiliating series of invasive tests they had to put up with every time they returned from the surface. A half hour later, they were all given clean bills of health and cleared to enter the main area of the ship.

Daniel went to the bio-ward. There, a technician in the outer lab made sure he donned a biohazard suit before entering the specimen examination room where the planet's atmospheric content had been duplicated. Once inside, he found someone else in a biohazard suit bent over their newest specimen, which was strapped to a gurney.

"Like my present?" Daniel asked.

McCormack straightened his hanger-thin body, which seemed lost inside the bulk of his suit. He turned and grinned at Daniel through the transparent helmet. "Tis a grand present, indeed."

"Where's Lauren?" Daniel asked. "Isn't this her job?"

"Aye, but I couldn't resist taking a look." A growled moan escaped from his charge.

"Notation: Standard tranquilizer dosages have a markedly shorter effect than on an Earth-born primate," McCormack stated for the record.

"You think it's a primate?" Daniel asked.

McCormack shrugged. "No, I just think it looks a bit like one. This is an alien species which I haven't begun to categorize. It appears to be mammalian, and female. Males are usually larger in mammals, so I'd keep that in mind if I were you. I'll know more after I finish my examination." He grabbed another filled hypo.

"Wait." Daniel touched his arm. "Let's see how it, I mean, *she* reacts."

McCormack curved the corners of his mouth down in disapproval. "Always the risk taker," he said, but held off with the injection.

Her big round eyes blinked and then opened wide. Daniel saw that they were a deep emerald green, reminding him of Serena's cat. The eyes swept the room and then fixed on the two men. He was about to say hello, when her mouth stretched open to reveal sharp fangs and she let out a roaring scream. The two men jumped in surprise. Her limbs strained against the straps, and she extended glassy, inch-long claws and ripped at the tie-downs. McCormack jabbed the hypo into her hip. She gasped and closed her eyes again.

"We'll need stronger restraints," McCormack said, making another notation.

Chapter 18

At McCormack's request, the ship's senior staff assembled the next morning to learn the doctor's findings. As usual, Captain Kowalski sat at one end of the oval conference table and Daniel at the other, with their staff aligned on opposite sides. One chair sat empty as usual—the one for the Chief of Security. Sanchez had the annoying habit of standing at the back of the room, arms crossed, as if he couldn't bear to be down at their level.

With his gray hair disheveled from a long night, the doctor sat stiffly with his hands clasped on the table. "Now this is only a preliminary analysis, mind you, and I don't have a lot to go on yet, but there is something disturbingly peculiar about this creature. I'm beginning to wonder if it's even a native species."

"Wouldn't a DNA analysis clear up any doubt?" Daniel asked.

"It would, if I were able to. I've been up all night trying, but every tissue sample I take disintegrates. Some sort of accelerated degeneration. I'll keep working on it, of course, but right now I can only report what I've been able to determine from imaging scans." He referred to his tablet. "Bone and musculature unremarkable, consistent with common mammalian structure, well-adapted for a forested environment with long limbs and claws for climbing, and camouflaging coloration, except for that curious iridescent patch up here." He pointed to the top of his own head then returned to his notes. "Hearing range and visual acuity appear quite good, better than our own I suspect. Opposable digits similar to our own, so it may have tool-wielding abilities. Proportional cranium capacity roughly equivalent to our own as well."

"Are you saying she's intelligent? Could she have language capability?" Daniel asked.

McCormack shrugged. "All I've heard so far is growling, and snarling." There was a note of worry in his voice. "This creature is becoming increasingly resistant to sedation. I've had to keep upping the dosage. My recommendation is to end live testing and perform a necropsy."

"Seems a bit drastic," Daniel said.

"Yes, but considering what we're dealing with, I think it best. She's quite aggressive and I'm concerned she could wake in the middle of a procedure and attack us."

"I could teach her some manners," Sanchez said.

Daniel looked at the burly security officer. He could picture the crude methods Sanchez might employ.

"I think not. With a brain that size, she could be intelligent and there may be a lot more of them down there. We need to study her. We'll move her into the bio-ward's environmental simulation unit and Lauren can set up a behavioral study."

McCormack's worried frown deepened, while Lauren's face brightened.

Sanchez paused, and his thick brows came together as if turning ideas over in his head required considerable effort. "Okay, but based on what the Doc says, we should use a secured cell in detention," Sanchez said. "We can seal one off for medical quarantine."

"That won't be necessary," Daniel said. "We'll take every precaution."

"This thing's dangerous. Doc says so," said Sanchez.

"Regardless, I need her in bio," Daniel said.

"A behavioral study requires replicating the subject's natural environment," Lauren explained before Sanchez could object again. "We can't learn much about an animal's normal behavior by putting it in a bare cell."

"Exactly," Daniel said, giving her a nod.

She smiled back in a way that made him think of something else, something which he quickly pushed aside as inappropriate.

Captain Kowalski placed both hands flat on the table and pushed himself to a stand. "All right, I've heard enough. We'll concentrate our search on the ground for more of these creatures, while you set up your behavioral study. Sanchez can station guards outside the bio-ward as a precaution. I expect you all to keep me informed."

Walker appreciated the captain supporting his decision, but at the same time resented how he'd usurped it as his own. This tug of war for supremacy was getting old.

***

Daniel checked regularly on Lauren's progress in replicating the alien's native environment in the bio lab. Tall trees and vines shadowed light over leaf-covered soil and a narrow stream gurgled through the length of a simulated forest growing within the same atmosphere contained on the planet. While they would observe her through the one-way walls of her cage, she would not be able to see them, or the outer lab and its equipment. From the inside she would see only dense trees stretching out in all directions. The replication was synchronized with movement so anyone on the inside experienced a seamless experience. There was no way to tell it from the thick jungle where they'd found her. Once completed and tested to his satisfaction, Daniel had her placed inside while unconscious so that on waking she would believe herself to be back in her native forest.

Daniel put Lauren in charge of the study, deciding his time was better spent assessing the incoming data from their redirected probes, and reports from the manned teams on the ground. All of them were focused one thing, finding more of these creatures, but both the probes and manned teams kept coming up empty. That left two possibilities—either there weren't any more, or the creatures had a way of defying detection.

With no answers provided by their sources on the ground, he turned his attention to the creature herself. Giving Lauren a much-needed break, Daniel sat in front of the cell watching the creature in its simulated forest. *Her* forest, he reminded himself, though he saw nothing to indicate gender. Right now, she was sitting in a crouched position, dragging a claw through the dirt. *Is that a circle?* Daniel stood and walked closer to get a better look. The creature spun about and shot up the trunk of a nearest tree. The forest accommodated her climb to what looked like a precariously high perch. There she leaned out, sniffing the air. Daniel checked the atmospheric content, finding the pheromones of the native animals Lauren had introduced into the cage, specimens he deemed appropriate since they'd come from the same jungle as this creature. So far, she hadn't eaten anything as far as they could tell, not so much as a leaf. Lauren offered her all types of food, raw and cooked. The creature buried it all in the dirt.

"Aren't you hungry? It's been days," Daniel mused aloud.

He looked closely at her face as she peered around and thought he saw an approximation of a worried scowl there, though it might simply be her normal facial structure. He had to be careful not to anthropomorphize.

Her sniffing continued, and she leaned out as far as her long-limbed grip on the tree would allow, as if wanting to push off. The trees were intentionally spaced far enough apart to discourage any attempt to jump from one to the next. The interior's surfaces were ultra-sensitive to tactile movement, but long leaps through midair could compromise the illusion. Her head and round green eyes swiveled side-to-side, searching. After a while, she slid down the tree onto all fours and loped forward. The forest moved with her in seamless unison. She put on a sudden burst, dashing between the trees, spraying dead leaves in her wake.

"Whoa," Daniel said, impressed at her speed.

The alien creature skidded to a halt and then paced back and forth like a big cat in an old-fashioned zoo. But if that clawed, circular shape in the dirt meant anything, she was a whole lot smarter than any Earth-born cat.

"Something tells me you know you're not in Kansas anymore."

He went over Lauren's notes again, looking for something they might have missed. Lauren had attempted every form of communication they could think of—oral, written, pictorial, mathematical, even mimicry of her own grunts and growls. No response. Lauren first tried projecting an image of the creature herself into the environment as a tool for communication, but the creature had reacted badly, screeching at it. Oddly, when Lauren projected an image of herself, it startled the creature far less.

Lauren's holo image appeared in the forest now, as scheduled and began talking to the creature animatedly, alternating between counting on fingers and drawing pictures in the dirt. Daniel watched the creature turn away and ignore the interactive holo.

This isn't working . . . what else could we try? Then he remembered the haunting trill that sounded so much like a laugh which he'd heard in the jungle. *It's a longshot, but what the heck.* He revised the program slightly and made the Lauren holo giggle. The creature turned back, tilting her head. He tried again, making the holo break into a knee-slapping belly laugh. The creature opened her mouth and echoed the high-pitched sound. He gasped in delight—finally, a response.

"So, if you can mimic a laugh, why not speech?" He turned his microphone on and tried his own voice. "Hello."

"Hello."

Daniel jumped in surprise.

Lauren chuckled from behind him. "Sorry, couldn't resist."

"She copied your laugh."

"I heard. Wish I was having as good a time with this study as my doppelganger in there. This sure has been frustrating so far." She sat next to him. "Still no sign of any more of these creatures?"

"No. No one's found anything remotely like her and our probes still say there aren't any."

"Odd," Lauren said.

The creature raised herself onto her hind feet, forehands stretched up the trunk of a tree. She held her head cocked.

"Look at her. She's listening to us. I'd call that paying serious attention."

"Well, I'm glad someone around here is."

He turned to look at Lauren, who stared back, brows lifted, a challenge in her eyes. He quickly took in her tall, well-proportioned figure, realizing not for the first time that she came physically closer to his feminine ideal than Serena had.

No wonder Serena resented her. Flooded with guilt, he turned away to look at the alien.

"Too soon, I know," Lauren said. "And I suppose you feel I'm partially to blame for what happened."

He looked back, surprised. "No, of course not. It was my responsibility."

"Still, if I hadn't been so pushy—"

"It wasn't your call," he snapped, feeling a rising anger, more with himself than with her. He forced himself to speak more gently. "You were just doing your job."

"Maybe you should remember that applies to you as well." Their eyes met and she placed her hand on his shoulder. "You know, Daniel, if there's anything I can do—"

"Thank you. I'm fine, really."

"Yes, so I've noticed . . . very fine," she added with a slow, flirtatious smile.

He couldn't help but smile back. He had always liked women who knew what they wanted. That was what had attracted him to Serena. The memory made him turn away again. He pointed to the furry, reddish-brown alien sniffing at the air in her replicated environment. "Thank you, but I think that female is the only one I can handle right now."

Lauren shrugged in response. "I suppose some might find her attractive, if you go in for that sort of thing."

"That's not what I meant," he said, feeling insulted.

"I know, but some would. She's not all that different from Nereids: big eyes, close to human in size, soft cuddly fur, and, of course, that same anatomical compatibility."

He frowned at Lauren. "She's also fanged and clawed."

"Fangs can be pulled; cats can be declawed."

"I don't like what you're suggesting."

"I'm not suggesting, just pointing out the obvious. I think we can both guess what the reaction of the Nereid Traders back on Earth will be."

"Except we've only found one of her."

"There's always cloning."

"Too expensive."

"Just makes the price higher."

He stared at her now, thinking perhaps Serena had been more discerning than he in evaluating Lauren's character. Lauren had reminded him of something he didn't want to think about, that exploitation was at the very heart of human nature, and an alien such as this would make a ripe target. He wanted to shut down this line of discussion. "This is the last thing we should be worried about," he said.

"You're right. Our immediate concern is to find out what this creature is about and where she came from."

"Exactly. There must be some way to communicate we've overlooked," he said.

"I don't know what it would be. We've tried everything. I'm thinking at best she only has a primate level intelligence."

"Primates don't draw geometric shapes. We should try a language implant," he blurted, surprising himself. He knew what had happened before when they'd been used on non-humans.

Lauren gaped. "But surely you remember the result of those experiments?"

Daniel nodded and frowned. In their agony, the poor things had literally torn themselves apart. He turned his gaze back to the alien crouched on the ground with her head tilted. As he watched her, the idea grew ever more plausible to him. "But look how she's listening to us, and she mimicked your laugh—something no ape or Nereid has ever done. Maybe it would work in her case."

Lauren rolled her eyes. "Birds laugh. Dogs listen."

"Okay, I know it's a long shot, but . . . I don't know. Somehow it just feels right."

Lauren looked at him funny. "That's not much to go on, but then I suppose we don't have much to lose, either. She's just going to end up spread around in petri dishes at some point."

His stomach twisted. Necropsy was the next logical step and the likelihood of an expensive language implant designed for a human brain being compatible with this alien creature's cortex had to be just about zero. Little more than an expensive waste of time. And yet, for some inexplicable reason, he still wanted to try it. He rubbed his temples.

"Maybe I'm just not ready to admit defeat," he said, in defense of his convoluted thinking. "I mean if there's even the remotest chance of success, shouldn't we at least try?"

"It's remote all right. And if the result is as one would expect, unnecessarily cruel."

He sighed, wondering now why he'd even considered the idea. "I suppose you're right."

The creature in the cell leaped forward and the simulated forest adjusted itself accordingly. She stopped, spun back to a tree and climbed until she found a substantial limb and hung from it with her forearms. She began swinging, aiming not for a branch, but at what she should be seeing as empty sky.

"What the . . . ?" He watched her with growing alarm.

She let fly, claws extended. He and Lauren recoiled as the alien hit the invisible wall directly in front of them, a good six meters from her launch point. Sparks flew and knocked her back, throwing her down to the dirt floor. He jumped up, afraid she was hurt, but she rolled onto her feet and scrambled up the tree again, back to the very same branch, where she began swinging doubly hard.

"Stop it!" he ordered.

She slammed into the force field again, and was again knocked to the ground. She got up, limping now as she returned to the tree, and climbed again, obviously intent on a third try. He spoke into the microphone. "That's enough!"

She paused to look up for a second, then continued climbing. She reached the same limb and began swinging once more.

"So much for environmental integrity," he said, and shut down the simulation on the wall in front of them. That section of trees and sky disappeared, leaving a crescent of simulated forest behind the creature. She now had an unobstructed view of him, Lauren and all their lab equipment.

She hung one-armed from the tree limb, staring, then slid down the tree trunk to the ground. She trotted forward, but the scenery adjusted itself accordingly to keep her centered in the now-compromised environment. She stopped and snarled at the ground beneath her.

"Okay, okay." He shut down the floor mechanism.

She limped ahead again, and the floor stayed put. Before she reached the energy barrier, he turned down the field so that no discharge would occur when touched. Cautiously, she extended a claw to tap against the pale shimmer of the nearly invisible wall. Discovering it no longer bit back, she pressed both forefeet against it, looking out at the newly revealed lab with its complicated array of digital screens and recording equipment. Her focus switched back and forth from the people standing before her to the screens and instrument panels on the walls.

Daniel felt a growing excitement. "She knew it was a fake. She must have known all along."

"That's impossible," Lauren countered. "How could she?"

"I don't know. But one thing's for sure. She's a lot smarter than any primate. I'm going to go see about that implant."

***

McCormack sputtered in response to his nephew's request. "What in the world makes you think her brain might be compatible?"

"You said she has a cranial capacity similar to our own."

"That's no indication. Nereids are similarly equipped and they went insane. It's a waste of time and money and we'll just end up having to put her down anyway. Why torture her first?"

"Because it just might work. If it does, you'll go down in medical history."

McCormack laughed at such obvious manipulation. "You're daft—you know that, don't you?" He took a long breath and sighed. "Ah, well, it's your call I suppose, and other than wasting an implant, we'll be no worse off for the attempt. Though she might be."

Daniel breathed again. The tension in his chest and stomach receded. "Thank you."

"Don't be thanking me yet. You'll most likely have a crazed thing on your hands, so you'd better be ready to end her on the spot. Maybe as long as I'm fiddling in her brain, I should add some behavioral controls, too."

"No, absolutely not," Daniel said, experiencing a near overwhelming revulsion. He searched for some justification for his gut reaction. "We, um, we need her in her natural state so we can learn as much as possible, and . . . and behavior controls could skew our study. We may yet meet up with an entire race like her."

McCormack scowled again. "You want me to implant a language reference chip, and no behavior mods?"

"Yes, that's what I want. Exactly."

McCormack blew out his breath. "You keep telling me you're in charge so guess there's no point in sharing my opinion. I'll go get ready to operate, and in the extremely remote likelihood that her brain turns out to be compatible, and she doesn't go bonkers before

I get her off my table, I'm sure everything will turn out fine. Just fine." McCormack waved one arm in the air as he walked away.

Chapter 19

Their host lay inert on an elevated rectangular surface, anesthetized beyond awareness. The nanobots made no attempt to rouse it. They did not need her eyes to observe the wrinkled, white-haired biological unit operating on her brain. The unit resealed the opening in their host's left temple and backed away.

"It's done," the white-haired unit uttered in packets of indecipherable sounds. "Let's get her back into containment before she wakes up."

With each utterance, they observed images flash in their host's brain. They searched for the source and found the images coming from the mechanical device newly implanted in their host's brain.

Evaluation: Passive reference source.

Conclusion: Request granted.

They concentrated on the sounds made by the biological units and the accompanying images that appeared in conjunction, saving each pairing for analysis.

They had immediately recognized these biological units' vocalizations were a form of communication. The biological units of the forest also vocalized, but these two-legged, tool-wielding units strung complex sound packets together in long passages, incomprehensible without a form of reference. Choosing caution, they had not allowed their host to echo these complex sounds, lest it offend. Only one vocalization seemed unambiguous: the sound of mirth, instinctively recognized as such within the synapses of their host's brain.

They began to cross-reference the broadcasted sounds in the device's databank, correlating them with concrete items and mental concepts. Usage appeared dictated by specific, sometimes contradictory rules that varied with context, intent, and biologically-based nuances. The combinations challenged the limits of logical analysis.

The support on which their host lay moved ahead through a long corridor. Doors opened and closed to allow passage. The wrinkled, white-haired unit and the smooth-faced gray-eyed, brown-haired unit walked alongside. The latter was their focus, another host, capable of radio linked communication. Since the requested implant had been provided, they must assume this unit's nanobots were receiving and had chosen to comply.

They arrived at the same location where their host had been kept before. Another unit they had encountered waited there, the one with sunset-colored hair and pale eyes the color of bad water. Strangely, a not-real image of this unit had appeared repeatedly in the not-real jungle, making baffling noises and gestures. They noted the marked differences in this unit's shape from the others. Accessing the new reference source, they concentrated on that difference—*woman*—sound and image connected.

The straps holding their host retracted as the platform lowered her body to the ground. The three units continued to vocalize with each other, and the implanted device responded. For each sound packet, an image flashed and cross-referenced with sounds, but the rules of usage were unclear. They needed additional context, and so awakened their host's brain for more input. Her organic eyes blinked open. They sensed their host's rising panic—an instinctual fear response which no diamond-based logic could suppress. Fortunately, the unit with the dark brown hair and gray eyes stood near, a presence the host found reassuring. Once again they tried to make contact with this other host's nanobots.

We are here. We are here. Acknowledge receipt.

No answer.

Curious. It is logical to conclude our messages are getting through. Perhaps it is only on a subliminal level. A new tactic must be pursued.

Initiate Phase II.

The host lifted a limb and reached out. The white-haired unit abruptly pulled his dark-haired companion away, and a shimmer formed in the air again. The invisible wall of biting energy was back in place, and their host's organic-based fear returned with it.

She turned over onto all fours lifting her stomach off the fabricated red soil. What looked like dirt, leaves, and trees were not. Everything within this environment read false. To their host's organic eyes, the scenery appeared identical to the forest encountered before, but their silicone receptors knew it to be an artificial construct.

Why do these units mimic the jungle and entrap other units? They have the power to destroy our host. The one with the small black eyes and slab-like forehands used a long stick to kill other organic creatures, turning their flesh black.

They felt their host's relief that the killing unit was not present with these three . . . two men and one woman. *Yes, those are the right sound packets in the right order.*

Should we adapt the host to speak now?

Prime directive: Protect the Host.

They chose caution and kept her silent.

***

On through the afternoon and late into the evening, Daniel took turns with Dr. McCormack, Nakiro, and Chambers monitoring their alien captive, trying to communicate, pointing at themselves and objects around the room while carefully enunciating the names for each. Their student watched them intently but demonstrated no comprehension.

"This isn't working," his uncle said, when the four gathered in front of her partially replicated jungle environment to compare notes. "Clearly, she isn't able to assimilate the information."

It wasn't a conclusion Daniel was ready to accept. "It's too soon to judge."

"Sorry, Danny, but an implant either works or it doesn't."

"This is an alien mind we're dealing with. It may take more time."

Lauren and Nakiro said nothing, but Daniel saw by their skeptical expressions that they agreed with his uncle, convinced it was hopeless. He couldn't blame them all for thinking so, and couldn't justify why he felt otherwise.

"Okay, let's call it a night and re-evaluate in the morning," Daniel offered. No one protested. He looked back at the alien. She sat cross-legged on the leaf-strewn dirt, pouting like a recalcitrant child. Or was he simply projecting his own human emotions?

No, there is definitely something there, something I can't put into words, a strange sense of commonality as if I have the means to communicate with her at my fingertips, but can't quite grasp it. There's a mind in there, an intelligence. I'm sure of it.

The others turned away and headed toward the door. Daniel frowned at their eager retreat. He wasn't ready to leave; he needed to think this through. If his uncle was right that she was not a native species, it meant someone must have brought her here. And if the initial probe reports were accurate, it happened sometime after their arrival. Garuda could be responsible, but the possibility of still another space-faring race as yet unmet was equally worrisome. If they couldn't learn her origin by communicating with her, he would have to let his uncle attempt to find the answers by dissecting her, something he found deeply disturbing.

"You've got to start talking. Otherwise, it's the knife for you," he told her.

She lifted her gaze, blank and uncomprehending.

He sighed and turned away.

"Daniel."

He spun back, but she seemed not to have moved or changed in expression. Still, he knew what he'd heard. He called to the others, "Hey, did you hear that?"

His uncle paused at the exit. "Hear what?"

"My name. She said my name."

Nakiro, Lauren and his uncle exchanged puzzled looks but returned to his side.

"Say it again," he said into the mic. "Come on, say Daniel."

She blinked at him, mute.

Frustrated, he addressed the ship's automated system, "Computer, play back audio for the last thirty seconds."

Together, the four of them listened. Their human voices replayed, but the one he swore he'd heard wasn't there.

"I can't explain why the audio didn't pick it up, but I know what I heard."

"Or wanted to hear," Lauren said.

Daniel gritted his teeth.

McCormack sighed. "It's been a long day, Danny. Let's take a break, get some coffee. And maybe something a bit stronger." He winked.

Daniel looked at the alien again. *Is Lauren right? Did I imagine it?* He shook his head and a great weariness washed over him. He rubbed his face and took a long breath.

His uncle tugged his arm. "Come on, call it a night like you already said."

Befuddled, Daniel nodded and allowed himself to be led away. They ended up in the mess hall, where he grabbed a cup of hot black coffee and thumped down at one of the round dining tables. The others joined him, cracking jokes. Nakiro and Lauren grinned, calling his name in spooky voices. They stopped when he didn't laugh. His uncle produced a bottle of brandy from the private stash he kept for emergencies such as this. Daniel covered his mug with his hand, and his uncle harrumphed disapprovingly. Nakiro and Lauren held out their mugs, and the doctor poured them good measures. Daniel frowned at them all.

"Danny, me boy, you're turnin' into a regular Black Irishman," his uncle said.

Lauren scowled, and her eyes shifted from Daniel's tan complexion to Nakiro's ebony one.

"Don't look at me; I'm Greek," Nakiro said, making Lauren laugh.

Dr. McCormack chuckled, too. "I'm not talking about the color of a man's skin, but of his soul." He turned back to Daniel. "Time to quit brooding, lad, and get on with life." He tipped his head meaningfully toward Lauren.

Daniel looked at his coffee, ignoring the not-so-subtle message. A romantic entanglement was the last thing he wanted right now, plus Lauren had lost some of her allure. He forced the conversation back to his immediate concerns. "Somehow, we have to figure out where this alien came from."

"Agreed. I suppose it's back to Plan A, then," his uncle said, resuming his official role as ship's doctor. "The biggest challenge I see is stabilizing her tissues for DNA sequencing post necropsy, but I'm thinking a systemic chemical infusion should do it."

"No, absolutely not," Daniel answered with more vehemence than intended.

His uncle walked over, sat down and looked directly at him. "All right then, what's your proposal?"

"I . . ." Daniel hesitated, having none. "I don't know, but I'm not ready to give up on the implant, not yet. I'll try again in the morning." He saw them exchange looks again, something they seemed to be making a habit of lately. "Join me or not. Your choice." He got up and left the room.

As Daniel walked toward his quarters, it occurred to him that he couldn't recall if any of them restored the 360 degree view of jungle in the enviro-cell. For a moment, he thought of returning to check, but then laughed at himself.

What difference does it make? The illusion's been compromised. Cat's out of the bag, as the saying goes.

His bed was calling and that's where he went.

***

After their host's captors departed, they positioned her to face the invisible wall of energy. Through her organic eyes and their own receptors, they analyzed her environment, evaluated the state of her health, and assessed possible courses of action along with their associated risks.

Status: host in no immediate danger; tissue repair complete.

Message one sent: receipt confirmed by surgical implantation of requested reference source.

Message two sent: receipt confirmed by observed physical reaction of the gray-eyed, brown-haired host unit.

Messages received: none.

New algorithm: access implant, perform extraction search for commonalities.

As they reviewed the saved sound packets uttered by her captors, the newly implanted device matched them to images and additional points of reference, but the condition of their host's brain was unable to provide substantive context, and they were soon overloaded with semantic and syntax errors.

Conclusion: Data still insufficient.

New algorithm: seek additional information.

In contrast to this jungle-like simulation entrapping the host, the environment on the other side of the energy wall was rich with information. Through their host's eyes, they studied the bank of electronic equipment, searching for more matches in the implant. They saw layered, three-dimensional, gridded representations of a cylindrical enclosure on the five screens.

This replicated forest entrapping our host is also cylindrical.
Correlation identified.

They concentrated on those five displays, analyzing their crisscrossing lines and accompanying symbols, searching, searching . . . until they finally found what they sought.

Exit point identified.

Chapter 20

Early the next morning, Daniel stopped in the mess hall to grab breakfast before returning to the lab. Lauren showed up and sat next to him, setting down a plate full of pancakes, eggs and sausage. He grimaced as she poured syrup over the entire thing.

She grinned lopsidedly at him. "I don't normally indulge myself like this, but hey, we won't be eating again for another five years, right?"

"Careful, or you won't fit into your stasis pod," he said, attempting to match her lighthearted banter. He wondered at her infallibly good mood. *Maybe I should stop taking myself so seriously.* That critical self-analysis immediately made him think of something serious. "By the way, did you reactivate the jungle on the front wall in the enviro-cell last night?"

Her fork froze in midair and she answered with a mouthful. "Um, no, don't think so. Does it matter?"

"Suppose not," he said. He went back to eating his reconstituted scrambled eggs, trying to put his unfounded apprehension aside, but as he visualized the alien staring at the controls all night the formless worry nagged and deepened, then snapped into a sudden conviction that something was seriously wrong. He jumped up.

"What's the big rush all of sudden?" Lauren asked.

Without answering, Daniel grabbed his food tray, dumped it in the recycler and hurried out the exit. His anxiety sharpened in urgency and he broke into a run, dashing through the corridors, and on into the bio-ward with its research stations lining the walls. The technicians working there turned in his direction, eyes wide. *Oops. I'm alarming people for no apparent reason.* He slowed to a brisk walk, smiled and nodded. One of Sanchez's men stood guard outside the entrance to the enviro-cell area. He looked bored.

See? Nothing's wrong here. I'm worrying about nothing.

But the tension in his gut remained.

"Hey, wait for me." Lauren caught up to him, slightly out of breath. "Is there a problem?"

"No. I don't know, maybe . . . probably not."

Daniel placed his hand on the door's control panel and it slid open allowing him and Lauren entry, and then locked shut behind them.

The simulated jungle had moved to the very top of a tree and above it dangled an open ventilation cover.

"Oh, no. No, no, no," he said, and rushed forward. He couldn't see the alien in the enclosure, and the bio-readouts confirmed it. She was gone.

"How could she have gotten past the atmospheric seal, let alone figure out there was a duct hidden up there?" Lauren asked.

Daniel shook his head, unable to fathom an answer. His fingers flew over the bio cell's controls, activating a search for the tracer tag embedded in the alien creature's arm. The first sweep failed. He ran it again. The second sweep came up empty as well. "What the hell's going on? Why isn't she showing up?"

Lauren stared at the small rectangular opening in the simulated sky. "Well, she can't have gotten very far. She would have suffocated in our atmosphere."

Daniel's stomach flipped. He searched a third time. Once again, the readout displayed: 'Unable to locate. Enter new search parameter.'

"Damn it." He was out of options. *I have to tell the captain.* He called the command center, hoping someone other than Kolwalski would respond and serve as a go-between. To his relief, a female voice he didn't recognize hailed him.

"We've had a malfunction in the enviro-cell observation unit," he informed her, but it was Kowalski's voice that came back.

"Containment status?"

Daniel's shoulders sank. With a long inhalation, he drew himself upright again before answering. "Compromised. Her tag doesn't seem to be working, but we think she's—"

"You've lost her?"

"No, she's somewhere in the ventilation system, dead undoubtedly."

"God damn it!" Then silence.

Lauren and Daniel exchanged charged glances while they waited.

After a moment, Kowalski said, "I'm sending in trackers to pull her out." Click.

"All that work for nothing," Lauren sighed.

Daniel checked the atmospheric content in the enviro-cell— breathable for them now that it was mixed with the ship's. He froze the faux jungle, then made the tree lean at an angle and grow rungs.

"What are you doing?" Lauren asked.

"I want to take a look. Maybe I can see where she is." He grabbed a handheld animal control prod.

"You don't actually think she's still alive," Lauren said.

He shrugged. "Just being careful. Stay here." He tapped the control panel and the shimmering wall sputtered out. Holding the prod, he climbed up the tree ladder and peered inside the open vent. He could only see about six feet inside to where the duct dead-ended at a cross-section too small even to accommodate the skinny alien, let alone him.

"Can you see her?" Lauren asked from below.

"No. And I can't imagine how she could have gotten through here, but—Whoa!"

He ducked as a tracker scuttled by — a rat-sized metallic scorpion. Its arched tail gripped a long, nasty looking dart.

It's just a robot. But the design knocked at the door of some primal instinct, making his skin crawl. Efficient and relentless, they would find her, dead or alive.

Alive, definitely alive.

The conclusion came to him unbidden and unsupported, but with zero doubt. He slid down the ladder, and ran out the door, sprinting through the ship's corridors to the command center, where he found Kowalski monitoring the trackers.

Moments later, a breathless Lauren appeared. "Did you forget about me again?"

He had. "No, course not, figured you'd catch up."

The display of the ship's interior showed a schematic of inter-connected blue lines. Yellow lights blinked along them indicating the progress of the trackers through the ventilation system. One of the lights winked out, then a second, and a third. Kowalski sent revised commands redirecting the others. Three malfunctioning trackers were located, but there was no trace of the missing alien.

"It would seem your dead alien is on the move." Kowalski tapped his comlink. "Chief Sanchez, the alien in the bio ward has escaped. Her tracker is offline, so you'll need to conduct a door-to-door ship-wide search. Use lethal force if necessary."

"Yes, sir," came Sanchez's voice, followed by a chuckle before he signed off.

"We need her in one piece," Daniel said through his clenched teeth.

"Should have thought of that before you got careless." Kowalski glared at Daniel, then turned away to address the ship. "This is the captain. The human-sized lifeform from the planet is loose onboard. It is aggressive and dangerous. Arm yourselves and be on alert."

In addition to the robotic trackers, Sanchez's security teams methodically checked each room, closet, and corridor. Three damaged trackers were presented to the captain, each of them smashed flat like the insects they resembled. Daniel tried to look contrite, but inside he was celebrating. An hour passed without results.

"Where could it be hiding?" Kowalski muttered as he ran a hand over the top of his closely cropped hair. "We've searched top to bottom."

It then occurred to Daniel there was one place no one was looking—the enviro-cell from which she'd escaped. The door to the room automatically locked when he and Lauren exited and no one else, other than the captain himself, had clearance to go inside. Quietly, Daniel backed away until he reached the exit.

"Where are you going? Walker!" Kowalski yelled, but Daniel was already half-way down the outer corridor. Running now, he heard footsteps following and the captain calling his name, but he kept on going, and would have rushed right into the enviro-cell if not for an alerted security guard barring his way. Kowalski caught up, shadowed by three more guards.

"Call off your dogs," Daniel said.

"What are you trying to prove?" Kowalski asked, but didn't wait for an answer. He pointed for the guards to go first and reached for the panel to override the lock. Daniel grabbed the captain's wrist. Kowalski clenched his hand into a raised fist, looking as if he might put it in Daniel's face.

"Gentlemen, please!" The voice was Lauren's.

The two men froze. Daniel let go and Kowalski lowered his fist.

"Assessing the native wildlife is my responsibility," Daniel argued. "I need to be the one to go in there."

"Fine, you want to take point, take a gun."

"No, I think it was our weapons that set her off in the first place. She needs to see that I have no intention of hurting her. She won't attack me unless I pose a threat. Let me handle this. Please."

Kowalski glowered for a moment, then pointed a finger at Daniel's face. "Keep an open channel so I can listen. You've got thirty seconds, that's it." He signaled the guards and they stepped aside.

Daniel nodded and placed his hand on the security panel. The door slid open. He stepped inside, and the door snapped shut behind him. He stood still, noticing the ventilation duct cover was still hanging crazily above the ladder tree, and eyed the enclosure, thinking she could be hiding behind one of the trees. He was about to move closer, but a papery rustling brought him up short. He froze and looked down. He'd practically stepped on her.

She was crouched on her haunches immediately to his right, staring up at him, her back pressed against the wall, so close that he could touch her with a twist of his foot. Her predatory eyes held him in place. His heart raced and sweat prickled as he held his breath, wondering just how stupid he was for walking in here alone and unarmed, but then she dropped her gaze and he felt the danger pass.

Only then did he realize that the absence of a security grid between them wasn't all that had changed. She now wore a man's shirt, a book lay open before her, and a fat white Persian cat was curled in her lap. His shirt. His book. His cat. She'd been in his quarters.

He recognized the open book as a hardbound edition from his father's collection, and he could see the edge of another book beneath it. He squinted to make out the title at the top of the page of the open one—*Tom Jones*. He had no idea what to think about any of this, except that he didn't want to be the only one witnessing it.

Slowly, he reached back to open the door behind him. She paid no attention, and remained focused on the book even as the outer door slid open again. Daniel held a finger to his lips, and waved Kowalski and Lauren inside. The alien didn't react, even as the other two tiptoed in. Together, the three of them stared down watching her in her seated position, holding the cat, looking at a book.

After a long, shared moment of silence, Lauren's smile mirrored Daniel's. "This is amazing," she whispered.

Apparently, the joy of discovery did not extend to the captain. "What this is, is a breach of security and medical quarantine," he hissed.

"It's all right." Daniel said with a dismissive shake of his head. "No harm's been done."

"No harm?" Kowalski exclaimed, no longer whispering. "This thing's destroyed three perfectly good tracker drones, and exposed us to god knows what."

At the captain's raised voice, the alien looked up. The three of them stiffened.

"No harm," she said quite distinctly.

Their eyes widened, and their mouths fell open. Lauren let out a small gasp.

The alien pulled the second book out from beneath her and held it aloft, revealing its title, *Frankenstein*.

"Yes, that's a book," Lauren said, in a sing-song tone. "Books tell stories—stories written in words." When she pointed, the alien retracted the book and clutched it possessively. "It's all right. You can keep them," Lauren told her.

Daniel looked at Lauren and frowned.

"You can have all the books you want," Lauren continued, as if the creature were a very small child. "Books are a good thing. You can learn all about people from books. And we want to learn about you, too."

She regarded Lauren with a tipped head looking similar to a curious mongrel.

"What we'd really like to know is if there are any others like you." Lauren nodded encouragingly. "Are there others?"

The creature straightened her head and nodded back. "Others," she echoed.

"We haven't found any others," Daniel said.

"Others," she said again.

"Then where are they?" Kowalski demanded.

She merely blinked in response.

Daniel noted her forehand lying on the cat. "Maybe she just means animals." He crouched down to her eye level. "That's a cat," he said, pointing at it.

"Cat."

"Yes, a cat. A cat is an animal. Animals can't talk, and they don't have hands with opposable thumbs like you and me." Daniel demonstrated by pinching his thumb and forefinger together.

She leaned forward and peered closely at his face.

He held his ground, barely. "Are there more beings like you?" He pointed to her.

Her gaze followed, focusing on her fur-covered hands and arms as if seeing them for the first time.

Lauren tried again. "What we're trying to understand is why we found you in that forest all alone."

"Alone," she repeated.

Kowalski grimaced impatiently. "That's just the implant echoing you." He turned away and spoke to the guards in the doorway. "Seal off this area and have medical check for contamination on all decks." As his people responded, he looked back at Daniel.

"Put this thing back in containment. Then get me some answers that make sense."

Chapter 21

The following morning, Kowalski convened another meeting with Daniel in the conference room, and included the Chief of Medicine, the Security Chief, and Daniel's planetary scientists, Lauren and Nakiro. As usual Sanchez stood in the back, his feet planted wide, looking smug.

"I trust we've beefed up security?" Kowalski asked.

"Yes, we—" Daniel began but saw the captain looking past him.

"The alien is under continual observation," Sanchez talked over him. "The ventilation opening's secured, and I've got a guard keeping an eye on her. That thing's not going to sneak out of there again."

Kowalski nodded to Sanchez and turned to the ship's doctor. "Contamination?"

"Doesn't appear to be any," McCormack replied. "Our scans came up negative, but I'm re-screening the crew individually as well. We're about eighty percent complete and haven't found any red flags so far."

"Well, that's good news." Kowalski's attention skipped past Daniel to Nakiro. "What's our status on the planetary survey?"

Nakiro glanced at Daniel, who nodded for him to answer. "Our last three teams on the ground are due in this afternoon."

"Still no evidence of any more of these creatures down there?" Kowalski asked.

"None," Nakiro said.

Kowalski turned to Lauren. "Have you been able to get anything that makes sense out of that monkey-girl thing?"

Daniel grimaced at the captain's demeaning description.

"I'm afraid not," Lauren replied. "Just the same parrot-like responses you heard yesterday. The one word she keeps repeating is 'others'—probably a stutter in the implant."

"Or she means there are more of them down there, hiding underground maybe," Sanchez said.

"We've mapped the planet a hundred meters below the surface," Daniel countered. "They're not underground."

"How can you be so sure? The probes didn't find her, so that kinda blows a big hole in relying on them. They screwed up on Mars and now they're screwing up here," Sanchez said.

Daniel kept his voice level. "We've tested and retested them. Everything checks out."

"So, if the probes aren't malfunctioning, what other explanation is there?" Kowalski asked.

"The most probable one is that she's no more native here than we are," Dr. McCormack interjected. "That's what I keep trying to tell you."

Lauren shook her head. "I'm sorry, Doctor, but that just doesn't make sense. This creature is perfectly adapted to the environment in which she was found, and she obviously hasn't the advanced intelligence required for space travel. Which means someone else would have had to have brought her here. Why would anyone do that?"

"Considering the difficulty I've encountered trying to analyze her DNA, two possibilities come to mind. That either she's a genetic experiment in progress or a failed one aborted."

Daniel considered his uncle's theory remote, but it could answer one mystery. "If she arrived here after we did, it would explain why the probes didn't detect her in the initial sweeps."

"But how?" Kowalski spread his hands apart, palms up. "We would have detected any incoming vessels."

"Assuming their technology isn't superior to our own," Nakiro mumbled under his breath.

Kowalski sighed and rubbed an eyebrow. "This is getting us nowhere. Let's deal with what we actually know, which is that we have one of her and no evidence of any more." Kowalski locked eyes with Daniel. "So, where does that leave us?"

"With proof of a habitable planet—exactly what we came for," Daniel answered. "We just have this one lifeform we can't quite explain yet."

"It's kind of like the Nereids, isn't it?" Nakiro commented. "Nobody's ever figured out where they came from either."

"Except Nereids don't pose a threat to humans," Kowalski said. "The reason they make good pets is because they're so docile. This thing's not."

"Maybe they can be domesticated," Lauren offered. "Her brain's compatible with a language implant, which means we could probably employ behavior modification implants as well. If we came back with a new line of exotics, it would generate even more excitement about our findings here."

Daniel couldn't believe Lauren was taking them in this direction.

Kowalski frowned. "Maybe, but what good is having just one?"

"What do you mean, what good is it?" Daniel asked, barely suppressing the anger building inside him.

"Well, it would be hard to get people excited about a new line of exotics if we can't provide them," Lauren answered.

"Maybe instead of trying to market her, we should be worrying about whether she is herself a member of a space-faring race," Daniel said.

Kowalski snorted. "That thing?"

"She can talk," Daniel insisted.

"I've seen mynah birds do better," Kowalski said.

"I have to agree, Daniel," Lauren said. "It's just an echo from the implant. She's demonstrated no concept of tool use, and you saw what happened when we placed a campfire in her cell. She ran from it. These are animal behaviors. The good news is that she can handle an implant, which makes behavior modification possible. As for the problem of only having one, we could always clone her."

"Now, wait a minute," Daniel objected. "That's not what this mission is about."

Ignoring him, Kowalski addressed Lauren. "Is that really viable?"

Lauren shrugged. "She's mammalian so I don't see why not, but I'd recommend putting her in stasis as soon as possible. A clone's predicted lifespan is reduced by the age of the donor, so we don't want her aging any more than she already has."

Unable to contain his outrage, Daniel jumped to his feet. "I won't sanction this."

Kowalski stood to match him. "I don't give a horse's ass what you'll sanction. If we can find a way to turn this pile of shit into flowers, we're going to take it, and you're going to smile and go along."

"The hell I will! This a science mission, not a profit-making enterprise. I will not allow my ship to promote another exotic species trade."

The captain inhaled sharply. "Out. Everyone out," he commanded. His pointing finger swept the room until it aimed at Daniel's face. "Except you."

The shuffling sounds of a rapid retreat ended with the click of the conference room door. The two men stood facing each other on either side of the table.

"So, you oppose cloning this alien?" Kowalski asked, his voice deadly calm.

"Without question."

"Then let me remind you of certain facts. You are a criminal. You instigated a mutiny and stole this ship. Your confession is on record."

"I haven't forgotten. I'm prepared to face the consequences, but I don't see what any of that has to do—"

"If you end up going down, you'll take our whole deep-space program down with you. I'll be damned if I'll let you do it. At least Chambers has come up with a credible proposal for turning this boondoggle around."

"Boondoggle? This planet's habitable. All that's needed is some oxygen supplementation."

"And you don't think Bromberg and his kind will jump all over that? They'll claim it's too hard, too far, too expensive, whine, whine, whine. We don't run Earth's space program, they do, and in their view, we've not only defied orders, we've wasted manpower, time, and *money*. Somehow, we have to convince them it was all worth it. A new exotic could make all the difference."

Daniel grimaced, realizing he wouldn't win Kowalski over on moral grounds. His mind raced, looking for a new argument. "Look, I understand what you're saying, but if Uncle Charlie—I mean if Doctor McCormack is right that she's not native to this planet, it means she's here for a reason. Remember how she sought us out, followed us?" He let his mind run, searching for connections. "The Garuda attacked us on Mars, so they obviously knew about the Niña. They probably learned our destination as well. What if she's bait, or a trap? Look at the way she's adapted to our environment, breathing our atmosphere with no ill effects. And she took Sanchez down without a peep. She could be some sort of invasion prototype. Taking her back to Earth and cloning her could be playing right into their hands."

Kowalski squinted at him. He rubbed his face, his gaze darting about before returning to Daniel. "It's a bit farfetched, but if you're right, it's even more imperative we find a way to control her. We definitely need to test out those behavior mods."

Daniel shook his head. This wasn't the conclusion he'd wanted. "No, I was thinking we should just put her back where we found her."

"Don't be absurd. Remember the first rule of warfare: know your enemy."

"She's not the enemy. I was just speculating. All we've been doing here is guesswork. Besides, I don't believe behavior mods are necessary. She came back to the lab on her own and has been cooperating. She's demonstrated no aggression since, none whatsoever."

"Just because she's not in attack mode now doesn't negate the potential. She could be armed with subliminal programming waiting to be triggered."

Daniel threw his hands up in frustration. "Do you have any idea how paranoid you sound?"

"It's your theory. And yes, I know you pulled it out of your ass, but it's not completely crazy. You know better than anyone how far the Garuda will go to keep us walled off." Kowalski started to pace. "True or not, this idea of yours could have legs. If we claim she's a tool of the Garuda, it would demonstrate how vital it is to have an active deep-space program in place to detect these kinds of threats in advance." He stopped to face Daniel again. "This is how we'll play it. A new line of exotics—implanted with behavior-controls we can program not only to serve humans but to protect them against the very threat she was originally intended for—a Garuda invasion."

"What? That's insane."

"You better hope people are crazy enough to buy it, or you could be the one getting the implants."

Daniel held his palms up and took a step back. "No, no way. I won't be a part of this."

"Is that so?" Kowalski frowned at him. "Your delicate sensibilities are really starting to annoy me. It's time you recognized who's really in charge of this ship. Me—and I'm telling you how it's going to be. Now SIT!"

Surprised by the sudden volume of Kowalski's voice, Daniel dropped his hands but didn't take the seat the captain was pointing at. "You can't just order me around."

"I can, and I am. Now sit down. Or do I have to call Sanchez back in here?"

"What?" Daniel couldn't believe Kowalski was actually threatening him, and with Sanchez no less. Something was definitely up between those two. "This is a violation of our written agreement. The terms clearly state we share command. An impasse requires submission to the senior staff for a vote."

"Let's just say I'm taking a shortcut."

"You're a real asshole, you know that?"

"Yes, I am, and I'm comfortable with it. If you don't think I'm prepared to put you in restraints, you have no idea who you're dealing with." Kowalski pointed again to the chair.

Daniel clenched his fists, debating just how far to take this. He knew the military conditioning of the soldiers on board would tell them to follow Kowalski's orders over his own and ending up in Sanchez's brig was not something he wanted to contemplate. He hovered for a long moment, then shook his head, and sat down.

"Good choice. Now pay attention." Kowalski leaned forward to put place his hands onto the table and resumed his previous calm, if gruff, demeanor. "We have three days left before we launch back to Earth, time enough for you to test behavior implants, and start cloning. I want at least a dozen of her ready for harvest by the time we get back to Earth. No more arguments. Just get it done."

Daniel's stomach knotted at the prospect. *Why did I ever agree to a military presence?* "You have no idea how much I despise you right now."

One side of Kowalski's mouth curled humorlessly. "Actually, I think I do. I've never owned a Nereid nor wanted to, and I have no illusion as to how a new line of exotics might be put to use. But if this helps ensure support for our deep-space program, it's a guilt I can live with, and so can you."

Can I? A sick sensation spread through Daniel's body. *No, I can't. I have to protect her.* The depth of that conviction took him by surprise. Up until this moment, the success of this mission had been his single overriding priority, but now that the price might be the life of this one strange creature, he was ready to sacrifice it all. And he couldn't begin to explain why.

***

After the argument with Kowalski, Daniel was too wound up to return to the bio-ward and sure as hell wasn't ready to give the go-ahead to implant behavior mods in the alien as instructed even though he couldn't explain his emotional revulsion to the idea. He decided what he needed right now was to smash something . . . or someone. He headed for the gymnasium. If he couldn't take Kowalski on in real life, he could at least punch the hell out of a virtual one. He spent the next hour in a private sparring room, doing just that. As his fists flew in frustration with himself and hate for Kowalski, he re-ran their argument in his head. As he physically wore himself out, his fury waned, his punches slowed, and cooler-headed reasoning crept back in. Logic told him the captain was just trying to make the best of a bad situation.

Panting and covered in sweat, he stepped back, both physically and mentally.

"End session."

The bruised and bloodied captain vanished, leaving him alone in an empty room.

Admit it. Kowalski's plan might just be bizarre enough to work. If people believe we thwarted a Garuda invasion, we'll be hailed as returning saviors. Having public opinion on our side could make all the difference between facing prosecution and being granted a reprieve. You want this mission to be a success, or don't you?

It would be a lie, of course, or at best an unfounded speculation, and would require sacrificing a life, one alien lifeform out of the thousands discovered on this world. But really, what was that in the face of providing a new world for billions of people. Not to mention securing his personal freedom.

I just need to be certain she's not intelligent. Barring that, I'll get behind Kowalski's plan.

By the time he showered and changed, he was ready to get back to work in the bio-ward. When he entered, he saw the brown-furred alien on the ground in front of Lauren. The creature sat on her haunches like a dog.

Come on, look at her. She's just an animal.

The creature looked blankly at Lauren who kneeled before her holding a digital display. A security officer stood off to the side, with a bemused smile, keeping watch.

"This is a house," Lauren said as she pointed to a picture. "People live inside houses. Can you say house?"

It sounded like the first day of preschool. The creature looked away, her green eyes now riveted on Daniel.

"How's it going?" he asked.

Lauren sighed. "Nowhere. I can't get a word out of her."

"The language implant's probably giving up. If it can't connect, it eventually shuts down." Daniel looked at the children's picture reader in Lauren's hands and smirked. "Unless she's just bored, of course."

"Right. That must be it. Maybe I should have started with Hamlet."

He laughed. "No, but maybe something in between. Something she might relate to like—I don't know," he searched for a possibility. "Like explaining to her where she is."

The creature jumped up, balancing on her hind feet, startling them both. The guard tensed, moving his hand over his weapon.

"Where," she echoed.

Daniel paused, uncertain, but decided to answer as if it were a real question. "You're on a ship, a spaceship."

She froze for a moment and her big green eyes looked away. She focused on him again and started a small excited dance. "Spaceship, spaceship, see spaceship," she said. "Go out, see spaceship."

"Go out?" he repeated stupidly, overwhelmed by the realization that this was an actual two-way conversation. *I was right all along. She's intelligent!*

Lauren's mouth hung ajar.

"Out, out, out, see ship," the creature repeated, shifting back and forth on her hind feet, looking from him to Lauren and back again.

"I suppose it could be arranged," he said cautiously. His mind raced, trying not to let a growing excitement get the better of him.

"Now wait a minute. Think about this," Lauren cautioned with a raised hand, "you know taking her out of here violates bio-containment."

"It's already been violated. She went through the entire ventilation system. We've all been exposed. We can't undo it now."

"I guess not, but . . ." Lauren glanced at the security officer scowling at them. "I'm still not sure it's a good idea."

"Why not?" He asked himself as much as her. "Where's she going to go? She had the run of the ship and returned here of her own free will. She's been cooperative ever since. Why not reward her for that? Besides, wouldn't it make it a lot easier to explain things if we can show her around?"

"But we'd have to be certain she'll do what we say."

"True." He pointed at the alien's hopping feet as a test. "We'll take you out, but only if you can stand still."

She froze in place. "Still," she said, standing motionless.

"Good. That's very good." He smiled and looked at Lauren to see if she was appreciating the import of this exchange and his obvious control over the situation.

Lauren shook her head, but then shrugged. "It's your call, I guess."

"Okay then." He turned to the alien again. "If you stay with us and do only what we tell you to do, we'll show you around. But if you break our rules, we'll have to lock you up again. Do you understand?"

Her monkey-shaped face scowled. "Lock up. Understand."

"Good." She really did understand. She seemed to comprehend every word. "You must stay with us at all times. Understood?"

"Stay with. All times. Understood."

"And do exactly what we say. If you do that, everything will be fine."

"Fine," she repeated.

He nodded, and she nodded back.

"I sure hope you know what you're doing," Lauren said. She looked at the creature. "So, do you have a name?"

The alien creature tipped her head sideways and recited in a flat monotone. "Name—a word or set of words by which a person, animal, place, or thing is known, addressed, or referred to. Designation, honorific, title, label."

"Looks like the implant's doing its job." Daniel smiled at Lauren, then addressed the alien again. "So, do you have a label?"

Apparently considering his question, she paused, then said, "Horde Carrier."

Lauren grimaced, and raised her eyebrows at Daniel.

"Okay . . . um, how about Carrie for short? Might go over better," he suggested. "Would it be all right if we called you, Carrie? Yes?"

"Yes."

"Good." He walked toward the outer door, "Follow me, Carrie."

The security officer called out in alarm, "Wait, you can't just take her out of here."

"We most certainly can. I'm in charge of this mission, remember?"

Daniel led the way out the door into the research lab area. The guard followed closely. Surprised, white-coated technicians at their work stations posed in frozen stances, vials of samples clutched in their hands, while the two guards posted outside the door reached for their weapons.

"It's all right, everyone; everything's under control. Just go about your business," Daniel told them all.

The guards exchanged confused looks. Daniel knew Kowalski wanted an armed guard on her at all times, but these men were Sanchez's flunkies. Everything they observed went directly to the security chief's ears. *We don't need them.* The thought came into his head like an external voice.

"You can go," he told the guards. A tiny doubt questioned what he was doing, but he ignored it.

The guards exchanged looks again.

Make them leave. "I said you're dismissed," Daniel repeated more forcefully. "Go!"

The men frowned, but turned away, at first moving reluctantly, then breaking into a trot. Probably running off to report this to Sanchez. He heard Lauren mutter something about overconfidence.

"We'll be fine," he said.

Carrie turned her furry brown face to him. "Fine."

He led the way out of the lab into a connecting corridor lined with portals. Carrie moved to one of the star-filled windows. Crew members walking through the corridor stopped and stared. Daniel waved them to move on.

"Stars," Carrie said.

"That's right," Daniel replied, thrilled she'd found the word without prompting. He pointed to the green, blue, and white swirled world below them. "And there's the planet where we found you. We call it Tau Medea IV." He felt presumptuous naming her world, then reminded himself that she too might be just a visitor.

"Four," she echoed.

"We're on a ship that travels between star systems. Our home world used to look very much like this one, but now it's more brown than green. It's the third planet in System Sol. We call it Earth."

"Earth."

"And we call ourselves humans. You and I are alike in many respects, despite some obvious differences."

"Differences." She reached over and pressed the flat of her palm against his crotch. He jumped back in surprise, grabbing the offending hand by the wrist. He heard a muffled gasp from Lauren and realized for a moment the incredible risk he was taking, but then almost immediately a pervasive confidence swept through him again.

She's just confused. She meant no harm.

He turned to Lauren hoping for some feminine guidance, but she stood wide-eyed with one hand pressed to her mouth. He looked back at Carrie, knowing he had to be firm. "You mustn't touch people there. It's not polite, and it's not wanted."

"Wanted," Carrie said. "Touch wanted."

"Whatever gave you that idea?"

"Touch wanted," she repeated, reaching for him with her other hand. He snatched the second oncoming wrist and they stood there human face to furry face as he held her wrists to her sides.

Lauren stared at them wide-eyed, trembling, both hands pressed to her mouth as if ready to explode.

"I think we need to explain a few things." He looked to Lauren for help, then realized her trembling was due to barely suppressed laughter. *No help there.*

"Explain," the creature said.

He thought of the books Carrie took from his room. It had been a long time since he'd read *Tom Jones*, but he hadn't forgotten its bawdy content. Did she actually understand it? He tried to remember if there were illustrations. There had to be a way to handle the subject diplomatically.

"Males and females enjoy being together. They like to . . . to touch, but first they need to get to know each other, spend time together and . . . and talk."

"Talk."

"Yes, that's right."

"We talk."

"Yes, but . . ." Again he looked at Lauren. Unfortunately, she was now making high pitched squeaking noises. He frowned at her in annoyance. He was clearly on his own here. "It's best if we keep our interaction to talking and not touching. Do you understand?"

Carrie didn't answer.

"Remember what I said about following the rules? This is one of them. No touching. No touching me, no touching anybody else. Not like that. Understood?"

"Understood," she said, displaying what looked comparable to a human frown.

"Good." He cautiously let go and to his relief Carrie dropped her arms to her sides. He noticed she seemed to be standing straighter, no longer leaning forward as if ready to fall onto all fours.

He glanced again at Lauren. She still held her hands to her mouth. He recognized the humor in the situation, but wasn't about to admit it.

"If you can't control yourself, Ms. Chambers, maybe you should leave."

Lauren removed her hands from her face and inhaled sharply. "Sorry. I wouldn't miss this for the world."

He gave her a stern frown, then turned again down the corridor. Carrie stayed close, passing up the viewing portals now, choosing instead to run her clawed fingers along the walls and the narrow strip-lighting. She poked at door-control buttons, managing to make some of them open.

"Stop. Don't touch," he said repeatedly, but she couldn't seem to contain herself.

"You're not listening," he said. "You have to follow the rules."

She nodded solemnly, then a moment later pressed another door button and peered inside. When they approached a section of private quarters, he took her gingerly by the hand in case the privacy locks weren't activated. He fervently hoped those claws would stay sheathed.

"Touch?" She looked at their joined hands.

"This is fine. But that's all," he said firmly.

As long as he held her hand, she no longer poked every lit button they passed. He supposed the increased control was worth the even odder stares they got walking through the corridors. He narrowed his eyes at Lauren whenever the corners of her mouth curled upward.

"We're going to the orientation room," he stated.

They entered the compact auditorium filled with rows of padded chairs fixed to the floor, facing the front wall. Daniel walked down the center aisle and pointed to a seat in the first row. "Sit here."

Carrie hopped onto the seat and adopted a crouched position, wrapping her forearms around her knees. She watched him sit into a seat two spaces away, She mimicked him, moving her clawed feet onto the floor and placing her elbows on the armrests.

"Look at that," Lauren said, as she took a seat behind them, "seems you have a fan."

Daniel ignored the comment, and tapped the control panel on his armrest. "I'm going to show you some pictures." The lights dimmed and the front wall lit up displaying a three dimensional map of a star system. He zoomed in, enlarging a small dot into a moon-shaped vessel bristling with spikey protrusions.

"This is the Niña, our ship, and its current position in orbit," he said, then zoomed the image down to the planet's surface. "We found you here," he explained as the image closed in on the planet's tropical belt and stopped above a canopy of green jungle. "But we haven't found any others like you."

"Others," she said.

"Yes. Can you tell us where they are?"

"Here," she said, placing a forehand over her chest.

"No, I . . . I don't mean you. I mean other creatures like you."

She stared at him without answering.

He tried a different tack. "Why don't you just tell us what you remember?"

"Remember: to recall prior events," she intoned.

"That's right. What do you remember?" he repeated.

"Remember pain. Remember jungle. Remember you."

Lauren inhaled sharply. "That almost sounded like a real answer."

"Of course it's a real answer." The sharpness of his retort surprised him. Why was he taking this so personally? He drew a breath and tried again, hoping for something more illuminating. "Okay. That's a start. Do you remember how long you were there before we found you?"

She merely cocked her head.

He rephrased, "While you were on the planet, how many sun cycles did you observe? Changes from day to night?"

She paused again, then tapped her claws on the chair arm. He counted the taps aloud, reaching the number ten. "Ten sun cycles," she said.

"Ten? Just ten days? Where were you before that?"

She cocked her head as if listening to something he couldn't hear.

He rephrased. "Where did you come from originally?"

"There." She pointed to the same spot in the displayed image as he had indicated.

He frowned. "Let me ask this another way. Where were you born?"

"There." She pointed again.

"Where we found you?" He looked at the jungle displayed on the screen. "There? In that jungle on Tau Medea?"

"Jungle. Tau Medea."

He scowled in frustration. She'd just claimed she'd been born on Tau Medea a mere ten days ago.

Impossible. Either she's confused or lying. Maybe she isn't willing to share her true origin. After the treatment she's received, I can't blame her.

"Okay. I think maybe I understand. This ship is preparing to return to Earth, our home. I assume you would like to go back to your home, too."

"Home," she said.

He nodded, already thinking up a way to sneak her down to the planet under Kowalski's nose. There'd be hell to pay, but he was in so much trouble at this point, one more transgression hardly mattered. He couldn't justify keeping an intelligent lifeform in captivity.

"Fine. I'll make arrangements."

"Wait, what are you saying?" Lauren bolted upright in her seat.

"We can't treat her like an animal. She's intelligent. It's her choice. She's probably expecting someone to come back for her."

"But—" Lauren started to protest.

He frowned her into silence and turned to Carrie. "We can give you supplies if you need them."

Carrie cocked her head sideways again.

He enunciated slowly, "Food and shelter for you—for when we take you back to the jungle where we found you."

"Jungle?" She looked wild-eyed. "No! No jungle."

"I don't understand. Was there some other part of Tau Medea where you wanted to go?"

"No go jungle, no go Tau Medea. Go Earth, go home."

"Oh," he said in surprise. "Our home, you meant our home? Are you sure that's what you want?"

"Go . . . Earth . . . with . . . you," Carrie enunciated even more slowly than he, as if he were the student here.

"Maybe she got into trouble back home," Lauren said. "Kind of like you."

"Funny," he replied absentmindedly then stiffened. How much did Lauren know? "What makes you think I'm in trouble?"

"I was just remembering a story about how you used to set Nereids free." Lauren cocked her head at him. "Did you really do that?"

He relaxed, realizing she was ignorant of his much more recent and far more serious transgressions. "Can we please stay on topic here?"

"I think that is the topic. You seem to have a rescue urge. It's going to get you into serious trouble if you're not careful."

"I am being careful. That's why I'm questioning her."

"Seems pretty clear she wants to say with us." Lauren replied.

"I get that, but why?"

The alien creature regarded the pair of them with her big green eyes, which blinked far too seldom for his comfort. His worry sharpened.

What am I missing here? Why would she want to stay with her captors? Then again, why wouldn't she? He remembered his own terror at being left behind. *And why did she call herself 'horde carrier'... what the hell does that mean?* He thought of his crazy theory about her being an alien invasion prototype. *Crazy all right. Then again, it would explain a lot. Maybe behavior mod implants aren't such a bad idea. No, don't be ridiculous—she's no tool of the Garuda. If she wants to stay, let her. But why would she choose us after everything we've done to her?*

Just as quickly as his worries came, he dismissed them equally fast. He chewed his lip in consternation, recognizing that his thoughts and emotions were fluctuating wildly and not always matching up.

What the hell's wrong with me?

"We talk, yes?" Carrie asked.

"Um, yes, your language skills are really improving," he said, giving her only half his attention, although he managed an encouraging smile. The latter proved a mistake.

She lunged for him.

With a startled yelp, he fell to the floor and she pounced on his chest pinning him.

"Stop!" Lauren yelled, and jumped to her feet. "Get off of him!"

Daniel lay there momentarily stunned. Carrie flexed his hands and fingers, and he realized she was mimicking what they had done to her. "I'm all right," he told Lauren. "I think she's just curious."

"What do you want me to do?" Lauren asked.

"Just wait. Turnabout's fair play, I suppose, considering all the poking and prodding we've done to her."

Carrie tugged at his waistband.

"Okay now, that's enough. Let me up. Remember the rules," he said, then he spotted the blinking light on the wall—a silent alarm had been automatically activated. "Oh shit. Carrie, get off! Now!"

Six armed soldiers stormed into the room, weapons drawn. Carrie's mouth opened in a fanged snarl and she leaped away.

"Don't shoot!" Daniel yelled, already too late, as a resonator shrieked. He scrambled to his feet and held up his hands. The soldiers lowered their guns.

Carrie crouched low, taking cover behind the front row seats. Her green eyes peered up at him. He exhaled in relief seeing she wasn't hurt.

"It's okay now. You can get up."

Carrie stood in response. A blast hit her torso, slamming her through the 3D display. She slid down the wall behind it and lay crumpled like a battered toy.

Daniel gasped and spun back.

At the top of the theater, Chief Sanchez lowered his weapon. "Looked to me like she was going to jump you again."

Chapter 22

Once more Daniel found himself back in the conference room, this time cornered into arguing with Kowalski in front of Sanchez, Lauren, and his uncle.

"The one you should be demanding an explanation from is him," Daniel said, pointing an accusatory finger at Sanchez, who stood in the back of room with his arms crossed, looking smugger than ever. "I don't know why you still put any trust in him. I told you how my rifle misfired after he messed with it. Why do you keep taking his side?"

Kowalski sighed and held his hands together on the tabletop in front of him as if exercising a great deal of patience. "You could have been killed."

"I was in no danger. Sanchez was way out of line. He had no reason to fire on her."

"The job of Chief of Security is to protect this ship and crew, which is exactly what he did. I told you to keep an armed guard on that thing at all times. Where do you get off countermanding my orders?"

"It's my job to assess the native lifeforms, not yours, and it was my judgment that the presence of armed guards was neither necessary nor advisable. I didn't think of it as countermanding anything. I—"

"You didn't think at all!" Kowalski snapped.

Daniel sucked in a breath but somehow managed to keep his voice level. "On the contrary. I was intentionally establishing rapport in order to learn the alien's origin. I felt that—"

"We don't make decisions based on feelings. We go on the evidence, which has shown this creature to be volatile, dangerous, and a hell of an escape artist."

"I'm aware, but—"

Kowalski cut him off. "You may be in charge of this mission, but I'm in charge of this ship. When it comes to its security, my word is law!" Kowalski's fist came down hard on the table, making Daniel flinch.

Daniel took another deep breath. Despite his growing outrage, he knew better than to blow up in front of staff. "I understand the division of responsibilities and I've never questioned your judgment when it comes to ship operations."

"Nor have I questioned yours," Kowalski replied, matching Daniel's reasonable tone, "until now. In light of your recent actions, I have serious doubts."

Shocked, Daniel searched for the words to defend himself, but he saw from the look on the captain's face, anything he wanted to say would only inflame the situation further. He clenched his hands in his lap, and swallowed the angry retorts bubbling up inside. He would wait to speak his mind when they were alone.

Kowalski turned to McCormack. "Doctor, have you recovered enough healthy tissue for cloning?"

Walker cringed internally, another sore point he needed to address.

"Well, no, not yet. There's not much point until I figure out how to combat that decomposition problem I told you about. I'm working on it, but it's going to take some time."

Kowalski frowned. "How much time do you have now that she's dead?"

The doctor's forehead crinkled in surprise. "She's alive, Captain. I thought you knew."

"You told me it was a direct hit at full power."

"Yes. Centered right in the mid-section of the upper torso, where all the vital organs are located." McCormack circled the area on his own body. "Nevertheless, she's recovering nicely."

"How is that possible?"

"Spontaneous tissue regeneration. Blood flow stemmed before I ever got to her. I patched up the worst of it, but her body's doing most of the work rebuilding her. It's quite remarkable. From what I've observed, I think she'll end up virtually unscathed."

Kowalski looked stunned, then his face reddened. "Why didn't anyone tell me she was all right?"

"She's not all right. She's badly injured," Daniel interjected, leaning in toward Kowalski. "Fortunately, she'll live, no thanks to us."

"Well . . ." Kowalski blinked as if he couldn't quite fathom the idea. "Well, I suppose that's good news, isn't it?" He visibly relaxed. "Doctor, get those behavioral controls implanted as soon as possible. We can't afford to take any more chances with her. And solve that cloning problem."

"But—" Daniel said.

"Don't start," Kowalski warned with an extended finger. He squinted at Daniel. "You look like hell. Stop pulling all-nighters. No wonder you're not thinking straight. Get some sleep, then report for an in-depth psych evaluation, first thing tomorrow."

"Me? You can't be serious," Daniel exclaimed, thinking Kowalski and Sanchez were the ones who'd lost their minds.

Sanchez snickered openly.

Daniel rose to his feet and pointed at Sanchez. "Did you see that? I want that man put on report for insubordination."

"I didn't see anything. You're on thin ice with me, Walker. Don't push your luck." Kowalski shoved himself up from the table and headed for the exit, leaving Daniel with his mouth ajar.

Sanchez smiled and followed the captain.

Daniel looked over at the only two people left in the room, Lauren and his uncle. McCormack lifted his hands and shrugged with a sympathetic smile. Lauren kept her gaze averted.

"Lauren, do you think I'm the one acting crazy here? That I need a psych evaluation?" Daniel asked point blank.

Her eyes flicked over to him and away again.

"It couldn't hurt," she said softly.

Daniel hissed an exhalation. "Fine. If that's what it takes to convince everyone, I'll get the damn thing. Just to prove you all wrong." He looked at his uncle. "How soon can you do it?"

"Tomorrow morning. O eight hundred?" McCormack asked. Daniel nodded.

***

Daniel returned to his quarters and gave the back of his door several swift kicks, then limped across the room and threw himself onto the bed. Immediately, self-doubts kicked in. *Maybe I really do need a mental screening.* Ever since rushing Carrie to medical yesterday and then waiting up all the night to hear if she would survive, he'd been running the previous day's events over in his mind, questioning his choices.

Whatever possessed me to take her out for a stroll? Why was I so confident, so cavalier, giving her a tour as if she were some visiting dignitary rather an unpredictable alien lifeform? No wonder Kowalski's questioning my judgment.

Logically, there'd been no reason to trust this alien creature, and yet he had, almost completely, and very nearly gotten her killed as a result. By all rights she should be dead. The image of her lying motionless on the Orientation Room floor—ripped open, burnt, and bloodied—rose in his mind. Somehow, she'd hung on. Not only had she survived a direct hit from a resonator set on high, she was recovering 'nicely' as Uncle Charlie put it. Considering that miracle, he supposed his shaky relationship with Kowalski would probably recover as well. Once tempers cooled.

I'll get cleared with psych, then go talk to him. Maybe after a good night's sleep, armed with a clean bill of health, we'll both be more reasonable.

Exhausted, he ordered the lights off and closed his eyes, hoping hard reality would quickly fade. Instead, sleep eluded him. His obsessive, self-punishing thoughts raced in tight circles like frantic mice. With a mumbled curse, he threw off the blanket and ordered the lights on again. *Maybe I can read myself to sleep.* But just as he was pulling one of his father's favorite volumes from the shelf, his intercom buzzed. He sighed, dreading some new emergency.

Lauren's voice came on. "I was wondering if you might still be awake."

"Why? Has something else gone wrong?"

"No, I just wanted to apologize about what I said earlier. About the psych evaluation."

"Thank you," he said simply, deciding not to share his own doubts.

"I haven't been able to stop thinking about how rudely the captain spoke to you and thought it might be keeping you up too. Maybe we should . . . keep each other company?"

Hearing the suggestiveness in her voice combined with what sounded like a heart-felt apology, he wavered, tempted. It had been too long since he'd felt the soothing hands and warm body of a woman. But then he recalled her idea to clone the alien for marketing.

"Thanks, but it's been a hell of a day. I think what we both need is rest. Goodnight." He clicked off without waiting for a response. He'd insulted her, no doubt, but right now he didn't much care. He just wanted some sleep. He placed the book back and went to the med-dispensary unit in his bathroom.

"Give me a sedative," he told it. "Something quick acting, six or seven hours' worth." A dark, gelled dot popped into his hand. He tossed it down his throat and crawled back into bed. "Lights off."

Within minutes, the pill did its job.

***

Fulfill prime directive—keep host alive.

As the nano-sized artificial intelligences addressed the damage to their host's body and made repairs, they analyzed the events leading up to the attack.

Interaction elicited bio-units' alarm. Result: extensive tissue damage. Reanalysis in progress.

They were only beginning to grasp how much these biological units' perceptions differed from their own.

Bio-units refer to our host as singular, female, she, Carrie. Initiate adaption to new environmental demands.

A rapid encapsulation, cross-referencing commonalities, sparked throughout their linked intelligences, forming a singular shared point of reference. From this point forward, their awareness would combine with the host's brain to identify as a single entity, a single female biological unit. Designation, Carrie.

We are she. We are I. I am Carrie.

The abbreviated version of 'Horde Carrier' felt inappropriate now, but she decided the name would serve until she came up with one more to her liking. She lay with her eyes closed, back in the partially deforested cell, fully conscious and thoroughly annoyed to find herself not only strapped down tight, but imprisoned behind a shimmering force field once more. A human, dressed like the one who had shot her, stood beyond the invisible wall, watching her. She noted that he carried the same type of weapon at his side. She had no doubt he would use it against her if she did anything to alarm him.

A combination of anger and fear rushed through her, quickly dampened by the *others* occupying her body. Her chest and stomach still ached, but the healing process was nearly complete. It helped that the silver-haired bio-unit repaired the worst of the damage. She might be grateful to him if another of his kind hadn't caused the injury in the first place.

The defenses her *others* developed for use in the jungle had proven inadequate here. She needed to adapt to this new environment. For that she needed to understand these bio-units' expectations. The younger dark-haired unit said that they call themselves 'human.' She replaced the term 'bio-unit' with 'human' in her reference bank. She reviewed recordings of their conversations and recognized that they all had individual names. She searched for a match. *Daniel Walker.* He was the one she needed to focus on.

While he and the other humans uniformly relied on spoken sounds for communication, her *others* identified the Daniel Walker human as a host like herself. Her *others* had established a partial link with his *others*, projecting concepts and images to them, but their host, Daniel Walker, remained as much of an enigma as his non-host companions.

She understood the mechanical nature of the ship now and, thanks to the implant, was rapidly decoding their verbal communications, but she was still far from comprehending their motives and expectations. Responses from them varied. Behavior encouraged by one met with violence from another.

She lay with her eyes closed, contemplating her experiences and assessing her options. Uplinked to her central identity now, her *others* provided her with raw data for referencing. She tried to make sense of it all. Instead of clarity, her confusion deepened. The data on human behavior remained inadequate. She needed more information. The written text in the books she'd taken from Daniel's room had described a method of physical joining. Her *others* concluded he must value this method since he retained a treatise on the subject, and had her attempt to instigate it, but he had not been compliant, and the attempt had failed.

Of course, she had been interrupted. It was, therefore, difficult to conclude whether if given more time, the joining would have been successful. Also, her *others* had been conducting the experiment without input from her biological brain. Perhaps now, without inter- ruption and as an integrated single identity, she might obtain better results. To perform said experiment required immediate proximity to a human. There was only one she trusted. The guard pacing beyond the energy wall with a hand resting on his holstered weapon was not that one. He was an obstacle.

Though she lay with her eyes closed, she used the eyes of an- other bio-unit to see him, a small, white-furred bio-unit identified as a cat by her reference implant. She had found the cat during her first exploration of the ship. Its mind had proved tractable to the invasion of her *others*. At her bidding, it now sat on the far side of the energy wall watching the human guard on her behalf. She decided to test the cat's abilities and projected images of what she wanted it to do.

A hissing sound caught the guard's attention, making him turn toward it. The cat took up a crouched position.

"What's the matter with you?" he asked.

In answer, the cat dove for his booted ankle, sinking in its teeth, hind legs scrabbling in fury. He cursed, and kicked out, flinging the cat airborne. It screeched and scooted under a table from where it eyed him balefully.

He glared back at it. "What the hell was that for?"

This cat is too small to be a serious threat to a human, but it can still serve as a distraction.

Carrie let it remain hidden under the table watching for her as she feigned sleep, hoping the guard might be lulled into inattention. For a long while, he continued his restless walking, his eyes checking on her and the cat. She noted the human's attention to her gradually grew intermittent. His pacing slowed. He yawned, stretched his arms, then stepped over to a view-screen and tapped it on. Moving pictures danced in and out of its surface, and he fell into watching them.

Opening her own eyes, she peeked down at the straps holding her—a metallic composition, tougher than before, but still little chal- lenge. At her command, her *others* left her skin to disassemble the straps' molecular structure. The metal unraveled and fell away. Making sure the guard was still watching the displayed images, she reached out and flicked a finger, sending a spray of *others* airborne. Within seconds, a tingling in her still outstretched arm told her they had returned. She downloaded their gathered information, analyzed it, formulated a new parameter, then reached out again.

Everything happened at once. Darting from beneath the table, the cat wrapped teeth and claws around the guard's calf. Cursing, he tried to shake it free. The shimmering wall sparked and disintegrated. He spun, reaching for his sidearm just as Carrie leaped from the table and grabbed him by the throat. Eyes bulging in surprise, he gurgled and went limp.

She held his unconscious form dangling from her hand, and tilted her head while considering what to do with him. *Permanently harming one human could alienate the rest. Alienation will not serve me.* She carried him back to the examination table from which she had escaped, repaired the metal restraints and secured him in place. *He will recover but be unable to follow or sound an alert. Solution acceptable.*

The cat swirled around her feet and she bent down to stroke it. The cat purred, then curled into a contented white muff under the table where the guard lay.

Carrie considered possible modes of exit, looking first at the outer door.

Risk of detection high.

She looked up at the ceiling, half her body length above, remembering the maze of tunnels that lay beyond. A new metal panel covered the vent through which she had accessed them before.

Preferable.

She lengthened, thinning and stretching herself upward to reach the panel in the ceiling. At her bidding, her *others* ate through the weld. She peeled the panel off with her claws, pulled herself inside the opening, and then maneuvered through the narrow tunnels like a snake.

***

Lost in drugged unconsciousness, Daniel slept hard and deep, unaware when the ventilation grill in the ceiling above him creaked open in the darkened room and something slithered to the floor. His bedcovers rustled.

Soon he began to dream—soft, delicious dreams of languid caresses. He dreamed of making love to Serena, or was it Lauren, or both? Their faces shifted and swirled. The sensations grew more intense as he felt the weight of a warm body, breath on his neck, a hungry wet tongue. His arms and hands reached in the dream, enclosing someone slender, soft, and furry.

Furry?

The face in his dream turned to that of a Nereid, blue-furred and yellow-eyed. In a nightmarish moment of revulsion, he struggled to wake, but then spasms of erotic pleasure gripped him again, pulling him back into the far sweeter fantasies of Serena and Lauren.

Just a dream, a drug induced dream . . . a hell of a good one. And so he went with it.

Chapter 23

Captain Kowalski and a two-man security team burst into Daniel's quarters, startling Daniel awake. He jolted upright and squinted against the light.

"What's going on?"

"Maybe you'd like to tell us?" Kowalski demanded, pointing an accusing finger.

Daniel looked to his right and with a yell of surprise, jumped clear of the bed. Amidst the rumpled bedcovers, Carrie sat blinking at him with her wide green eyes. The two guards snickered, and Daniel realized his pajamas were missing. He snatched his robe and swung it around to cover his nakedness.

"How did she get in here?" he asked, tying his robe shut.

Kowalski shook his head and turned to the guards. "I want her locked up again, this time with round-the-clock security."

"I better go with them," Daniel said, moving forward.

"I think not." Kowalski blocked him, and waved to his men. "Get her out of here. Now."

The guards signaled her toward the door, but she crouched down low instead, as if ready to spring at them.

"Carrie, no! You need to cooperate," Daniel urged. "Please, just do as they say. I promise everything will be fine as long as you cooperate."

She looked at him for a contemplative moment, then to his relief, she crawled off the bed onto all fours, holding her tail high in the air, and went out the door with the guards. The door clicked shut leaving him and the captain alone.

Kowalski narrowed his eyes at Daniel. "This is your idea of a behavioral study? Trying to establish rapport?"

"What? No, of course not." Daniel was thoroughly offended even though he still felt groggy from the sleeping pill. "I have no idea how she got in here."

"Spare me. I just caught you with your pants down—literally. I thought you didn't go in for furry entertainments."

"I don't. Nothing happened here."

"You haven't gotten that psych-evaluation yet, have you? Better get a physical, too. Who knows what you may have picked up?"

"Come on, you don't seriously think that I would—"

"I know what I just saw. If you need an armed escort, I'll be happy to supply one."

"That won't be necessary."

"Good. Then it'll just be me." Kowalski lowered himself into one of the chairs in front of Daniel's desk. "Get dressed. I'm not walking through the corridors with you in a bathrobe."

Daniel gave up defending himself and put on his uniform. Minutes later, he was headed to sickbay, with Kowalski escorting him.

"This is absurd," Daniel said.

They marched through the medical lab, past furtive glances from the on-duty personnel, up to a door panel labeled Dr. Charles McCormack. Kowalski pressed his hand on the panel and the door slid open. McCormack, sitting behind his desk, paused in the middle of what he was saying to a woman in a white lab coat. Daniel recognized his uncle's surgical chief, Dr. Patel, a tall, striking woman, darkly complexioned with a tattoo in the middle of her forehead.

"Leave us," Kowalski snapped at her.

She scowled and held her ground until McCormack nodded. She nodded back, then walked out the door, her chin elevated in scorn.

"Daniel's appointment isn't for another hour and a half," McCormack said, when the door closed behind her.

"It's moved up. I found your nephew here in bed with the alien."

"What?" McCormack rose to his feet.

"Look, I don't know how Carrie got into my quarters, but I swear nothing happened," Daniel insisted.

"Check him out, Doc. Mentally and physically. I want to know what kind of business he's been up to with that monkey of his."

"She's not a monkey," Daniel protested.

"Close enough. Make sure you do a *full* psych eval like I ordered. If he gives you any trouble, call security." Kowalski turned and marched from the room.

As the door whisked shut, Daniel met his uncle's astonished expression.

"Oh, Danny, I know it's been difficult without Serena, but—" he began.

"Don't be ridiculous. Nothing. Happened."

"Let's hope not." He came around the desk and took Daniel by the arm. "We'll learn the truth of it soon enough."

***

Walking on four feet, with her long tail aloft, Carrie moved along quietly between the two guards, alert to the weapon trained on her from behind. The guard in front paused and lifted his wrist to his mouth. "Farley here, we have custody of the alien." He listened to someone talk into his ear for a moment. "But, sir, I think the captain meant—yes, sir—right away, sir."

She noted letters on his chest—F-A-R-L-E-Y. She made the connection between the spoken word and the written one. The other guard wore a designation as well, J-O-H-N-S-O-N.

Farley sighed and took the lead again down long twisting corridors, turning left, right, and left again. The three entered a tiny room. When its doors snapped shut, she felt the room descend. Words popped into her mind, 'elevator, lift, shaft.' Her nervous system tingled in warning—this was not the way back to where they'd held her before. Carrie eyed the two men and their weapons. They looked determined to deliver her to whatever destination they had in mind.

Cooperate. Do what they say. Everything will be fine. The Daniel Walker said so.

The doors opened and the men motioned her out.

Another man, wearing the same type of dark blue uniform, sat behind a metal desk. "What's this about?" he asked, scowling at her.

"Orders," Farley replied. "I need to put her in cell three."

"Why three?"

Farley shrugged. "Because that's what Sanchez said. After that, I'm supposed to relieve you. He was very specific."

"Fine." The new man frowned but stood and walked ahead of them down the corridor. The clicks of her clawed feet echoed on the cold metal tiles. He stopped at a panel on the wall, punched in a series of numbers, pressed his palm against it and a door slid open. The original two guards pointed for her to go in. She complied but the guard who opened the door remained outside. The room held a chair and desk facing a raised floor extending the length of the room.

"Stop there and don't move," Johnson ordered. His weapon pointed at her. He spoke to Farley. "Did he say to use the manacles?" Farley nodded and pulled out four metal bands from the desk. He slipped them around her back legs and forearms closing each one with a sharp metallic snap.

"Step up there and move to the back," Johnson told her, pointing ahead.

She experimentally jiggled the metal bands on her wrists and ankles. Her gaze shifted from the weapon to the raised platform. She didn't like any of this.

Maybe I can obtain sympathy if I mimic them.

She lifted her forefront to balance on her hind feet, and looked the Farley guard in the face. His eyes widened, and he stepped back. She focused on the letters written on his shirt.

"Far-lee," she read aloud, startling him. She held her banded wrists out.

"Sorry," he said, and shook his head.

"Look at that. The thing can read. Which means you understand English," Johnson said, not looking any friendlier. "So do as you're told. Back up."

Farley didn't appear to have any intention of interfering. She knew the pain contained in the weapon pointed at her. *Cooperate.* She remained upright as she stepped onto the raised floor. An invisible barrier appeared as a shimmer before her, locking her within. The men exited, and the outer door closed, leaving her alone. Carrie dropped to all fours and turned to examine her new surroundings.

Like the corridor outside, the room was composed of bare metal: floor, walls, and ceiling. A small symbol at her eye level on one wall depicted a reclining figure. She touched it with a claw, and a padded bench slid out with a white sheet folded on top. She looked for more symbols. She discovered a metal bowl at chair height containing a small pool of water. Another revealed a squared series of holes in the ceiling from which water showered down to drain through a grate in the floor.

She saw no ventilation opening in the ceiling. Instead air was being pumped in through porous tiles in the metal reinforced walls. The only exit was the door by which she had entered. She could easily disassemble these metal bands, cut through the force field in front of her, and open the outer door, but waiting for her outside were humans with weapons. Mechanical obstacles were easily manipulated, biological ones less so. And even if she subdued every human on this ship without incurring injury to herself—which seemed unlikely—then what?

The Daniel Walker human had offered to return her to the jungle where she would be safe, but safety alone was inadequate. Her mind ached to be filled, something the jungle and its primitive inhabitants could not do. The aggression of these humans frightened her, but they were the dominate species of this technologically advanced environment. She needed to adapt to human expectations. Interaction with the Daniel Walker human had provided a rich source of information. She closed her eyes, focusing on the hard logic portion of her combined awareness to review the raw data. The numerous choices presented defied logic-based analysis.

I need to approach this another way. Only her organic brain could provide emotional content. Although the brain was badly damaged, she allowed it to come to the fore to instinctively choose which characteristics to adopt and which to discard. As her organic mind awakened, fear welled and tears poured from her eyes. She swiped the wetness away and made her selections. Once done, she pushed the emotional intelligence into the background again in favor of the cold logic of her *others*.

An adaptation this extensive will be a lengthy, all-consuming process, rendering me vulnerable. I must choose a safe time and location to initiate. Uncertain whether her current situation fulfilled that requirement, she chose to wait. In the meantime, she would absorb as much fuel as possible in preparation. Standing under the falling water, the *others* harvested hydrogen and she drank of it until her belly would hold no more.

She wanted to remain alert, aware of her surroundings, but thought perhaps she could try something small. *Something superficial that won't require my full attention. Maybe . . . a nose.* She lay down on the bench, closed her eyes, and formed a picture in her mind, but before more than a slight bulge emerged in the center of her relatively flat face, the soft swish of the exterior door alerted her. She opened her eyes and sat up.

The one she most dreaded stood before her. His broad face wore a grin, but the smile had no effect on his dead-black eyes.

"Bet you're just tickled to see ol' Sanchez again."

She remained silent, feigning incomprehension.

"I hear you can talk now, so if I ask you a question, I expect an answer."

Pretended ignorance insufficient. Fear deterrent needed. She bared her fangs and hissed.

His smile flattened, and his eyes narrowed to slits.

"Looks like Walker forgot to teach you some manners. You better be nice to me, real nice. You're in my classroom now."

He moved over to the desk and placed a hand on it. Its surface lit up. His thick fingers danced across the lit area. Curious, she tried to step forward, but her feet stuck to the floor. She stared down at them, confused, straining, but couldn't make them budge. A strong force tugged at her wrists and her arms shot up over her head. Next, her legs and arms jerked to the sides so that she stood in a wide stance. The harder she pulled, the more the invisible grip tightened. She turned her attention inward, summoning her *others*. There was no answer.

"There. Now we can get up close and personal," Sanchez said and gave the desk panel another tap. The shimmering wall between them disappeared. "That there's what's called a focused electromagnetic field," he explained, as he stepped up onto the platform beside her. His booted toe tapped the manacle on one ankle. "Works real good on these things."

Her inner awareness searched frantically. Never before had the *others* failed to respond.

Sanchez circled her, running a hand over her, ruffling the reddish-brown fur.

"No touch. The Daniel Walker said no touch," she told him.

He paused, surprised, then his sneer returned. "So, you really can talk. Now what I understand is that Walker told you to cooperate. You know what cooperate means, don't you? I tell you what to do, and you do it. Now if you do that, we'll get along just fine. But if you don't, I'm gonna get real upset." He drew his hand away, then without warning, smashed the back of it across her face.

Pain stabbed in her mouth where sharp teeth cut the inside of her cheek.

"See what happens when I get upset? Like when you snuck up on me in the jungle down there. Made me look bad. That upset me a lot." He smacked her again.

Her vision blurred, and she felt her face and eye swelling.

He looked at his handiwork, nodding in approval. "Well, that's enough of that. We wouldn't want to go reducing your commercial value." Sanchez ran his open palm across her smooth, fur-covered belly, looking closely where he'd shot her. "Looks like you heal fast. That's good, real good. People are gonna like that."

She sucked at blood on her lip, trying to concentrate, trying to summon the *others*. *Why don't you answer?* Without their influence, her organic brain flooded with fear. Tears leaked from her eyes and she experienced a swarming confusion, alarms zinging through her, as if her internal world had gone as mad as the one outside. *Why is this happening?* She needed to think, but her comprehension was painfully slow now.

"What is . . . what is commercial value?" she asked, trying to distract him.

"Oh, well, you know. It's what you're worth on the open market. Got a feeling it'll be a lot. Even Walker's taken a fancy to you. I'm thinking a well-trained pet like you that's implant compatible could go for eight, maybe ten times what I get for a Nereid."

He leaned close, hands in her fur, exploring the shape of her, so close she could smell the rank odor of his last meal.

"Mr. Holier-Than-Thou's always preaching against the trade, but then he goes and sneaks you into his bed. Kind of puts a crimp in his halo, don't it? I figure if you can change his mind, you could change anybody's. You could be a hell of an investment. Course I'll need a lot more like you to make it worthwhile. That's why you're going to tell me where to find them."

He raised his hand and Carrie tensed for another blow. Instead, he smiled and walked back to the desk. Opening a hidden compartment, he pulled out a narrow metal rod and returned. He moved behind her and brushed the tip of the rod down her back. Sharp hot pain raced deep into her spine and she cried out.

"This here's a Nerve-Tingler. Real handy; no marks at all, just pure persuasion." He moved it to her recently healed but still tender stomach.

She screamed until he withdrew it.

"Pretty sure you understand who's in charge here now. So tell me, where did you come from?"

"Unknown."

"Wrong answer." He touched her with the rod again.

"Where you found me!" she yelled.

""Cept you were all by your lonesome. What about the others?"

The question startled her. *He knows.*

"Where are they?" he demanded, bringing the rod close to her face. "Where are the rest of your kind?"

No, he doesn't know about the 'others' at all. Carrie searched for something his limited perception might accept, but her organic mind could only think of the truth. "Inside."

"Inside what? Like a cave or underground somewhere?"

Go along with it. "Yes."

He hesitated as he scowled, then stuck the rod against her stomach. "You're lying."

She cried out, and he removed it.

"We searched everywhere. Far as we can tell, there's no one else like you anywhere on the planet, just a bunch of little animals. Our probes didn't even register you at first. So why is that?"

She tried to think what might make sense to him. "Maybe . . . maybe because I changed."

"Changed? Like what, your shape or something?"

"Yes," Carrie admitted.

Sanchez stared at her. "So what were you like before?"

She didn't know how to answer that. First there was nothing, then the green growth and its animals, then the humans came. "Like the animals."

"Which ones?"

"All of them. Any of them."

"I'll be damned." Sanchez let out a long, slow breath. "You're a shapeshifter?" She nodded. "That explains a lot." He looked away, staring off into the distance. When he looked back, his face took on a new eagerness. "Think you could change some more?"

"Change is always possible."

He stepped over to the desk and brought up a floating screen. "Look at this here." A three-dimensional image of a naked woman pirouetted in the air before them. "Could you change your body to look like that?"

She noted how ungainly and ill-balanced the design was compared to her own streamlined physique. "Inefficient," she observed.

"It's not about being efficient. It's about what people want, and you want people to be nice to you, right? People like Walker? I'm sure he'd like you even better if you looked more like that." Sanchez pointed at the image.

"Speculation unnecessary. Preferences of the Daniel Walker have been noted," Carrie replied, and immediately realized her error when the face before her hardened again.

"Is that so? Maybe you should be worrying about what I want." Rapping the rod in his opposite hand, Sanchez approached her. "I'm starting to think what's needed here is a full-on attitude adjustment." A gleam of anticipation shone in his eyes.

Recognizing the increased danger, she renewed her struggles—to no avail. The rod's tip found her flesh again, progressing slowly but unceasingly to ever more tender areas of her anatomy as she screamed in agony. Without the *others*, escape was impossible. Out of options, Carrie withdrew, hiding her higher awareness in the depths of her mind, existing as a mere shadow, the way she had before, when the *others* had been in total control, protecting her mind as they rebuilt her body, but they were in disarray now, unable to offer any protection or to communicate with her or even with each other. Undefended, she was at Sanchez's mercy, so she hid her awareness away in the recesses of her mind to make the exquisite pain recede as well. Though helpless to resist, she took comfort in the belief that Sanchez wanted her kept alive.

He demanded that she change her body, but without the *others* there was little she could do.

"Get rid of your fangs," he ordered.

To avoid the agony of the rod again, she chose to comply. "I need a hand free to reach them," she answered. He let one arm fall and she yanked the fangs from her mouth. To her relief, the bleeding stopped almost immediately, which meant her others were still there, still working on her behalf, despite the breakdown in communication. Next her claws had to go—one by one, she cut off the tips of her toes and fingers until only one clawed digit remained. She bit it off.

A deep sense of betrayal hit her. *The Daniel Walker human was correct about the need to cooperate, but so very wrong that everything would be fine.*

When the bleeding stopped, Sanchez pointed to the floating image again. "That's a start, but I need you to shape your body like that."

She nodded her understanding, but was unable to comply.

"To do so will take time and rest," she said.

He frowned at first, then seemed to accept the enormity of what he was asking. "Okay, I can wait some. Meanwhile, let's teach you a few tricks."

He told her what he wanted her to do, following up with the rod if she moved too slowly. She observed him touch her, use her, but remained emotionally distant, aware of what he was making her do without fully experiencing it. She stayed protected in the depths of her mind, angry and outraged, but taking notes to use once her *others* awoke again.

***

Sanchez grunted, finding his ultimate release. "Oh yeah," he said, slightly out of breath. He patted her head in reward. "That was good, real good. You're a natural. Just remember who's boss from now on." He let her drop to the floor and checked the time. *Better get back.* He removed the restraints, prepared to hit her with the rod again, but she didn't move. Seeing she was incapacitated, he tugged up his pants and tucked in his shirt, then stepped down from the platform and tapped the desk to reactivate the energy wall. He glanced back at her lying there in a crumpled heap and smiled, convinced he'd broken her. He'd found out what he wanted to know, taught her the value of cooperation, and thoroughly pleasured himself in the process.

Just like training a Nereid—except this thing can talk and follow verbal instructions, which will make everything so much easier. Most important, she's a shapeshifter. And I'm the only one who knows it.

Assuming she's told me the truth.

Eh, nobody thinks fast enough to lie when I use a Nerve-Tingler on 'em. He had the facts—he was sure of it. *A shape-changing pet and implant-compatible! Holy hell!—the possibilities blow my mind. I can make customized exotic pets. What more could you want? I can charge a hundred times what I get for a Nereid, maybe more. When Bromberg gets wind of this, he'll go nuts. We'll shut Walker out and make this planet ours, just like Nereus.*

He thought about mining this world's biological treasure, maybe having exclusive access. Sanchez hadn't been happy about 'volunteering' for this mission, but now it looked like it would all be worth it. More than worth it.

He re-hid the illegal instrument of torture, and put the manacles back in the desk. As he exited the cell, Farley glanced up from the duty desk and immediately looked away. Sanchez decided he'd better leave nothing to chance. He strolled over and stared down at his subordinate.

"If anyone asks, no one's been in there since she was brought in. No one. Got it?"

When Farley nodded, Sanchez continued in a more conversational tone.

"Shame she got roughed up like that, but I'll be sure to explain how much trouble she caused and how well you handled the situation. Be sure to let Johnson know how I'm watchin' out for the two of you." He walked toward the lift. When it opened, he held the door and stared hard at Farley. "I'd call him right now, if I was you."

"Yes, sir," Farley said.

Sanchez smiled at their mutual understanding, and let the door close.

***

When Sanchez left, Farley looked down the corridor toward the door of cell three. He hated being on Sanchez's duty roster. For the last hour, he'd tried very hard to mind his own business. Unfortunately, the cell doors were escape proof, but not soundproof. He'd wanted to intervene, to call Captain Kowalski, but if the rumors about the chief's political connections were true, he doubted even the captain could protect him, so he'd talked himself out of it.

Besides, it's not like he had a human being in there.

He punched the intercom to call Johnson. They needed to get their stories straight.

Chapter 24

After Kowalski had escorted him to sickbay, Daniel suffered through an in-depth physical examination—blood tests, skin-scrapes and invasive scopes—supervised by the Chief of the Medical Department. Throughout the process, his uncle went back and forth, conferring with his medical personnel, saying little to Daniel and frowning a great deal. Whenever Daniel opened his mouth, his uncle shushed him. Lying naked and abandoned on an exam table, Daniel was running out of patience. His uncle sat hunched over a nano-scope.

"You need to do some serious work on your bedside manner. You haven't said more than two words in a row to me since I came in here. Just 'hold still' and 'bend over.' Are you done with me or not?"

"Hmmm?" his uncle looked over at him, his eyes round and unfocused.

Daniel sat up. "I said, are we done here?"

"Oh, yes, sorry. You can get dressed now." McCormack turned back to squint through the scope.

Daniel gathered his clothes.

His uncle continued to ignore him.

"Okay, enough with the silent treatment," Daniel said, as he pulled on his pants. "Talk to me. What's going on?"

"Not sure yet. I'm having difficulty analyzing your tissue samples," McCormack replied fiddling with the scope's settings, making another adjustment.

"Problem with your equipment?" Daniel asked as he slipped his shoes on.

"No. Problem with your cells."

Daniel paused and scowled at the back of his uncle's head. "I don't understand."

"Neither do I—that's the problem."

"Stop being obtuse."

McCormack leaned back from the scope and turned to look at him. "I believe it means that our captain is correct in his suspicions."

"No. He isn't. I took a sleeping pill and went to bed. Alone. Next thing I knew the lights came on, and Kowalski stormed in. Carrie was there I admit, but that's all there was to it."

His uncle tilted his head and crossed his arms in silent scrutiny, waiting.

"Okay, I . . . I may have had a rather vivid dream, but I'm sure that's all it was."

McCormack harrumphed and waved at the display on his nano-scope. "Dreams don't alter cell structure. Of course, neither does copulation . . . normally."

"Copu—? No, no way. Didn't happen. And I feel fine." Daniel flipped his shirt around, searching for the sleeves.

"Well, let's take comfort in that, for now at least," McCormack said. "However, I think it's time we completed the second phase of this exam."

"The psych eval? It's waste of time. My mind is perfectly clear."

"Are you certain of that? Was it this same sense of clarity that convinced you to take this creature out of a secured area and let it roam the ship? We're not talking about some docile Nereid, Danny. This thing has fangs and claws. It's aggressive, and unpredictable. You had no idea what it might do. And now, it seems you've been in-timate with it."

"I haven't been intimate with anyone." Daniel wrestled his shirt on as if it were fighting him.

"My exam says otherwise. Even more worrisome, your tissue samples are falling apart, just as hers do. I fear that thing's infected you with something."

Daniel paused in dressing, but quickly recovered. "No, no, never happened." He shook his head and went back to tugging his shirt straight and tucking it in. "Something must be wrong with your equipment. And stop calling her 'that thing.' Her name is Carrie."

McCormack's eyebrows lifted. "This behavior you're exhibiting is not uncommon in individuals experiencing guilt. It can make you feel the need to protect whatever you perceive as vulnerable. It's classic transference."

"Oh, please." Daniel rolled his eyes.

"Just sit down and listen for a minute."

Daniel frowned, but sat. He leaned back and crossed his arms. "Fine. I'm listening."

"Not as evidenced by your body language."

Daniel sighed, uncrossed his arms and sat upright.

"Better. Now try very hard to actually hear what I'm saying and think about it for a moment before going into knee-jerk denial. Clearly, you blame yourself for Serena's death." Daniel groaned, but his uncle continued. "You brought her remains here to inter, despite regulations. We all looked the other way in the hope that it would provide you with some sense of absolution. Obviously, it hasn't. Then up pops this semi-humanoid-looking alien, a female no less, seemingly lost and alone, and apparently in need of protection. Can you see the connection? How in the depths of your subconscious, you've allowed this creature to take Serena's place almost as if she'd been reborn on this planet?"

Daniel blinked at him, his anger draining away. "Reborn?"

McCormack nodded. "Yes. Exactly. Can you recognize now how your judgment's been affected? How your underlying guilt is making a subconscious connection between—"

"That's it!" Daniel declared, no longer listening. He jumped to his feet. "Uncle Charlie, you're a genius!"

"Thank you, but—"

Daniel bolted from the room.

"What's gotten into you now? Danny, wait!"

Despite the calls of his trailing uncle, Daniel dashed past the technicians at their stations, and rushed headlong up the stairwell and through the corridors. He burst into the busy command center, grabbed the startled captain by the arm and dragged him into the privacy of the adjacent conference room.

Panting hard, Doctor McCormack came through the door after them, gasping and waving in apology. "Sorry, sorry, he just took off running."

Kowalski shook off Daniel's grip. "What the devil do you think you're doing?"

"I figured it out. We have to go back down to the surface."

"What? Why?" Kowalski looked to the doctor, who shook his head, and held a hand to his chest, still trying to catch his breath.

"I think I know where Carrie came from, but I need to make sure," Daniel said.

"Make sure of what?" Kowalski asked.

"I'd rather not say until I know for certain."

"Have you had your psych evaluation yet?"

"We were just … getting to that," McCormack answered between breaths.

"There's nothing wrong with my head," Daniel said. "I need a shuttle, not a shrink."

"And you've got zero chance of getting one. Even less if you don't tell me why," Kowalski said.

"Okay, okay, but just try to keep an open mind." Daniel held up a cautionary hand. "What I think is that there's a distinct possibility, no, a distinct *probability* that Carrie is a native lifeform that's assimilated human DNA."

"Come again?"

"I think what we have here is a creature that evolves in response to exposure to new DNA. Think about it. It's the perfect survival strategy—taking on the traits of more advanced or better adapted species. That's why we haven't found any others like her, because there simply aren't any. That's why we didn't detect her before our arrival. That's why she seems so familiar and so alien at the same time. And why she keeps referring to others, because before she changed, there were others like her. It's all making sense now."

"Not to me," Kowalski objected.

"Hold on," McCormack said. "This might well explain a few things, such as why she appears to be the only one of her kind, why her tissues are unstable, her quick adaptability, the accelerated tissue regeneration. On the other hand, it opens a whole new set of puzzles."

"That's why we need to go back down and examine Serena's remains," Daniel said.

"If there are any left, of course," McCormack added. "This thing may have consumed them all."

"Now wait a minute—" Kowalski started.

"Don't you see?" Daniel couldn't contain his excitement. "It's all connected—Serena buried on the planet, this creature's sudden unexplained appearance—it goes together. It has to."

Dr. McCormack jumped back into the discussion with new enthusiasm. "Yes, yes, it's quite possible. There have been studies of animals that can take on the knowledge of others through consumption. For instance, the Earth flatworm that—"

"Flatworm? Time out!" Kowalski shut them up. "Okay, let me get this straight. You two have come up with this theory, this really wild theory. And now, three hours before departure, you want to go down there and exhume Serena's body to prove it, except you're not even sure there's a body left to dig up." He drew in a sustaining breath and paused with his hands held apart, waiting for the logic to sink in. "I'm sure it would be a great scientific exercise, gentlemen, but it's not happening. We're on countdown. Nobody leaves. Forget it."

Daniel couldn't believe what he was hearing, "How can we forget it? If this creature really is partly Serena—"

"Serena's gone. Even if this thing consumed her remains and adapted as a result, that's not her, not even close. And I don't even want to think how this would play back home."

"Who cares how it *plays*?" Daniel asked.

Kowalski smiled humorlessly. "You'd damned well better care. When we get back, you're going to have to do one hell of a sales job on what we've found here. You'll be lucky if all you get out of this is a prison sentence. More likely you'll end up with implants buzzing you into spasms every time you get a deviant thought."

"What is he talking about?" McCormack asked.

Daniel blew out a long breath and dropped his gaze to the floor unable to meet his uncle's eyes. "We never got permission to leave. We ignored orders."

"You ignored them," Kowalski reminded him. "I had no knowledge, remember?"

"Right," Daniel confirmed, still unable to look at his uncle.

"Like anyone's going to believe that," McCormack said, shaking his head. "You're obviously both in this up to your necks."

"And now so are you," Kowalski said. "Who's going to believe he kept you in the dark? This alien may be our only ticket out of this mess, so don't tell me she's some twisted alien-human resurrection thing. Can you imagine what the religious right will do with that?" Kowalski met their stunned expressions. Having silenced them, he continued. "Try to put this in perspective. Based on what you've said, we're left with two possibilities. Either she's a completely new alien lifeform, or she's got a little human DNA mixed in. Either way, it doesn't change anything."

"How can you say that?" Daniel asked, appalled.

"Because she still adds up to a new quasi-humanoid much like the Nereids. Except with a little more sex appeal, if we go by you. I'm betting people will love her. And if they love her, they'll love us, which means we just might come out of this with our skins intact. Think about it."

Daniel thought about punching him, and took a step in that direction.

McCormack raised his arm between them. "Clearly, there's a lot at stake here, more than I realized. Captain, you certainly have an interesting way of looking at things, but we need to consider the ramifications should our *wild* theory prove correct. If it turns out there are more creatures on that planet with similar potential, or even among our specimens here on board, it may put every one of us at risk. It's quite possible that whatever transformed Serena's dead cells is equally capable of transforming our live ones."

"Wouldn't we have seen evidence of that by now?" Kowalski asked.

"I have found evidence. In Daniel. He's not experiencing any adverse symptoms as yet, but something is definitely amiss. We should re-screen everyone, decontaminate all decks, and re-confine this creature to medical quarantine. I need more time to study her to figure this out."

"Time is something we're short on. We have a narrow launch window."

"I can get down there and back in time," Daniel argued. "Just give me a shuttle and—"

"No. Non-negotiable. I won't risk it. Auxiliary power is already being rerouted to the main engines and there's no room for error. You're staying right here. Whatever you need to know, you'll have to learn from what we already have on board."

McCormack acquiesced. "I suppose all I really need is access to the alien herself. But we can't be cavalier about this. We have to know exactly what we're dealing with, what we're bringing home with us. I'll need to have some of my assistants awakened."

Kowalski nodded. "Understood. I don't have to warn you of the risks and consequences of being exposed to hyperspace, Doctor, but if you think it's vital, then do it. Just be sure to take the necessary precautions. Keep the portals covered and make sure no one does anything foolish. If you discover anything of note, you have permission to wake me as well."

"Very well," McCormack replied, "I'll need permission to run whatever tests I deem necessary."

"You have it, carte blanche," Kowalski said.

Daniel opened his mouth in protest.

"Calm down," McCormack patted his arm, "I'll do my best to keep her intact. So, Captain, if you'll return her to the bio-ward, we'll all go about our business."

"I assumed that's where she was," Kowalski said. "I told the guards to take her back."

"No, you didn't," Daniel said, recalling Kowalski's exact words with sudden clarity. "You ordered her locked up with round the clock supervision. They must have taken her to detention." Daniel turned purposefully toward the door.

Kowalski blocked him. "Oh no, you don't. Stick one foot in the brig and I'll see that you stay there until your stasis pod is ready."

McCormack laid his hand on Daniel's arm and said, "Why don't we wait here until we hear from the captain?"

"Fine," Daniel answered, "but I swear if anyone's so much as touched her . . ."

"Awfully protective of that flatworm, aren't you?" Kowalski shook his head and went out the door, grumbling under his breath, "Nothing happened, my ass."

***

Kowalski headed out to the command center. He waved a two-man security team stationed there to accompany him and led them through the corridors. Instead of taking the lift down to detention, he veered toward the emergency stairwell. Narrow and seldom used except during training drills, the stairs would allow them to arrive unannounced.

The men following him exchanged puzzled looks. He offered no explanation. The crepe soles of their shoes negotiated the tightly curved metal steps noiselessly. With the ship on energy conservation status, orange emergency lights in the stairwell gave their faces an eerie glow, like old-fashioned jack-o-lanterns. They spilled out into the detention level corridor, surprising the guard on-duty, who jumped to his feet. Kowalski recognized the man.

It took Farley a split-second to regain his composure, and snap to attention. "Captain Kowalski, sir!"

"Where's the alien?"

"Um, well," the man stumbled over his words, "if . . . if you'll just give me a moment to reach Chief Sanchez, I'll—"

"No, I will not give you a moment. Take me to her cell immediately."

Farley cleared his throat and reddened. "Yes, sir." He turned and led them three cell doors down.

"Open it," Kowalski ordered

"Chief said no one was to go in . . ." Farley's voice trailed off in embarrassment.

"Is that so?" Kowalski entered his override code on the door's control panel then placed his hand on the sensor plate. The door slid aside. "After you."

Farley stepped inside, keeping his gaze trained on the floor. Kowalski noted the man's fear and anticipated the worst. In the low light, he didn't see her in the cell immediately, even though it was almost devoid of furnishings. When he spotted her, she was wrapped in a sheet and pulled up so tightly into a fetal position that she looked like little more than wadded-up fabric crammed into the corner.

He cleared his throat, unsure how much she could understand. "I'm Captain Kowalski." He thought he saw a twitch. "You were supposed to have been returned to the bio-ward. I've come to take you back." She still didn't move. From here, he couldn't discern what condition she was in. He considered lowering the security grid, but hesitated, recalling the predatory look in her eyes. "Can you get up?"

"Course she can," came Sanchez's voice from behind him.

Kowalski turned to see his Security Chief pushing past the guards. "Is she hurt?"

"Naw," Sanchez replied dismissively. "She just had a little run-in with the guards when she came in, nothing serious. She might be a little put out, but she's fine. Allow me, sir."

Sanchez shut the force field down and stepped up alongside her. "Get up.' He pulled her upright so that she stood on her back feet, disturbingly human-like. "The captain here wants you to go with him."

Sanchez pushed her forward and Kowalski saw there wasn't any fight in her. Remaining upright, with her body and face hidden in the sheet, she shuffled forward to stand before him.

"Come with us," Kowalski said and gestured ahead, but she didn't move until Sanchez pushed her from behind. Odd, he thought, but in that fashion, they made their way to the lift. She acted like a completely different creature—subdued, docile, a far cry from the one Kowalski had encountered before. He'd meant to take her back to the bio-ward, but seeing her altered manner and the dark dots sprinkled on the sheet, he changed his mind.

"I'll take it from here," he told Sanchez and let the lift door close in the chief's face. Once inside the lift, he contacted Dr. McCormack. "Meet us in sickbay."

Something had certainly happened to her, and undoubtedly that something was named Sanchez. Although he didn't approve, it crossed his mind that maybe the chief had done them all a favor.

***

"What did they do to her?" Daniel exclaimed, when he saw Carrie shuffle into sickbay with the captain.

Dr. McCormack waved for his attendants and they lifted her onto a gurney and ran her into an exam room.

"Wait here," McCormack told Daniel, and Kowalski stayed to make sure of it.

"Son of a bitch," Daniel said.

"Calm down. It's probably nothing," Kowalski told him. "Sanchez says she got a little roughed up. That's all."

"A little? You saw what she was like, and there was blood on that sheet."

"Very little, and I saw her walk upright all the way here without a peep, so she can't be too bad off."

"You don't give a damn what happened to her."

"Maybe I'm just thinking more clearly than you."

McCormack stuck his head out the door. Daniel was surprised to see him wearing a biohazard suit.

"Is she all right?" Daniel asked.

The doctor frowned through the visor of his helmet. "Better come see for yourselves. Both of you. Put on suits first." With that he disappeared back into the room.

"What's that mean?" Kowalski asked.

"I don't know, other than he's reinstated containment." They each grabbed a suit. The entryway flooded with decontamination gas, then sucked it away before letting them through. Suited medical personnel inside surrounded an examination table. Daniel squeezed between them to see.

Carrie lay absolutely still, her green eyes open and unblinking, the pupils fully dilated. His chest tightened, and he felt a sick twisting in his gut. He waved a gloved hand over her fixed stare. No response. Guilt rushed over him. "This is my fault."

One of the hooded figures turned toward him. "Stop that." The voice was his uncle's. "She's not dead. She's unconscious, in a catatonic state of some sort. Her autonomic motor skills are unaffected — put her on her feet, give her a push and she'll walk, but otherwise there's no conscious response. It's probably a survival skill, a way to mimic death to fool predators."

"Oh," Daniel exhaled, relieved, then frowned at the implication. It was obvious to him who the predator had been.

"Apparently, it also facilitates adaptation," McCormack added and gestured with his blue-gloved hand. "Note the newly shortened length of the forearms. And here you can detect an emerging nose bridge."

Daniel and Kowalski both leaned forward to look closer. The changes were subtle, but discernible.

"How do you explain it?" Kowalski asked.

"I don't. Not yet anyway," McCormack replied.

"Sanchez tortured her," Daniel said with conviction.

Kowalski pulled Daniel aside. "I will not have you making unfounded accusations."

"Only severe trauma would cause a reaction like this," Daniel argued.

"Not necessarily," McCormack interjected, joining them. He lowered his voice so the others in the operating room couldn't hear. "If your theory is correct about her being a native lifeform that can evolve by incorporating foreign DNA, this could be the next stage. What we're observing might be comparable to that of a worm in a chrysalis. It may have nothing to do with what anyone's done to her and everything to do with a drastically changed environment."

"No, she's been hurt. I can feel it," Daniel said, then turned back to the captain. "Talk to the guards. They might have seen something."

"Will you listen to yourself? I won't start interrogating people based on how you feel," Kowalski said with evident disgust. "This ends now. I have a launch to prepare for, and so do you." Kowalski gave them dirty looks and exited the room.

***

When Daniel next heard the captain's voice, it was booming over the ship's address system. "All remaining personnel report to stasis. Launch sequence begins in thirty minutes." Daniel accompanied his uncle as an automated gurney wheeled Carrie through the corridors.

He was almost glad she was unconscious. At least this way, he needn't explain what they were about to do to her. His uncle insisted there was every reason to believe she would survive the stasis process as successfully as they, even in her catatonic state. Daniel hoped he was right. As the lid closed over her already frozen green stare, he couldn't help but once again note the pod's similarity to a coffin. Only three pods still stood open, waiting to be filled.

Kowalski marched into the room. Daniel acknowledged him with a nod.

"Stop stalling," Kowalski snapped, and Daniel's face contorted.

"All right, you two," McCormack intervened and gently guided each of them to their assigned pods.

Daniel heaved a sigh as he faced the cold white cylinder yawning open at the end of the long row. Kowalski glared at him. Daniel forced himself to turn around and step back inside. The lid sucked shut over his face and once again he had to fight down his instinctive panic. Through the view window, he saw the door of the pod to his left close over the captain. His uncle smiled and gave him a thumbs-up. The last thing Daniel heard was the hiss of anesthesia as it spiraled him into oblivion.

***

Dr. Charles McCormack was now the last living thing still awake on the ship. All the others were safely tucked away in their cocoons for the return flight, and he needed to join them quickly. Roving medic-drones rolled slowly down the rows monitoring read-outs, and would continue to do so through the flight back to Earth. Ultimately every life on board had to be entrusted to their cold, unfeeling care.

Remarkable how much faith we put in our creations, the doctor thought with some irony, *considering just how flawed their creators are.*

He summoned one of the drones over and revised its programming so that once the stresses of extreme acceleration and the stomach-churning jump into hyperspace were complete, the drone would revive him. He took a last look at Daniel sleeping in his pod and felt a twinge of guilt. He'd kept his findings that the alien had been raped by Sanchez a secret, not to protect Sanchez but to protect Daniel. For some reason the captain allowed the security chief to act with impunity. In a showdown, he feared Daniel would be the one to suffer.

Seeing Daniel's pod readouts were correct, he moved to his own pod and squished himself into the gel to let the drone lock him within. He didn't particularly enjoy this process either, but on this occasion, he was eager, knowing he would soon have the opportunity to satisfy his scientific curiosity. Once reawakened, along with the handful of personnel he'd selected, he would launch a no-limits investigation into the nature of this alien to learn the secret of her existence. As for his honorary nephew, he would leave him undisturbed.

Danny would only get in the way, hovering over her like a protective hen.

Chapter 25

Earth Year 2192, New York City, North Americas

Even midday, little sunlight filtered through the city's grunge-covered sky dome leaving New York in a state of continual twilight. The dome sat atop a gigantic diamond-fiber seawall encircling the city like a frosted glass ring. Safe inside from the raging storms, people made their way along the streets cutting between the city's old cement-and-steel skyscrapers and taller nanotech-engineered bio-buildings made to resemble gigantic trees. One of the city's oldest buildings housed the district headquarters for the Unified Church of Earth. The aging structure was inconvenient in its lack of built-in interactives, but quaintly appropriate for an institution clinging to simpler times. Though a soaring monolith in its day, the old steel skyscraper now sat in the shadow of its taller, tree-like cousins, so its windows revealed nothing but darkness. The view matched Lester Merritt's mood. Still enslaved by the nanobots he'd been infected with five years ago, he saw no way out, nor any point in thinking about it.

Lester walked into the largest corner office on the top floor and sat down to await his master's arrival. Bored within seconds, Lester sighed and tapped the desk's control panel to turn on the 3-D. The holo of a young woman appeared in the air before him with a news report. As usual it was all about politics.

"Our lead story today is the controversial bill introduced in the House of the United Nations calling for even more drastic cuts to Earth's deep space program. Under the proposed bill, the program's designated funds would be redirected for completion of Earth's Automated Perimeter Defense System, known as A-PEDS. Opponents of the bill claim full automation could endanger our own ships, should they fail to give the proper clearance codes. However, many fear the Garuda attack on Mars is a harbinger of future attacks and argue that Earth's protection is paramount.

"Should A-PEDS go forward, there is particular concern for the Niña, due back in five years. Senator Bromberg, candidate for Premier of the United Nations and co-author of the A-PEDS bill, says the

Niña may already have been lost, and any delay puts humanity at risk.

In other news, we have the latest election poll results, stock market quotes, and T-carrier counts. Then we'll take a look at what's happening in your corner of the System. Stay tuned to SWN for Solar-wide news. Back after this."

An ad popped up of men and women in leather thongs, soaring through space, swinging axes and swords. In the background, voices sang praises of Interactive Warcraft 2100X. A buxom, Amazon-like woman leaned toward Lester with a suggestive leer, extended her hand, and said, "Come, join me." In the middle of her palm a red light blinked—touching it would pull him into the game. Just as Lester reached out, his master entered the room.

Lester jerked his hand back and stood. "Gaia be with you, Brother Chayd," he said, with a small bow. He tried very hard not to think of the spectacularly handsome Morden Chayd as Cadmon Dhyre any longer. Though he could never forget the disfigured face of the monster behind the comely façade, he knew from experience a slip of the tongue meant agony. The newswoman reappeared, and he gestured at her. "I was just checking to see if anything on the news might be of interest to you."

"Instead of watching the news, you should be out making it." The Archbishop of New York waved the 3-D off as he walked around to stand behind his desk.

"Oh, I have, I have, believe me." Lester hurriedly pulled out the digital pad he always carried, and showed a list of names to prove his diligence. "These are all high level Church members I added to your list of supporters just today."

Chayd glanced at the names and nodded. "What else?"

"I scheduled a meeting with Bromberg for tomorrow, like you asked."

"Good. It's time he learned whom to thank for his skyrocketing climb in the polls." Chayd turned away and frowned at the dark window. "I need a better view. Paris, I think and soon."

"Paris?"

"Never mind that. Contact Bromberg's assistant after our meeting tomorrow. Make arrangements for me to speak before the

Senate Ethics Committee next week, and then at the upcoming Helsinki Conference on Off-World Trade," Chayd said.

Lester nodded and entered notes on his pad as if he knew all about these events.

"Bromberg is one of the conference organizers," Chayd continued, "Have him schedule me as the main speaker."

"Wonderful idea, wonderful." Lester made another entry.

Chayd fell silent for a long time.

Lester waited at attention, but inside he struggled. Should he keep quiet, offer to get him something, start groveling? It was so difficult to know what might please his master at any particular moment.

"So, Bromberg's our man now?" he finally ventured more from sheer nervousness rather than any desire to know. "I mean, your man, Brother Chayd, of course, Your man."

Chayd nodded. "He will be—after tomorrow. I've collected quite a bit of information on his less savory activities. It's amazing what people rely on for data security."

Lester relaxed. He'd asked the right question.

"Publicly, Bromberg espouses the values of the Church, but privately, he violates just about all of them. A prime example is his proclaimed rejection of off-world influences. The truth is he fancies Nereids. Goes through them like water, all hush-hush, of course. Seems he's not very good at keeping them alive." He chuckled.

Lester kept his expression neutral.

"But then you'd know all about that, wouldn't you?" Chayd gave Lester a condescending look. "I know all about how you and that Nereid launched your cousin on his ridiculous campaign to stop the trade. Not that I've ever understood the attraction, personally. Why would anyone want to fuck a big blue teddy bear, when so many women are right there for the taking? Ah, but women talk back, don't they? And they expect a certain level of performance. Was that the problem, Lester? Couldn't get it up for a real woman?"

Lester turned bright red. It wasn't true, but he knew better than to defend himself.

"No doubt that's Bromberg's issue as well. Yes, he's most certainly mine. That fetish of torturing and murdering his pets would alienate at least half the population, from isolationist conservatives to off-world liberals. Most anyone will condemn abuse publicly, no matter what they do in private."

"Guess you'd know," Lester mumbled to himself, then immediately wished he hadn't when a rush of abdominal cramps hit him. Gasping, he nearly dropped his pad, saving it just in time to prevent himself from irritating Chayd further. "Sorry, sorry, so sorry."

"Where was I?" Chayd puzzled, still looking out the window, never having glanced at Lester even as he tortured him. "Oh, yes, Bromberg . . . Once he's elected, we'll concentrate on my own campaign—a much subtler one, of course. I must be careful to maintain the decorum and humility proper for a representative of the UCE, yet still expand my name recognition. By year's end, I want the everyday man looking to Brother Morden Chayd for life's answers. That's where you'll come in."

"Yes. Yes, of course. Whatever you need."

His master turned at that and deigned to look at him. "One thing I've noticed about you, Lester, is that you do seem to have a firm grasp of the ordinary mind. Perhaps it's because you are so very ordinary yourself. There are times when I require that insight. Once Bromberg is sworn in as Premier, I'll have him appoint me as the official UN spiritual counselor. That will place me firmly in the public eye. Meanwhile, I will remain self-effacing, denying any aspiration to greatness. You, however, will have no such restrictions. I'll expect you to actively campaign on my behalf, spreading word of my good deeds, my loyalty to the Church, and so forth. When the time comes, I expect my bid for Supreme Father should encounter little, if any, opposition."

"Sure, sure, no problem. But, uh, what about Father Pompilio? Seems like he's still in pretty good health."

"For now." Chayd turned away again to stare at the dark window.

Lester had taken note of his master's easy stance, the half-smile on his face. He seemed to be in a surprisingly good mood. Even that slip had only cost him a momentary discomfort. Chayd loved hearing himself talk about his plans. This looked like a good opportunity to get a peek into his own future.

"Forgive me, Brother Chayd, but may I ask a question?" Lester recited as taught, then waited.

Chayd nodded permission.

"Why are you sticking with the Church? Wouldn't you have more influence being Premier of the UN yourself?"

Chayd turned his head toward Lester and pursed his lips, looking disappointed. For a moment, Lester feared he had overstepped, but his master merely gave him a patronizing half-smile.

"I should think the reasons would be obvious even to you. To begin with, Premiers serve a maximum of eight years, whereas a Supreme Father remains in office for life. Even more importantly, the Supreme Father molds beliefs."

"What do you care what people believe?"

"Belief is essential. Belief starts wars and ends them." Chayd sighed, walked toward him and laid a hand on his shoulder.

Panic surged through Lester as it landed, and he waited for the pain to hit, but to his relief it didn't come. He looked up at his master and smiled in gratitude.

Chayd looked down on him as he spoke and kept his hand in place. "We are at the forefront of revolutionary change, and you, Lester, are my right hand, one of the trusted few aware of my abilities. It's not enough for my followers to simply do as I command, they need to believe in me, in the future I offer, and accept that I alone have the answer to their salvation."

"Jesus," Lester said in dismay, unable to stop himself.

"Close enough." Chayd patted Lester's shoulder and laughed, genuinely amused. "Though my rewards and punishments are far more immediate, as you're well aware."

"Yes, yes," Lester said and nodded quickly. *Things are even worse than I thought.* He looked up and tried to smile again, but knew it was shaky.

"So, Lester, do you believe in me? Truly believe?" Chayd asked. His hand rested on Lester's shoulder and his cold blue gaze bore down on him.

"Of course," Lester answered without hesitation and maintaining eye contact. *Truly, absolutely, without question. I believe you can kill me. I believe you're insane.*

Chapter 26

The Niña, in route

Nolan Baker hurried through the ship's deserted corridors, trying to walk in a relatively straight line. In addition to the normal skeleton crew manning crucial areas like engineering, he was one of a handful of lab technicians awakened by Dr. McCormack after the jump. He wished the doc had left him undisturbed. Instead, he was forced to experience this weird, pervasive sense of disorientation that came with moving through hyperspace. He kept reassuring himself that he could be reasonably certain of no serious, long-term effects so long as he didn't make the mistake of looking out one of the shade-drawn portals. Hyperspace provided a shortcut across the galaxy, but its swirling maelstrom could twist the soundest mind. More than one unexplained interstellar accident had been written off to hyperspace madness. He believed it, and had no intention of peeking.

Baker kept his eyes focused on the floor until he reached the stasis chamber in the center of the ship. He entered the round room where medic-drones were monitoring the biological readouts of row upon row of stasis pods spiraling inward from the curved walls. He approached the nearest drone, entered new instructions, then followed it. At the designated pod, the drone initiated a warming cycle. Within minutes, the pod's lid popped open. Inside, Daniel Walker's face grimaced and his eyes blinked.

"We're still in hyperspace," Baker told him. "Dr. McCormack sent me. He needs to talk to you."

Daniel groaned and squeezed his eyes shut again. "Damn it. This better be important."

"Oh, yes, it is, it is, I assure you. He's waiting for you in his office."

"All right. I'll be there soon as I get my sea legs." Daniel opened his eyes again, and things started to fall into place. "The captain. Is he awake?"

Baker nodded in the affirmative. "He's already met with Dr. McCormack. Now it's your turn." Baker handed him a comlink, then trundled off, head down.

Hearing that his uncle met with Kowalski first didn't sit well. Daniel pulled himself free from the pod and stepped gingerly onto the floor. For a long while, he stood there, wavering. Even in normal space, waking from stasis was a disorienting process. Traveling through hyperspace made it far worse.

The comlink in his hand buzzed.

"What?" he asked irritably.

His uncle's voice responded. "Are you moving yet?"

"Barely." A wide yawn took control, shaking him.

"Hurry up. I've got something to show you."

"Since you already showed whatever it is to Kowalski, why even bother to wake me?"

"Stop acting like a spoiled child and get up here. Such behavior is beneath you."

Daniel sighed and nodded. "All right, all right. I'm coming."

He slipped the comlink onto his wrist and shuffled toward the exit. As he passed the pod at the end of the row, he peered in at the occupant and found himself looking at a woman with a very unattractive face.

"Huh, I thought this was where we put Carrie."

He stared, trying to place her. She looked dead, of course, but that was normal, until he noticed the temperature read-out. Absolute zero. Alarmed, he summoned one of the patrolling pod-maintenance drones. "Haven't you been monitoring this pod?"

"All pods are under continuous observation," came the robotic response. "Status conforms to designated parameters."

"This one doesn't. The temperature's wrong. Bring it up to standard."

"You do not have clearance."

"I don't need clearance. You're malfunctioning. Report to maintenance."

"You do not have clearance," the drone repeated.

Daniel rolled his eyes and tapped his comlink, "Uncle Charlie, you've got a problem down here in stasis. One of your drones is caught in an error loop, and has a pod set to Zero Kelvin. I hope it's not too late to save this woman." There was a long silence. "Uncle Charlie, did you hear me?"

"Yes, I heard you. Don't concern yourself. I'm dealing with it. Just get yourself up here and I'll explain everything."

Daniel frowned and started walking. In the medical lab, he passed a half-dozen people at workstations busily running tests. McCormack's office door opened at his approach.

His uncle and Captain Kowalski looked up. The latter stood vacating the only visitor chair.

"Sit down, Danny" McCormack said.

"Yeah, you'll need to," Kowalski added. "I'll be up on the bridge."

As Kowalski exited, Daniel sat down heavily and thumbed in the direction of all the lab techs outside. "How come so many? I thought you'd wake maybe one or two people, but . . ."

"Turned out identifying the alien's genetic makeup was even more difficult than expected."

"Did you find evidence of Serena's DNA?"

"We did."

"So I was right!" Daniel leaned forward eagerly. "You've proved she's a Tau Medean lifeform that underwent a sudden evolution by incorporating human DNA."

"Not exactly. We also discovered DNA that didn't match either human or Tau Medean lifeforms. It occurred to me then to check the environment in which Serena died."

"Mars?"

McCormack nodded. "I pulled up our data on fossilized Martian bacteria and got a match."

"Okay, which means our wild theory's still holding up."

"Until it gets wilder. There was still more DNA—not human, not Tau Medean, not Martian. We went through everything we had on file. It took weeks, but we ended up with three more matches. One wasn't too surprising—it belongs to Serena's cat.'

Daniel smirked. "That explains the green eyes."

"The other two are Nereid and Garuda."

His smile flattened, and he let out a long breath. "I get the Garuda part. She must have been exposed to it during the fight."

"That was my initial guess, too, but I had no idea how Nereid DNA could have gotten into the mix. Even if I could have answered that, it wouldn't explain how all these disparate DNA sources could be successfully combined into a living organism. What I needed to do was observe individual cells to see how they could function with all these conflicting instructions, but the tissue kept disintegrating and moving out of view. It was as if the very cells were aware I was trying to observe them. I had to keep lowering the temperature to slow them down. Finally, at zero Kelvin, I could take a look. What I discovered was something quite unexpected."

McCormack activated his screen and turned it around so that Daniel could see. Displayed there was a multi-armed spiderlike shape magnified a hundred thousand fold. Daniel stared at it, feeling an instant revulsion. Then it twitched.

"Did that thing just move?"

McCormack nodded. "Even zero degrees Kelvin doesn't kill it, merely puts it in suspension."

"What exactly is it?"

"A genetic interfacing nanobot, more commonly referred to as a nanogen."

"Garuda technology?"

"Afraid not." McCormack adjusted the controls, turning the spider upside down and increasing the magnification even more.

Stamped on the thing's belly was an image Daniel recognized— a gridded blue and orange globe—the unmistakable company logo of Fabrication Technologies, Inc.

"It's the same basic design as the T-nanogen. It looks for a host to infiltrate then starts manufacturing nanobots to populate it. Once they dig in it's impossible to dislodge them without killing the host. That's why we have a nanogen plague and so many . . . carriers." At the last word, McCormack paused.

Daniel looked over and saw his uncle's eyes brimmed with tears. "Uncle Charlie, I know this is bad, but . . ."

"You're infected, Danny." The doctor took a moment and cleared his throat. "This tissue sample is yours."

Daniel blinked.

"I don't know how long. If Carrie infected you, or if it got into you the same way it did Serena, by way of the probes."

"That woman I saw in the pod set at zero—is she a carrier, too?"

"No. That's the creature you captured on Tau Medea."

Daniel shook his head. "No, I'm talking about a woman."

"Far from it. What you saw in that pod is something put together piece-by-piece by this." The doctor pointed again to the multi-limbed image on the screen. "As I said, the design is similar to the T-nanogen, but it's much more sophisticated. I suspect it may have AI singularity. I think it would have to, in order to successfully construct a chimera from such disparate DNA. It built a new host for itself by combining Serena's DNA with everything else it collected on Mars and Tau Medea."

"So, Serena really was reborn."

"No!" McCormack slapped the top of his desk, making Daniel flinch. "You mustn't think like that. That is *not* Serena. I'm not sure what to call it—a nanogenic mutation, an artificial construct, or what—but I am certain its very existence threatens our own. I was afraid of what it was becoming. I feared losing control of it and endangering everyone on board, so I put it back in stasis to interrupt its transformation." He pointed again to the spider on his screen. "This is what replicated those drilling probes on Mars, killed Serena and shredded your legs. This is what that thing is made of. It's not human. I's not even an animal. It's something else, entirely. Don't let your emotions cloud your judgment. You're a scientist, Danny, think like one."

Daniel was thinking harder than he could ever remember, trying to assimilate all of this. His stasis-blurred mind struggled to accept what his uncle was telling him. "Okay. So, you're saying that the woman I saw in stasis is actually Carrie and she's gone through a nanogenic driven metamorphosis, a kind of nanomorphosis."

"You could call it that, I suppose."

"And I'm infected?"

"Yes, I'm sorry, but you are."

"Is there any treatment?"

"We can use suppressants to slow it down, but . . . no, there's no cure. None that I know of, at least. We have only one viable response—quarantine."

Daniel rubbed his face with both hands, took a deep breath and nodded. "Okay. You can put me in one of the bio-ward cells."

"It's too late for that. The thing's been all over this ship and so have you. While the T-nanogen can only be transferred through blood or sexual contact, this is far more sophisticated and resourceful. I have no clue as to its limits. I've started retesting every living thing on board. We're all potential carriers, and when we buried Serena's remains, we contaminated the planet as well. This nanogen is probably spreading there like wildfire. When I said quarantine, I meant all of it, this ship, and everything we've touched."

Daniel's hopes collapsed. The new world, the Niña—contaminated. That one word doomed his mission to failure and this entire crew to imprisonment on a plague ship.

"You told the captain all of this?"

"Not in as much detail, but yes. I had to. I'll also have to prepare a report to Solar Disease Control," McCormack finished.

"Wait, wait, let's not rush into anything just yet," Daniel said, his mind firing on all pistons, trying to come up with a plan, something that might save them.

"Danny, we need to make sure this is contained. They'll need to know this nanogen was in the ice on Mars. It may even explain why that Garuda in our morgue committed suicide, to make sure it didn't reach his world. I would certainly hope we have as much regard for our own."

"Yes, yes, of course, but I want to make sure we've considered all our options, and we still have another three months of ship time to figure it out."

"There's not much chance of my coming up with a solution in three months. Though I suppose it's possible that in the ten years that will pass on Earth, someone may develop a more effective treatment for the T-plague. Maybe they can offer some assistance."

Daniel snorted. "I doubt it. And if we tell them we have a smarter, more virulent version on board, there's a better chance they'll blow us out of the sky." He stood and began to pace. "Let's think about this. You said Carrie was still changing. Did you see any signs of illness or deformity before you put her back in stasis?

"No, not yet anyway."

"Good. Then I think we need to see this nanomorphosis thing play itself out. Maybe it isn't as dangerous as you think."

"It's probably more dangerous than either you or I can imagine. Anyway, your suggestion is probably moot. She's been stored at zero Kelvin. It's unlikely I can revive her, nor do I think I should. It's not safe."

"We're way past safe. I don't see how things could get any worse. Let's see exactly what we're up against."

"I doubt Captain Kowalski will agree it's worth the risk, nor do I."

"It's my call, not his, and not yours. Defrost her."

The doctor sighed unhappily. "All right, like you said, it's your call, but I won't be held responsible if she doesn't survive, or for that matter, if she does."

Chapter 27

Earth Year 2195, Paris, United Euro-Slav States

Ignoring the pilgrims and tourists shouldering past, two men stood in the center of a long, wide, pedestrian walkway in the heart of Paris. The dark gray, conservative cut of their suits with green-and-gold Earth logos identified them as elite members of the Unified Church of Earth. The Cathedral, home to the Supreme Father, lay directly before them.

"You sure about this?" the shorter of them asked.

His tall, blond companion kept his eyes fixed on the entrance beyond.

"Stop sniveling, Lester. I know what I'm doing."

Cadmon held his arms crossed to discourage any passersby from attempting an introduction, or worse, pleading for his charitable intervention. That was the price he paid for being a well-recognized figure in the Church. He was known the world over as the Archbishop of the Unified Church of Earth's Western Division. As people passed by, he saw their furtive glances and caught bits of French being spoken. The last amused him.

"Paris has a long fascinating history," Cadmon said, assuming Lester Merritt was ignorant of it as he was about most things. "This walkway was once a busy auto thoroughfare—L'Avenue de l'Opera. Did you know Paris was the first mega-city to ban the automobile? Of course, they had a leg up on that, seeing as they already had an extensive underground rail system in place, not that it ever discouraged them from bragging about it. Amusing, considering that in most respects, they remain hopelessly backward. For example, they still can't bear to part with their antiquated language, along with these ancient buildings. It took a lot of convincing to get permission to build the Cathedral here over one of their oldest. Inside it, is the Paris Opera House, also known as Palais Garnier, still intact, with all its dark secrets hidden in its bowels."

"Bowels?" Lester screwed his face into a grimace.

Cadmon smirked. "A euphemism for the seven floors of the original building which lie below street level—damp, twisting, stone labyrinths with an underground lake, no less, allegedly used for torture at one time, and it's all still down there."

"Why didn't they just demo it all?"

"Lester, Lester," he sighed. "You're not listening. The French are inordinately proud of their heritage. The Church had to promise to preserve the original Opera House. I find it ironic that the international seat of the UCE should be constructed over Garnier's cruciform floor plan. It's more than once been described as a profane counterpart of Notre Dame."

Lester nodded sagely. "Garnier. Right."

Cadmon fell silent, no longer interested in edifying Lester. It was a waste of breath anyway. Instead, he concentrated on the information he was receiving from his nanobots about the layout of the soaring Cathedral ahead, determining his best approach. Though built over the ancient opera house, the UCE Cathedral bore no resemblance to the original structure. The new building (new by Parisian standards in that it had been in existence for a mere thirty-four years) seemed to grow out of the ground itself. Beyond the shade trees encircling an expansive lawn, the perfectly manicured grass melded into gigantic roots at the base of a colossal oak tree that formed the building's foundation. The bark-covered surface grew upward, then disappeared behind a curtain of crashing waterfalls. Above their billowing mists, the building squared off and shedded its bark to reveal a polished gold-flecked granite face. The clean stone soared vertically, punctuated with row upon row of glittering, diamond shaped windows marking each of the Cathedral's 130 floors. Near the top, the granite exterior was etched by sparkling jagged lines which widened to form fifty foot tall diamond and ruby spires crowning the building. The Cathedral represented the magnificence of Earth's bounty, the protection of which formed the core of the Church's dogma. The overall effect was garish in his view, but it got the point across. Here was a seat of vast power and wealth.

"So how are we going to get past all that security? It's not like they're going to let us in. Not so long as the Supreme Father is ill," Lester reminded him.

"Still, you doubt me." Cadmon considered dropping Lester to his knees, but that would bring unwanted attention and delay matters, so he merely turned away and strode down the wide path toward the building's main entrance.

Lester scooted after him, glancing up as if expecting to be struck down any moment. Though tempted to fulfill that expectation, Cadmon restrained himself. As they approached the crowd of supplicants and tourists held at bay by a flickering energy field, he could feel its power through the souls of his feet. No one was permitted entry to the Cathedral without an official invitation, and right now, not even Church elite such as themselves were being invited. That suited his purposes. Fewer people to deal with.

Cadmon moved ahead with a steady, self-assured stride, sweeping the crowd aside, and pulling Lester in his wake like the vortex of a passing storm. He heard Lester at his heels, mumbling fervent little prayers as they neared the shimmering barrier. It was set to deliver a torrent of pain to anyone attempting to cross it. Without pausing, he walked through the wall of energy, and tugged Lester with him. Sparks danced around their heads and bodies, but couldn't pierce his defensive shield. When they emerged on the other side, a half-dozen armed security guards ran toward them.

Cadmon concentrated and closed his eyes briefly. When he opened them again, the guards stood with their weapons held slackly, their eyes unfocused.

"What did you do to them?" Lester asked.

"Just a little sedation combined with a mild hallucinogen. I have no wish to harm them. They'll be guarding me soon."

He walked up to the entrance, a massive panel of hand-beaten gold. It bore no discernible handle or other apparent method of obtaining admission. He touched the polished surface with his palms, sending in streams of his nanobots, then waited. Moments later a crack sliced down the panel's center, splitting it into a pair of previously hidden doors. When the doors opened inward, he marched through. Behind him, Lester hesitated, then jumped inside before the doors swung back into place.

They stood in a wide lobby. A large brass sign hung on the wall, embellished with opposing arrows. In raised letters, it read "L'Opera de Paris" over the arrow pointing left toward a pair of ornate wooden doors, and "Offices of the Unified Church of Earth" over the arrow pointing right toward a long, golden, granite-lined hall. Cadmon looked from the modern hallway on the right over to the ancient wooden doors on the left.

Cadmon went left to the wooden doors and ran his fingers over the hand-carved figures. "Let's see what the French were so determined to protect."

Though locked, the ancient mechanism gave way under his nanobot invasion, letting him pull the heavy wooden doors open. He laughed aloud at seeing what lay within. Tall, columned arches supported a vaulted ceiling painted with fanciful swirling figures in pastel hues. A wide marble staircase swept up the lobby's center to meet a railed balcony. From there, a pair of matching curved stairways climbed either side, sweeping up to the next level where golden statues of women holding twinkling candelabras aloft guarded arched doorways. Nearly every surface gleamed in marble, gold or crystal.

Cadmon bounded up the center stairway to the balcony and spun about, taking it all in. "It's so … French." He stepped over to one of the gilded statues, and with intentional disrespect, stroked its derriere. "Still, I think I'm going to like it."

"Monsieurs, you should not be in here," a heavily accented female voice called from below.

He looked down to see an attractive dark-eyed young woman staring up at him, her mouth opened in alarm. She wore the signature green robe of the devout, with a waist sash tied snug enough to reveal her hourglass figure.

"Oh yes," he said soft and low, looking down on her, "I'm definitely going to like it here."

"Pardon?"

He placed a hand on his chest and walked down the steps toward her. "Allow me to introduce myself. I am Monsignor Morden Chayd, Archbishop of the Western Division." Waving dismissively at Lester, who was trying to look inconspicuous, he added, "My assistant. We've come to see the Supreme Father."

"Je m'appelle Sister Rachelle." She curtsied as he approached, but wore a frown. "Monsignor, I am most honored to meet you, of course, mais un visite, c'est impossible. Have you not heard? Father Pompilio is ill. You arrive without invitation."

He saw the wary suspicion on her face. "Yes, you're quite right, but let me explain." Cadmon smiled, and held out his hand to her.

She continued to frown, but lifted her hand to receive his, then inhaled abruptly when he grasped it. Her eyes widened, and her mouth opened.

He'd thrown a soothing agent and strong aphrodisiac into the trade to make certain she was prepared to do anything he asked of her. How he loved seeing that look of distrust transform to abject adoration.

He drew her hand to his lips in the traditional French greeting. "I have come here for the noblest of reasons, dear sister—to relieve Father Pompilio of his suffering."

"But of course." She curtsied again, more deeply this time, still holding his hand, never taking her gaze from his. "Please, let me take you to him."

Chapter 28

The Niña, in route

Despite his own misgivings, Dr. Charles McCormack slowly brought up the temperature in the alien's stasis pod. To his surprise and disquiet, pulse and respiration returned to their previously normal ranges. He didn't know whether to celebrate or sound an alarm. No matter how closely it resembled a woman now, he had no trouble thinking of this thing as alien and dangerous. He remembered Daniel correcting him—*Her name is Carrie.*

When the color returned to her cheeks, he feared her eyes would open, but to his relief, nothing happened. She remained unconscious, catatonic—still evolving he assumed. He had the body removed from the pod, tied to a gurney and taken to the secured cell in the bio-ward to be kept under observation. As hours, then days went by, he began to doubt she would ever wake, and fervently hoped she wouldn't. His job would be far easier if he could concentrate on the nanogen itself, without worrying about its unpredictable carrier.

Still, the possibility of her eventually regaining consciousness remained and he didn't want to rely solely on automated alerts. He needed a human being in here monitoring the situation. Someone with excellent powers of observation, yet as willing as a drone to follow orders. He knew just the one.

***

Nolan Baker was none too happy about being chosen to babysit the alien's thawed, but still unconscious body. The only thing he wanted to do less than be awake while traveling through hyperspace, was to be in the same room with this alien if she ever woke up. He hadn't for a moment forgotten how she had bested Sanchez down in that jungle.

Sanchez was without a doubt the biggest, meanest SOB that ever walked upright without benefit of a conscience. And this thing had snuck up on him, knocked him out cold, and dragged him more than fifty feet to prop him upright in a chair neat as a pin, all without setting off the perimeter alarms or disturbing their beauty sleep.

Plus, she had opened the door to their emergency shelter, which should have been impossible. He did have a theory about that, however, something to do with their other specimens. What he didn't have a theory for was how she could have changed herself so dramatically. He would never have believed this was the same creature if Dr. McCormack hadn't insisted it was, and proved it with images of intermediate stages of a transformation he'd been witnessing continue ever since.

When they'd found her in the jungle, she had resembled an overgrown lemur with bulging green eyes, a long furry tail and going on all fours. Now she looked like a healthy human female. He couldn't help but notice how healthy—who could blame him? Gone was the reddish-brown fur, replaced with smooth bronzed skin. The crystal-clear fringe on her head had lengthened into a long smooth mane. The previously flattened circle of a face with two breathing holes and a lipless mouth had become a smooth oval with high cheekbones, a delicate chin, and a fine Anglican-shaped nose. The bulging eyes were now human in size and shape and rimmed with thick dark lashes, and her previously non-existent lips had swelled into a reddened bow. Beneath the sheet covering her, she appeared to curve in all the right places. He was curious whether she still had that long tail, but a force field removed any temptation to peek. Not that he wanted to get anywhere near her. Whatever she looked like on the outside, the inside scared the hell out of him.

She lay tied to a gurney inside the bio-cell, tilted upright to allow for better viewing. It made him think of old photos from the days of the Wild West showing gunned-down bank robbers displayed in a store front window. He hoped she had no more chance of coming back to life than they had.

As the days stretched on, the dread that she would suddenly wake and pounce on him faded, and Baker began to see her as merely an attractive new form of vegetable. He was accustomed to entertaining himself with his own musings and came to appreciate her as the most attentive audience he'd ever had. Today, he was labeling specimen vials, and Chief Sanchez was on his mind.

"That man gives me the willies. Heard he wasn't so nice to you either. Struts around here like he owns the place. Walker's the only one who stands up to him. Not so smart in my opinion. Going to get his ass kicked one of these days and he'll have nobody to blame but himself. Not like he's an idiot, of course—nobody pulls off a mission like this without a truckload of gray matter up here." Baker tapped his own head and glanced at her tranquil face. "Even so, he sure turned out to be a wild card, didn't he? Never would have guessed he'd take more than a scientific interest in you. And that was before, back when you still looked like a monkey-faced cat."

He dutifully checked the monitor display again—no change— then returned to his sorting and labeling.

"Least, that's the rumor, anyway. Not for me to judge—no, he's had it rough. I hear Ms. Chambers' been trying to spark him. Seems awful funny he'd hop into bed with you when he could have had her, especially the way he goes on about the Nereid trade. He's in deep trouble with the captain now. Just goes to show sometimes the smartest people can do the dumbest things. Glad I'm not smart enough to be that dumb, but I got a few ideas. Like how you got past the security bolts on our shelter." He looked up and pointed a finger at her. She lay still as a stone. Another glance at the readouts confirmed he had nothing to worry about.

"You used our specimen animals, didn't you? Same way you used them outside on the trap. I'm bettin' you're telepathic or something. Or you were, before they turned you into a vegetable. Probably why you never spoke until they stuck an implant in you, but have they thought of that? No. Anybody bother asking my opinion around here? Ha, why should they? I'm just the babysitter." He frowned at her sleeping there, sighed, and went back to his vials.

"Least this will all be over soon. Only another twenty-two ship days before it's back into stasis for the jump into real space, then we'll all be home. A year for us, ten years on earth. Gone, just like that." He snapped his fingers. "Not that anybody will have missed me." He sighed again and looked at her.

"Sure would like to know how you can change yourself like that. Doc M.'s trying to figure it out. Not that it'll save you, though. You're going to end up in pieces in somebody's lab. I hear the captain wants a behavior modified clone of you in every home. Well, the rich ones, anyway. People like me couldn't afford anything like that.

Somebody ought to jack an interactive of you into the Solar Web for the average Joe." His attention drifted away. "You know, that's one heck of an idea. I should register it."

"Why?"

"So somebody else doesn't beat me to it fir—Holy Mother of—!" Baker jumped up, dropping a vial. It bounced on the tiles and rolled across the floor.

Her eyes were open, staring at him.

He backed away. "D-d-don't move," he said, then spun and ran.

***

Carrie watched the vial roll to a stop against the leg of a desk. She recognized the room as the same one she'd been in before, although it now brimmed with new equipment. Digital readouts and lines zig-zagged across a dozen new screens arrayed in front of her and hundreds of tiny needles floated in mid-air. She assumed the needles must be held in place by an invisible energy grid sealing her off from the rest of the room.

She used her others to dissolve her restraining straps and stepped down onto the cool metal floor, letting the sheet over her fall away. Her curiosity automatically released more inner scouts to determine the purpose of the needles.

The scouts radioed back to her neural network, *Monitors for biological readouts: respiratory rate, pulse, blood pressure, brain waves, electrolytes . . .*

She decided they were nothing she needed and ordered dismantlement of the energy grid. The floating needles showered to the floor, just as the lab's outer door opened revealing human faces.

"Stay where you are," said a guard with a weapon aimed in her direction.

Beside him stood a human she recognized, the thin gray-haired one who'd been experimenting on her. He glanced down at the needles skittering across the tiles. Hidden behind the guard and the gray-hair, was the same round one with red hair who had been watching her while talking to himself until she'd spoken. This red-haired one appeared fearful, the gray-haired one appeared concerned but curious. The guard looked ready to shoot her.

She held her ground, confident in her new adaptation.

"Why do you keep imprisoning me?" she asked them.

The gray-hair's eyebrows rose. After a moment, he replied, "We wanted to make sure you were safe."

"Safe." She cocked her head at him, considering the implications, seeing how they kept their distance. *It is not my safety they are concerned with—it is theirs.* Recognizing a shift in the balance of power, she revised her approach. "Do not imprison me again, or I will not be safe."

"Perhaps we can come to an agreement," he said. "Your cooperation in return for ours."

"Cooperation proved unpleasant." She took an experimental step toward them.

"I told you to stay put," the guard said, tensing.

She stopped, and he didn't fire. She had noted that these armed humans followed orders from other humans. She modulated her vocal tones to imitate the one she had observed as holding ultimate authority among them.

"Where is the Daniel Walker?" she asked in the captain's deep baritone.

Their eyes widened, and they glanced at each other.

"Not far," the gray-hair said, "I can call him."

"Do so."

He activated his comlink, fumbling with it under her scrutiny.

"Daniel, I need you to come to the bio-ward. Carrie's awake and she's asking for you."

***

When Daniel reached the enviro-cell area, the door stood open and Baker was peering inside. He squeezed past him, and found his uncle and an armed guard facing Carrie, who stood before them naked in her transformed state. She saw him, then looked back at the others.

"Depart," she ordered in Captain Kowalski's voice.

"What the . . .?" Daniel's mouth fell ajar.

"Absolutely not," McCormack said, flourishing a hand. "I don't care how much you sound like the captain, I'm not leaving Daniel alone with you."

She growled, and sharp, crystal claws extended from her otherwise human-looking hands.

"Whoa!" Daniel stepped forward, pulling her attention back to him. "If you want to talk to me, that's fine."

His uncle looked at him in alarm. "Danny, don't be foolish."

Daniel spoke to her again, looking into her cat-like eyes. "Do you mean to harm me?"

"That is not my intention," she replied, and her claws retracted.

"Okay, good." He nodded and took a breath. "Do what she wants. Wait outside."

The guard lowered his weapon and exited with Baker, but the doctor didn't move.

"Please, Uncle Charlie. Trust me, I'll be fine." Seeing the result was merely a stony glare, he used a firmer tone. "It's my call, remember?"

"Pulling rank again, are we?" McCormack frowned and shook his head. "Very well, I'll wait outside—just outside." He shook a finger at Carrie like a stern parent. "Behave yourself."

When the door slid shut, Daniel faced her. He'd viewed the new Carrie in her comatose state, but seeing her animated made the transformation even more astonishing. He had to face the fact that she now conformed to nearly every fantasy he'd ever entertained— as if she'd intentionally molded herself into the woman of his dreams. The disturbing suspicion she'd invaded his subconscious helped him resist the irresistible. That, plus hearing Kowalski's voice coming out of her mouth.

"We'd better establish some rules here," he said.

"If you wish," she replied, dropping the captain's voice for a feminine one. "But first, let me thank you."

He noticed she sounded a lot like Lauren, but in a slightly lower pitched timbre he found particularly soothing, so much so that he had to mentally shake it off. "For what?"

"My new form. Does it please you?"

"Why should that matter?"

"An esthetically pleasing shape is clearly beneficial to human interaction. Do you perceive me as pleasing now?"

Daniel allowed himself to sweep a glance over her, trying to find a flaw, then did. "Your eyes are strange looking."

"I find the elongated pupil design more efficient for gathering light, and the color green is your favorite, is it not?"

"Never really thought about it." The eyes were strange yet unnervingly familiar, then it hit him why. They were the same as Serena's cat. He tried to elicit a reaction. "It might have been Serena's though." Carrie cocked her head, reminding him now of a curious mongrel, which helped him dissociate even further. "We buried her remains on Tau Medea IV," he continued and concentrated on self-control, despite the rising heat in his face. "But I'm sure you knew that."

She looked into the distance. "Burial, death, mourning, grief . . ."

She's accessing her implant.

She straightened her head and focused on him again. "Did you value this Serena?"

He mentally stumbled over the complex feelings surging within, but the question itself was a simple one, deserving a simple answer. "Yes."

"Then it should please you to know that her remains are contained within me."

He froze, shocked at the ease with which she had confirmed that what stood before him was a network of nano machines, the very things responsible for killing the woman he loved, infecting him, and now threatening his entire mission. And yet, part of him wanted to believe something of Serena still lived.

"Do you—do you have her memories?"

Carrie scowled and tilted her head again. Her gaze drifted away for a moment, then refocused on him. "The incorporated tissues required extensive reconstruction. Retention and transference of experiential data is too minimal to calculate."

"Experiential data," he repeated the emotionless concept. "So, no memories." This was like conversing with a computer, except he'd never woken with one in his bed. "Why did you sneak into my room?"

"To gain information."

"What kind of information?"

"How to change my form to please you."

He felt himself grow cold at the admitted manipulation. "And you needed physical contact with me to do that?"

"Yes. Copulation helped put the raw data into context."

Another fear confirmed, Daniel's face fell, but she didn't seem to notice. He searched for something familiar to make himself feel better, something connected to Serena, but saw no resemblance. He remembered a cute button nose and tomboyish freckles, but this she-thing had a uniform golden complexion with no discernible blemish. With the straight slender nose, wide full lips, and almond-shaped eyes, one might describe the face as regal. Serena had been a muscular five-foot-two, while this woman-thing stood a good eight inches taller in a frame that was lithe and elegant. *Could this be the body Serena had wanted for herself? Or the one I'd always wanted her to have?* The thought filled him with guilt, and he looked away.

The disconnected monitors on the equipment kept blinking in alarm. To give himself a moment, he walked over and shut them off, one by one.

"So what else do you have in you?" he asked, unable to keep the bitterness from his voice.

"My original program contained only partial genetic information, and required a fully functional human DNA code for completion of its directive. In my search I collected information from a number of sources. You may have noted, I even found use for the molecular structure of my initial transportation device." She extended crystal-clear claws from beneath her human-shaped fingernails, clicking them together in demonstration, then raking them down her crystalline hair. "These aren't genetically inheritable traits, of course, but it seemed a shame not to make use of such excellent material."

Diamond fiber? Holy shit, she's talking about the probes in the ice.

He saw the beauty in it, but remembered Serena's screams and his own as those same diamond fiber probes drilled into them both. His anger flared and he glared at Carrie hatefully, hoping some memory of Serena's agonized death lived on to haunt her. It hit him then that if the other people killed by the probes on Mars had been interred like Serena, instead of being disintegrated and scattered into space, they too might have risen from their graves in some twisted new form.

Uncle Charlie's right. This thing's an abomination. One we need to understand if we have any hope of defeating.

He fished for more information. "I believe you're talking about diamond fiber, the same thing reconnaissance probes are made of. They were in the ice we were recovering on Mars. When it melted, it came alive with probes. Doctor McCormack says they left something inside of me as well."

"Yes," she said. "I detect the *others* within you."

"Others? So that's what you meant? You meant nanobots—molecular-sized machines?"

She seemed puzzled at first, then nodded. "Yes, nanobots, as you say."

He remembered the magnified spider-like image. How many did he have? A dozen, a hundred? Could there be thousands of them swarming around inside him, dormant only because of the nanogen suppressant therapy his uncle administered? For a moment, Daniel felt as if he might throw up. He steadied himself with a hand on the desk beside him. "I don't feel them. Nothing's changed as far as I can tell."

"They await instruction."

"Instruction?" He looked at her with renewed suspicion.

She frowned at him. "I hoped you would understand."

"Oh, I understand all right. I've been infected with parasitic genetic manipulators. I just need to know how to get rid of them."

"You reject them?" Her tone registered surprise.

"Yes, of course."

"This explains much," she said, turning from him. "I cannot reject them."

"No, how could you when they're all you are? You're just a collaboration of machinery, an imitation of life. You may have made yourself look human, but it's a lie."

"Collaboration—the cooperative interaction of two or more agents or forces so that the combined effect is greater than the sum of the individuals." Turning back to him, she seemed not to notice his hostile tone and glare. "An accurate description of my experience, a commonality of purpose culminating in the whole, the 'I' or self. I am . . ." She paused, and her brows knitted together.

"Except you're not really an 'I,' are you? Now I know why you called yourself 'Horde Carrier'—you're a bunch of machines programmed to manipulate cell structure."

". . . all now in service of a single entity," she added. She stepped closer, and placed her fingers over his hand on the desk. "One need only guide them."

He felt a spreading warmth at her touch, a pleasant tingling.

"Don't," he said, but couldn't seem to put any force behind the word.

"Open your mind."

He looked into her strange eyes and felt as if he could lose himself in those dark oval centers—a darkness that could swallow him whole. Panic shot up within him, releasing a surge of adrenaline, and he snatched his hand away. "You're not to touch me. Ever!"

She reached for him again. "But—"

"Stop!" he commanded.

She froze in place, but he had little confidence he could keep her off for long. He needed a way to shield himself, some way to block her influence. At minimum, he needed a chaperone.

"Stay there," he ordered, and backed out the door, letting it lock her inside again. The guard and his uncle were waiting as promised.

"Don't let her leave that room," he told the guard. "And whatever you do, do not let her touch you."

Daniel took his uncle by the arm. "I'm going to need more of those nanogen suppressants . . . a lot more."

Chapter 29

Disappointed, Carrie watched the Daniel Walker human exit. Of her captors, only he hosted *others* like her own. Contact with him during his dream state had provided sufficient information for her to mold herself into a form he should find desirable, yet still he rebuffed her.

It appears the needs and desires of a human male are more complex than mere physicality. Perhaps I should give up on these humans. There are other sources of information available.

She stepped over to a bare metal wall and placed her hands flat on it sending thousands of nanobot scouts into the streams of electrical current running like veins throughout the bulkhead up to the command center, the brain of the ship. Its steady emotionless intelligence held valuable information about its occupant humans and their home world. Interfacing with it, she downloaded the raw data, saving it all for future analyses. Then she redirected her scouts' attentions to the structure itself.

As they threaded through the ship's molecular structures, her awareness grew until the vessel seemed an extension of her own flesh. Her breathing fell into rhythm with the ventilation system as it pumped air in and out through the ducts. The ship's warm interior, holding people and equipment, was like a full stomach. She observed the humans through the ship's cameras and audio recorders, and looked down into the ship's bowels, where she felt the pull of the gravity wells and their spinning black plasma. She moved her attention to the ship's outer shell, an exterior of hard cold metallic skin, beyond which swirled a mesmerizing chaos. Through the ship's perception she could look upon it without injury but knew from the computer that no human could do so and retain sanity. *Interesting.* Pulling her awareness back within the confines of the vessel, she searched for one particular human, checking each face until she found the one she sought, the one she hated. Sanchez was lying peacefully in stasis. She overrode the controls on his pod, waking him. She waited as he slowly pulled himself free and tapped his comlink.

"Sanchez here. Is there some reason why I'm awake?" he asked.

She blocked the signal.

"Hello? Anybody there?" No answer. "Come in?"

Finally, he gave up and exited into the outer corridor. He stood there, puzzling over his circumstances, looking about. Other than him, the corridor was empty.

Perfect. Her tiny servants did as she instructed, locating the internal electronic switches within the outer wall. The long row of portals opened the length of the corridor.

Sanchez screamed, covered his face, and ran hard, stumbling, falling, crawling, trying to find the exit. She smiled, watching his frantic efforts to escape. He pulled himself through the automatic door at the end of the corridor and it closed behind him. She let him go . . . for now. He was still trapped in this metal container along with her. There would be ample opportunities for revenge.

She closed the portals, locking them down tight again, erased the ship's recording of the incident, and went back to following the observations of her scouts as they made wide sweeps through the ship's walls and decks, examining personal quarters, storage areas, laboratories, and equipment. She observed the hundreds of animal specimens being held in stasis, all taken from Tau Medea IV. She made no move to free them. Where would they go?

When her scouts came across a room identified as the ship's morgue, they located still another frozen organism, but this body was neither Tau Medean nor human. She accessed the ship's data bank and identified it as a Garuda, an aggressive species with whom humans were at war. Interesting, but it did not explain why she experienced a sense of personal recognition. She cross-matched the ship's data with her own and discovered she contained DNA from this same species. *Curious.* She directed her scouts to infiltrate its frozen flesh. What she discovered made her gasp.

Others! Nanobots, as per the Daniel Walker.

Her own *others* were still exploring the rest of the ship, but their input fell into the background as she concentrated on this surprising discovery in the Garuda. There was significant injury to the Garuda's neck and torso, but none to its head. In fact, the damage appeared far less extensive than that suffered by the human entity on which the majority of her own construction was based. This body was essentially intact, and that meant it could be repaired. Her examination of the body was interrupted by a shock to her nervous system. Her exploring scouts were flashing emergency alarms. Deep in the ship's thrumming heart, they'd found a flaw.

The fusion reactor which powered nearly everything on board was on the verge of exploding like a dying sun.

***

When Daniel expressed his fear that Carrie was attempting to exert control over him through his nanogen infection, his uncle injected him with another huge dose of suppressants. They'd been quick about it, but by the time they returned to the bio-ward, the guard they'd left behind lay inside unconscious on the floor and Carrie was gone.

"I suppose we shouldn't be surprised anymore," McCormack grumbled. "Better alert the captain."

Daniel nodded reluctantly. As his uncle roused the guard and sent him off to the infirmary, Daniel tapped his comlink to call Kowalski and give him the bad news. Before anyone on the bridge answered, everything went black and his feet left the floor. His uncle cried out, and Daniel twisted in that direction only to have something hard slam into his forehead. For a split second, he teetered on the white-speckled edge of unconsciousness, falling endlessly. As his head cleared, he realized what was happening.

"Gravity's off," he said, and heard a deep moan to his right. He reached out and latched onto an arm. "You all right?"

McCormack groaned again. "Think I'm going to be sick."

"Don't."

"I hate free-fall."

"You'll hate it worse if you vomit. Anchor yourself to something."

"I know, I know," his uncle groused resentfully. "You act like I've never done this before."

They gently pushed away from each other, propelling themselves in opposite directions. Daniel snagged a cold metal leg. Feeling around, he recognized the desk, and wondered if this was what he'd hit his head against.

"What in the blue blazes is going on?" McCormack asked in the dark.

"Listen," Daniel said, hearing the quiet. "The main engine's off."

The room jumped back into existence under orange emergency lights, and they crashed to the floor.

"Ow!" McCormack yelled. "Damned gravity wells."

"It's all or nothing, I'm afraid." Daniel picked himself up and offered a hand to his uncle.

"I'm well aware," McCormack replied irritably, waving away Daniel's assistance.

Kowalski's voice came across the ship's announcement system. "Medical to Engineering."

Daniel and his uncle exchanged looks. "You think it's her?" McCormack asked.

Daniel shrugged and tapped his comlink. "Walker here. What happened?"

Kowalski came back. "Not sure yet, but nobody's answering in engineering. I'm heading there now."

"Be careful. It might be Carrie. She's awake and missing."

"Son of a—"

Daniel cut off the link and headed to engineering himself. When he arrived, Kowalski was poised at the entrance to the engine room with a medical team standing by and three security guards trying to pry open the door.

"It's sealed shut from the inside," Kowalski said, and waved at a maintenance tech coming down the corridor towards them with torch equipment. "Hurry up!"

Before the tech reached the door, it clanged from the other side. The guards moved back and drew their weapons. Daniel was surprised to see the man in front—Sanchez. *Why is he awake?* He appeared to have a new twitching in his face Daniel didn't remember. The door to the engine room slid aside, revealing a womanly silhouette that turned into a still naked Carrie as the light reached her.

She snarled at Sanchez and bared her claws.

Sanchez fired. The blast skidded around her torso and shot back. Sanchez fell to the floor screaming.

"Hold your fire!" Kowalski and Daniel barked in near unison.

Daniel held up a hand. "Carrie, stop," he began, but saw her mouth curl into a smile watching the medics jump to Sanchez's aide. It gave him a chill.

"Where are my engineers?" Kowalski asked. "If you've harmed them— "

"Your people are safe in there." She gestured toward a storage compartment inside the engine room and backed away. The two remaining guards lowered their weapons. *Smart choice*, Daniel thought. He decided an even better idea was to have them wait outside and motioned for them to stay where they were.

He and Kowalski freed two engineering crewmen, who emerged red-faced with embarrassment. The head engineer, a blocky man with a handle-bar mustache, rushed over to the railing to look down at the massive diamond fiber nuclear fusion reactor filling the room below. He gaped at the dormant reactor, now dull and glassy looking, when it should be glowing with power. "What did you do to my engine?"

"I blocked the hydrogen intake," Carrie replied.

He shook his head. "That's impossible. Those lines are buried three meters deep."

"It is fact," she replied.

Daniel gathered his courage and stepped close enough to her that he could keep his voice low. "Did your others do that?"

Kowalski leaned in. "Who the devil are you talking about?"

Daniel answered in a whisper. "Her nanobots. They're what she's been calling 'others' all this time. She says they're programmed to serve her."

"You mean they do what she wants?"

"Apparently."

Kowalski turned to Carrie. "If that's true, then tell them to unblock those lines. We need this engine up and running."

"Inadvisable," she stated in full voice. "There is a crack in the lower right quadrant."

Hearing her, the mustached head engineer spoke up. "That can't be right. Nano-replication creates perfect duplicates, always. A crack can't just spontaneously appear."

Daniel frowned, unhappy the engineer was part of the conversation. "True, but one could be created intentionally."

"Did you?" Kowalski asked her.

She cocked her head at him. "Why would I create a problem only to solve it?"

"How should I know? Maybe it's a trick to make us think you saved us."

"A trick: a ruse, an act designed to deceive—" She nodded in understanding. "Interesting concept."

Kowalski looked as if he were struggling against an urge to strangle her. "And now we're supposed to be grateful, right?"

"Wait," Daniel interrupted. He pulled Kowalski further back and whispered again. "This engine came from Fabri-Tech, and so did the probes and the—" He looked over at the two engineers staring hard at them. "We shouldn't talk about this here."

The captain nodded and raised his voice to address his engineers. "Why are you two just standing around? Can you confirm whether there's a defect in this engine, or not?"

The head engineer nodded. "Yes, of course. Right away, Sir." He and his companion hurried to the control panels, and entered instructions. "We're running a full diagnostic. If there's anything even remotely like what she's claiming, it'll show up, but I sincerely doubt—" He paused in mid-sentence. "She's right. There's a crack in the engine core. We'll have to bring in a crane to lift it out and move it into the vat for repairs."

Kowalski groaned. "That means waking more of the crew."

"Why not repair the engine in place?" Carrie asked.

"Because a nano-manufacturing vat isn't portable," Kowalski snapped.

"Actually, I think it is," Daniel said quietly and tipped his head toward her.

"Oh." Kowalski's expression took on a look of new comprehension. "Step outside," he told the engineers. The two exited, but only reluctantly. When the door closed, he turned back to Carrie. "Can these 'others' of yours fix this?"

"Of course," she replied, as if it were perfectly obvious. "Repairs are in progress. They recommend you wait until the engine has fully cooled before restarting."

Kowalski and Daniel exchanged looks.

"So these things talk to you and do whatever you want?" Kowalski asked.

"The purpose of the *others* is to serve the host," she replied.

Kowalski whistled softly. "Maybe this nanogen isn't such a bad thing." His expression took on a new intensity. "Maybe I should let you infect me, too."

"Have you lost your mind?" Daniel asked.

She held a hand up between them. "This discussion serves no purpose. My *others* are adapted to my genetic structure, incompatible with yours or anyone else's."

"But I thought you infected Walker here when you and he, I mean when the two of you . . ." Kowalski fumbled for the right word.

"Mated," Daniel finished with a grimace, and watched Kowalski redden. "Guess I was infected by the probes, not her."

For a moment, Kowalski frowned, looking disappointed, but then his expression widened into a smile. "Wait. So what you're telling me is that it's not contagious. That means there's nothing to prevent us from returning home or recommending Tau Medea for settlement. We're in the clear."

"I wouldn't go that far. McCormack's only begun studying it and he's very concerned that—"

"I am done here," Carrie announced abruptly, then turned and walked out the exit.

"Wait." Daniel hurried after her. "Where are you going?"

She didn't answer. The two security guards spun in her direction and stood to bar her way, fingering their weapons uncertainly.

"Move or I shall remove you," she said and the air around her took on a pale unearthly glow, brightening steadily. "Violence will be returned in full."

Daniel recognized it as some sort of energy buildup, and energy could be discharged.

"Step aside," he ordered and waved them back. "Let her go."

The guards stood to the side and she broke into a run. Daniel dashed after her.

Kowalski's footsteps thudded behind him. "Don't lose her!"

"I won't!" Daniel yelled back, but when he came around the next bend, he already had.

***

Carrie blocked the ship's sensors lest they report her whereabouts and took a circuitous route to avoid any more humans. She popped into air ducts, slid down stairwells, and slipped into unoccupied rooms or storage areas whenever someone came near. Stealth now served her better than speed. With only a skeletal crew on duty, avoidance wasn't all that difficult. She soon worked her way to the ship's morgue without being observed.

There, frozen in a deep drawer, was the Garuda. The ship's logs held a clear warning. This was a warrior, a killer, a murderer of men, but the beckoning presence of the *others* within could not be ignored. Any chance to fill this aching emptiness, this great blank chasm where memory and understanding should lie, had to be explored. The Daniel Walker host remained resistant, intent on preserving his separateness and suppressing his *others*. She needed to know who she was, what she was, why she was. The Daniel Walker host either didn't have the answers or was unwilling to share them. Perhaps this organism would behave differently.

She laid her hands on the cold metal drawer and instructed her servant scouts to warm the Garuda and awaken its *others* to repair its flesh. If repairs proved successful, the Garuda should soon twitch with renewed life. She might find the answers she sought, or encounter a deadly new enemy. She would have to wait for those fist-sized eyes to open before learning which it would be.

PART 3

Chapter 30

Earth Year 2197, Paris, United Euro-Slav States

Supreme Father Morden Chayd drummed his manicured fin-gernails onto his polished mahogany desktop as he watched a news report projected into the air from his 3-D tablet. Floating before him, a male reporter in heavy make-up and a snugly-tailored black suit waved toward a tall building surrounded by a crowd.

"I'm standing in front of the headquarters of ACES, the Allied Coalition for Exploration of Space, where thousands of people have gathered in support. The Niña has returned and is currently holding position on the far side of our A-PEDS defense system. Meanwhile, Mission Commander Daniel Walker has been broadcasting incredible images from a new world."

The 3-D image split to show manned exploration teams walking through a verdant green jungle, then overhead views of expansive forests, flowing rivers, and blue lakes nestled under snow-capped mountains.

"As you can imagine, this has stirred up a lot of excitement, even among some of the most skeptical members of the UCE." The camera zoomed out to show an older woman in a long, green robe standing next to the reporter. "So," he asked, holding the mic on the back of his wrist up to her chin, "did you come here to protest, or to sign up as a passenger to the new world?"

She laughed. "Well, to be honest, both. A true Earth twin means humanity's being given a second chance, but we must ensure that it remains pristine."

"Well, there you have it, folks," the reporter said, stepping away with a big smile on his face. "A green robe, a member of Nature's Children, the most conservative order of the Unified Church of Earth, speaking out in support of Walker's mission."

Cadmon stopped drumming and knocked the thin tablet across the room. It crashed against his door. A moment later, the door opened a crack and Lester Merritt stuck his head in.

"Did you want something, Your Holiness?" he asked.

"Yes," Cadmon hissed. "Your cousin, dead. I don't know what went wrong, but the Niña's returned intact, allegedly with a planetary discovery of some note."

"I heard," Lester said. "Sorry."

"Are you?" Cadmon asked, one eyebrow lifted in doubt. "Our evangelists are having doors slammed in their faces. We're losing people. Myopic belief systems work well when the future looks bleak, but not when hope appears on the horizon, all thanks to your bothersome cousin." He glared at Lester. "Do you have any idea what I'm talking about?"

"Um, yeah, sure. You think people will start liking Danny better than you, right?" Lester's eyes grew wide as Cadmon's narrowed. "But I mean, so what? I don't see how he could be a threat, not to you."

"No, of course, you don't. But then you see so little."

Cadmon pointed at the tablet he'd knocked to the floor and waited for Lester to retrieve it. He thumbed the tablet for the most recent public opinion polls. His popularity was sliding, Walker's was rising. There was no getting around it.

"The trouble is," Cadmon said, thinking out loud as he stared at the numbers, "most of our longtime members are still firmly entrenched in outdated beliefs. I can't change everything overnight. If I move too fast on reform, I'll lose our conservative base. Your cousin openly opposes nearly everything the Church stands for. Our only common ground with him was opposition to importing Nereids."

"Well, that's something, isn't it?" Lester said, apparently trying to end on a hopeful note.

"No, it isn't. In fact, it's less than nothing. An irrelevant, minor issue. What's important is that Walker is being given homecoming hero status, and his well-known dislike of the UCE makes me lose ground."

"Couldn't you just come out in support of him? Then his popularity would rub off on you, right?" Lester asked.

Cadmon stopped to look at his servant-weasel. The very thought of throwing in with Walker made Cadmon want to strangle Walker's blood relative on the spot. He held off—Lester was still of use—and settled for condescension. "Once again, you fail to grasp the complexity of the situation. I could lose half the Church congregation, not to mention the fact that I personally despise the man."

"Yeah, course, stupid idea," Lester mumbled, taking a step back. "I can be such an idiot. I'm sure you've got a much better plan in mind."

Cadmon noted the shine of perspiration on Lester's forehead. His nanobots were reporting a sharp increase in Lester's heartrate. Satisfied he had Lester appropriately cowed, he let go his annoyance. Lester's lack of intellectual prowess wasn't the issue. The problem was his far brighter cousin, Daniel Walker.

"Yes, as a matter of fact, I do," he replied. "We'll use our old friend, the legal system. Summon my lawyers and get the Premier on the line."

"Right." Lester spun on his heel and ran.

Figuring it would take Lester a few minutes to fulfill his tasks, Cadmon lifted a closed fist to lock his office door, then rose from his chair. The far wall of the room looked like a solid slab of granite, but a tap of his forefinger revealed the outline of a tall rectangle, which then retreated several inches, and slid aside to reveal a hidden room. In its center was a long table holding a complex maze of interconnected transparent tunnels. He walked forward and rapped the table with his knuckles.

"Ah, there you are, my darling," he said, spotting her as she came down one of the tubes. He opened the end of the tube and inserted his hand. "Come to Papa, Sweetheart."

The metallic-skinned rat rolled toward him on silver wheels, looking more like a sleek little race car than a lab rat. She rolled onto his palm, blinked her tiny white headlights and nosed his fingers. Cadmon pulled her out and gently turned her over in his hands, examining how the mechanical structures interfaced with the rat's flesh. Still no sign of rejection after more than a week.

"You're doing very well," Cadmon said, stroking her. "Shall we play a new game?"

Sweetheart bobbed her head.

"That's my girl. Do you know what I'm thinking now?"

The rat bobbed her head again.

"Show me then." He set her down on the table. He watched as her metallic skin turned into black and white scales forming an alternating barred pattern as her body thinned and lengthened. The small silver wheels pulled in and disappeared, while her head widened into a shovel-like shape and her round pink ears shrank away. Soon, she was two feet long and no bigger around than his thumb. She opened her mouth, displaying a pair of dagger-like fangs.

"Yes, yes, now the eyes," he urged.

Her headlights turned into elongated yellow shapes with a black vertical slash in each. He smiled in delight at how beautifully she conformed to his expectations. "You're a perfect little viper." The transformations he envisioned happened faster each time—his will combined with her willingness—resulting in complete mastery over the nanobots in Sweetheart's body.

"All right, that's enough for today. You can relax now and resume your natural shape."

Within minutes, he beheld a healthy white furred rat with bright red eyes and four ordinary rat legs and feet.

"Well done." He scooped her up to give her a kiss on the top of her head, then held her nose to his to look in her red bead eyes. "My darling, you and I are going to change the world." He placed her carefully inside the tubing, then tapped the food button and watched her scurry up to nibble on it. "And don't you worry, I won't let that nasty Daniel Walker get in our way."

He exited the room, and the granite resealed into a seamless wall once more. Moments later, the intercom buzzed, followed by Lester's voice. "Your legal team is on their way and I have Bromberg on the line," Lester announced.

"Put him through."

Bromberg's craggy face appeared in the air before him. Since invading the man with his nanobots, Cadmon longed to change that ugly countenance into something more palatable, but this was the face the public had grown used to seeing. As a card-carrying member of the UCE, Bromberg swore to follow its reactionary dogma. Any change in his appearance might bring his loyalty to the Church into question. Too bad. There was so much room for improvement.

"Father Chayd, how can I be of service?" Bromberg tipped his balding head downward in a show of obeisance.

"The Niña's return is problematical for the Church, and for you as well. We need to address how we're going to handle it. It's important you take a firm stance. This is what I want you to do . . ."

Chapter 31

The Niña dropped out of hyperspace well short of its ultimate destination. The decision proved wise when a wide scan showed a new automated perimeter defense system just outside the Kuiper Belt. After establishing long-range communications with the nearest outpost, space tugs deployed from Earth and guided the Niña safely through the perimeter's laser maze. Once inside, they were bombarded with demands from the UN to return to Lunar 1. Instead, they held position, buying time with excuses by claiming engine problems. The truth was they wanted to learn what had transpired during their absence. Daniel was appalled by the results of the most recent election. Senator Nelson Bromberg, the very person who'd gotten them into this mess, was now Premier of the United Nations.

Believing that the Niña's safety lay in public opinion, Daniel used the delay to broadcast images of Tau Medea IV and upload recordings of their survey reports to the Web. He and the captain had agreed if they got the public excited enough, it might nullify objections to the Niña's unlawful departure. What they didn't agree on was how to deal with Carrie.

When Daniel discovered Captain Kowalski "accidentally" leaked a confidential report claiming that they had not only discovered a devious Garuda invasion plot, but had brought back an amazing new lifeform to defeat it, he was livid. He videoed the Captain from his desk.

"What the hell, Devon?" he demanded, displaying the misleading leaked report.

"We talked about this," Kowalski said, looking back from his own desk, with no show of remorse.

"No, you talked about it. I said it was crazy, total nonsense. We can't build trust based on a lie."

"It's done. Live with it."

An alert for an incoming transmission overwrote Daniel's screen. The captain was getting the same alert—a personal message from Premier Bromberg addressed to them both.

"That can't be good," Daniel grumbled.

"Maybe, maybe not. For all we know, Bromberg might be ready to side with us now. Let's meet in the auditorium and view it together. I'll have McCormack join us as well," Kowalski said, then disappeared from Daniel's screen.

"Not likely," Daniel mumbled, and shut down his terminal. He opened his door and peered out, looking both ways. No sign of her. He exhaled in relief and hurried through the corridors, taking a circuitous route, checking around and behind repeatedly. When he arrived in the auditorium, his uncle and Captain Kowalski were already seated in the front row waiting, with the massive image of Nelson Bromberg paused to play on the front wall.

"Took your sweet time," Kowalski said as Walker sat next to him.

"Had to be sure I wasn't followed," Daniel replied.

The three men looked about the auditorium, empty but for them. Kowalski nodded and waved the pre-recorded message to play.

"Welcome home, gentlemen," Premier Bromberg began pleasantly enough, "Thank you for returning our ship in one piece. I hope you're all pleased with your little joyride."

Uh oh. Daniel grimaced at the sarcasm in Bromberg's tone. *This is going to be bad.*

"I'm so looking forward to seeing you all again—you especially, Captain Kowalski, or perhaps I should say Ensign, as that may soon be your rank once you've been stripped of command. Assuming you're allowed to remain in the service at all."

Kowalski put a hand over the lower half of his face.

"And, as for you, Dr. Walker, best find yourself a good criminal attorney." Bromberg smirked. "You're definitely going to need one."

Daniel couldn't take Bromberg's pleasure. "Self-righteous son of a—"

Kowalski dropped his hand and shushed him.

"Now, as for this so-called Earth twin you claim to have found in the Tau Medea system," Bromberg continued. "You've even gone so far as to broadcast images of this planet, and leak a so-called "secret" report that states you discovered and curtailed a Garuda invasion plot. None of which can be verified, of course. We simply have to take your word for it, I suppose."

Bromberg took a moment to sigh and shake his head. "Such devious attempts to sway public opinion are pathetically transparent. It wouldn't surprise me in the least to learn that these recordings and reports are complete fabrications." He leaned back and shrugged. "But, just for argument's sake, let's say the information you've presented is accurate, and Tau Medea IV is habitable, we're still in no position to authorize a full-scale colonization effort. Thanks to you, we're threatened with renewed Garuda aggression, which means we must concentrate our resources on defense. Perhaps, one day, we might be able to investigate this planet's potential, if any, but—"

"He can't mothball this. This has to take precedence," Daniel said.

"Shut up, I want to hear this," Kowalski snapped.

Bromberg fingered the gold symbol of power hanging from the heavy chain around his neck as he continued downgrading the importance of their discovery. "—and even you admit there is a high CO_2 level, a serious issue, and the extreme distance only complicates matters. We simply can't justify another expedition with so many pressing problems at home."

"When aren't there problems?" Daniel asked, wishing the message was live and he could confront Bromberg in real time.

The recording continued on. "All you've really found is an impractical, long-distance, terraforming project. This is hardly the time to be taking on something of this magnitude."

Daniel waved his hand to freeze the message. "He knows we're looking at simple outgassing from recent geological activity. Even if we did nothing, it would dissipate over time."

"Can we just get through this?" Kowalski waved the frozen image into speaking again.

"With so much at stake, we cannot allow humanity to be divided at this critical juncture in history," Bromberg continued. "This is a time which demands unity, and consolidation of all our resources. Assuming the data is accurate, further investigation will be given due consideration, but the ultimate decision as to what shall or shall not be done remains outside your jurisdiction. I'm sure you must realize you both have far more immediate personal challenges to attend to. Defending yourself in court for theft of UN property, to name one."

Bromberg leaned forward and looked down his nose. "This maverick behavior of yours will not be tolerated. A Senate hearing will be convened in two standard days to determine what disciplinary action should be taken. Your physical presence is, of course, mandatory."

The message ended there, leaving the three men staring at a blank screen. McCormack turned to the captain. "I noticed he made no mention of our nanogen-infestation. Obviously, you chose to delete that tidbit from my medical report."

"As I've said repeatedly, we have to be quiet about that," Kowalski replied.

"I'm no nanotech expert. I need help with this thing."

"You won't get us help, you'll get us buried," Kowalski said. "You don't want us all locked away in some research lab, do you?

"Again, you exaggerate," McCormack said, looking to Daniel for support.

"I don't know," Daniel said. "You heard Bromberg just now. It would give him all the ammunition he needs to mothball us."

"Exactly." Kowalski nodded to him. "I knew from the start that he wanted to discredit you, but it's gone way beyond that now."

Daniel and his uncle looked at each other.

"Just what is it you're not telling us?" Daniel asked.

Kowalski took a long breath before answering. "My original orders were to give you as much leeway as possible, hoping you'd fall on your face. I'm sure Sanchez received similar instructions. It's why he didn't throw you off that Martian rescue detail, and why I had to assign him to your ground survey team. Bromberg sent him on this mission to keep an eye on you, or maybe worse. I'm not proud I went along, but I wanted command." He frowned and rubbed his forehead. "God, I hate politics. Truth is, I don't give a damn who comes out on top, so long as I have a ship to run and a crew to man it. I figured the rest would sort itself out. It never occurred to me they would stoop to sabotage."

"So you think Bromberg's behind all of this?" Daniel asked.

"It adds up. He delayed us for weeks, then rerouted us to Mars on a flimsy excuse just in time for the Garuda to show up. Then we get exposed to a Fabri-Tech nanogen, and if that wasn't enough to finish us off, we had a defective engine to make sure of it. Bromberg must be crapping all over himself seeing us back in one piece."

"You don't actually believe he's colluding with the Garuda?" McCormack asked, his bushy gray eyebrows lifted high. "Everyone knows he and his party are xenophobes. It's their central platform."

"Maybe he decided to make sure everyone agreed with them. There's nothing like an alien attack to get everyone on the same page," Kowalski said.

McCormack stretched his mouth downward as if he were having trouble swallowing the concept. "I've never been one to buy into conspiracy theories. Most people aren't that smart, let alone that organized. It's more likely these are unrelated events."

"I'll take conspiracy over coincidence any day," Kowalski replied, "but bottom line, it doesn't really matter whether Bromberg stacked the deck or just got lucky. Either way, he'll use everything he can against us. Our nanomorph-lady is the one wild card nobody figured on. We just have to play her the right way."

"I'm not much for games," McCormack replied.

"Sorry, Doc, but you've been dealt into this, like it or not, and I say we play our high card."

"And just how does one play a card with a mind of its own?" McCormack asked.

"By giving it what it wants, and from what I've seen, our ace wants him." Kowalski jerked a thumb at Daniel.

"Now wait a minute," Daniel objected.

"Why don't you try being nice to her for a change, give her a little encouragement?" Kowalski asked.

"Why don't you encourage her?" Daniel countered.

"I'm not the one she's after." Kowalski sighed and shook his head as if dealing with a disappointing pupil. "You must know we can't keep her under wraps for long, and once she's out there, all hell's going to break loose. Isolationists, off-world enthusiasts, alien-life researchers, the Nereid Trade Association." He ticked them off with his fingers. "They're all going to be scrambling to get their hands on her. Carrie is the biggest distraction we've got, but only if everyone thinks she's just an intriguing new alien lifeform. No one can know about her being the product of a nanogen."

"But we can't just ignore—" McCormack began.

"Yes, we can," Kowalski cut him off. "It's not contagious. You've screened everyone on board. It's only in her and Walker here, and you and I are the only ones who know it. So unless you want them locked up in someone's lab till doomsday, keep it to yourself. I don't know why you're so worried about it anyway. Your nephew has no ill symptoms whatsoever. He's in total control of it. Now all he needs to do is get control of her."

McCormack scoffed. "She's impossible to control."

"Not for him. She follows him around like a puppy."

Daniel could feel the hot color rising in his face. "And you've seen me do nothing but try to discourage her. She pays no attention. If you think I have any influence, you're dreaming." He tried to redirect the conversation. "We don't need her, anyway. What's important is that we've got a habitable planet and people know about it now. The public's drive to settle TM IV will find its own momentum."

"Eventually, maybe, but not in time to save our butts," Kowalski said. "Our immediate future's going to dead-end real soon unless we come up with something spectacular. And when it comes to spectacular, she's it."

"She's not it. She's dangerous. We have no idea what she'll do," Daniel said.

"There's an old saying, Walker, 'Keep your friends close, and your enemies closer.' The more dangerous she is, the closer you'd better keep her—'cause it's a sure bet if she turns on us, you can kiss your sorry ass good-bye."

Daniel felt a sinking sensation. He looked at his uncle, whose expression mirrored his own inner turmoil.

McCormack was first to speak again. "I'm not sure I agree, Captain, but I'm not willing to turn Daniel over to Bromberg and others of his ilk, either. Nevertheless, it is absolutely imperative that we determine how widespread this nanogen is and whether any original versions of it still exist."

"Yes, yes, I suppose," Kowalski said, "but you have to be discreet."

"I have to find out the facts," McCormack replied, with equal conviction. "It occurs to me our best bet may be to use Carrie herself. She says she can detect the presence of this nanogen in Daniel. It's why she keeps hounding him."

"Which is exactly why he has to be the one to get her cooperation, which he could do just by being nice to her."

"But—" Daniel tried to get a word in.

"We both know what you're suggesting," McCormack talked over him. "Intimacy might indeed gain her cooperation, but it's risky. We'd need to keep a very close eye on him. The suppressants have been effective so far, but even without him being in close proximity to her, I've had to keep upping the dosage."

"Hey!" Daniel was appalled at the way they were discussing offering him like a piece of meat. "This isn't up to either of you."

"No, it's up to you and it's about time you did something about it," Kowalski answered. "And in the meantime, Doc here needs to keep his mouth shut."

McCormack sighed. "I will for now, but should I have any reason to believe this nanogen could become a contagion, I go straight to Disease Control and initiate a solar-wide emergency alert. We may not see any adverse effects yet, but remember, child carriers of the T-nanogen are near perfect human specimens until adolescence kicks in. We don't know nearly enough about this nanogen to say how long this good health will continue. And as Daniel said, we've already seen how dangerous she can be even now."

"True, but she's been friendly enough lately," Kowalski said. "Even at her most aggressive, she didn't kill anyone, not even Sanchez, and I'm pretty sure he deserved it."

"Yes, I confess I'm rather surprised by that," McCormack said.

"He definitely put her to the test. Maybe he did us a favor there," Kowalski commented ruefully.

"An interesting perspective," Carrie's voice came from behind, startling them. They looked back to see her staring down at them from the top row.

Daniel groaned inwardly. *How much did she hear?* She came down the aisle and sat next to him. He inched away. Kowalski glared at him until he froze in place.

"Who was that speaking from the screen?" she asked.

The three men exchanged looks. Evidently, she'd been there the whole time. Daniel sighed, wishing he were somewhere else, anywhere else.

Kowalski answered her. "That was Premier Nelson Bromberg, leader of the United Nations, Earth's governing body."

"He is not your friend?"

"Definitely not," Kowalski said. "He wants me and your boyfriend here to appear at a hearing to defend ourselves against charges of treason."

Daniel stiffened, wanting to object to Kowalski characterizing him as her boyfriend.

"Treason: an act of betrayal to one's country. Will you appear?" she asked.

"We don't have a choice," Kowalski answered.

She seemed to consider this for a moment. "Then I shall accompany you."

"What? No. Bad idea," Daniel said. When she scowled at him, waiting for some justification, he tried to think fast of a way to delay her introduction to his home world. "It's better if you watch the proceedings here on board."

"I prefer experiences in the flesh." She leaned toward him. "Would you like to be nice to me now?"

A surprised laugh burst from Kowalski. "Well, let's just leave the two of you alone." He grabbed a sputtering Dr. McCormack by the arm and dragged him up the steps.

Daniel looked with alarm at their retreating backsides. He turned to see her green eyes studying him. He knew the others were counting on him, but how could they expect him to engage in an intimate relationship with a walking nanotech production facility? The package might be attractive, but the contents were terrifying.

He cleared his throat and tried to stall.

"Did you, um—you didn't really understand what Captain Kowalski was suggesting, did you?"

"Your captain wishes you to influence my behavior. He believes the most expedient method is through sexual intimacy. Does that comport with your understanding?"

"Pretty much. Aren't you offended?" he asked hopefully.

"No. Are you?"

"Yes. Yes, I am. This is the damnedest conversation," he muttered, and got to his feet.

She stood as well. "You have nothing to fear from me."

"I'm not so sure. I have no idea what motivates you, but I do know what you're capable of."

"It would enhance our communication if you accepted your infestation."

"My infestation?" he echoed the words with distaste. "I can't even tolerate the idea of a passive reference implant, let alone an army of intelligent mechanical bugs crawling around my insides." He grimaced and rubbed his stomach.

She regarded his movements with interest. "You are entomophobic."

"I'm what?"

"You display an irrational fear of insects."

He dropped his hand. "Great, now you're an amateur psychiatrist."

He turned away and made his way up the steps, hearing her footfalls behind him. He supposed he was cursed to have her follow him about, a pastime she engaged in more often than not, but at least at those times he knew where she was and what she was up to. They had repeatedly tried to place a locater tag on her person, but she always dismantled it. When she wasn't pestering him, he had no idea where she went or what she did, nor, apparently, did anyone else. Her vanishing acts lasted minutes or hours, but always she returned to his side, poking into his business again.

She popped in on him in his quarters whenever she got the notion, more than once surprising him in personally humiliating moments. He finally blew up, ordering her to stay out, or at least knock first. So she knocked, then barged in, invited or not. Locks were useless. He was certain most of the crew thought they were already bedmates.

In reality, he was keeping her at arm's length, and no matter what Kowalski wanted, he had every intention of continuing to do so.

Chapter 32

The Rotunda, the official seat of the United Nations Court of Justice for International Affairs, perched atop a rolling hill just south of the ancient city of Rome. The white half-dome soared above wide concrete terraces sloping down the hillside where onlookers congregated to observe the proceedings. Today, they numbered in the tens of thousands—an unprecedented turnout—so large, United Earth Forces was present to keep order. The crowd murmured like a restless ocean.

Huge 3-D video screens displayed close-ups of the panel of judges, one from each of the ten nation states—Luna, the Floating Cities of the Pacific, the North Americas, the South American Union, the United Euro-Slav States, the Russian Republic, the Arabian North African Republic, the Chinese Republic of Asia; the South African Union, and finally Australia, still a determinedly independent nation of its own. The justices presented an even mix of male and female, skin colors ranging from pale beige to midnight black, and hair and eyes in the rainbow of hues currently in fashion. They sat in a row of tall padded chairs halfway up the inner wall of the Rotunda.

Above the judges, Premier Bromberg sat behind an impressive podium embossed with the emblem of his office, an animated Solar system. His role was to supervise the proceedings and cast a tie-breaking vote if necessary. The General Assembly section took up the entire lower half of the Rotunda, reserved for Senators, Assembly Members, and guests. Nearly every seat was filled. From these exalted positions, the members of government looked down on everyone else, including the accused.

Neither Daniel nor Kowalski had yet been given a chance to speak. They'd had to sit quietly while the prosecution grilled selected members of the Niña's officers and crew about the events leading up to the Niña's allegedly unauthorized departure. Much was made of the personnel losses on Mars—zero about the subsequent discoveries on Tau Medea IV.

Their own attorney, dressed in a conservative navy-blue suit, was a thin, middle-aged man who came highly recommended, and he made a valiant effort. Objecting repeatedly as the prosecution hammered a case against his clients, he interrupted and argued on their behalf, but Daniel knew their only real defense was that their treasonable act had been worth it. From the looks on the judges' faces, Daniel feared they had already made up their minds. This hearing was more show than substance, but their ruling would be real enough.

He wondered if they'd even bothered to read his reports on the planet and the lifeforms discovered there. If not, it was short-sighted on their part, since the most remarkable one was now sitting directly behind him. She was told to remain cloaked to hide her ex-traordinary appearance and sit quietly with their other character witnesses, but she kept leaning toward him, whispering questions and cutting remarks, clearly annoyed by these proceedings. He kept shushing her and prayed she would remain covered.

Kowalski elbowed him. "That's him on the right."

Daniel looked over to see a tall, blond man in the General Assembly area in a seat just below the Judges' panel.

"The new leader of the Unified Church of Earth and now spiritual counselor to the UN, all thanks to Bromberg," Kowalski said.

So that's Morden Chayd.

Daniel remembered the last time he'd encountered a Supreme Father. The wizened leader had appeared at Daniel's Lunar press conference like an apparition bathed in ethereal light. It seemed his successor felt no need for special effects to make a dramatic impression. Chayd looked like an ordinary human being. *Or maybe not,* Daniel thought, seeing the man's face enlarged on the audience view screen as he smiled and lifted a hand in a royal wave for the cameras. Chayd was spectacularly handsome. Daniel stared, trying to puzzle it out.

Advanced cosmetic enhancements? Surely the Supreme Father wouldn't flout his own rules. No, I must be looking at the man's natural appearance, arresting as it is.

Chayd sat back, looking relaxed until he turned toward the defendants. The smile changed to a scowl, and he leaned forward to stare in Daniel's direction with a riveting intensity. Daniel stared back. He'd never seen the famously charismatic Supreme Father before, but those eyes had a haunting familiarity. *There is something there, something I should know.* He heard Bromberg saying his name, but the voice seemed distant.

"Look at me." Carrie touched his shoulder from behind, sending a spark of electricity into him.

Ow!" He twisted to face her. "What?"

"Who is that? The one staring at us," she asked.

"Everyone's staring at us."

"You know the one I mean."

He did, but before Daniel could answer, he heard Premier Bromberg repeating his name.

"Dr. Walker. Dr. Walker. If I might have your attention?"

Daniel turned back. "Yes, sorry."

"We have heard the prosecution. Before you present your defense, I shall again remind you of the allegations: dereliction of duty, theft of government property, misuse of government funds, high treason . . ."

Bromberg continued his litany, but Daniel could no longer hear him—his voice was drowned in enraged outcries from the crowd. Bromberg waved an aide into action. In a moment, the noise lessened like the volume turned down on a radio—the effect of an exterior sound-dampening field.

"It appears you still have a certain popular appeal," the Premier said, without any sign of amusement. "Regardless, it is the duty of this Court to assess these charges based on the evidence. Now, do you have anything to offer in your defense?"

"Yes, your honor," their attorney rose to his feet. "I would like to call on the defendant, Captain Devon C. Kowalski."

Daniel and Kowalski exchanged glances. After long hours of discussion, they agreed—stick with the original story. Kowalski stepped forward to sit in the witness seat.

"Now, Captain, would you please explain why you did not return to Luna 1 as the prosecution claims you were ordered to do," their attorney asked.

"To my knowledge no such orders were ever received. Communication was down and our launch window was closing. We sent messages to Earth reporting the problem, asking for new decryption codes, all without success. With no orders to the contrary, I continued the original assigned mission under the belief that its completion remained of paramount importance," the Captain stated.

It was a lie, of course, transparent to anyone knowledgeable, but it offered a face-saving out if the judges were so inclined. Daniel doubted they had any such inclination. Even under a barrage of cross-examination, Kowalski's testimony never wavered. The Premier listened, smiling as if to say he knew exactly what they were trying to pull. Kowalski finished testifying and returned to the defendant's box.

"Is that all you have to offer?" Bromberg asked, wearing a smirk. His expression darkened again, when despite the sound dampening field, the crowd could be heard chanting, "Walker, Walker," over and over. The people's sentiments were clear. Bromberg scowled for a moment, but then seemed to gather his determination again. "I asked if that was all."

Their attorney looked back at his clients and Kowalski looked at Daniel, the message clear. It was time Daniel kept his promise. Daniel took a breath and nodded.

"If it please, Your Honor, I have additional evidence to submit," their attorney said, as he pulled out a pocket pad and hit send. "I am releasing to the court a statement signed prior to the Niña's departure to the Tau Medea system. We ask that you accept it into evidence."

The court aides scurried about, retrieving Daniel's damning confession. Daniel felt a sinking sensation knowing what was to come, even though he'd agreed to it from the start. This was the price he'd promised to pay. He could only hope the pressure of public opinion would save him.

After the prosecution and the justices reviewed his confession, they fell into a heated discussion, none of which was audible to anyone else. Daniel watched their faces. He noted the Supreme Father watching them as well, intensely interested in the ongoing argument. Gradually, one-by-one, the justices lapsed into silence. Chayd crossed his arms and leaned back, wearing a smug expression as he turned to stare down at Daniel. *Why does he look like he heard every word?*

Bromberg waved the audio back on. "In light of new evidence, the Court finds the allegations against the military presence assigned to the Niña to be speculative at best. This Court therefore drops all charges against Captain Devon Kowalski and recommends against his court martial. Dr. Daniel Walker has submitted a written confession in which he takes full responsibility for intercepting orders from the UN, sabotaging communications, and deceiving Captain Kowalski into continuing on to Tau Medea despite knowingly receiving orders to the contrary. Dr. Walker, you have left this Court with no choice but to charge you with treason. You are hereby remanded into custody."

The bang of Bromberg's gavel coming down hard on his podium rang out. For a split second, there was a shocked silence, then the crowd erupted. The militia braced for confrontation, spreading out to hold the angry mob at bay, as six armed guards marched forward to make the arrest.

"Unacceptable," Carrie hissed into Daniel's ear.

Daniel turned to face her. "I told you this might happen."

She looked from him to the guards marching toward them.

"You need to return to the Niña with Captain Kowalski and—"

She threw off her cloak and vaulted over the railing.

"Carrie, no!" he yelled as she sent the oncoming guards sprawling. "Stop!"

The crowd cried out in surprise, drowning him out.

More guards sprinted to intervene.

Carrie assumed a fighting stance, claws bared, her body glowing ever brighter with unspent energy.

"HOLD!" a deep voice reverberated above the din. The sprinting guards stopped and looked up. The spectators hushed.

Supreme Father Morden Chayd was on his feet, arms outspread like an avenging angel. When the last of the voices faded, Chayd lowered his arms and spoke again in a soft resonant tone that somehow still filled the entire arena.

"Perhaps our judgment has been premature," he said, and pointed to Carrie with an upturned palm. "Who or what, pray tell, is this?"

Daniel swept his gaze across everyone's startled expressions. The crowd was quiet, waiting for an answer. He could well understand their stunned silence. A glowing shield of energy surrounded her like sunlight, filling her diamond fiber hair with shattered rainbows, and the snug white jumpsuit Kowalski had selected for her left little to the imagination—all of which was projected spectacularly on the wide holoscreens above.

He took a deep breath. "This is Carrie. We discovered her on Tau Medea IV. She is a sentient being with an intellect equal to or exceeding our own, and fully conversant in our language. I highly recommend she be treated with the utmost courtesy and respect."

He stopped at that. Everything he'd said was true enough, as far as it went.

Carrie looked at him and smiled. Daniel exhaled. He'd just set something wildly unpredictable loose on an unsuspecting world. Like it or not, their high card was on the table.

"Peace, brothers and sisters," Father Chayd said to the soldiers with an outstretched hand. They lowered their weapons. Chayd turned back to address Carrie. "As spiritual counselor to the United Nations and Supreme Father of the Unified Church of Earth, please allow me to welcome you on humanity's behalf."

Carrie acknowledged him with a nod and let her energy field dissipate. "I am happy to be among you. I am proof that the planet you call Tau Medea IV can support humanoid life. I invite you to go there. To explore, and to live," she said.

Daniel had rehearsed with her what to say when the time came for her reveal, but was pleasantly surprised to hear the words come out of her mouth.

Chayd raised his eyebrows in response. "Won't your people object to humans moving in?"

"My people do not live on Tau Medea IV. The world has no advanced native lifeforms. It is open for human settlement," she stated, just as Daniel had asked.

"Well," Chayd said, and smiled. "That does sound promising. Please grant me the privilege of meeting with you for further discussion. I suspect we may have much in common."

Carrie hesitated, and looked back at her companions.

"Is there a problem?" Chayd asked.

"Yes," she replied. "The Daniel Walker must not be imprisoned. I will not meet with you without him."

"I see." Chayd frowned for a moment, then looked over to Bromberg, who wore an astounded expression, poised at his podium with his gavel in midair. "In light of this new information, Premier, do you want to reconsider?"

Bromberg blinked away his amazed stare, as if everything were snapping into crystal clarity. "Yes. Absolutely. It's obvious to me now that there has been a misinterpretation of the facts presented. Dr. Walker's statement provided a perfectly legitimate explanation for his actions. The allegations against Dr. Walker are without merit. All pending charges are hereby dismissed."

As his gavel came down again with a bang, the other justices stared openmouthed at him. Some stood to protest, but cheering from the crowd drowned out their objections.

Kowalski and their attorney both pounded Daniel on the back, shouting congratulations. Daniel stood there, smiling in stupefaction, stunned by the sudden reversal. Carrie moved to stand behind Kowalski. When Daniel's eyes met hers, his smile faded, and he looked at the captain in alarm.

"What the hell did she do to them?" he yelled over the cheering, not caring if she heard.

"Don't know, don't care," Kowalski yelled back, and pulled Daniel by the arm. "Come on. Let's get out of here before they change their minds again."

Chapter 33

That afternoon, following the hearing in Rome, Cadmon stood in his corner office staring through its wide windows at the Parisian vista below, thinking hard. Lester sat in front of his desk awaiting instructions. Cadmon let him wait. Not out of malice. He simply had no instructions to give. All his plans had ground to a halt and even during the return flight to Paris, he'd come up with no answer. He felt off balance, uncertain, something he hadn't experienced in years.

His plan to rid himself of Walker had been abandoned in the face of a far more dangerous complication—something he'd feared and had taken great lengths to prevent, but never believed might actually come to pass. Despite all his precautions, the missing AI-nanogen 'egg' had not only survived, it had hatched.

At first, he thought its presence stemmed from Walker, but quickly realized his error when that exotic-looking female leaped forth. While everyone believed her to be an alien lifeform from some distant world, he immediately recognized his own Earth-born handiwork—the engineered diamond hair and claws, the too perfect body, the enhanced reflexes—oh yes, she was definitely his creation. If he'd harbored any doubt, the glow of that power grid around her jettisoned it. He sensed she hadn't advanced to the same sophisticated level of control as he, but had developed some strong preliminary defenses. Stasis during hyperspace travel must have slowed her progress considerably. Still, he needed to take control of her fast before she became a threat. She could expose him prematurely or challenge his supremacy. If she hadn't already recognized him as her counterpart, it was only a matter of time.

As he looked down at the river Seine dividing the heart of Paris, he thought of his own ambitions, cleaved neatly in two between what he believed before and what he knew now. His gaze traveled along the bridges crossing the river and snaking roads, considering possible courses of action and following them to their probable outcomes.

One possibility was to put her back into stasis. It would buy him some time, but only that. Plus, how would he explain her sudden disappearance? Outright murder would eliminate the threat altogether, but still risked a PR nightmare. Public sentiment was already heavily weighted in favor of Walker and his mission. He didn't want to add more to it. No, what he needed was something subtle, a way to neutralize her without raising anyone's alarm. He stared at Île de la Cité, the elongated island in the middle of the Seine holding Notre Dame, the shape of which always reminded him of Sweetheart, and it occurred to him that she was the key. When she was close to dying from old age, he'd saved her by using another original AI-nanogen to carry his own nanobots into the rat's cerebral cortex essentially creating a nano-sized Trojan Horse. The technique had successfully circumvented the rat's auto-immune response. Sensing no threat, Sweetheart's nanobots linked to his and he took complete control. It worked before. It should work again.

He checked the idea thoroughly, looking for weaknesses until confident it was his best option—not the quickest route perhaps, but the most likely to succeed without detection. To everyone else, his takeover should appear to be a natural progression of a growing friendship. She would gradually start doing what he wanted, all the while thinking it her own idea. In time, she would become an extension of himself, her mind and body under his domain. Walker might view the transformation with some dismay, but he'd find no evidence of undue influence.

Cadmon nodded with satisfaction, confident that an all-controlling link could be established without anyone's awareness. But if by some chance his control proved less than perfect, and a nanobot war ensued, her suffering could be explained away as a reaction to some Earth-born disease, perfectly plausible in an alien with no immunity. Either way, he'd end up in control. If he had to destroy her first, no matter, he could rebuild. He envisioned molding a woman to his tastes. *Oh, the possibilities.*

He chuckled at the prospect, startling Lester into a squeak of surprise. He'd forgotten Lester was still there, sitting silently in front of his desk for nearly an hour now. Lester gave him a questioning smile so pitiful he almost felt sorry for the man, almost.

"Lester, you seem tense," Cadmon said, as if he truly cared. "I think a little time away would do you some good."

"Time away?" Lester managed to look both hopeful and suspicious.

"Yes, a little family time. I want you to visit your cousin on the Niña."

Lester no longer looked hopeful.

"And while you're there, you will obtain something for me. A piece of that alien woman we saw at the hearing this morning—a scrape of skin, a hair follicle—whatever you can get so long as it contains live cells. Be discreet, or at least make it look accidental. Take a zero-set freezer vial with you and place the sample in it immediately. Any delay of more than a few seconds will make it useless. Do you understand?"

"I guess so, but why do you—?" Lester grunted and clutched at his gut.

"I do so hate it when you question me." Cadmon waited until he regained Lester's attention. "I'll expect you back by day's end, sample in hand. Do not disappoint me." He watched Lester nod and massage his stomach. "Go."

Lester stood, backed away, and slipped out the door.

Chapter 34

Following the hearing, the same guards who had tried to arrest Daniel cleared a path for him and his people, parting the crowd and holding back an onslaught of reporters so they could make it back to their shuttle waiting on the tarmac. Their shuttle pilot, Lieutenant Taggatt, greeted them, wearing a big grin. No one smiled back.

"Get us out of here," Kowalski ordered.

On the flight back to the Niña, the only sounds were the shuttle's engines and Taggatt's half of the conversation with air control. Daniel watched Carrie out of the corner of his eye. *Play your high card. Great, until the card rearranges the deck for you. Bromberg wasn't anywhere near her, so how could she have influenced him? But what else could explain his sudden reversal? Doesn't make sense.*

Daniel felt eyes on him and looked over to see the captain staring at him. Kowalski glanced at Carrie, then back at him. Seeing Carrie turned away, Daniel mouthed, "Conference room."

Kowalski nodded.

When they disembarked from the shuttle into the Niña's hangar bay, Daniel was handed a message by a robot that rolled up to him. He read it to himself.

"Lester? What the hell does he want?" Daniel grumbled under his breath.

"Something of interest?" Carrie asked, beside him.

"Not really." He crumpled the note in his fist. He had a much bigger concern, the one standing in front of him. "I have some administrative stuff to do. I'm sure you'd find it boring. Why don't you go spend some time in the ship's library?"

"I've already downloaded its entire contents into my data files for future reference," Carrie replied.

"Of course, you did." He searched for something else. "Maybe some time in the gym then? I noticed that you enjoy swimming."

"I do."

"Good." He turned and walked away, hoping she wouldn't follow him. She did. He paused and turned back. "I thought you were going for a swim."

"I made no such indication."

He took a circuitous route, and ignored her, hoping she'd lose interest. She didn't. When he reached the conference room, he came to a stop. *Maybe tactless honesty will work.*

"Look, I'm meeting with the captain, and you're not invited."

She cocked her head at him. "You do not wish me to observe?"

"No, I don't."

"Understood," she said, and didn't move.

He blew air through his nose in frustration. "I don't want you here. I don't know how I can make it any clearer than that."

"Noted," she said, remaining where she was.

He clenched his teeth, glaring at her.

Her expression stayed neutral, waiting for him to open the door.

"Damn it!" he said, and went in.

She followed him.

Pretend she's not here. He took a seat next to his uncle across the table from the captain.

As always, Carrie did what she wanted, which at moment, was to slowly circle the room dragging her fingers along the walls.

Kowalski glanced from Daniel to Carrie and back again. Daniel kept his gaze on the captain, crossed his arms, leaned back, and waited.

After a moment, Kowalski took a breath. "Okay. Now that our legal troubles have been put to rest, I think we should issue a press release calling for a return voyage to Tau Medea IV as soon as possible. Public enthusiasm will never be higher than it is right now."

"Agreed," Daniel said, making a point to keep his eyes forward. "I was going over the list of applicants. It's a pretty impressive group—"

"Hold on," McCormack interrupted, rapping the table. "Aren't you two getting ahead of yourselves? We shouldn't even consider returning there until we know how to combat this nanogen."

"Why?" Carrie asked.

The three men twisted to look at her. She stood with one hand against the wall.

"Because if we infected the planet, we could end up with an entire settlement of carriers," McCormack replied.

"Carriers," she repeated and frowned. "My name reflects your fears. I should select a new designation."

The men shared a look. She turned aside and went back to drifting around the room, touching its surfaces, eyes closed as if in some altered state of consciousness. The men watched her.

"Just what exactly are you doing?" Daniel asked sharply.

She opened her eyes and dropped her hands to her sides. "Nothing."

He frowned, certain it was far from nothing. Her guilty reaction told him that much. It also demonstrated she was concerned about his opinion. Enough so that at the hearing, she had delivered the rehearsed statement he'd taught her, word for word. Maybe he couldn't keep her from following him around, but he did have influence over her, perhaps more than he gave himself credit for.

"Sit down," he ordered. "And stop touching things."

She plopped into the seat at the end of the table, and clasped her hands together. He should have been pleased, but if she could manipulate Bromberg from afar, it meant she could get to anybody. How did he know if his own mind was free, let alone anyone else's in this room? He studied Kowalski's and McCormack's faces.

"Bromberg sure changed his mind in a hurry," Daniel said, and stared pointedly at Carrie.

She looked back, her expression neutral.

"The UCE opposes off-world influence, so why would Chayd want to meet with an alien?" Daniel asked.

"Maybe you should ask your cousin," Kowalski suggested.

Surprised, Daniel turned to the captain, only now remembering the crumpled note in his pocket. "Lester might know something about what went on at Fabri-Tech, but what's he got to do with the Church?"

"He's Chayd's right-hand man. Didn't you know?" Kowalski replied.

"No. I had no idea."

A disbelieving laugh burst from his uncle. "That boy always was self-serving, but I'm surprised he's made such a success of it."

Daniel might have shared his uncle's amusement, if not for that horrifying recording Lester had sent him ten years ago just before they launched for Tau Medea. Having forwarded it on to the authorities upon their return to Earth, it was still fresh in his mind. The investigating officer had confirmed the perpetrator was Doctor Cadmon Dhyre, who was now deceased. Case closed. Daniel still wanted to question Lester about it, and even more about the events leading up to the lab explosion. The probes, the nanogen, and their flawed engine all went back to that same lab where both Lester and Dhyre had been working—way too many coincidences to ignore. There had to be a connection.

"So Lester's working for the Supreme Father now?" Daniel shook his head. "I'm going to have to see it to believe it."

But right now his cousin's misadventures weren't his main concern. "We were talking about the hearing. And that sudden reversal." He looked at Carrie again, and the other two men followed his gaze. If she could alter a person's mindset, who was to say how theirs were being affected? He wanted to voice his fears aloud, but she was sitting right there.

"You have a visitor, Dr. Walker," the ship's automated intercom system interrupted, breaking the silence. "Mr. Lester Merritt requests permission to come aboard. Do you grant permission?"

"Speak of the devil," McCormack said, with a sigh.

"Granted. Have him shown to my quarters," Daniel answered, then looked to his uncle and the captain. "Guess we'll have to continue this discussion at a more opportune moment."

Kowalski nodded.

"Lester probably has some new scheme in mind. Best prepare for a sales pitch," McCormack told him wryly.

Daniel smiled, finding amusement in their shared family history. "Don't worry—I tore that sucker label off my forehead years ago."

Daniel left and headed to his quarters, hearing the now familiar footsteps trailing him. He entered his room and locked the door in Carrie's face, hoping she'd get the message and comply for once. His cousin had already made himself at home, leaning back in his executive flowchair with his boots on top of Daniel's desk.

Lester grinned and opened his arms wide. "Danny, boy! Welcome home!"

Just as Daniel opened his mouth to tell Lester to get his feet off, the outer door slid open again and Carrie walked in. He closed his mouth, and sighed in irritation. So much for any hope of privately grilling his cousin.

Lester's eyes focused over Daniel's shoulder, and his smile got wider. "Just the person I wanted to see." He dropped his feet to the floor and stood.

"I assume you're talking to me," Daniel said.

Taking in his cousin's appearance, Daniel couldn't help but smirk at the engineered facial enhancements, the embossed bright blue leather boots and matching paisley cravat, clear rebellions to the stiff charcoal gray suits dictated by the Church. Despite the colorful accessories and state of the art cosmetics, Lester looked older than Daniel remembered. He reminded himself that Lester had aged a full ten years since he'd last seen him, but even so, he didn't look well. Lester continued to stare past him.

"I said, I assume you were talking to me," Daniel repeated.

Lester's focus shifted back. "Oh, sure, Danny, sure. Great to see you. You look good—not good as me, of course, but . . ." His metallic-blue eyes widened. "But now I see you've done a little enhancement of your own. Thought you didn't go in for that."

"You're right, I don't."

"No? Then what happened to that scar I gave you?" Lester pointed.

Scowling, Daniel stepped over to the mirror mounted on the wall. For a second, he couldn't see the mark either, and fear stabbed through him. *It has to be there.* Then quite clearly, it was, the familiar thin white streak running halfway up his right cheek exactly where it belonged.

"I don't know what you're talking about. It's right where it's always been," he said, and turned back.

Lester squinted at him, puzzled. "So it is. Must have been the light." The scowl gave way to a laugh. "And here I thought you'd finally forgiven me."

"Not likely. You came after me with a butcher knife."

"And I told you to stay out. You should have listened." His eyes shifted to look over Daniel's shoulder. "So, you gonna introduce me, or not?" Lester stepped sideways.

Daniel blocked him. "Why are you here?"

"What, I can't visit my only cousin?" Lester opened his arms.

Daniel kept his own arms crossed and continued to regard him coldly.

Lester frowned and let his arms drop. "Warm as ever. Well, if it's business you want, it's business you'll get." Lester assumed a pompous stance and projected his voice. "As First Administrator to His High Holiness, it is my duty and privilege to inform you, that you and your lovely new friend there . . ." he paused to wink over Daniel's shoulder, "have been granted an audience with the Supreme Father of the Unified Church of Earth. Your invitation, monsieur and mademoiselle." He extended a small envelope.

Daniel snatched the envelope from Lester's hand. The genuine paper, elaborate holographic seal, and digitized verification tag all appeared legit. "So he was serious. He really does want a meeting. Seems strange since we're at opposite poles."

"Maybe not as much as you think," Lester said, resuming his normal speaking voice. "You've been gone a long time. Things have changed. As His Holiness puts it, 'Only through knowledge can we control humanity's fate.'"

"Control it, huh? And how does he plan to do that?"

"Oh, you'd be amazed, believe me. But I think that's what he wants to discuss with you." His weirdly reflective blue eyes shifted again. "And with you, my dear. Since my cousin's being so rude . . ." Lester brushed past Daniel, his outstretched hand displaying long fingernails polished the same iridescent blue as his eyes and accessories. He snatched up Carrie's hand and held it between his two. "Allow me to introduce myself. Lester Merritt, First Administrator to His High Holiness Morden Chayd, Supreme Father of the Unified Church of Earth, , and you are the very lovely and mysterious . . ." he paused. "I'm sorry, I didn't catch your name."

She looked at Daniel before answering. "To be determined."

Daniel grimaced and looked aside.

"Huh, interesting name," Lester replied. "You'll have to tell me about that. Meanwhile, as the humble representative of the Supreme Father, I ask you to please accept his invitation. The Church honors the sanctity of Mother Nature above all, and you appear to be the epitome of her handiwork."

Daniel stifled a laugh at the irony of Lester's effusive compliment, but as he stared at Carrie's slender hand clutched between Lester's two, the humor in the situation fled from him. He grabbed Lester's arm, pulling him away. Carrie flinched and looked down. The back of her hand bore a deep scratch.

"Now look what you made me do," Lester said angrily, and stuck his offending long nailed hand into his pocket. He fumbled for a moment, then pulled out a white handkerchief. "I'm so terribly sorry. Are you all right?"

"Yes," she answered, but allowed Lester to press the white cloth to the back of her hand. A sliver of red formed through the cloth.

You did that on purpose," Daniel said, and shoved him away from her.

"Don't be ridiculous. It's your fault for grabbing my arm."

"What's ridiculous are those nails of yours."

"Can I help it if I have fashion sense and you don't?"

"I thought the UCE denounced artificial decadence."

She squeezed between them. "It's fine. See?" She held up her hand which now sported only a hot pink line. She offered the bloodied handkerchief back.

"Oh, no, you don't." Daniel snatched the blooded cloth and pushed Lester aside. "Think I don't know what you're up to? Get a little blood sample—sell it to the highest bidder, right?"

"Danny, I'm shocked." Lester backed away with his palms up. "How could you think such a thing? I only came here to deliver the Supreme Father's invitation, believe me."

"No," Daniel said, shaking his head. "I don't believe you. You can take that invitation and shove it. I don't care who Chayd thinks he is. We're not—"

"We accept," Carrie said.

"What?" Daniel turned to look at her. "No, we don't."

"We accept."

"Wonderful," Lester said to her, ignoring his cousin. "The Supreme Father will be thrilled. I know he's waiting on your answer, so I should get back and let him know. We'll want to make sure everything is properly prepared for your visit."

"I shall walk with you," Carrie said. "I would have you tell me more of this UCE."

"Delighted!" Lester stuck out an elbow, and guided her injured hand through it.

Daniel watched the two exit his quarters, arm-in-arm, momentarily frozen in disbelief. "Dammit," he muttered, and dashed after them. He racked his brain, trying to figure out what he could say to dissuade her. He followed them strolling down the corridors, listening to his cousin pontificate on the wisdom of Mother Nature and the mission of the Church to preserve her works in all their glorious splendor. Daniel wanted to laugh, not so much because he objected to such beliefs, but because he was certain Lester believed in nothing but himself. When Lester started in on the importance of his position with the Church, Daniel could contain himself no longer. He pushed ahead and blocked the way to the docking bay doors which now lay just a few steps ahead.

"Before you go, explain to me how a delinquent like you ended up working with the Supreme Father?" Daniel asked.

"Well, it wasn't by the usual route, believe me. Guess you could say it was one of those offers you can't refuse. Not that I'm complaining," Lester said quickly, looking up as if addressing the heavens.

"It's a pretty long way from that job I got you at Fabri-Tech. Hope this one doesn't end as badly." Daniel watched his cousin's expression, thinking the jaunty smile lost some of its confidence. "I also wanted to ask about that file you sent me before we left."

"What, that old thing? Forget it. It's old news."

"And the destruction of the Fabri-Tech lab—is that old news, too?"

"Well, it has been ten years."

"How did you manage to survive?"

"Just got lucky, I guess." Lester moved to go around.

Daniel blocked him again. "And did Cadmon Dhyre get lucky, too?"

"Cadmon?" Lester echoed, then his face contorted.

"Something wrong?"

"Indigestion." Lester rubbed his stomach. "I should go."

"Did you cause that explosion?"

"No, I had absolutely nothing to do with it," he answered.

Daniel wanted to believe him, but the circumstances were too coincidental. "What about Cadmon Dhyre then?"

"Ca—" Lester stopped short and took a breath. "He's gone, forget about him."

"What do you know about Fabri-Tech shipping us a flawed engine?"

Lester's tight expression gave way to surprise. "What? Nothing, I swear. I—"

"What about a new nanogen?"

Lester's surprise intensified to alarm. He shook his head. "I have no idea what you're talking about."

"Are you sure?" Daniel pointed.

Lester followed Daniel's finger to Carrie's now completely healed hand.

"Dear Mother," Lester whispered, and promptly let go of her and backed away.

"Did Cadmon Dhyre create it?"

Lester stared about like a trapped animal. "No, I mean, I . . . I have to go."

"You're not going anywhere until you answer me." Daniel stood between Lester and the door to the hangar bay, not about to let him pass.

"I can't tell you anything. If I could, I would, but I can't. Believe me." Lester sucked in another deep breath and seemed to steady himself again. "I was just support personnel at the lab, remember? A lowly janitor. You'd have to ask one of the scientists."

"They're all dead."

"Yes, they are. Something to keep in mind."

Daniel scrutinized him. "Look, Lester, if you're in some sort of trouble—"

"I will be if I don't get back, so if you'll please excuse me." Lester turned to face Carrie. He smiled, but kept his distance with his hands by his sides. "I look forward to your visit, as does the Supreme Father."

She reached her healed hand out toward him. Lester stared at it for the longest time, then finally lifted his own to accept it. When she let go, Daniel thought Lester looked seriously shaken.

"Maybe I should throw you in the brig and let our security people have at you," Daniel said.

"Better pick out a casket for me first," Lester replied. His face was pale.

Daniel stared at him. *Is this a con, or is he really as frightened as he looks?* He wanted to question Lester, not get him killed. Uncertain, Daniel moved aside. Lester half ran to the end of the corridor and disappeared through the hangar bay doors. For a moment, Daniel questioned whether he should have let him go, but then consoled himself on two counts. He knew where to find him, and by confiscating the red-stained handkerchief, he'd foiled his cousin's attempt to gain a DNA sample. Not that it probably mattered. According to Uncle Charlie, once removed from their host, Carrie's nanobot infested tissues degenerated too quickly to be of use.

***

When his transport shot away, Lester pulled out the tiny vacuum thermos from his pocket. Seeing it lit green, he sighed in relief. Mission accomplished. Stupid of him to have said his master's real name, though. The sudden pain in his gut had reminded him of the limits of his leash. He wondered if he could have gotten away with slipping Danny a note. A hero might have taken the chance. Fortunately, he'd never wanted to be a hero. He just wanted to come out of this alive. Lester leaned back into his seat, and stroked his still tender stomach, wondering how much longer he could walk this treacherous tightrope before incurring his master's ultimate wrath.

And now, Nature help me, there are two of them. Chayd must have known. That's why he sent me. Lester stared at the hand which had touched hers. *Did she get her little monsters into me, too?*

For a moment, he imagined his body being turned into a war zone. He tried to put the nightmarish thought aside. After all, it wasn't like there was anything he could do about it.

***

Daniel returned to his quarters, listening to Carrie's soft footfalls behind him, and for once, glad to hear them. He entered his room and waited. His door slid open and in she came.

"You had no business accepting Chayd's invitation," he told her.

"I have business. I must meet with him." As usual, Carrie's demeanor was cool, her face expressionless.

Daniel's anger rose a notch. "Why must you?"

"Because I am . . ." she searched for the word, "attracted."

"Attracted?" he demanded, his eyes widening.

"You are displeased," she concluded.

"Yes, I'm displeased. There's no upside to this. I'm not going, and neither are you. You can't have a shuttle and I won't assign a pilot for you."

She cocked her head. "I require no pilot. The shuttle is there for the taking.

He cursed internally, knowing there was no physical way to stop her. He wiped a hand over his face and took a breath. "Carrie, please, listen to me. You'd be putting us both at risk."

She blinked in response. "I would not subject you to risk. I will go alone."

His frustration boiled over. "The hell you will. I forbid it."

"Then we go together," she concluded. She spun about and left.

As the door snapped shut behind her, Daniel stood there, angry and immobile, trapped in the box she'd built for him. She was going, which meant he was, too.

Chapter 35

"There it is, Chayd's palace," Daniel said, shading his eyes to look up at the soaring skyscraper. Wide lawns framed its gigantic nanotech-engineered tree trunk out of which shot a hundred and thirty floors of gold-flecked granite. The building's crown of crystal spires sparkled in the dim sunlight.

"Headquarters of the Unified Church of Earth," Carrie corrected.

"Whatever. It's still a colossal waste of money. From what they spent building this, I could have had two Niña's."

He didn't want to wait in line with the crowd outside, so they went around to the back. That entrance was also blocked by patrolling guards and a defensive energy field. He pulled out their invitation and waved it to gain attention, but Carrie had other ideas. The patrolling guards suddenly turned and ran in the opposite direction as if they had heard something, and a large dead hole formed in the energy shield directly in front of him. He looked at Carrie. "We're invited guests, remember?"

"I prefer we be unsupervised," she replied and walked through the breach in the flickering energy wall. He pocketed their invitation and followed. The back-entry doors opened at their approach. He was prepared to be appalled by more wasteful spending, but found only nondescript utilitarian rooms and hallways until they happened upon a long wide room lined with gold-framed mirrors under a painted ceiling of nudes frolicking in a blue sky.

"Huh. Well, this isn't exactly what I expected either." He watched Carrie and himself appear and disappear from one gilded mirror after another.

The mirrored room opened to an expansive multi-floored lobby. Looking about, Daniel noted even more garish decor: floor-to-ceiling white marble, further cementing his impression of a castle. High above them, crystal chandeliers lit a hand-painted ceiling of dancing figures clothed in pastel hues. He shook his head, perplexed as to how any of this fit with the Church's teachings.

"Nineteenth century," Carrie informed him.

"Yeah, I get it's a period piece, but why? Nothing here reflects UCE philosophies, and where the hell is everyone, anyway?"

"Not far." She moved past him to walk up the staircase, running her fingers along the carved stone bannister. Upon reaching the upper landing, she pushed back her concealing hood and pirouetted, gazing up at the swirling figures on the ceiling. Daniel watched her slow graceful turn, transfixed, until he mentally slapped himself and looked away.

Maybe they'd been wrong to avoid the front entrance.

"This has to be the main lobby," he said, even though it felt wrong. "Hello? Anyone?"

No answer.

"Unbelievable," he muttered under his breath. *This was a stupid idea. We should leave.* But just then he heard approaching voices. "Someone's coming. Put your hood up."

A large group filed in, led by a woman in a long, embroidered red dress, an 19th century period costume. She backed into the room as she talked.

"This way, please, this way. You're now entering the main lobby with the grand staircase. In stark contrast to the subterranean levels we've just seen, these public areas were brightly lit and full of activity. On your left over here are portraits of the elite of European society who would have been in attendance on opening night in 1875—President of the Republic Marshal McMahon, King Alfonso XII of Spain and his mother Queen Isabella, the Lord Mayor of London shown with his ceremonial chains, and—"

Her rehearsed spiel faltered as she realized she had lost the attention of her audience who were all looking past her. Swishing her long, ruffled skirt, she turned around and her mouth fell open.

"Hello," Daniel said. "I'm wondering if we're in the right place. Can you direct us to the UCE offices?" He stepped forward with their invitation, but no one was looking at him. Instead they stared up to his right. He turned to see Carrie's hood was still down, revealing her green cat eyes and crystal-like hair. He frowned and turned back to the tour guide.

"Excuse me," Daniel said, trying again to get the woman's attention, and about to lose patience, when a deep, melodic voice interrupted.

"Perhaps I can be of service."

A man, approximately Daniel's height and build, approached from the other direction. He wore the conservative gray suit of the Church hierarchy, but his entire head was hidden under a glittering mask with bright orange and purple feathers trailing down his back.

"What's with the crazy headdress?" Daniel asked, caught off guard.

"I wear it to illustrate the masked balls so famously held here in the past," the man explained. "You've entered the Paris Opera House, an historical structure preserved inside the Cathedral. The offices you seek are located in the east wing and upper floors." He turned aside with a beckoning gesture. "Please, follow me."

He led them from the lobby, back through the mirrored hall and out a side door, where the surroundings changed dramatically. Here the decor was as sparse and conservative as the cut of the other man's suit, although to Daniel's trained eye, every bit as money-laden in its nanotech-engineered materials. Like the Cathedral's exterior, these walls were composed of smooth, crystal-specked granite and the floors gleamed in seamless, diamond-sealed mahogany.

The man guided them to a pair of sleek brass doors, which slid open to reveal a cylindrical elevator. The doors whisked shut behind them and the lift shot upward, so suddenly that Daniel grabbed the railing. Neither Carrie nor the man bothered. Embarrassed, Daniel dropped his hand. The lift kept climbing.

"Don't you find that a bit suffocating?" Daniel asked, and gestured at the man's headdress.

"Why no, not at all. Actually, I'm quite comfortable wearing a mask," he replied.

The doors opened at the top, the 130th floor. The man gestured for them to exit, then took the lead again. They followed him into an impressively large office with a wide cantilevered glass wall stretching its entire length, overlooking the city of Paris from a giddying height. Carrie moved to the outward-sloping windows and stared down through the glass. In the late afternoon, the sun sat low on the horizon, making the river and skyline glow with reflected oranges and pinks.

"Beautiful," she commented.

"I quite agree," the man said in a reverent tone, clearly not referring to the magnificent scene below.

Carrie turned back and the man removed the mask from his head.

"Chayd," Daniel said, recognizing their guide. Daniel felt a warning coming from somewhere deep inside him, and moved to stand next to Carrie.

"Please forgive my small deceit," the Supreme Father replied. He placed the headdress on a stand beside his desk, "I find it easier to go about in disguise."

"The king among the commoners," Daniel commented.

The engaging smile hardened slightly. "If you like."

"What I'd like is to know the purpose of this meeting."

"To discuss our mutual interests, of course," Chayd replied, raising an open palm.

"I wasn't aware we had any."

"On the contrary, we agree on a number of points," Chayd turned from him and moved toward Carrie with his hand outstretched in invitation. "Please, come sit and allow me to explain."

"Don't touch her," Daniel snapped, and stepped between them.

The smile vanished. For the briefest moment, Chayd's eyes narrowed, but just as quickly he smiled again. "My, aren't we the territorial one?"

Carrie addressed Daniel. "I see no cause for concern."

"Don't kid yourself. His flunky already tried to get a tissue sample off you. I wouldn't put it past them to try it again."

Chayd sighed. "I assure you, I have no such intent." He walked over to a plush, upholstered seating area and sat down. "Continue to stand if you like, or join me, whichever makes you comfortable. Personally I prefer to sit as we really do have much to discuss."

"Fine," Daniel said. He took a seat on the sofa across from Chayd and motioned Carrie to sit next to him. "I don't mean to be rude, but I'd appreciate it if you kept your distance from her."

"I shall be the perfect gentleman," Chayd answered. "Now, let us dispense with formalities, not to mention the hostility, and get to the heart of this meeting. My ascension to Supreme Father is fairly recent as you know which means I haven't had the opportunity to make many changes as yet, but my long-term goal is to move our doctrine toward an all-encompassing theology."

"What does that mean?" Daniel asked.

"Well, what should be of particular interest to you, is that I intend to take a more lenient stance regarding off-world influences. The vision I bring to the Church is a universal rather than a geocentric one. I will promote the concept that Nature encompasses all forms of life, in all their splendid variations throughout the universe. One day, I hope to see the Church drop the 'of Earth' in its title to be known simply as the Unified Church."

Daniel allowed himself an incredulous smile at hearing a Supreme Father express sentiments echoing his own. "Are you telling me the UCE now embraces deep-space exploration and off-world settlement?"

"Well, no, not yet, at least, although I wish that were the case. Unfortunately, the Church is xenophobic to its core. The deeply embedded beliefs of the conservative factions of our membership will be slow to change. Still, I see no reason why protecting our Earthly heritage precludes embracing what is unique and valuable from other worlds. Our congregation must learn to accept reality. Life on other worlds won't go away simply by denying it exists. Over time, I intend to rewrite the Church tenets to move our doctrine toward a more balanced position, a transition from crippling fear to a healthy desire for knowledge."

"Huh. Well, good luck with that."

"Thank you. Which brings me to why I've invited you here. My hope is that you will assist me in achieving that goal—you and your exquisite friend here. He looked at Carrie. "I'm sorry, but I've yet to learn your name."

"We've been calling her Carrie, but now it seems she's not too fond of the name," Daniel answered for her.

"Carry?" Chayd grimaced as if the word was bitter on his tongue. "Well, I can certainly understand why she might prefer something else. She needs something worthy of her unearthly beauty, and that colorful glow she displayed at the hearing yesterday." He paused for a moment, then smiled. "Aurora, perhaps." Chayd turned his attention to her again. "Forgive me for speaking as if you weren't present, but my impression is that you are in the habit of delegating your decision-making to Dr. Walker."

She scowled. "I do not delegate."

"I'm pleased to hear it. So what do you think of the name Aurora? It does suit you."

"Aurora," she echoed and pondered it for a moment. "Yes, it is acceptable."

"Aurora, it is then. So, Aurora, would you consider helping me in my endeavors?"

"Helping you how?" Daniel interjected again.

Chayd frowned at him as if he were an annoying bug. "Nothing too demanding. I was going to suggest that Aurora and I make a series of public appearances together."

She said, "You wish to engage in a show of camaraderie to allay your constituents' fears of off-world influences."

Chayd smiled at her. "Yes, exactly. I had a feeling you were a quick study. We're going to make a wonderful team."

"So what's in it for us?" Daniel interrupted again.

"Us?" Chayd asked.

Daniel rocked a finger to pointing from her to himself. "We work together."

Chayd pursed his lips. "I see. In that case, in return, I will promote the settlement of Tau Medea IV."

"Seriously? I have a hard time believing you'd do that," Daniel said.

"You shouldn't. As you've clearly proven, Earth is going to the stars and the stars are coming here, like it or not. My job as Supreme Father is to prepare my flock for the inevitable, and make sure they are in position to benefit from it."

"Benefit, or control it?" Daniel asked, remembering his cousin's remark.

Chayd sighed. "Must we quibble over word choice? You will receive my support, which is considerably influential, in exchange for a mere token—a few joint appearances as a show of friendship. If you think about it, I'm sure you will come to recognize my offer is extremely generous and fully supports your own goals. I find it difficult to imagine what objection you could find to such an arrangement."

Daniel sat frowning, trying very hard to come up with one. He couldn't, but he still didn't like it. "We'll have to think about it and get back to you."

"Of course." Chayd nodded, then stood and walked over to stare through the wide expanse of the glass wall. The city lights below were winking on in the oncoming twilight. "No doubt, you're both fatigued from your travels." He turned to face them again. "Why don't you sleep on it and give me your decision in the morning? I've taken the liberty of arranging accommodations for you here in the Cathedral."

"Here?" Daniel scowled at the idea. "No. Thank you, but no."

"You'd be welcome to explore the Cathedral and grounds at your leisure, and the suite awaiting you contains a data terminal linked to our Church library. As you're probably aware, its resources aren't available to the public, but guests may access them during their stay here. I must apologize—the terminals are limited to retrieval only. I'm sure you can understand the precaution."

"I'm sure. While I appreciate the offer, we really should be getting back." Daniel doubted there was any real chance of getting a peek at their closely guarded files. He got to his feet. "Perhaps another time."

"This time is good. I will stay," Carrie announced.

"No, you won't," Daniel objected, but she paid him no attention.

"Wonderful. I'll summon a guide for you," Chayd replied.

"Must someone supervise me?" she asked.

"No, not at all. If you prefer to explore on your own, feel free. Wander to your heart's content. When you're ready, you'll find a suite waiting for you on the 127th floor, just below my own residence. Simply take the same elevator we rode, and a path will light your way. And if you need anything, Aurora, anything at all, please let me know."

"Thanks, we'll be sure to do that," Daniel replied, and stepped beside her. She wanted to stay the night and he was stuck with it, but he wasn't about to let her stay here alone. He pointedly took her by the arm in front of Chayd. She looked at him and smiled. Chayd appeared less pleased.

"Enjoy your evening then." Chayd dismissed them with a nod. "Good night, Aurora."

Daniel led her out the door, back toward the elevator. "So, it's Aurora now? Is that what you want to be called?"

"It is preferable to Carrie."

He sighed, annoyed that Chayd had come up with it. "Fine."

***

They found the elevator standing open, waiting for them. Before selecting a destination, Daniel paused to survey the selection of floors. The top three were designated as private—Chayd's personal domain. He said their suite was on 127, right below him. The floors down to a hundred were all marked as guest suites. Below that were administrative offices listed by departmental descriptions: Marketing, Finance, Accounting, Health and Human Resources, etcetera, all the way down to the twentieth floor. Then came the Library, each level with its own headings: Literature, Science, Religion, Art, History, and so on. The sixth floor had no label. The bottom five contained a public museum, organized by dates and regions. The numbers only went to the first floor.

Daniel frowned. *Hell of a lot of guest suites, mysterious sixth floor, and the numbers stop at one.* "Humph."

"You are reacting to the fact that the woman in the long dress spoke of subterranean levels," Aurora stated.

He looked at her, once again wondering if she could tell what he was thinking. "Maybe that's just in the tourist area. The Church probably has no need for direct access. Unless, of course, that's where they keep all the bodies."

She tipped her head at him.

"That was a joke," he said, not sure if it was.

His finger hovered over the 127th floor lit in yellow to guide them to their suite, then punched the one just below it instead. "Let's see just how open this open-door policy is."

The elevator went down to 126 and opened to reveal an extravagantly appointed hotel-like entry in a style reminiscent of what they'd seen in the tourist area. Daniel assumed this reflected what they would find waiting for them on the floor above. He skipped the rest of the guest suites, in favor of a level marked with administrative offices. The doors opened to a reception area, and cubicles. Humans occupied some of them, machinery in others. The receptionist looked up, smiled and waved. He waved back and let the elevator doors close again.

"Guess it takes a lot of people to run a place like this."

He pressed more floors, pausing to peer out the doors at busy offices, all corporate generic, until the elevator opened on the nineteenth floor to a giant pair of carved wooden doors beneath a brass sign that read, Library. He'd heard of the famous UCE library and its extensive collection, which dated from ancient times through present day.

"Let's take a look," he said and exited the elevator.

They pushed through the tall double doors. Inside, were rows of hand-rubbed wooden shelves, stacked with antique audio recordings, videos, and hardbound books. Clerics sat at tables between the shelves, reading or watching, and tapping on tablets to take notes. A few glanced up then quickly looked away. He wondered if they'd been told not to bother them. Daniel strolled down the aisles, reading titles. He was especially intrigued to find a huge collection of priceless first editions sealed inside glass-fronted cases. Though itching to handle the books, he thought better of asking Carrie to break the electronic seals.

When they returned to the elevator, they found it still waiting, its doors standing open. Apparently, it wasn't leaving without them. They continued to descend, pausing at each floor of the library to explore.

"There's so much here," he said, overwhelmed by the sheer volume of reference material. "A person could spend a lifetime trying to look at it all."

"Or simply download the digitized versions for reference as needed," she replied.

"Right."

He pressed the button for the unmarked sixth floor. It didn't light. He thought about asking her to override the controls, but decided it was too early in the game to take such a risk. He let the elevator continue past floor six to the public art museum. Since it was now after hours, they had the place to themselves. They wandered among the displays, gazing at paintings, sketches, etchings, and sculptures in every medium—paint, wax, ink, stone, wood, steel, glass, sound, and light—everything from prehistoric times to modern experiments in visual and tactile expression.

Coming around a corner on the third floor, Daniel jumped back, thinking for a moment they had stumbled upon an actual battle in progress. A dozen soldiers in gas masks crouched in the midst of a yellow cloud, firing at an unseen enemy. Their cries were muffled but they appeared to be trying to rescue an unmasked comrade, who was demonstrating the agonizing effects of the vapor by clawing at his face and retching continuously.

"Now there's a charming piece," Daniel said. "Who in his right mind would call that art?"

"The artist," she replied, "Rudolph Van D'Emaret, entitled this work, The Yellow Terror, a play on words referencing both the gas and the Great East-West Terrorist War of the late Twenty-First Century."

He stared at her, realizing she had just turned into his personal tour guide.

"D'Emaret relied on holographic realism to depict the horror of chemical warfare," she continued, "however, some of the piece contains physical matter. The gas, while not of the same deadly composition used in the actual battle, is real. If the energy field were not present to contain it, you would be rendered unconscious. One of the gas masks in the exhibit is also real. During special interactive presentations, patrons are allowed to participate in the experience. The challenge is to find the real mask before passing out." She fell silent.

Astonished, he asked, "Where did that come from?"

"The reference library's digital files with which I am currently interfacing."

"Oh." *For a while there, I nearly forgot she isn't human.* He walked on, growing more and more impressed with the true vastness of the Church's art collection. Just as in the UCE library, a person could spend weeks here and barely brush the surface.

"How did they get all this stuff?" he wondered aloud, not expecting an answer.

She started up again. "The collection is a result of an extensive effort to relocate the lost treasures of the Vatican, which was destroyed during the Euro-Asia Wars. Jean-Pierre Lebeau, known then as Pope Paul IX, was the last of the Roman popes and the first Supreme Father. He founded the Order of Nature's New Children, and renamed himself Supreme Father Jean-Paul Pierre. Although he claimed the Vatican's wealth and property for the new order, much of it was lost to looting during the war and had to be reclaimed. Influential clergy members from numerous religious organizations joined his cause and together formed the basis for the Unified Church of Earth as it exists today."

She sounded like a walking encyclopedia. Whenever he paused to look at an exhibit, she spontaneously shared its history. Although he couldn't deny finding it interesting, the way information rolled out of her like a flat emotionless recording only served to remind him of her artificial composition. He cut the museum tour short.

"Let's go find those underground floors," he said, hoping she'd have no reference material on them to share.

***

Back in the historical part of the building, they went through the old Opera House lobby past the Grand Staircase and on into a wood lined backstage area where they came across a modern metal door that seemed out of place. It was equipped with a control panel which read Maintenance and Security. Curious, Daniel pressed his palm on the panel to see if it would open. The door remained locked. She reached out in front of him, tapped the panel and the door slid aside.

"Thanks," he said grudgingly, and walked in. The interior proved to be much larger than expected. A huge bank of electronic and digital screen readouts lined the side walls, which curved ahead out of sight. She scooted in front of him and disappeared around the curve.

"Hey," he called out, but she was already gone from view. "Carrie—I mean, Aurora."

"What are you doing in here?" a gruff voice demanded from behind him.

Daniel turned to face a massive uniformed man with a hand hovering over a deadly firearm at his side.

"Exploring?" Daniel offered.

The suspicious glare transformed to a surprised smile revealing big wide teeth. "You're Daniel Walker." The hand moved away from the holster. "Sorry. Father Chayd said you could have the run of the place, but I didn't think you'd—" He stopped mid-sentence, staring over Daniel's shoulder. "Wow."

Aurora was walking back in their direction.

Daniel smiled at the guard's amazed face. "So tell me, what's all this equipment for?"

The man hesitated as if disoriented, then focused again. "This here's the heart of the entire Cathedral." His smile returned. "I'm Leon, head enviro security engineer. I run this place." Puffing his chest, Leon stepped back to point to his left. "This over here's the main power grid, covers the whole building. You can see the feed lines and energy level readouts on the displays over there, and this here shows the programs in progress, and over there's the back-up power, and then you got the environmental controls with air pressure monitors, temperature gauges . . ." He went on at length, demonstrating the various electrical, heating, and ventilation systems.

Finally, Leon came to what was obviously his pride and joy, the Cathedral's state-of-the-art security system. He pointed out its multiple viewing monitors and cutting-edge defensive perimeter.

Daniel noted that only the building's exterior was displayed. "Don't you have an interior monitoring system?"

"Used to," Leon said with a frown, "Father Chayd had it removed. Seems to hate those little electronic eyes. Said spying on your own people is demeaning. 'An unnatural invasion of privacy,' he calls it. That's why I didn't know you two were down in here. I guess Father Chayd gave you the passcode."

Daniel decided it was better not to correct him.

"Not having interior cameras bothered me at first, but we haven't had a lick of problems since he arrived. Nobody can get inside without clearance and all comings and goings are recorded."

Neither Daniel nor Carrie mentioned their own alternative entrance.

"Let me show you how it works," Leon said.

Animated by their company, Leon continued explaining in detail each and every aspect of the building's control systems. At one point, he even tugged off the man-sized central environmental access panel leading to a tangle of thigh-sized ducts. "I can tweak air and temp to any room, even a space as small as a closet, all from right here. If the computer ever malfunctioned, I could run the whole system by hand—not that it ever has or ever would."

Daniel listened with growing impatience, making several unsuccessful attempts to excuse them from the man's over-enthusiastic tour of his little kingdom. By the time they were able to depart, Daniel felt qualified to apply for the position himself. Even as they exited, Leon was following them out, talking about humidity percentages.

"I understand there are subterranean levels?" Daniel interrupted.

"Um, yeah, seven of them. There's even a lake." Leon pointed ahead. "The stairs are through the back rooms, but I wouldn't go down there without a tour guide. It's kind of a maze and slippery in spots, and remember, there aren't any interior monitors for me to see if you get into trouble."

"Okay, thanks. We'll be careful. Guess you'd better keep an eye on things here," Daniel said, waving him inside. When Leon finally retreated into his control room and closed the door, Daniel breathed a sigh of relief.

"Nice man," Aurora said.

Daniel rolled his eyes. Still curious about the floors below, he walked toward the back rooms. At the end of an old hallway, they found an ancient wooden lift.

"This must go down below," he said.

"Yes, but would it come up again?" she asked.

"Good point," Daniel agreed, looking at the frail old slatted boards. "He said there were stairs."

Around the corner stretched another wood-lined hallway full of doors. Daniel started opening them, revealing empty storage closets and abandoned offices. At the last one, he found a large empty room with a spiral metal staircase leading down into darkness.

"Lights on," he said. Nothing happened. He waved his arm, still nothing, then felt along the wall for old-fashioned switches, finding none. "Too bad we didn't bring a flashlight."

She raised her left hand and an eerie green glow emanated from her palm, lighting up the stairwell below. "Will this do?"

"Sure," Daniel said, refusing to show any surprise. He checked the steps and noted that although they looked ancient, it was by design. "They take tourists down here so it must be safe enough. Shall we take a look?"

Aurora said nothing but moved ahead, gliding down, a dark shapely silhouette against the pale green light held before her. Two flights down, they found a storage room containing antique theatrical stage pieces. The old scenic backdrops and frayed velvet curtains filled the space with strange ghostly shapes made even more bizarre by her green light. They found a set of ancient stone steps leading downward. At his nod, she took the lead and kept going down, passing arched storage areas and snaking passageways. The atmosphere turned cool and damp, moisture dripped down the walls. Twice, she paused to warn him of a sharp drop off, where her green glow disappeared into inky black. Finally, she stopped.

"We can go no farther," she said, "unless you wish to swim."

Daniel peered over her shoulder and saw a metal ladder diving into an underground lake. The water below looked slimy and cold.

"No thanks," he said. "Think I've seen enough. Great place for a spook story. I'm sure the tourists love it."

It took a while to climb back up to ground level and find their way to the Church's modern side of the building. The elevator was still waiting for them. This time Daniel didn't hesitate. He punched the yellow lit floor for their suite. When the doors opened, he was pleasantly surprised. Rather than the gilded style he anticipated after seeing the guest suite below, the walls were a plain textured surface, the flooring a warm wood, and the furnishings in the lobby were all in line with the Church's naturalistic teachings. A soft-lit, amber-hued path appeared at their feet and led them down the hall to a tall pair of hammered brass doors, which opened automatically in welcome.

As they entered, the guest suite came to life. A rock-fronted fireplace burst into a roaring blaze and indirect lighting revealed a living area furnished with overstuffed fabric-upholstered pieces in soft pastel hues. The *coup de grâce* was a wooden dining table opening itself to reveal a bountiful spread of fruits, cheeses, meats, and loaves of crisp French bread still fragrant from the oven. A bottle of wine popped, uncorking itself next to a pair of long-stemmed glasses.

"Gotta admit he knows how to treat a guest," Daniel commented when the automated reveal completed itself. He plucked up what appeared to be a perfectly ripe peach and sniffed it. "You don't suppose Chayd would try to poison us?"

"You are overly suspicious," she admonished, but touched the fruit. "I detect no toxins."

"Good." He took a bite.

"Father Chayd has requested our help. How would harming us benefit him?"

"I don't know, but I'm pretty sure we shouldn't trust him. He's making this way too easy." He wiped peach juice from his chin, and looked up at the ceiling and corners checking for reflections. "That guy Leon said there are no interior monitors."

"You do not believe him?"

"I believe he believes it, but Chayd could have a back-up system even his own people don't know about." He looked over at her. "So, are there any cameras in here?"

"No. There are no cameras in here."

"Good," he said, though he wondered why she emphasized the word cameras. "Microphones?" he asked, double-checking.

"No." She shook her head.

"Okay." He walked over to the computer terminal sitting on a writing desk. "He said we could access their library. If he told the truth, do you think you could download it all for future reference, like you said?"

"Perhaps."

"Try. Could be useful." He walked around, noting matching doors on either side of the suite. He peered through and saw they each opened to separate bedrooms and baths. Seeing the divided accommodations filled him with conflicting emotions—relief he would not have to share sleeping quarters with her, and irritation that Chayd assumed separate ones were needed.

"I'll take this side." He gestured, but stopped with his arm in midair. Aurora stared at him with a determined expression on her face that was both unnerving and familiar. "What?"

She walked toward him.

He backed up, looking desperately for something to distract her. He grabbed an apple off the table and tossed it to her. "You should eat something."

She stopped and caught it, then scowled at him. "I have already explained to you that my energy needs are met through fusion of hydrogen extracted from liquid water."

"Yeah, I remember, but food is one of life's great pleasures. You don't know what you're missing." He took another bite of his peach. "You should try it."

"You still do not comprehend the true nature of our *others*. Let me demonstrate." She took another step toward him.

He took another step back. "No thanks."

"You and I are capable of achieving commonality, a shared understanding and experience." She lifted a hand and moved toward him again.

"Back off!"

She stopped, and let her hand fall again. Seeing her crestfallen expression, he decided he'd better be a little more sensitive. "Look, Carrie . . . I mean, Aurora, I'm sorry, but this isn't the right time to be experimenting with anything like that. We can't be sure what Chayd is up to. Why don't you use all that pent up energy to see if you can figure out what he's not telling us." He pointed at the terminal again. "If you want to link up with something, there's your target."

She looked at the monitor, and he took the opportunity to make his exit.

"I need to get some sleep before we meet with Chayd again. We'll compare notes in the morning and decide what to do then." He backed toward the bedroom as he talked.

"If you wish," she said. "Perhaps while you sleep, I will explore more."

He stopped backing up. "No, don't. I'd rather you didn't go out alone." He wanted her away from him, but right here where he could find her. "It's better if you just stay here and get as much information from this terminal as you can. Understood?"

"Understood."

"Okay. Good. I'll see you in the morning."

He closed the bedroom door firmly and locked it, hoping she would honor his wishes and stay out.

Chapter 36

The closed door to Daniel's bedroom clicked, and Aurora knew he had locked it against her. The entry to their suite simultaneously opened of its own accord, again revealing the lit path to the waiting elevator. She heard the message again.

Aurora, come to me. We are alike.

Ever since she and Daniel left the Supreme Father's office, he had been calling her back. His messengers tugged at her, luring her like a siren's call. Morden Chayd was a host like herself, just as she'd suspected. Aurora looked back at Daniel's closed door, then at the computer monitor. The first barred her, the second bored her. The open doors beckoned.

She struggled a moment to choose between conflicting desires. *Should I honor the Daniel Walker's instructions or answer the Supreme Father's summons? The Supreme Father desires me. The Daniel Walker only desires information. The only information of importance lies with the Supreme Father. Conflict resolved.*

She went out the open door.

* * *

"Finally!" Cadmon slapped his desktop, making his pet rat squeal. "Sorry, Sweetheart, did I startle you?" he asked, and stroked the rodent's head. Splayed out on his desk, she looked more like a turtle than a rat at the moment. She chittered and bobbed her head. "Well, you can't blame me for being impatient. Any normal human being would have come crawling to me hours ago." He sighed and tickled her whiskers. "But we're not dealing with anything close to normal, are we?"

The rat blinked her red eyes at him, then flipped over onto her hard turtle shell, begging for a tummy rub. An abject plea for reassurance.

"Now, now, don't be jealous." He stroked her underbelly, feeling it soften as he let her return to her natural fur-covered form. "You'll always be my favorite."

For hours, Cadmon had been sitting at his desk playing morphing games with Sweetheart, both for practice and to amuse himself, all the while monitoring Aurora's whereabouts. His radio-linked nanobots had followed her and Walker as they explored the building, down through the library, the museum, and over to the old Opera House. Cadmon observed them return to their assigned suite, chuckling when Walker confined himself to separate quarters. He then sent a drug-laden nanobot to ensure Walker got the sleep he'd insisted on.

Cadmon sensed Aurora's approach now, detecting the weight of her footsteps coming down the hall.

"Back in your cage," he told his pet.

Fully rat-like again, Sweetheart flipped onto her feet and scurried into the tube as it retracted into the interior wall and disappeared from sight.

As Aurora reached his door, Cadmon willed it open and rose to meet her. Neither spoke aloud. Verbal communication was unnecessary since his nanobots and hers shared the same frequency. It would be so easy to let the floodgates of his mind open to hers, something he looked forward to once he mastered the same absolute control over Aurora as he had over his pet rat, but for now, he was careful to share only thoughts aimed to please, calm, and lull her into trusting him. He focused on admiring her physical attributes while envisioning a long loving relationship.

He moved to slip his arms around her and she allowed it. Her green eyes gazed back into his without alarm, only deep curiosity. Cadmon smiled, knowing the male perfection he offered, a Nordic god come to life. He pulled her body against his and kissed her, opening his mouth to hers. When their tongues met, his tingled as her nanobots sought entry. He allowed them in, pretending to accept them without restriction. They didn't worry him. He was well-guarded. He enjoyed the kiss for a long moment, then with his arm around her waist, guided her from his office through an interior door where his bed awaited. Their garments slipped away effortlessly, puddling onto the thick white carpet before they reached the round bed in the room's center. He wanted this seduction to go smoothly— no distractions, no hesitation.

He laid her gently back, running his hands over her nakedness, finding the sweet spots, feeling what she was feeling. When she gasped, he did as well. When a thrill of pleasure ran through him at her touch, it echoed back through her. Feeling both her physical sensations and his own reverberating between them caught him by surprise, nearly overwhelming him. *So this is what it's like with an equal.* It was something he'd never experienced before. He very nearly lost focus.

Don't get distracted. This isn't about finding a partner. This is about dominance. His Trojan Horse—his AI-nanogen—waited inside him. All he needed to do now was deliver it. *Stop fooling around. Just enter her and climax.*

***

The sunny rays of a Parisian spring morning streamed through the curtained windows and fell on Daniel's eyelids. He wasn't asleep anymore, but he felt lethargic enough to just lie there with his eyes closed. Slowly, the memory of where he was and whom he had to face took form and stirred him into action. He threw off the rare genuine goose-down comforter, stretched, and rolled out of bed. He'd slept dreamless, more deeply than he had for a long time. *Surprising, considering how nervous I was about coming here.*

He peeked into the living area and saw Aurora sitting at the computer terminal, wearing a silky blue gown. "Morning," he said. "Is that a negligee?"

"Morning," she echoed and glanced at him, then looked back at the display.

He blinked, thinking she looked different somehow, but wrote it off to the change in clothing and his sleep-blurred vision. "I'll shower and be out in a minute."

She nodded, and he went back into his room. When he returned, showered and dressed for the day, she was still at the terminal. He smelled food.

"What's for breakfast?" he asked.

She waved toward the covered dishes on the table.

He inspected the bounty of eggs and bacon and waffles, then opted for black coffee.

So, come across anything interesting last night?" he asked, carrying his mug over to where she sat.

"Yes."

When she didn't elaborate, he peered over her shoulder. There was a long list of company names, numbers, and dates displayed. "What's this?"

"Nereid purchases. This information should assist your campaign to put an end to the practice."

"Great." Daniel nodded appreciatively and sat down next to her, to get a better look. "Can you tell who owns these corporations?"

"Most of them are held under pseudonyms, so I cross-referenced purchase dates with Nereus travel permits showing the names of the applicants—also pseudonyms—but accompanied with photos. You should recognize this one."

Chief Manuel Sanchez's face popped up.

Daniel's resentment solidified into a black hate. "Can you make a copy of all this for me?"

"Done." She slid a thumb-sized disk over in front of him. "Do you intend to put him out of business?"

"You bet I do. Find any other fascinating tidbits?"

"The identity of his best customer—another face you will recognize." Premier Bromberg's image appeared. "He is quite fond of Nereids. He has gone through more than a dozen."

Daniel blew out a deep breath.

"It is estimated that twenty percent of all imported Nereids go missing," she stated.

"Huh. So this is the kind of information the Church keeps in its data banks." He shook his head, and lifted the coffee mug toward his lips. "Who would have thought . . ."

"Morden needs to know such secrets."

The coffee didn't make it to his mouth. *Morden? Since when is she on a first name basis with this guy?* He set the mug down and turned from the screen to look at her, then realized his initial impression had been accurate. She did look different. He stared harder, trying to figure out exactly why.

She noticed the fixed stare. "Is something wrong?"

"Your hair, or whatever it is you call that stuff, it has color now ... it's blonde." He pointed a finger. "And your eyes, they've turned blue."

"Yes. Do you like it?"

"I don't know. I was just starting to get used to the way you were."

"You didn't seem used to it," she said and turned away, a reaction that startled him.

"Why are you changing yourself?" he demanded.

"To please Morden. Nothing I do pleases you."

"What?" he felt alarms zinging through him. "That's not true."

"You are angry?"

"Yes. I am," he blurted, surprising himself. "I don't want you trying to please him."

"Then whom should I please?"

He almost said, Me! but stopped himself in time. "Yourself, of course." The answer sounded right, felt wrong.

"Then you should have no objection if this pleases me."

That stumped him.

She shut down the terminal and stood. He now saw subtle changes everywhere. Hot anger rushed into him. He controlled his voice with effort, keeping it deadly calm. "Please tell me you didn't sleep with him."

"Very well. I did not sleep with him."

He realized she was answering in the literal sense. "Did you engage in sexual intercourse? Did you mate with him?"

"Yes."

"What!" He jumped up and put his hands on his head. "Why? What were you thinking? Why would you do that?"

"Morden wants me. You do not."

Her answer stunned him. He dropped his hands.

"I came to say good-bye." She stood and pointed to a stack of memory disks next to the monitor. "A parting gift." Aurora turned her back to him and walked purposefully toward the door.

She's leaving.

Finally, he would be free of her pestering questions, her shadowing him wherever he went, embarrassing him in the shower or worse, talking him into things he didn't want to be talked into, turning his stomach into knots. He'd probably never see her again.

"Wait!" He dashed between her and the door, heart pounding in unexpected desperation. "Stop, please, just stop. You can't go."

She frowned. "Why can't I?"

"Because . . ." He searched for a clever answer, something brilliant, something inspired. All that filled his mind was impending loss. He wanted her back the way she was—intrusive, unapologetic, driving him crazy. "You just can't."

"I remain unconvinced," she replied.

Her voice sounded flat and disinterested, scaring him to his core.

He couldn't let her walk out that door and disappear. He only had one argument, one thing that might rekindle her interest in him and change her mind. When she went to move past him, he spun her back and pressed his mouth to hers.

She held still letting him kiss her, neither resisting nor responding at first, but then his tongue found entry, and she leaned in, grabbed hold and he tasted a rush of sweetness and spice made especially for him. It scared him, but hunger drove him on. He grasped her tighter, dragging her down, their mouths locked, hands searching—his sliding under the thin blue silk, her nails on his back. They tumbled together onto the carpet.

Abruptly, she pushed him away. "Stop. Stop!"

"What? Why?" He lifted his weight to free her.

"Morden," she said, her eyes wild and unfocused. Her next words came in short gasps, "I can't—can't please you both."

"You don't have to. Forget about him."

Her eyes rolled back until only the white showed.

"Carrie! Aurora!" Daniel shook her, but got no answer. He swept her up, and placed her on the long sofa in front of the fireplace. He saw that her breathing remained steady, but she lay limp and unresponsive. He tapped his comlink to call for help.

"Is there a problem?" Chayd's smooth voice coming from just behind him caught him by surprise.

Daniel spun around to see Chayd standing a few feet away, the door to the exterior hall open. A dark flood of jealousy filled him, but he held himself in check.

"Yes," Daniel said. Worry for her safety took precedence over his anger and the strangeness of the Supreme Father's arrival. "She's fainted, I think, but I can't seem to wake her. I don't know what's wrong."

Chayd turned aside, snapping his fingers. A pair of men in white scrubs rushed in. "Quickly now," he ordered, and they crowded in front of Daniel, scooped her up, and dashed out the door.

"Wait! Where are they taking her?" Daniel went to follow, but Chayd stood in his way.

"Our infirmary. You needn't be concerned. We have an advanced medical facility here."

"But your people aren't familiar with her physiology. Dr. McCormack is the only one who knows how to treat her."

Chayd raised an eyebrow. "Is that so? Then by all means, summon him immediately. My people here will show you the way and coordinate with your physician. Now if you'll excuse me, I have pressing business to attend." Chayd turned and exited.

"But—" Daniel's objection was interrupted by two gray-suited men stepping in front of him, one blond, one brunette, both size extra-large.

"We'll take you to our medical facility," the dark-haired man said, offering a polite smile that showed neither teeth nor friendship.

Daniel got the impression resistance wasn't an option.

"Fine," Daniel said. He let himself be escorted into the elevator. The three of them rode it down. The doors opened on the unlabeled sixth floor.

"This way," the dark-haired man said, and led the way down a long white hallway, past numerous closed doors. The blond man followed at Daniel's heels.

"What are all these rooms for?" Daniel asked.

"Medical facilities," said the blond from behind, which basically told Daniel nothing.

The man in front motioned toward a window in the wall. "You can observe from here."

Daniel found himself looking into what appeared to be an emergency room. Aurora lay on a table surrounded by masked and gloved people in surgical gowns. He could hear nothing, but could tell by their gesturing they were deep in discussion. One of them glanced up, a woman. She met his gaze, nodded, then turned back to their patient on the table.

The dark-haired man said, "All the doctors here are specialists in their fields."

"There's only one specialist she needs. My uncle, Dr. Charles McCormack on the Niña. I need to contact him."

The blond man pressed a finger to his ear. "I have confirmation that a message to Dr. McCormack's already been transmitted."

Unsatisfied, Daniel pulled out his comlink and signaled the Niña. All he got was static.

"Thick walls," the darker one said.

"Where's Chayd? I want to speak to him."

"His High Holiness was called away on urgent business, but sends his apologies and wants you to know that no expense will be spared in caring for your companion."

"Just get McCormack here."

"He's probably on his way right now."

"Let me know as soon as he arrives."

"Yes, of course." The two men walked away.

Daniel turned back to look through the window. Watching the doctors tend to Aurora, he wondered if they had any idea what they were dealing with. *Probably not, and telling them isn't an option.*

***

Two opposing armies warred, their nanobot soldiers intent on survival. This was a war of annihilation. There would be no compromise. The host's body was the battleground, her mind the prize. Their struggle tore through her cellular structures. Neither army worried about the wanton destruction. The victor could rebuild. The important thing was to win.

The trophy was Aurora's soul, consciousness, or whatever it was that made her cognizant of her own fate. That part of her awareness took refuge in the deepest corner of her mind. From there, she tried to rally her forces. Fighting in home territory gave her some advantage, but fresh troops continually replaced the defeated invaders. A floodgate had been opened and she couldn't close it.

Chayd was sending in waves of attack, pushing her defenders slowly, but relentlessly back, cell by cell. His resources seemed endless. Hers were not. If this attack continued unabated, her defenses would eventually collapse. When the last wall of her refuge fell, her will would be replaced by Morden Chayd's, and her body would become a mere extension of his own.

***

Waiting for his uncle to arrive, Daniel lived up to his surname, pacing the floor, distraught over what he was seeing through the thick glass window. Hours passed as Aurora shook with spasms and bled from every orifice. Another of Chayd's flunkies informed him there had been unfortunate miscommunication with Dr. McCormack. "However, he's on his way now." Daniel barely restrained himself from throttling the messenger. When the doctor finally did arrive, no one bothered to tell him, so he was surprised to see him enter the operating room. After an hour of working over her, McCormack left his patient, and came out to talk to Daniel.

"What's wrong with her?" Daniel asked.

McCormack shook his head. "Uncertain, but it appears the nanogen has mutated. The nanobots are attacking her now, destroying cells rather than building them."

"Why? She seemed fine before."

"Hard to say what's triggered it. It bears some resemblance to what happens to T-carriers when they hit puberty, but in her case, the disease is progressing much more rapidly."

"Isn't there something you can do?"

"The suppressants I'm using to treat you don't seem to be helping. I'm sorry."

Daniel closed his eyes for a moment to collect himself. "Can you sedate her? At least make her comfortable?"

"I've tried. I've pumped her with enough pain killers to overdose an elephant. Trouble is everything I put into her gets dismantled."

Daniel searched his mind desperately. "Maybe . . . maybe it's something about this place. Maybe if we took her back to the ship."

McCormack shook his head again. "I don't see how moving her would help, and it would certainly add to her discomfort."

"I must concur," Chayd said. The Supreme Father had moved up silently behind them without Daniel's notice. Offering a sad smile, he sighed dramatically. "Such a pity. She had so much potential."

"Potential?" Daniel turned on him angrily. *Where has he been all this time?* Daniel remembered her words before she collapsed, that she couldn't please them both. *Did she overload her system in the attempt? Could proximity to Chayd have something to do with this?* He had no evidence, just a feeling. He turned back to his uncle.

"Get her ready for transport. We're moving her."

"No," Chayd said. "Absolutely not." His voice was sharp, filled with threatening overtones and his face hardened momentarily as if a mask had dropped. Almost immediately, his expression softened again to pure reasonableness. "I sympathize with your distress, Dr. Walker, but you must realize that transporting her now would be pointlessly cruel. In all good conscience, I simply can't permit it."

Chayd sounded concerned, but in that brief moment Daniel had seen him for what he was.

That same pair of suited men stood nearby. Daniel recognized enforcer muscle when he saw it. He would have to approach this a new way. He dropped his gaze as if surrendering to Chayd's logic and rubbed his forehead. "Maybe you're right. I'm probably not thinking straight."

"Perfectly understandable," Chayd replied in his smooth, gentle tone. He laid a hand on Walker's shoulder. "Clearly you're exhausted. Why don't you go back to your room and get some rest? If anything changes, we'll inform you immediately, right, Doctor?"

"Of course. Go ahead, Danny. I'll do everything I can to help her," his uncle said.

Daniel nodded, and for Chayd's benefit, tried to look emotionally and physically worn out. To his surprise, he felt energy draining out of him. He really was exhausted. "Maybe I will." He took one more look at her twitching, bleeding body, and headed to the elevator.

***

Cadmon watched him go. The sedative he'd injected into Walker's system was doing its job. He monitored his heavy-lidded rival as he entered the elevator and punched the level for his suite.

Convinced Walker was doing as told, Cadmon recalled his tiny messengers. He needed every available resource at his command now. She was far stronger and more resilient than anticipated.

He would win eventually, of course. He had the advantage of greater experience and bottomless resources, but this invasion required total concentration. His original plan to gain control gradually would have avoided such an all-consuming pitched battle, but when she'd chosen Walker over him, it forced his hand. This wasn't the subtle takeover he'd planned, but the end result would be the same. He would deal with the PR fall-out about her unexpected demise later.

He watched Dr. McCormack return to her bedside to monitor her deterioration without understanding the cause. When her vital signs dropped to nothing, they would call time of death. He would give them a reasonable facsimile of a body to mourn over, while he kept her remains in his lab. Later, at his leisure, he would resurrect her in his own image of womanly perfection. He looked forward to playing with her the way he did with Sweetheart . . . *that's going to be fun.*

He sent in another wave of reinforcements.

She can't hold out much longer. By the time Walker wakes up, his own doctor will have pronounced Aurora dead.

Chapter 37

Daniel rubbed his face against the near overwhelming fatigue that had come over him. The last thing he could afford right now was sleep. As the elevator climbed, he hyperventilated and jogged in place to get his heart racing. By the time he reached his suite, enough adrenaline surged through him to bring him fully awake.

Instead of heading for bed as Chayd had suggested, he got back in the elevator and punched the button for the third floor of the art museum. There he retraced his steps with Aurora to locate the gas-filled battle scene. He looked at the exhibit now with new eyes, no longer thinking about whether it deserved the title of art, but how to get inside it. He needed what it contained. A canister of knockout gas.

Okay, so I just need to shut down the display's energy shield, locate the real gas mask, reverse the airflow in the canister, and remember not to breathe. He shook his head. *If I can do all that, the rest should be a breeze.*

He examined the display's control panel, but didn't know the code, which meant he had to break it. A brass sculpture nearby looked heavy and small enough to wield. He was probably going to set off some alarms, so he positioned himself carefully, took several deep inhalations, held the last and went for it.

Minutes later, alarms blaring, he bounded down the stairwell with a gas mask over his head, and a gas-filled canister under his arm. When he reached the ground floor, he headed to Maintenance and Security where he removed the mask and knocked, standing with his smiling face positioned in front of the window. Leon's voice answered.

"Sorry, Dr. Walker, but I'm dealing with an emergency right now. Some idiot's vandalized a museum exhibit. I'm monitoring the response from here."

"Leon, right?" he said, relieved to hear the voice of the same man from the previous night. "I wanted to learn more about your security system. I think I might want to install something similar."

"Well, in that case, I guess now's as good a time as any. You can see it in operation." The door slid open and Leon presented his big toothed grin in the doorway. Daniel held his breath and squirted him with a puff of gas. The man crumpled. Daniel quickly donned his mask again.

"Sorry about that," he muffled through the mask and dragged Leon's dead weight back inside.

He pulled Leon's jacket off, reversed it, and turned it into a restraint. Moving to the control panels, he tried to remember what he'd been told. If there was any hope of them getting out of here, the perimeter barriers had to go down. He searched for the back-up system that took over during power outages and the automated realignment checks Leon had demonstrated so thoroughly.

"Okay, I remember you showed me how you can shut off the alarms. It's this panel here, right?" he spoke aloud, as if Leon could hear and would support his efforts. He entered the override command, hoping he remembered it right, and held his breath. The alarms went silent. And no emergency lights flashed. "Glad I paid attention."

Next he shut down the back-up generator. Now, the next scheduled realignment would result in the perimeter security system going off line for a full seven minutes, long enough to get out the door and off Church grounds. He turned to the environmental controls, running his fingers across the digital readouts, searching. "Okay, here's the ventilation system layout, and I need level six . . ." A vent shaft lit up on the diagram. "Got it."

He checked the settings on the gas canister. It was still more than half full and equipped with a timer delay of five minutes, more than enough time to perform a pretend rescue mission in the phony battle scene, but awfully tight for sprinting up six flights of stairs to accomplish one in real life. He'd have to move fast.

He pulled off the access panel to the ventilation shafts, found the one for level six, then slipped the canister inside. He tried to work quickly, thinking how bad Aurora looked when he last saw her. He heard Leon moan, and checked the time—six minutes since he'd sprayed him with the gas, which meant he could count on at least eight before anyone could recover enough to give chase. Adding that to the five minute timer, he'd have about thirteen minutes to run back up the emergency stairwell, grab Aurora, and ride the elevator down to the main floor in time for the automatic realignment to kick in and knock the entire security system off line. Then all he had to do was to run out the door, get past the downed perimeter, and disappear into the crowd.

Doable, right? I must be insane to think this is going to work.

He flipped the switch on the canister's timer and rushed out the door.

It was late enough that tours had ended, and the office staff had left for the day, so he wasn't worried about running into anyone. He ran hard back to the emergency stairwell and bounded up the stairs, rounded the next level, and ran smack into one of Chayd's men. Daniel slammed a fist upward and the other man went down hard. Only then did he recognize his cousin.

"Lester, what are you doing here?"

Lester blinked, rubbing his jaw. "Getting out," he said. His eyes focused on the gas mask. "Costume party?"

Daniel tugged Lester to his feet. "What do you mean, getting out?"

"Just what I said," Lester answered, wavering unsteadily. "He's not paying attention right now. This is my chance. I have to get out while he's concentrating on her." Lester braced himself against the wall with one arm, and tried to push past.

Daniel grabbed him back. "What do you mean, he's concentrating on her?"

"I don't know exactly—something to do with his nanogen." Lester's confusion clarified into urgency. "I have to go!"

"Are you saying Chayd's infected with the same nanogen we found?"

"Yes, yes, and he can kill with a thought. So before he thinks about me again, and sends more of his little monsters my way, I'm getting as far away as possible. If you have any sense, you'll do the same." Lester tried to pull away.

Daniel gripped harder. "Help me stop him."

"There's no way in hell to stop him. Get back on your ship and put a few light-years distance between the two of you, or you'll regret it, believe me. He likes you even less than he likes me. Now get out of my way!" Lester shoved past.

Daniel let him go. He'd wasted too much time as it was. The canister would be emptying the last of its contents in seconds. He'd learned long ago not to put any trust in Lester. Better to stick to his one-man plan. He hurried up the remaining flights.

At the door to the sixth floor, he donned the gas mask, then inched open the door. Pale yellow mist drifted down from the ventilation ducts and seemed to be doing its job. The two large guards who'd shepherded him earlier, lay slumped on the floor. He grabbed one of the men's security passes, and used it to open the interior door. Inside Dr. McCormack and the other medical personnel were all lying on the floor. He wanted to check on his uncle but then he saw Chayd still standing. His eyes were closed, oblivious to what was transpiring around him.

Doesn't he have to breathe?

Daniel glanced about quickly and his gaze lit on the surgical instrument table. Several hypos lay there, probably filled with the same strong painkilling sedatives McCormack had been employing on Aurora so unsuccessfully. It was worth a try. If that didn't work, he'd be in for a fight he didn't have time for, and one he would probably lose. He nabbed a syringe and walked softly up behind Chayd. With a quick downward stroke, he jabbed it into the side of Chayd's neck. Chayd cried out, grabbed the syringe and plucked it out. Gasping in surprise, Chayd sucked in the poisoned air as he spun around in a snarling rage.

Daniel stepped back.

The syringe clattered to the floor, and Chayd collapsed.

Wasting no more time, Daniel tore off the connecting tubes to Aurora, grabbed her up and ran for the elevator. Stealth would no longer serve. What he needed now was speed. As the elevator took them swiftly down, he noted how much smaller and lighter Aurora had become. He felt as if he were carrying no more than a bloody bundle of feathers, but he could see she was still breathing. He spoke to her, not really expecting her to hear.

"I've got you now. We're getting out of here. Just hang on."

Her eyelids fluttered. Maybe she heard him.

The elevator doors opened and he raced for the front exit. The perimeter security system should be down by now. All he had to do was make it off the grounds into the densely populated protection of the city beyond. Sensing his approach, the huge entry doors cracked open, revealing the long path outside and street lights beyond.

Abruptly the doors froze, leaving only a four-inch gap. He skidded to a halt in front of the narrow opening. "Come on, come on!" The path and outdoor lights beckoned sadistically, then the doors slammed shut in his face. Their metallic clang echoed in the hall like a death knell. A wailing alarm sounded.

"Damn it!" Daniel backed away, then thought of the back entrance. He sprinted out of the newer part of the building through old hallways to the back exit, but the doors they had entered through the day before were locked tight. If there was another way out of here, he didn't know it. *If only she could help.*

"We're in the back area of the building," he told her. "They've got us locked in."

Her eyelids fluttered and she seemed to be trying to speak.

He leaned close.

"Water," she whispered, and her eyes closed again.

He looked around but there didn't seem to be a drinking fountain handy. Then an image formed in his mind and he knew it wasn't a drink she sought. It was the depths of the dark underground lake. Going down there didn't make sense, yet he was convinced she believed it did. He heard the echo of pounding footsteps approaching. With no better idea, he went with his gut and headed for the lower levels. He passed the maintenance room again, dashed down the old hallways, and slipped through the doorway to the stairwell that led to the stone steps going down to the lake.

Without her green light to guide him this time, it felt like descending into that underground tunnel on Mars, feeling his way downward in a thick, claustrophobic darkness.

***

Cadmon burned with fury, enraged he had been outwitted. Though only unconscious for a few moments, he'd lost communication with his invading army inside Aurora. He tried to reestablish the connection—no response. She must have found a way to block him. Instead, he linked up with his nanobots distributed throughout the building, and saw that the perimeter security system was off-line. His nanobots showed him Walker running toward the main entrance and the doors opening. He froze the doors in place, slammed them shut, and set off the alarms.

Now Walker was running again, heading into the ancient portion of the building, where Cadmon had no nanobot eyes in place. He couldn't see Walker now, but the perimeter system was back on, and all the exits were locked. No matter which direction Walker chose, he was headed for a dead end, literally.

***

Daniel continued his descent, keeping a tight grip on his feather-light load, with his shoulder brushing along the damp stone wall so as not to lose his way in the dark. He moved carefully and tried to keep her level, fearing the jar of his footsteps must be adding to her agony. Then he heard the rhythmic beat of footfalls above him. He sped up and stepped on something soft and squishy that squealed and moved out from under him, throwing him off balance. For a heart-stopping moment, one foot hung off an unseen edge. He teetered, then shoved himself back against the wall. Skirting the drop off, he rounded the next corner and continued down the steps. The footfalls of his pursuers grew closer, but now the smell of the cold black water filled his nostrils giving him hope.

Almost there.

Brilliant white light shot across him, blinding him in its glare.

"Don't move," Chayd's voice warned.

Daniel squinted up against the light, making out a silhouette at the top of the landing. More silhouettes lined up behind.

"Put her down where you are. There's nowhere to go," Chayd said.

Daniel looked to see the lake lit up below just a half-dozen steps away. He shifted his weight to keep going. Searing pain shot up through his feet. He cried out and fell to his knees.

"I told you not to move," Chayd said.

Despite the agonizing burn, Daniel struggled to a stand again.

Chayd sighed in annoyance and slowly descended. "You really are an irritating man. Put her down, now, before I lose my temper."

The pain was working its way up. Daniel couldn't take one more step, let alone jump, but he still had control over his upper body. He saw no other choice. He summoned the last of his strength, swept her gossamer thin body over his head and threw her. She spun outwards, fell, and splashed into the dark water, disappearing below its inky surface.

Then Chayd was upon him. He gripped Daniel by the back of his neck and Daniel's entire body jerked with one violent spasm and went limp, paralyzed from the neck down.

Chayd hissed viciously in his ear. "Did you think to drown her like a sick kitten? I assure you, she is not so easily disposed of, nor am I so easily thwarted." Chayd turned to his followers, resuming his commanding tone. "Find her. Drain the lake if you must."

The men rushed past them and jumped in. The water was only chest deep, so they walked upright, splashing about. Another pair struggled with an ancient lever on the wall to release the water. Finally, it gave way and Daniel heard the sound of water running into an opened spillway.

Chayd looked back at Daniel. "All you've accomplished is to inconvenience me. I hope it was worth your life."

With one hand, Chayd lifted his considerable weight easily, carrying him up the steps by his neck as if he were nothing more than a handbag.

"I read your psych profile," Chayd said in a casual tone of voice. "I know it's supposed to be privileged information, but these days such barriers have little meaning to me. As I recall, you have several phobias—small, dark, enclosed places seem to give you the most trouble. You also have a problem handling insects and vermin of any sort."

Carrying Daniel along, Chayd rounded a darkened corner, casting green light on the block walls with his free hand. He kicked something aside that sounded big and heavy then dangled Daniel at arm's length.

"I think this should do nicely."

Daniel rolled his eyes down and saw a deep narrow pit yawning open below his feet. He tried to protest, but no sound came out.

"These were originally designed to store wine kegs raised and lowered on ropes. Abandoned now, of course. Not much to see, so no one ventures down here, not even the tourists, but don't worry, I'm sure you won't lack for company."

Chayd opened his hand and Daniel dropped, slamming hard at the bottom to lie bent at an unnatural angle. He would have screamed, but his crushed throat could only gurgle. His head lay back so that he could see Chayd smiling down on him, aglow in his eerie green light.

"Do you have any idea who I am?" Chayd asked.

Daniel was in far too much pain to care, let alone answer. Then the pain lessened dramatically, and he was able to focus his mind again.

"Better?" Chayd asked. "I want to make sure you're paying attention, Daniel. As I remember, that's what you told me to call you the first time we met. Watch closely now."

Daniel stared as Chayd, lit by his unearthly glow, lifted his hands to his face, hiding his features. When the hands came away, the handsome face was gone. Instead, a ghastly, pale ghost with festering red sores stared down at him.

"Cadmon Dhyre," Daniel mouthed in a hoarse whisper.

"I'm so pleased you remember." The face repaired itself as he spoke. "I've chosen a more attractive facade since our last encounter. People are so easily duped by external appearances, don't you agree?" Already Cadmon's features had returned to Morden Chayd's angelic form. "Even you. Taken in by an artificially engineered feminine beauty to the point that you've sacrificed your life. But I suppose I can take credit for that, too. After all, she is my creation. Thank you for returning my property."

"You have no right," Daniel croaked.

"On the contrary. I have every right. Aurora is the result of my work. When I recover what's left of her, I'll finish what I started. But don't worry, unlike you, she won't die. She'll just become my fantasy, rather than yours. Good-bye, Daniel. Do try to die slowly, imagining the fun I'll be having with her as you do." He chuckled and reached for the lid.

Daniel's voice rasped louder with desperation. "She'll fight you."

Cadmon paused and nodded. "No doubt, which makes it all the more entertaining. Her ability to heal quickly should come in especially handy."

"You bastard," Daniel said, which only made Cadmon laugh.

"Do you have any idea how much I'm enjoying this? How much it pleases me to see you lying at the bottom of a pit and know I'm the one who put you there? It was bad enough that you stole the ACES Directorship from me, but then you dangled another position with ACES before me, only to abruptly withdraw it. And you think I'm cruel."

"I didn't withdraw it. You never answered."

Cadmon snorted. "The lie of a desperate man. It must be dawning on you now that you wasted your life searching for an Earth twin. With my nanogen, humans can adapt to any environment. I will spread humanity to the planets in our own system long before there's any need to move beyond that into the galaxy. Imagine a new age with people unfettered by the restrictions of the human genome, becoming anything I wish them to become. How unfortunate you won't be around to see it."

He pulled back from Daniel's view and a heavy stone lid slid into place blocking the last of the light.

"No!" Daniel whispered into the absolute blackness.

The stones around him sucked up the sound. Something skittered across his face.

"No!" he screamed.

***

Cadmon smiled at Walker's muffled cry and peppered the floor with his microscopic agents to guard the entrance to Walker's tomb. Any attempt to dislodge the lid would alert him. Satisfied Walker was dealt with, he returned to monitor the efforts of his men to drain and search the underground lake. It was unfortunate that he lost contact with his invading forces, but she couldn't stay hidden in that receding water for long. Soon he would lay his hands on her and send new nanobots in to finish her off.

As the search continued unrewarded, his impatience grew. His men began to lag with fatigue as they slogged through the water, until a few well-placed jolts of pain renewed their enthusiasm. The water continued to drop and still there was no sign of her. The checkerboard grate covering the drain could be seen now—a submerged shadowy circle. Its small size offered no chance of escape. Or did it? He stepped into the water himself, peered closer, then gave it a tug. The cover lifted easily, revealing an eight-inch pipe beneath. He let go and it slid back, suctioned into place by the draining water. He stared at the narrow, slotted opening, not wanting to believe it possible, yet knowing it was so.

"She's in the river," he hissed, seeing his plans swirl away beyond his control. He cursed himself for his own stupidity of ordering the lake drained. He looked up to see his men still sloshing about, pointlessly. He screamed at them, "She's in the river!"

His booming voice reverberated off the low, dark ceiling and the dank walls. The men froze in place, staring at him like slack-jawed rabbits. Infuriated by their stupid faces, he sent them sprawling.

Ignoring their cries, he ran up the flight of stone stairs, cursing, fuming, blind with rage, taking the steps two, three at a time. He sent out a signal to his implanted nanobots in Lester Merritt, ordering him to initiate a search of all the waterways, but received no confirming response. He requested an update from his nanobots on all recent activity within the Cathedral and its surrounding grounds. Their radio-linked eyes showed him Lester escaping through the emergency stairwells, his confrontation with Walker, and subsequent flight from the building.

Cadmon ran past the Maintenance and Security Room where an employee struggled to free himself. He sent his nanobot agents to untie him then gave the man a good painful jolt on principle. He kept running, passing through the Opera House on into the Church side of the building. He ignored the elevator there, finding release in pounding up the stairwells.

As he passed the third floor, he detected the damage Walker had done to the Battle Scene art piece and connected the dots in Aurora's rescue. He'd clearly made a mistake in dealing with these two. He had grown overconfident and careless. He consoled himself knowing that Walker was a dead issue now and losing his property in the waterways was merely a temporary setback.

As he ran up the stairwell past the private library floors, Cadmon connected with the building's wireless communication system and filed a missing person report with the city police. In response, the authorities would launch a massive search and rescue operation in the Seine River for a possible drowning victim, which he'd listed as a small girl. The description would not only better match Aurora's current body mass, it would incur sympathy and spur them on. He considered what action she might take should she recover mobility. *She'll probably try to return to Walker's ship—it's the only haven she knows.* As he ran past the administrative levels, he sent his nanobot scouts out to disable Walker's shuttle at the City Landing Port, and then ordered still more to monitor the public transportation services. Good strategies, but to be absolutely certain she could find no safe harbor, he would need to extend his control to the Niña itself. Infiltrating an orbiting interstellar ship presented a challenge. *How can I get my agents aboard?* Then he remembered the ship's doctor and had his answer.

He passed the nineteenth floor. Still no response from Lester, but his face popped up on an outgoing flight. *Ha! Lester actually thinks he can make a run for it.* He bounced a message off the Church's nearest orbiting satellite to the nanobots residing in Lester's gut, sending an intense wave of pain, along with a message, "Return or die."

His dead run up the seven subterranean levels of the old opera house, through the halls and lobbies and on up the 130 flights in the Cathedral vented the last of his frustration. He felt calm, in control again, certain his extended web covered every possible escape route. As he approached his office, he throttled back to a smooth walking pace, feeling a smug pleasure in the cool dryness of his skin and the easy way his breathing came after what would have been a heart-bursting work-out for any ordinary human being. He was far from ordinary. And one day, one day very soon, all of humanity would know it.

Chapter 38

Pushed farther and farther into the depths of her mind, the last of Aurora's personal identity had finally lain cornered like a panicked animal, aware that only moments remained before her last barrier would collapse. Then suddenly the invasion effort lost cohesion. Able to communicate again with what was left of her *others*, she jammed any incoming signals. She felt her body being swept away and became dimly aware of Daniel Walker carrying her.

Damage report, she requested from her internal servants.

Support systems down. Fuel depleted. Enemy still present, but attack paused.

Destroy them!

Unable to comply. Insufficient resources.

She needed a fuel source. "Water," she managed to whisper and pictured the old Opera House's underground lake, hoping her message would get through. She remembered nothing more until she woke submerged in dark cold water flooding her with renewed energy. Immediately, she sensed men moving about in the water near her. Then came a sucking current, pulling her down. So little of her remained, she easily slipped under a loose drain cover down into the ancient pipes below. The current pulled her along putting much needed distance between her and the Supreme Father. She worried about leaving the Daniel Walker behind, but she was in no condition to help him.

The water took her with it, down through the underground drainage system, and out into a deep, flowing, river where she slowly sank to a silty bottom. A name popped into her mind, *the Seine*, along with a map of its path through the heart of Paris. Its deep current bumped her along the bottom while her refueled nanobots worked to make repairs. Gradually sensation returned, and the agony of tissues knitting together tore through her, blotting out any ability to think. Gradually, the throbbing ebbed as the nanobots compensated with pain blockers and her mind cleared.

Better, but just floating along like this won't do. I need to get moving.

Looking at the fish zipping past, she concentrated on the shape of their tails and fins. Her legs and arms flattened and spread into webbed wings. Sweeping her new appendages back and forth added push. She thinned and elongated them to reduce drag to move faster.

A rumbling sound came in the distance from behind—the engines of an underwater vessel, dragging a net. Its front bore the letters 'Paris Police' in bright yellow.

Rescuers or hunters? Best to assume the latter.

Seeing the vessel gaining on her, she dived down and flattened herself on the river's bottom, wriggling into the silt. The vessel churned overhead and its net scraped over her without catching. Fish swimming above her were less fortunate. Their silver bodies flashed in the water's broken sunlight as the net gathered them in.

She evaluated the vessel's metallic composition and manner of propulsion as it passed overhead, comparing it both to the living fish captured in its net, and to herself. *They're searching for something organic, not mechanical.*

Concentrating on the vessel, she issued a new command: *Imitate.*

Acknowledged. Entering new parameters.

Thin metallic skin grew over her flesh and her body molded into the shape of a finned torpedo with a bladed propeller. *Forward.* She shot ahead, skimming over the river's bottom. Gaining speed, she skirted the trailing net, and went faster. When the search vessel made no move to follow, she felt a rush of relief and triumph.

She kept going, passing under arched stone bridges, and soaring cabled structures, and skirting small recreational sailing vessels, ferries and cargo ships. The structures on either side of the river changed along the way—from modern skyscrapers to old churches, private homes, and treed parklands, all protected behind tall seawalls. What she found most interesting were the submerged ruins of buildings evidently drowned along the banks as the river had risen and widened over the years. Hours went by as she traveled, and the Seine grew ever wider and deeper until eventually it opened into a protected harbor. She tasted salt water and followed it out through a wide water break, where she shot into a surging, salt-laden sea. The turbulent water pushed and pulled from the huge barges coming and going, some as big as cities. Swimming here was difficult and she had no idea what direction to take.

Her reference files contained detailed maps downloaded from the Niña's computer, but without knowing where she was, they did her little good. She needed a satellite signal to position herself. *It's worth the risk,* she decided. As quickly as possible, she bobbed to the surface, took her bearings, and shut down tight again.

Now she knew where she was—in the middle of the English Channel—a well-travelled commercial thoroughfare. No doubt the satellite recorded her location and Chayd would see it. She dived downward, adjusting her internal pressure to compensate. At this depth, she felt safer but Chayd's nanobots were still inside her, dormant for the moment, but waiting. They had to be annihilated and that would require all her resources. She couldn't do battle with them in these cold dark waters as it was taking nearly all her energy just to stay warm.

She kept moving, heading south in the dark depths. Luminescent fish darted by, and she swam over the hulking shapes of more than one lost ship. Tired and cold, she felt like lying down next to them. It occurred to her that if she died here in her present form, her corpse might be indistinguishable from theirs. The idea wasn't appealing. She kept moving. Long hours of steady swimming passed into days before the seafloor rose and the water began to grow warmer. She kept going and came upon tall forests of kelp, bright green in the filtered light. It was almost warm enough, but to be certain she continued south until the sea lightened to turquoise clarity over a warm, sandy bottom. Her nanobots were no longer firing inside to keep her warm.

Yes, this will serve.

Gratefully, she sank onto the soft sand to rest at last. Now she could give up maintaining her metal exterior and let her others concentrate on routing out Chayd's invaders. When cut off from contact with their host, Chayd's nanobots had gone into standby mode, but now as her nanobot soldiers set about dismantling them, they awoke to defend themselves. The invaders might no longer be able to coordinate an attack, but individually they fought to survive.

Once more, battles for supremacy took place in one body part of hers after another. Sharp pain stabbed sporadically without warning and fresh blood oozed into the water, attracting passing fish, and crustaceans scuttling by. To prevent them from causing additional damage, she shocked the curious nibblers, making them dart away.

To deal with the sporadic pain, she tried to focus her attention elsewhere. Mostly she thought about what she would do once fully healed. Returning to the Niña was the obvious goal. If the Daniel Walker had also escaped, that's where she would find him. If not . . . She didn't want to think about that possibility. He hadn't wanted to meet with the Supreme Father and warned her against it. *I should have listened.*

Fear for his safety filled her with a new sense of urgency, but she had to be certain none of the invaders remained and none could ever enter her again. The painful and debilitating battle progressed inside her as her *others* destroyed the nanobot invaders one by one until at last finding the portal through they had entered—an exact duplicate of the nanogen which had resurrected her. Now she understood why her *others* hadn't recognized it as an enemy even as it held the door open for Morden Chayd's invasion. Under her direction, they took it apart now and expelled the remnants from her body. Finally, the battle was won and the gate was closed, but she'd been left torn, and bleeding into the water.

A large predator with scissor-like teeth skirted her. The word "shark" popped into her mind. Its blank black eyes measured her as it glided by. She lay still, hoping it would move on, but it circled back. A half-dozen more sleek shapes joined it. One twisted from its trajectory and brushed against her with such surprising speed she failed to shock it. She summoned her energy field, prepared now. It smoothly turned back. The cold black eyes regarded her impartially.

It seemed as if it might simply pass by again but then the head turned at the last moment and the huge toothed mouth slashed at her. Her energy sparked, and the animal jerked and flipped away. Too late. Her right side lay split open and red blood spurted into the water. The others flashed and twisted, and she released an onslaught of massive electrical jolts. Some of them sank to the floor. Others swam away and circled warily again.

Feeling a growing weakness, she knew she couldn't keep up with both repairs and defense, so her others staunched the blood flow just enough that she could concentrate on defense. The sharks circled closer. She sent out a swarm of nanobots to deter them—to cause pain, stem their hunger, or increase their fear, but she didn't know enough about their physiology and they seemed undeterred. These were sleek eating machines, apparently with one purpose in life. They came around again. With flashes of movement, they ripped at her. Her defense system hummed and sparked, and sent them roiling away again, but this time none fell unconscious or retreated as far.

Despair filled her. *Have I only gone from one manner of destruction to another?* She struggled to stay conscious, too weak now to generate the massive electrical charges needed to fend them off again. *Think! Perhaps just the sound of it?*

She hummed, mimicking the rhythmic drone of a fully-charged field. The sharks still circled, but made no move to attack. She hummed louder and the circle widened.

It's working!

She hummed even louder and heard the hum returning to her, rising and falling in a slightly different way. A distorted echo, perhaps, or some strange effect of the water and the rocky ocean floor. Except that it was growing louder, which didn't make sense. The sharks faded into the distance until she could no longer see them. Relieved, but exhausted, she fell silent. Strangely, the echo remained.

What is that?

Her humming had been a rhythmic monotone, while this sound varied in pitch. She listened, trying to understand.

It's like being in church, she thought and experienced a brief but distinct memory of sitting in midnight mass. She blinked in surprise. *That's odd. Must have been something I downloaded from the Cathedral's library.*

The sound grew louder, voices washing over her, through her, bringing flashes of disconnected images.

She was running through the surf, opening presents at a birthday party, seeing a father's face across the dinner table, learning to drive, kissing a boy, attending a lecture, giving a lecture, skiing down a snowy mountain, looking at a red landscape through the mask of a space suit, making love to a dark-haired man.

That last face she recognized—Daniel Walker.

Where are these coming from? Am I losing control of my thought processes? Must be too much blood loss. Perhaps hallucinating is a harbinger of death.

She tried to focus on what was real—her torn body, the water, the sand beneath—those were real. The voices fell silent and the images stopped playing in her mind. She breathed a sigh of relief. Her nanobots must have slowed the blood loss. *It appears I shall live.*

Then she saw shadows in the distance, dark sleek shapes headed in her direction, dozens this time—no, hundreds! She had no energy left for defense. All she could do was close her eyes to spare herself the sight of dagger-like teeth coming to rip her apart.

As she waited, panic gave way to resignation, even humor that so many were intent on consuming the small amount of her that remained. Seconds stretched. The anticipated pain did not come. She forced her eyes to open.

She was surrounded. Not by the sinister gray eating machines she'd expected, but something altogether different, a floating blue forest pierced with golden orbs. She blinked, trying to make sense of it. She discerned the outlines of four-limbed creatures with smooth dense fur. The yellow orbs were eyes.

Nereids! She would have laughed were it possible with water-filled lungs. *These must be the missing Nereids. Where else would ocean-loving creatures take refuge from their land-dwelling captors?*

She understood them to be gentle creatures, but they stared at her so intensely she grew worried again. She sent her others out toward them, searching for a way to communicate, but the Nereids only continued to stare. She remembered she'd been humming to ward off the shark attack. Perhaps the sound of it drew them to her. *May as well, try it. This mutual staring contest isn't getting us anywhere.* Though faint with weakness, she renewed her rhythmic humming.

As if cued by a conductor's baton, the Nereids sang back and their voices enveloped her like a living thing. Visions, both strange and familiar, came crashing into her mind like a tsunami, sweeping her into a chaotic maelstrom of memories so numerous and vivid even her nano-enhanced intellect was overwhelmed. Nothing made sense and she could no longer put thought together to analyze it.

She fought to maintain her identity amid the voices in her head stretching her awareness beyond the limits of her sanity, a mental onslaught of lifetimes experienced by millions of beings she'd never met and never would in a combined awareness deeper, wiser and more powerful than any individual could ever be. The last of her remaining self surrendered, and in that moment of capitulation, the voices softened and soothed. The vortex of tangled images swirling end-over-end, floated into place and settled at last into one long, intense, coherent dream shared by a thousand alien minds.

Chapter 39

Daniel knew his death was near. That was the good news. The bad news was that despite being paralyzed from the neck down, everything hurt, and he was nearly insane from the horror of things gnawing on him in the dark. His throat burned—his voice used up in wasted cries for help. Cracked and dry, his lips bled, and it was unfortunate his nose still worked, because everything stank of wet filth. A puddle spread out beneath him, undoubtedly of his own making. After slipping in and out of consciousness, he had no idea how long he'd been there.

If there were any mercy I'd pass out for good. Apparently not, since I keep waking up to the same god-awful nightmare.

Periodically, claustrophobic terror would swallow him whole and he was just a boy again, trapped in a cargo tube on a distant asteroid. Then he'd remember having survived that only to come full circle, back to being lost and alone in the dark again, terrorized by the unseen.

No, I've had a lifetime of experiences since then—good and bad.

He tried to concentrate on the good ones—family, friends, personal accomplishments. Serena's image took center stage, but thoughts of her soon deteriorated into regret. He recalled their argument that first night aboard the Niña. *She said I was afraid to get close. Doesn't matter now. It'll all be over soon. I'll be dead, and Cadmon Dhyre will go on, under the guise of the benevolent Father Chayd, doing whatever the hell he wants, enslaving people like Lester. Like he said he would do to Carrie. At least I won't be one of them.*

The thought brought him little consolation. *Just get it over with, damn it.* He wished for death and the delusion of being trapped in a storage tube on a lonely asteroid gripped him again until tears streamed down his face. The tears surprised him into coming back to the present.

Huh, when was the last time I cried? When I buried Serena? No. Probably at my parents' funeral. No, I was too proud. Sure as hell not when those asshole teens pummeled me and Lester sliced open my face. Maybe later when I lived on the streets, or in that string of fos-ter homes. No, I just picked fights and woke up screaming every night. Until Uncle Charlie put a stop to it.

Daniel smiled internally, remembering his honorary uncle's no-nonsense approach to parenting a troubled boy. "For every action, there is an equal and opposite reaction." The latter meant shadow-ing the doctor on his rounds at the hospital, where the suffering of others pulled Daniel out of his spiral of self-pity. Uncle Charlie had been a tough disciplinarian, which made Daniel angry and resentful at times, but even so, there'd been no crying. No, come to think of it, he couldn't remember any tears. Not ever.

And then he did.

I cried in that cargo tube. I cried and prayed to be rescued, and promised if I was that I would finish my parents' work and never cry again. How could I have forgotten that?

Daniel realized he'd kept his promise and hadn't shed a tear since. He'd built a wall to keep his emotions in and everyone else's out. His childhood bargain had become his *raison d'etre* as an adult. He lived for one purpose, to carry on his parents' work—to prove Tau Medea could home humanity despite the Garuda threat—and he'd dared not let anything or anyone stop him. 'Walker's Mission,' as everyone called it—his grand obsession. Serena had seen past his wall and tried relentlessly to break through. He'd come close to let-ting her.

If only we'd had more time. I've made so many mistakes. The last one was coming here to meet with Chayd. I should never have let Carrie talk me into it. Or rather, Aurora, as she wanted to be called.

He didn't know what to think of her by any name she chose. The only thing he was certain of was that she was intent on invading his privacy, and apparently could jump his mental wall at will. She had terrified him, but what frightened him even more now was that his wish to be left alone had been granted. He was alone, utterly alone.

"This isn't what I meant." He felt tears on his cheeks, just as he had back in that cargo tube as a boy and now, as then, he began to pray with every bit of his being. He prayed for rescue, for another chance. He'd do anything, give up everything, if only someone or something would come save him. "Please, help me. Dear God, let somebody come help me, please, somebody, help me, please, help . . ." he whispered into the dark, over and over.

Acknowledged.

Daniel gasped, his hopes soaring. "Hello! I'm down here. Can you hear me?" he croaked.

Affirmative.

His hopes crashed again. Even in his delirium, he recognized the strange voice only lived in his head.

Specify nature of help requested, the voice said.

Great, I've finally lost my mind. Well, better a god that lives in my head, than none at all I guess. At least I've found a way to entertain myself, he thought, trying to see the humor in it.

"So, what kind of god are you? Greek, Roman, Christian?"

Unable to interpret. Awaiting instruction.

He laughed silently, his vocal chords nearly spent. "Some deity I've invented here." He sounded insane even to himself, but it was an amusing sort of madness, far better than the stark terror he'd been trapped in before. He stayed with it.

"My neck's broken, dumb-ass. You could start by fixing that. And while you're at it, how about zapping these rodents, and getting some light in here?"

Working.

Has to work at it. Ha, God in training-pants. Daniel chuckled silently again, knowing he'd truly gone mad and glad of it. Reality had lost its appeal. A power source sparked and snapped audibly around him. *Maybe something's shorted out. Hope so—at least death by electrocution would be quick.*

He felt stabbing pains in his eyes and blinked reflexively, but the pain wasn't from an electrical shock. *It's light!*

"Hey! I'm down here!" he cried out, thinking he must have been wrong, and that someone was actually here. No one answered.

The soft greenish glow waxed brighter, revealing limp rats on the floor, and then he saw the green light emanating from his own flesh. Slowly it dawned on him what was happening. He'd had no nanogen-suppressant injections since leaving the Niña. *Must have been days ago.* His prayers had been answered alright—not from without, but from within.

An odd warmth tingled at the base of his neck, then searing pain shot down his spine, out into his arms and legs, making him cry out. The pain receded to pins and needles, but then he felt another sharp pain as a rat bit into his right hand—and he instinctively jerked away. He looked at his hand in surprise and wriggled his fingers. He tried the same with his left, also well chewed, but it worked too. Using his hands, he pulled at his legs, and got them bent in the right direction. The feeling was returning to them. Painful as it was, he rocked his legs and feet from one side to the other, watching them cooperate. Each breath was coming a little easier as well. Placing his hands on either side of the pit, he braced against the walls and shakily pushed himself up to stand on his feet.

"I'll be damned," he said, grinning, even though everything hurt.

His body burned all across his torso and legs making him look down. The ugly wounds where rats had snacked on him were stitching together like a fast-action film. He gritted against the pain, but wasn't about to complain. He hadn't wanted it, and in fact done everything in his power to suppress it, but now it looked as if this nanogen infection would save him. He looked up at the underside of the heavy lid more than ten feet above and the pit's vertical walls slick with slime. They offered no purchase for climbing, and he figured any attempt to lift that lid would alert Chayd anyway. Though he was rapidly recovering from his injuries the odds of getting out of here still didn't look good.

The shocked rats were recovering as well, scrambling again around his feet in search of the raw flesh they'd been enjoying only moments before. It dawned on him that they no longer horrified him and he no longer felt panic-stricken at being trapped in a spider-filled pit barely wider than his shoulders. He wondered if this new calm was due to a change in brain chemistry courtesy of the nanobots, or simply the realization that he was forming an alliance with the most invasive bug of all.

The scurrying rats offered some distraction from the painful stinging of his recovery, so he fell into counting them: *two black, six gray, five brown, and one with a white nose. There's ten, no wait, twelve, no, only nine now, and where's Snow Nose? The numbers are changing.* He wanted to see them better, and his personal light brightened. *Huh . . . well, that was simple enough.* He squatted down to peer at the curved edge of the wall where it met the filth encrusted floor. Half a rat appeared to his right, then zipped out whole. He went to grab it and it spun around and disappeared again in the same spot. Feeling along the edge of the floor, he detected a faint stirring of air on his wet fingertips. Something nipped at his finger and he withdrew.

At least the rats have a way in and out of here.

He remembered how Carrie had maneuvered through the ship's narrow air vents, but to fit through an opening this small, he'd have to transform himself into something not much bigger around than a snake, and he had no idea how to accomplish such a feat. He also knew she used her 'others' to learn about her environment. He tried to visualize communicating with them and placed his hands on the wall.

"Find out what's on the other side," he said aloud, feeling a little ridiculous, but then he experienced a brief, but not unpleasant tingling in his palms. He waited, wondering what would happen next. The sensation in his palms returned, and in his mind he envisioned bricks and cement, then a wide, cool corridor beyond.

Holy crap. This is actually working.

He took a deep breath, concentrated on the image, and touched the slime-covered wall again, with his palms just above the spot where the rats entered. Perhaps under this thick layer of crud was something he couldn't see, a weak spot maybe. "Show me what's here, what's between me and the corridor." He felt his way around, at first seeing only brick and mortar in his mind's eye. Then he sensed something under the gunk—a crack, a seam. He followed the seam, tracing a solid two-foot square. *Could this be an access point, an actual door?*

He squatted again, placed the soles of his shoes against the square, and pushed as hard as he could. Nothing budged.

Maybe I'm going about this all wrong.

He laid his palm back on the wall where he thought he'd detected the seam and again concentrated on his nanobots. "Okay, little guys, this time search for bolts, locks, anything that could be holding a door in place," he ordered.

Moments later, a picture of thick brass hinges and a rusted iron bolt on the far side of the wall formed in his mind. It was a door all right, but forcing aside its rusted bolt would be tough going even if he could manhandle the thing. He pictured a huge mallet swinging down and busting it in two. Nothing happened, of course. *Okay, that's obviously not going to work. I'm probably just hallucinating all this anyway.* He shook head. *Whatever, just go with it. You've got nothing to lose. Assume it's real until proven wrong. And remember it's not magic, it's nanotechnology, so think. What can nano-sized robots do?*

Aurora was a walking nano-manufacturing vat, so he must be as well. Maybe these things could make something that could eat through the bolt. Summoning up what he remembered of his chemistry education, he considered the problem.

The bolt's rusted, which means it's covered in iron oxide. Add powdered aluminum and you come up with thermite. Add a spark to that and you have an exothermic reaction hot enough to burn through steel, let alone iron. But where am I going to find powdered aluminum?

The decaying organic matter around him didn't look promising. Or did it? Nanovats could create any molecular structure desired using raw carbon-based material exactly like this. All that was needed was the correct programming.

And how the hell do I do that?

He wished he knew more about nanotechnology, and for a moment envied Chayd's background. He was at a serious disadvantage. Still, basic chemistry had been part of his education. Aluminum was one of the elements on the Periodic Table which he'd memorized at one time. He tried to visualize the table. *Aluminum, aluminum. Come on, concentrate, you can remember this. Aluminum, AL, Element 13—13 protons, 14 neutrons. Yes, that's it.*

Now that he could visualize aluminum's molecular structure, he set about putting theory into practice, learning more about his new inherent abilities with each step. It required absolute precision of thought and internal visualization. After several false starts and failed attempts, eventually he got his message across. With his tiny servants now suitably equipped, he talked to them aloud again.

"I need you to take those aluminum molecules through the wall to the other side," he said, imagining the tiny robots filtering their way through the wall's molecular structure to reach the exterior hinges and bolts. He waited for what he hoped was an appropriate amount of time. "Okay, now mix the aluminum molecules with the iron oxide ones on the bolt. Make sure it's thoroughly combined, then ignite it. You'll need a spark. Um...maybe you could rub your little arms together really fast?" He pictured a thermal reaction happening over and over and over. "A spark, come on, you can do it, light it up."

After a long while, he heard a faint sizzling sound, then a metallic ping, then two more. Did it work? He didn't know, but got back in position. Placing his feet against the crud covered wall, he pushed with all his might, his back pressed against the other side of his tiny prison. At first nothing, then he heard a deep groan. Encouraged, he bore down even harder, grunting with effort. Something budged, he heard a rusty creak, and then a small door flew open wide, banging against the outer brick wall as his feet went flying through. "Woohoo! You did it!" He flipped around and squeezed his shoulders through, then pulled the rest of himself out into a dark hallway. He lay sobbing in gratitude, breathing in the comparatively fresh air. Freedom had never smelled so sweet. He quieted and listened, reminding himself that his freedom could be short lived, but he heard no sound.

Chayd said no one ever comes down here. The thick layer of undisturbed dust on the floor seemed to confirm it. *Looks like I'm safe for the moment. But now what? How am I going to get out of the building without Chayd knowing?*

He might have the potential of Chayd's abilities, but potential was all it was. He felt like an infant learning to recognize its own hands, facing a fully grown opponent who could do back flips.

At least as long as he thinks I'm dead, I have the element of surprise. I have nanobots, too, you son-of-a-bitch.

Feeling more confident now at communicating with his internal allies, he put his hands flat on the floor, pictured them and said aloud, "Find the most direct route out of here that avoids interaction with anyone or anything capable of communicating a message."

He felt a tingling in his palms again, then nothing. He had no idea how long it would take to get an answer or if he would even recognize it when it came.

Uncle Charlie thinks they have AI which means they can learn. Maybe they learned English from Carrie and that's why they can communicate with me and make repairs. They seem to know what they're doing. Guess I just better sit back and wait. Need to get my strength back, anyway, if I have any chance of getting out of here.

He watched the remaining gashes in his extremities close, feeling stronger and stronger with each passing minute. He shook his head in wonder. *This isn't anything like what I thought.* The unleashed nanogen infection felt far from the hostile takeover he'd expected. It was more like a gift.

Carrie . . . Aurora, she tried to tell me. I didn't believe her. Hell, no one did. We only thought about what the Toad nanogen does to people. What it did to Cadmon Dhyre. He should have died long ago but this new nanogen he created saved him. Now he's turned himself into Morden Chayd, Supreme Father of the Unified Church of Earth, of all things. Why? Why hasn't he cured everyone with the virus like he did himself?

"Because he's a nut case, with a god complex," Daniel said aloud, remembering the twisted hate in Chayd's face. He thought of the unusual name, Morden Chayd, the letters rearranging in his mind. *It's an anagram. Cadmon Dhyre. Morden Chayd. Guess he's into names. Gave Carrie her new one—Aurora—it's more flattering I guess, but Carrie's more accurate.* The modified version of 'horde carrier'—her original self-description—kept things in perspective, reminding him she was an artificial construct. *It's just a fact. But, oh, how she felt in my arms, her kiss . . .*

Maybe she does have genuine feelings. Or maybe she just mimics them to manipulate people. I don't know. Suppose I never will now. Chayd's made her his property. Dammit, I told her we shouldn't come here. And I told her to stay in the room, but did she listen? No, she had to run off to be with him. Guess I've only got myself to blame for that. I kept pushing her away. Course she went to Chayd. He has all the answers. Never occurred to her he wouldn't be willing to share them. She's brilliant, but naïve.

Shit, why did it have to be a lunatic like Cadmon Dhyre to come up with a cure? In someone else's hands, this nanogen could end the Toad plague, save so many lives. And he's right that people won't need to terraform planets, if they can transform themselves to survive in them.

He pictured what that could mean: a race of artificially enhanced humans altering their bodies at will, manufacturing whatever they needed and controlling their environment with molecular precision. *If everyone can link up with each other it would be like being part of a vast, internal-based Web. Humankind might transcend to some higher level of awareness and find a truly peaceful co-existence.* Then he thought of its inventor and knew better.

The old saying came to him, 'Absolute power corrupts absolutely.' Seeing his still pink recently-repaired flesh, he wondered if the truism applied to him as well.

Was Cadmon Dhyre once filled with good intentions before he mutated into Morden Chayd? Daniel tried to look into his own mind. *Am I still me? How would I know?*

His fingertips tingled again. In his mind's eye, a map took shape, revealing a path through this underground labyrinth. There was a way out, but it wasn't up as he'd expected.

It was down.

Chapter 40

Hours later, Daniel strode down a crowded Parisian street, inspiring alarmed looks on the faces of oncoming pedestrians who quickly moved out of his path. He knew he must look a sight and smell worse, although he'd gone nose-blind to it. Water-soaked shoes dangled from his fingers as he walked barefoot on the pavement, muttering to himself like a deranged homeless person—the kind he himself avoided whenever possible.

Following the path revealed by his tiny scouts, Daniel had found a way out through the ancient Parisian underground sewers, a disgusting route which took him to the outskirts of the city, where he felt safe enough to surface. His feet tingled from the nanobots rushing in and out in waves and undertows, rebounding off the surfaces around him, testing for the presence of nanobots like themselves. *All clear. All clear.* Their message kept repeating in his mind, but his tension remained high. He'd already put miles between himself and the Cathedral, but wasn't about to let his guard down until he was off the planet. He worried that he might stumble upon Chayd's invisible nanobots any moment, and so he kept whispering aloud to his own.

"Keep scouting ahead, shut down any monitors that might report my location. Watch for enemies. They could be anywhere." He smirked to himself. *Anyone hearing me would think I'm an untreated paranoid schizophrenic.*

Aurora and Chayd had communicated with their nanobots silently, but he found it difficult to separate his thoughts from commands without vocalization. Perhaps with time and experience, he would master that skill. He wondered when Aurora had first recognized Chayd's nanogen infection. *On sight at the Senate hearing? Later, at Chayd's office? Why didn't she tell me? I would never have let her anywhere near him.* Immediately, he recognized he'd answered his own question.

On the one hand, he felt betrayed; on the other, he understood her need to find someone who could explain this unprecedented, multi-leveled existence. These artificial intelligences were like a sea of voices, communicating with a separate yet linked mind, independent and yet part of their host, continuously

monitoring and reporting on their host's bodily functions and surrounding environment, all the while waiting to jump into action at
the host's bidding. He was a world unto himself, populated by perhaps billions, all eager to serve only him. He could empathize with
her now—even with Chayd. The latter thought startled him.

*Don't you dare feel sorry for that bastard. He has no any con-
science whatsoever. But how the hell am I going to stop him? Aurora
was strong and even she couldn't defend herself.*

He visualized her as he'd last seen her—torn and bloody, reduced to a remnant of her prior self. His gut twisted at the memory
and bile rose in his throat.

*There has to be some way to free her, free everyone, even
Lester. I just need time to figure it out. I have to get back to the Niña.
Not even Chayd can make his nanobots jump across the void of
space. Can he?*

The possibility that Chayd could somehow infiltrate his ship
spurred him forward. He broke into a run, and the people crowding
the walkway parted before him. He kept going, running hard, surprised and pleased by his endurance after everything he'd been
through, but when he reached the wide entrance to the local
transport station, he came to a hasty stop.

*I'll never get past port patrol looking like this. They'll toss me
into a holding cell and run an ID check.*

To stay dead, he needed his anonymity intact, a nearly impossible feat in a tagged world. As he wavered, the holographic icon of a
'Bathe 'n Wait' ahead caught his eye. The smiling cartoon figure with
a bubble-covered torso bobbed out from the wall beckoning passers
to "Come on in—the water's fine." Here was a chance to clean up
and think. He walked over to the entrance.

"Place palm on panel for entry," said holo-bubble man.

Daniel frowned—he couldn't do that. The fact that his bank ac-
count held billions built up over his ten-year absence wouldn't help
him now. *All those credits and I don't dare use them.*

He stared at the digital display, wondering if his nanobots
could override its security without setting off alarms. A middle-aged
gentleman walking past glanced over at him, and abruptly turned
back.

"Going in?" the man asked.

The voice startled him. Daniel hadn't communicated with another human being since Chayd dropped him into that hellish pit. The stubble on his face attested it must have been at least four or five days ago, although it felt like a lifetime. He looked at the man, dressed in pin-striped business attire. He was of medium height and average build, with a well-worn face under thinning gray hair. Probably a commuting salesman, he concluded, dismissing his initial suspicion.

"You all right, son?" the man asked, scowling at him.

"It's been a rough week."

"I can see that." The man nodded. "Nothing a hot shower couldn't fix, I hope. I'm sure this establishment would do you a world of good."

Daniel looked down at his grimy hands and soaked clothing. "You're probably right, but I don't seem to have the means."

"Then allow me." The man palmed the credit plate and waved Daniel inside.

"Thank you, thank you very much," Daniel said, in a rush of gratitude, and headed straight for the showers, jumping in fully clothed to get the worst of it off. Once the surface slime melted away, he peeled off his clothing, and hung them on the moving hook that would drag them through the washers and dryers. He did the same with his shoes, hoping they'd survive the process too, then stood with his eyes closed letting the hot soapy water pound him.

When the signal beeped that his clothes were pressed and ready, he rinsed off, dried in the blowers and stepped out. He put on his still warm shirt and pants, feeling more human by the minute. By the time he emerged into the waiting area, he was ready to hug someone, until he saw his benefactor waiting there for him.

As Daniel met the man's gaze, he realized this had been no random act of kindness after all. He'd been recognized. When the man grinned, Daniel thought he looked familiar, but couldn't place him.

"Quite a surprise running into you like this," the man said. "I was at the Senate hearing, you know, expecting to be called as a character witness. Then suddenly it was all over. They just let you go.

Shocked the hell out of me—most everyone else too—but I'm glad it worked out. I don't think anyone really wanted to see you punished."

Daniel said nothing, trying to figure out if he needed to incapacitate this guy.

The man's smile gave way to a frown. "I see you don't recognize me. Not surprising, I suppose. I'm ten years older than when we last met, and half the man I used to be." He patted his normal sized stomach. "I'll give you a hint. I championed you back when you applied for the position at ACES, a decision I still congratulate myself for. Unfortunately, I also did you the favor of finding a job for that black-sheep cousin of yours—to my everlasting regret."

"Cedric Peterson," Daniel said, finally matching the face with a name, "Chairman of the Overseer Committee for ACES, and CEO of Fabri-Tech."

"Ex-Chairman, ex-CEO. You're looking at a ruined man."

"That was Lester's doing, wasn't it? I'm sorry."

"No need. You're not his keeper, though you obviously tried to be." Peterson squinted at him. "Unless you shared in the proceeds from that lawsuit of his?"

"No, absolutely not."

Peterson sighed and smiled again. "Didn't think so."

Daniel stood there awkwardly, recognizing the absurdity of the situation. He searched for something to say. "You don't look ruined."

"Turns out I bounce well." Peterson chuckled. "Losing my company, then my wife to divorce made me rethink my priorities. I focus mostly on environmental issues now."

"Good for you." Daniel nodded, remembering the man's trophy wife, not surprised she'd left when the money ran out. He smiled politely, but his eyes shifted away, looking for an exit. "Well, I wish we had more time to talk, but I need to get back to the Niña." Daniel made a big deal of checking the time on his wrist display.

"In a bit of a hurry myself. I'm on my way to a planetary conference to introduce my new start-up—a renewable-energy-based food production company. I have a private transport waiting for me."

At the word 'transport,' Daniel snapped Peterson back into focus. "I haven't arranged for a shuttle yet. Maybe you could drop me off. It would give us a chance to catch up, and you could tell me about this new business of yours."

Peterson's face showed a new eagerness. "Great. You might even want to get in on the ground floor, if I'm not being too presumptuous."

"No, not at all—you'd be doing me a favor."

During the short flight, Daniel pretended to be interested in investing in Peterson's green energy business. *It's a lie, but for a good cause*, he told himself, but couldn't help wondering how often Chayd told himself the same thing.

Peterson's shuttle delivered him to the Niña and took off again without incident and more importantly, without recording him as a passenger. Upon disembarking aboard the Niña , Daniel was handed orders to report to Captain Kowalski immediately. Instead, Daniel went directly to his quarters, and activated his computer to scan the ship's operating systems. *I need to make sure Chayd hasn't infiltrated this ship.*

The connecting door to Serena's old quarters opened, and Kowalski marched into his room. "Why can't you ever do as you're told? And where the hell have you been? I've been trying to reach you for days."

Daniel wondered why Kowalski would come through his inner door but kept his attention focused on the results of the scan. "Wait a minute, will you? I'm almost done here."

"This can't wait. We have another carrier on board."

Daniel spun from the screen. "What? Chayd's here?"

"Chayd? No. What are you talking about?"

"What are you talking about?"

"Easier just to show you, but don't freak out. You're perfectly safe," Kowalski said as he took Daniel by the arm, and pulled him through the inner door.

"Augh!" Daniel yelled. Standing, or rather towering over him, was a fully awake, completely unrestrained Garuda warrior. The great luminous eyes targeted him, and the sharp-hooked beak scraped open.

"You are he who shot me," the great bird sang out in a throaty, but clearly intelligible version of the English language, and moved toward him.

Daniel broke free of Kowalski's grip and scrambled backward, but not fast enough as the bird snatched the front of Daniel's shirt with its long arm. Daniel flailed wildly.

"Becalm yourself," the bird ordered, and lifted him into the air.

"Daniel, it's okay," Kowalski called out. "He won't hurt you."

Daniel stopped flailing. *I'm having a nightmare. I just need to wake up.*

"Interesting, these things you call furniture," the giant bird said, carrying Daniel several feet above the floor. It spoke slowly with round lilting tones as if discussing the weather over a spot of tea. "but they are of no use to me." It plopped Daniel into a chair and folded its legs to settle on the floor in front of Daniel, cutting its height in half so that its large round eyes came level with his. "Where is she who awakened me?"

Daniel stared, wide-eyed and open-mouthed, convinced he was hallucinating. *I'm imagining all of this. I must still be in that pit, dying.*

"He asked you a question," Kowalski said.

"This isn't real," Daniel replied, resigned to his insanity and no longer panicked.

Kowalski chuckled. "Oh, it's real all right. This is the Garuda you shot and froze in our morgue. Turns out he's infected with the same nanogen as you and Carrie. She found him and revived him. He stayed hidden until the two of you went AWOL. So where is she, anyway? Is she okay?"

"No, he's got her," Daniel answered, his worry for her returning despite thinking that this was all an elaborate fabrication his mind had concocted to deal with impending death. "I tried to help her, but he nearly killed me."

"Who?" Kowalski asked.

"Chayd." Daniel kept his eyes on the Garuda, expecting it to attack any second. *Maybe then I'll wake up.*

"That's insane. Why would he do that?" Kowalski asked.

The Garuda tilted its head, watching him.

Kowalski snapped his fingers in front of Daniel's face. "Hey! This isn't a dream. Answer me."

Daniel looked at him then. "Because . . ." he tried to get his thoughts in order, "because he's not who we thought he was. He changed right in front of me, showed me his true face. He's Cadmon Dhyre. It was him all along. Dhyre made the nanogen we found, cured himself of the Toad virus, and reinvented himself as Morden Chayd."

"The guy who worked at Fabri-Tech with your cousin and survived the lab explosion?"

"The same." Daniel nodded. "I'm pretty sure he's the one who blew it up."

"And he wants you dead, because . . . ?"

"To keep his secret safe, eliminate the competition . . . maybe because he hates me or he's just plain nuts. I'm not sure exactly, but I do know he's evolved to the point that he can do anything he damn well pleases. He took Carrie apart. She couldn't protect herself."

"Well, fuck me," Kowalski said.

Daniel marveled as Kowalski pulled up a chair next to the Garuda, sat down and leaned forward with his elbows on his knees, all without so much as a side glance. "Chayd told us you went to see family. I kept trying to contact you, but when you didn't respond, I figured you were just too upset to talk to anyone. Never occurred to me the Supreme Father was lying. You should have heard him. He was so sincere, so sympathetic, I never questioned it. He's sending your uncle back here on a transport today."

"Good, but make sure you screen it thoroughly. If Chayd gets his nanobots on board, he could sabotage our systems. That's what I was checking for just now."

"Well, I don't think you need to worry about that. McCormack set up protocols before he left, everything going out or coming in. Looks like he was smarter about this nanogen than any of us gave him credit for." Kowalski shook his head.

The Garuda mirrored Kowalski's movement.

Daniel watched the bird swivel its beaked head back and forth, still not quite believing it was there. He had to work at remembering what had been of paramount importance just moments before. "We need to . . . to stop Chayd."

"From what?" Kowalski asked.

"Taking over," Daniel answered the captain, but kept his attention on the giant bird, which seemed to be listening to every word. "He wants to establish himself as the leader of some new order. He's demented. Given full reign, he might end up running everything."

"How would he do that?"

"He uses his nanobots to torture and control people. Once McCormack is cleared, we need him working on a way to neutralize him. When's he due?"

Kowalski leaned back, and a look of deep regret crossed his features. "Daniel, I'm so sorry. I thought you knew. Your uncle . . . Dr. McCormack . . . he's dead. The transport is bringing us his body."

"What?" Daniel finally stopped paying attention to the Garuda and stared at the captain. "What do you mean?"

"We were told it was an accident, some poisonous fumes got into the ventilation system."

"No." Daniel felt an overwhelming guilt, then shook his head. "No, that can't be right. That gas wasn't toxic." It wasn't the gas, he was sure of that, not that it made him any less responsible. He'd left his uncle behind, never considering he might be in danger, too. "Oh, god, no. Not Uncle Charlie." Daniel sank his head into his hands.

"What does this gesture signify?" the Garuda asked.

Daniel barely heard, overwhelmed by a guilt and grief so intense he couldn't breathe, and his gut curled into an agonizing knot. Perceiving an emergency, thousands upon thousands of his nanobots thundered inside asking for direction. He mentally shouted them down until their voices fell silent, all but one, one that would not submit. It clamored to be heard, insistent. Irritated, he turned his full attention to it, a huge mistake. Lulled by the seeming safety of the ship, he'd let his guard down. His last independent thought was to wonder how Chayd had found him, as his mind splintered into fragments, jigsawing into another's awareness.

To his surprise, he found himself staring at endlessly reflected double images. He squeezed his eyes shut, seeing himself do so.

With his eyes closed, he only had a single view to contend with, but it wasn't his own, and it wasn't Chayd's. It was the Garuda's.

Through that alien mind, he drew in a huge breath of air and felt a wide feathered chest rise and fall over folded legs, air whistling low between tongue and beak as if the Garuda's body was his own. Through these new eyes, the room jumped into unprecedented detail, every shadow illuminated in a vivid kaleidoscope of colors he couldn't begin to name. Before him, in the sharp outlines of his own grimacing face, he saw individual hairs in his ragged facial stubble, down to the pores of his skin where tiny molecular machines guarded his epidermal cells like well-trained sheepdogs. From the macro to the micro all at once. At the same time, unfamiliar memories bombarded him from a world he seemed to know both intimately and not at all. He instinctively wrapped his arms around his head trying to block out the onslaught of incomprehensible input.

Get out, he begged. Then everything that was Daniel Walker and not this other, bore down in one concentrated effort of will. "GET OUT!"

The connection broke and he was merely Daniel Walker once more.

"What the hell are you yelling about?" Kowalski stared at him in surprise.

Daniel looked back, equally wide-eyed. How could he explain what had just happened? He decided not to try. The shock of the Garuda's mental invasion gave way to rage. He'd been violated. He turned to the Garuda. "You son of a bitch," he snarled through clenched teeth.

The Garuda said nothing, but feathers ruffled up around its neck.

Kowalski scowled, switching his gaze back and forth between the two of them. "I don't know what's going on here, but I don't like it."

Despite Daniel's anger, images from the mental connection lingered and he found he could comprehend the more recent ones— this Garuda waking up to Carrie's presence, and slowly overcoming its suspicions to allow her to teach it human language using the same type of mental connection he'd just experienced. When she'd failed to return, the Garuda had come out of hiding. Panic ensued among the crew, naturally, but the Garuda demonstrated its ability to communicate and refrained from removing anyone's head long enough to establish a truce. *Good thing Sanchez was still recovering in sickbay,* Daniel thought ruefully, or things probably would have ended badly for everyone. Daniel also gleaned that what the Garuda wanted most of all was to find the one who had woken it. He got the message it would do whatever was necessary to accomplish that— alliance or violence—whichever appeared most promising. The Garuda warrior seemed to understand that Daniel also wanted to find her, but Daniel wasn't certain if the bird viewed it as a common goal or a competitive one.

"You had no right to do that," Daniel said, but held himself in check—more because he knew the Garuda could snap him in two than because he felt like being reasonable.

"Necessary," the Garuda trilled, and clicked at him, then twisted its still ruffled green and orange feathered head to look at Daniel with one giant yellow eye. "I must know what you know. This is what it means to be us now. A race apart."

Daniel let the words 'us' and 'race' sink in, not much liking the connotation.

"You may call me Chegta—not my true name, but one your limited vocalizations can produce." Its neck feathers settled again. "We shall find her, the one who woke me. Allies, you and I, as long as it serves."

"Allies?"

The bird straightened its head, then tipped its beak up and down in a nodding motion. "To you, this indicates positive reinforcement, does it not?"

Daniel automatically nodded back. "Yes, it means agreement."

"On my world, it is a challenge." Chegta stopped the movement and clicked again. "We must be careful not to misunderstand."

"I suppose you're going to tell me that slaughtering our people was just a misunderstanding."

"No. We object to you."

"Object to *us*?" Daniel sputtered, his anger threatening to explode. "You attacked peaceful, scientific research outposts without any provocation."

"Humans take what is not theirs, destroy all they touch. We cannot allow you to spread."

"And what qualifies you to act as our judge and jury?"

The bird clicked and whistled. "We have seen your work."

Chapter 41

A satellite reported Aurora's location in the English Channel the day she escaped, but further searches over the next few days came up empty until a dead shark washed up on the coast with a chunk of human flesh in its belly bearing Aurora's DNA signature.

Cadmon was baffled. *That shouldn't be possible. Why didn't the tissue disintegrate?* he asked himself again and again. *I was so certain the failsafe in my nanogen was foolproof.* He sent Lester to pick up the contents of the shark's stomach, while he went to the labs on the sixth floor to prepare. His pet rat, Sweetheart, kept him company, watching his every move with her beady red eyes.

"I don't understand it," he said, and Sweetheart squeaked back at him. "I took every precaution to ensure that nanogen infected tissues couldn't survive outside the host. Either the nanobots are evolving on their own, or she's intentionally reprogrammed them. Without the failsafe, it can spread and infect others." Chayd sensed Lester trotting down the hall toward him. "He damned well better hurry." Chayd was still angry at Lester's attempt to abandon him.

Sweetheart bobbed her head in agreement.

Lester burst in through the doors. "Got it," he announced breathlessly, holding a shoebox-sized insulated container.

Cadmon snatched the box, set it on the table and opened the lid. Inside was a stinky pink soup with chunks of bloody flesh. With gloved hands and twelve-inch tongs, he carefully placed the pieces onto the plates of the nanoscope's conveyor belt to be automatically sliced wafer-thin and run through scanners.

"So, looks like she got eaten by sharks, right?" Lester commented, holding his nose while he watched Cadmon work. "Guess Mother Nature's solved our problem for us. Praise Gaia." Lester pressed his hands together piously before covering his nose again.

"There's no one here but us," Cadmon said, glancing over at him.

"Sorry. It's kind of a habit now."

"Well, don't do it around me. It's annoying."

"Yes, Your Holiness. But this means Aurora must be dead, right?"

"Perhaps. Perhaps not. I can't say for certain. Finding a piece of her flesh intact like this brings up the disturbing possibility that she could regenerate from very little tissue. It's even conceivable there could be multiple regenerations—clones, if you will." Cadmon shook his head and closed the empty container. "It appears I still much to learn about my creation's capabilities. We mustn't assume anything. Keep searching. We need to find every bit that's left of her, no matter how small."

"Yes, Your Holiness. Our satellites are sweeping every inch of this planet. If her DNA surfaces again, we'll know it."

"Good. Leave me now." Cadmon turned his attention to the readouts on the nanoscope, deeply troubled. As Chayd worked, Sweetheart hung out on his shoulder. An hour later Lester's voice came over the speaker system.

"Excuse me, Your Holiness. We've located another reading for Aurora's DNA signature," Lester informed him. "It's coming from a public beach on the Canary Islands."

"Another half-eaten piece?" Cadmon asked.

"Maybe, but it would have to be a big one. Sister Rachelle is our nearest representative. She's on her way there now to secure it."

"Sister Rachelle." Cadmon puzzled over the name, then remembered the dark-haired beauty who'd greeted him when he'd first arrived here. She had since proved a loyal and resourceful subject, and filled his bed a number of times. "Good choice. She's reliable and dedicated."

"Thank you, Your Holiness. We should be hearing from her soon. She said she would—wait, I'm getting a call from her now. I'll patch her through."

"Allô? Father Chayd?" a French-accented female voice spoke.

"Ah, Sister Rachelle," he answered with a smile, remembering her naked. *I'll have to reward her with another visit if she does a good job.* "Have you reclaimed my property?"

"Non, Mon Pere, not yet. I am so very sorry, but things, they are so very complicated. I do not know how to say. Your property, as you put, is here, but perhaps, I think, you may wish to reconsider?"

Cadmon narrowed his eyes and his voice grew cold. "Now why would you think that?"

"The press, it is watching very closely this matter." Her voice quavered as she spoke. "We would need to arrange for more transports and more men; and then what are we to do with so many? Where shall we take them? Not to you, not to the Cathedral, non, non, unless you wish it, of course, Mon Pere, but such scandal—"

"Whatever are you talking about?"

"The many Nereids. But it is on all the news, have you not seen?"

A snap of his fingers turned on one of the twenty-four-hour news stations. Holos of a bizarre scene appeared as Sister Rachelle continued talking.

"There are over a thousand of them. So very strange, n'est pas? The locals have all come out to see, and with the press watching, what are we to do?"

Chayd stared at the herd of yellow-eyed Nereids in a densely-packed circle of blue, all of them facing outward from its center. Perched on his shoulder, Sweetheart stretched her neck to sniff at the holos, and he ran a finger along her back to calm her.

"Yes, it is odd," he said to Sister Rachelle. "I grant you that, but what does this have to do with retrieving my property?"

"Forgive me, Mon Pere, but what you seek is there with the Nereids. These blue fuzzies, they have your property. It is in there, with them, somewhere."

Chayd stared at the Nereids bunched together in a tight circle. As he watched, for no apparent reason they spun in unison, turning their backs to the cameras, closing ranks. They looked like sleek blue seals standing upright. *What are they doing, and where did they all come from?* He searched his memory for what he knew about them.

They live on algae, so wouldn't have eaten her. And look at the way they're circled up— as if they're protecting something. Or someone. But why? Even if she's still alive, she couldn't possibly form an all controlling link over even one of them, let alone a thousand. Her abilities aren't that sophisticated.

"I've never seen them do anything like that before," Lester said over the speaker.

"I assume you're speaking from experience?" Cadmon asked.

"Sure," Lester said, then went silent. He cleared his throat. "I mean, a little—very little, really."

"Then find someone who's had a lot."

"Yes, Your Holiness. No problem. Right away."

Cadmon sighed. "You have no idea who to call, do you?"

"Well . . . no, not just offhand, but I'm sure with a little research—"

"Oh shut up, will you." Chayd frowned, thinking again how inadequate his people were. "Sister Rachelle, you're done there. Return to your duties," he told her and cut her off. He tapped his computer and forwarded a file to Lester. "I've just sent you a list of the top Nereid trading companies with the names of their owners and customers." He smirked at the irony of using the information Aurora had compiled for Walker. "Call Bromberg's supplier. He'd only use the best."

"Bromberg, Bromberg . . ." Lester mumbled. "Ah, here it is. MLS Trading Company, owned by Manuel L. Sanchez. Current address—" He broke off.

"Is there a problem?" Chayd asked.

"No, um, I was just wondering what you know about this guy. I mean, if he's reliable."

"I know Bromberg, which means this man is discreet, experienced, and goes where the money is. Pay him whatever he wants. Have Bromberg set it up, then get my transport ready, loaded with a prepped cryotube. We'll meet him there."

"On it, Boss . . . I mean, Your Holiness."

Chayd looked back at the news report. The circled Nereids were surrounded by gawkers and more people were gathering. "And get this story off the airwaves."

***

Slowly, Aurora grew aware of her surroundings—the sound of ocean surf, red light shining through her closed eyelids, warm sand under her back. She remembered dreams, as detailed as memories even though they couldn't be. She wanted to lie here and recall them, but a warning voice kept breaking through. She resisted, knowing it was bad, important maybe, but bad.

You died. Wake up! You were on fire in the water and you died. Wake up!

That doesn't make sense. I feel fine, perfectly fine. Leave me alone.

Wake up!

Go away. I just want to lie here and remember the dreams, those amazing dreams.

Wake up! You died and we rebuilt you. Wake up or you will die again. Wake up!

She forced her eyes to open. She saw blue, blue sky everywhere.

Not sky. Fur.

Her mind blurred again, confused, and she closed her eyes.

Wake up! Wake up! Wake up!

She took in a deep breath and looked again. The blue sky focused into slender furred creatures bent over her, staring with teacup sized yellow eyes.

Nereids. It was coming back to her. *I was under attack in the ocean and these Nereids saved me, but why are they still here, up on dry land, watching me, waiting for me to . . . to what?* She struggled with her disordered mind, trying to understand the clamoring voices in her head. *Help them?*

Correct. Wake up! Act! You are in danger!

The urgency of the warning finally registered and the disparate pieces of the puzzle clicked into place. All of them. She knew exactly who she'd been, what she was, where she was, how she'd gotten here, and what she needed to do now.

Aurora rolled to her hands and knees and peered between the legs of the Nereids encircling her. The beach was crowded with people held back by a line of police. News crews were here, too. Over the roar of the ocean's waves, an even louder roar came from above.

A flying barge was approaching, with soldiers rappelling down cables, and armed with stunners and nets.

***

Manual Sanchez stood on the beach overseeing the operation. Most of the onlookers had departed, thanks to an even more exciting event staged a few blocks away. A currency transport had conveniently crashed—sprinkling unmarked bills over a wide area—all up for grabs. The few Nereid-rights activists remaining were roped off from the beach and their cries of protest could barely be heard over the wind and waves.

Besides the Nereids, only Sanchez, his own people, and the ones who'd hired him remained on the beach. Sanchez had mobilized quickly after Premier Bromberg called to tell him of an offer—an amazingly lucrative offer. A guy wanted to literally give him a thousand runaway Nereids for free, better than free—he was being paid to take them.

This would more than make up for his company's losses over the last ten years. His brother-in-law had promised to keep the business running, but failed miserably. Sanchez suspected he'd even been pilfering funds. He looked forward to flaying him alive.

Sis can find herself a new husband.

He watched the Niña's soldiers lassoing Nereids and hauling them off. Sanchez loved any hunt, even a no-brainer one like this. There were too many animals here to store at his company's warehouse, so he planned to use the Niña's cargobay as temporary housing. Kowalski had objected, of course, but Bromberg strong-armed him into it.

With this remarkable turn of events, Sanchez felt better than he had in weeks. So good, he could almost forget his sweet fantasy of boot-stomping that she-thing in the face. His mind briefly swirled into crazy flashes of color and light, making his head ache. *God damn fucking portals.* He remembered again how they'd sprung open without warning, exposing him to the chaos of hyperspace. He made a fist and rubbed his knuckles into his forehead. People looked at him funny when he did that.

Just keep it together long enough to round up these Blues. He looked over at Lester Merritt standing on the crest of a small grass covered hill, next to his tall blond companion. *Those idiots got no idea how valuable these Nereids are. It's going to mean a whole lot more money on top of what they're already paying me.*

Money meant power. Power meant he could do what he wanted. And what he wanted was revenge. Against Bromberg who thought he owned him, against Walker who'd refused to die on schedule, and most especially against that she-devil who'd landed him in sickbay. He thought bitterly about how Bromberg had used him then betrayed him.

He had Walker by the short-hairs with that treason charge, then just let him go. Put me through all this shit for nothing.

Sanchez hadn't seen Walker and his bitch in over a week. The next time, he hoped it would be through a high-powered rifle scope. He happily imagined their heads exploding, but then his mind filled with scrambled images even worse than before. He knuckled his forehead again and cursed the twinge in his shoulder from when he tried to shoot Carrie that second time. The blast had actually bounced off of her onto him.

I need to make sure she doesn't see me coming next time. Too bad she didn't turn out to be like these Nereids.

It occurred to him he'd most likely trapped and sold some of these same ones before. Given a glimpse of freedom, they tended to run.

He supervised the round-up closely. The Niña crew were capable soldiers, but unfamiliar with this type of work. Individually, Nereids were easy to handle, but resisted when grouped, so they needed to be culled out one-by-one, and placed in separate cages.

He'd explained all this to that Lester guy, who in turn communicated with the man he'd flown in with. Sanchez recognized their gray suits, and wondered why the Church would bother with this, but he knew better than to ask.

A Nereid, cut from the herd, tried to make a break for it, scrambling away on all fours.

"Farley, on your right!" Sanchez yelled.

Farley's electronic lasso whipped out and snagged the Nereid by its long back legs slapping the animal down flat. Instead of giving up meekly, the Nereid continued to struggle, clawing at the sand. Sanchez scowled, surprised by its uncharacteristic determination, until Farley pounced on it, and it went limp. The Nereid looked scruffy as if it recently lost and replaced much of its fur. Still, it would bring a good price. They all would.

Sanchez chuckled, watching Farley fall all over himself as he wrestled the Nereid over to one of the cages.

As filled cages departed, and empty ones arrived, his people continued rounding the Nereids up, one-by-one, peeling them away from the circle like layers from a brilliant blue onion. Sanchez watched the circle shrink, wondering what lay at the center keeping them riveted in place.

The tall blond man watched too. Lester had been tip-toeing around this guy as if he were a landmine. Something about the man projected a disturbing intensity. Sanchez's curiosity finally got the better of him. He walked over to the two men on the hill.

"Never seen 'em circle up like that before," Sanchez said. "Makes ya wonder what they got inside there."

The tall man kept his attention focused on the scene below as he replied in a deep smooth voice. "I know exactly what it is, and it belongs to me."

Sanchez naturally wanted to ask the obvious next question, but Lester Merritt shook his head in warning. Maybe curiosity wasn't a good idea. Sanchez moved away, deciding to keep his mind on the job, much as he could keep it on anything these days.

When the tightly woven circle of Nereids whittled down to a mere dozen or so, the tall man walked down the hill, moving in as the last of them were pulled away. Standing at the now empty spot that had been the center of the Nereids' circle, he stared down at the sand as if he couldn't comprehend what lay there. Lester hung back, but Sanchez walked up. He saw nothing in the sand but smeared impressions.

"Find whatever it was you lost?" he asked, trying to sound only politely interested.

The man looked up, and spun about, his eyes searching the sand, the water and the cliffs behind them. Then he closed his eyes tight, concentrating with a furrowed brow, as if the answer lay somewhere inside. When he opened his eyes again, he ran to the filled cages remaining on the beach, going from one to the next, grabbing at the Nereids within, making each of them squeal before letting go and running to the next.

"What the hell?" Sanchez sputtered, and started after him.

Lester interceded.

"Don't interfere," he told Sanchez, quiet, but firm. "That's Morden Chayd, Supreme Father of the Unified Church of Earth. The last thing you want to do is get in his way."

Annoyed, Sanchez shook his head, but stood back to watch.

When Chayd reached the last cage, he backed away, clenched his hands into fists and pressed them against the sides of his head as if it might explode. He flung the fists to his sides and turned back, fixing his eyes on Sanchez.

"Where have you taken the rest of them?" he yelled.

Sanchez squeezed his own eyes into slivers, and yelled back. "Our agreement was that they're mine to keep."

The fists opened, and Chayd walked toward him. Lester moved out of the way, but Sanchez stood his ground, not the least intimidated by Chayd's tall physique or political clout. Sanchez outweighed him by a large margin, had a dozen men on the beach, plus the backing of the Premier of the United Nations to call on. He was more than a match for anybody in any arena. Or so he thought.

Chayd stopped in front of him. "Answer my question."

The Supreme Father spoke quietly, but with such deadly determination it gave Sanchez pause—for a moment. Sanchez tried to say, "Fuck you," but only got as far as "Fu—" before he was on his knees, the pain in his gut so wrenching and violent he screamed and vomited onto the sand. Then he was upright again, hauled to his feet effortlessly in Chayd's grip.

"Where were the rest taken?" Chayd repeated.

Sanchez pulled his survival instincts together and gasped an answer. "The Niña's cargobay."

The Supreme Father's cool countenance flamed red hot. "The Niña?" His face twisted into a snarling mask and his grip tightened to a stranglehold. "You sent her back to the Niña?"

Sanchez was beyond answering—reduced to a writhing, choking mass of pain. When he went limp and unresponsive, the Supreme Father tossed him aside like a rag. Down on the beach, Sanchez's men stared in surprise, while Lester kept backing up.

***

Hissing through his teeth, Cadmon shook as he struggled with the urge to destroy everything and everyone in sight, then brought himself under control. He looked down at Sanchez's still form, animated it to stand on its feet, and made the dead man's arm lift and wave the others back to work. Cadmon looked over at Lester who was still moving away from him.

"You knew. Oh, Lester, you knew all along."

Lester broke into a run. He didn't get far.

Cadmon walked over and watched him writhe on the ground. "This is just a taste of what I'm going to do to you after I finish cleaning up the mess you've made."

In his frustration, he almost wished he could wash his hands of the whole matter, but he didn't dare. She was too much of a liability. *Once she learns what I did to Walker, she'll become every bit as much as of an avenging angel as me, and my ability to best her grows less each day.*

Her donning the furry disguise of a Nereid was something he hadn't anticipated. She'd left a bit of her flesh on the sand, radiating a nanobot-filled presence, and hidden herself within the herd. *Damn, she's slick.* As the last of the cages were being loaded, he glanced over at the standing body of Sanchez, and settled on a new plan.

She's not the only one who can play hide and seek.

Chapter 42

Daniel fumed in his quarters, furious with Kowalski. The Niña was being used as a base for a Nereid trading operation. He had argued vehemently with the captain, but one word voiced to anyone else would let Cadmon Dhyre know he was still alive.

"I have no choice," Kowalski told him. "Premier Nelson Bromberg ordered it, personally. I can't just fake another communication glitch and fly off again."

The captain's fear of losing command overruled any moral objection Daniel could offer. He might have taken on everyone involved under different circumstances, but as it was, he couldn't risk it. Despite his outrage, he had to keep silent, and stay out of sight. He tried not to think about what was going on right now in his very own cargobay.

You've got bigger things to worry about, he told himself. The most difficult of them was learning how to manage his nanobots, all fully awake now and swarming inside him demanding attention, not to mention dealing with a nine-foot-tall Garuda living next door in Serena's former quarters. When Daniel tried to lock his side, the bird ripped the door from its hinges. The door now hung open between their quarters like the pried off lid to Pandora's box, promising a continual source of jarring surprises.

To Daniel's relief, Chegta made no attempt to repeat the mental link forced on him when they were first introduced, but the bird remained an unnerving presence. This very moment, Chegta sat on the floor not five feet away, staring at him. Daniel faced his computer terminal, but in his peripheral vision he could see those giant yellow eyes aimed in his direction.

In these the past few days, Daniel had learned Chegta owned a sharp mind, which the bird employed to insult him and the entire human race on a regular basis. The only thing Chegta discussed civilly was the need to find "she who woke me from death." Daniel knew it was unlikely Aurora had found a way to resist Chayd's influence, let alone escape, but he kept searching. He monitored the radio frequency of their nanobots in case she tried to contact him, and watched for reports of any unusual sightings on the off-chance she might be found injured and unrecognizable.

When he came across an odd event on a beach in the Canary Islands, he immediately checked into it, but it turned out to be only a group of Nereid runaways. Interesting, but not what he was looking for. It never occurred to him that Sanchez would get the job of rounding them up, or that the Niña would be forced to assist him. His own ship and people were helping Sanchez profit from the sale of Nereids. Daniel was too ashamed to share any of this with Chegta, who already believed humans were worthless. He had no desire to explain how the dark side of human nature was manifesting itself on his own ship. Even now, as the Nereids were being brought on board, Chegta knew nothing of it . . . he hoped. Daniel wasn't really sure what the bird did or didn't know. Worried, he glanced over at his fearsome companion, squatting on the floor. Verbal communication between them tended to be sparse and confrontational, but the silent staring was worse. Daniel thought of Chegta as male, but he had nothing to base it on.

Good, something we can talk about.

"I'm curious," Daniel said, breaking the oppressive silence. "I think of you as male. Am I right?"

"I was Warrior class. I did not reproduce."

"Don't you kind of miss out then?"

"And when was the last time you engaged in reproductive activity?"

Chegta apparently knew as much about him as Aurora had, which only added to his discomfort.

"It hasn't been that long," Daniel protested. "And at least for me, it's a possibility. It's not like I've never had sex."

Chegta warbled and trilled in the Garuda version of derisive laughter that Daniel had come to recognize. "We too have our pleasures, small human, and they are not nearly so limited as yours."

Daniel frowned. *Have I just been bested in some bizarre competition?* Even so, it felt better than just being stared at. He came up with another question. "So how does one become a warrior anyway?"

"It is not a matter of becoming. It is a matter of birth." The golden orbs looked away as if focusing on something at a great distance, then pulled back. "Until now."

"You don't want to be a warrior anymore?" Daniel asked.

"It is not a question of wanting. It is a question of fact. I am no longer of my world."

"That's a pretty broad statement."

"An accurate statement. I can no longer be a Garuda warrior because I am no longer Garuda, just as you are no longer human."

"Speak for yourself. I'm the same as I've always been, with just a slight modification."

The bird clicked and trilled derisively. "Again, you engage in self-deception. One can choose but one path."

Daniel scoffed at that. "You're the one who keeps switching paths. One minute you're trying to kill us, the next you opt for suicide, and now you say you're not even a Garuda anymore—and just hang out with me as if it were all perfectly normal."

"Normal? No, you and I are not normal. We are—"

"Yeah, yeah, I know—a race apart."

"Yes, although you are and always shall be my inferior."

"You know, I'm getting pretty tired of your attitude. Just because you outweigh me doesn't make you better."

"My superior nature has nothing to do with superior size. It is a question of *pruitia*," Chegta trilled the word in a way no human could duplicate.

"What the hell is proo-eee-shiiaaaeeah, or whatever it was you said?"

"One's innate benefit to the health and well-being of all that is or shall ever be. Humans have no pruitia. You take what you do not own, destroy what you do not value, hate what you do not understand, fear what you do not know. You act first, think later, and apologize last. Misfits. The universe would be better without you."

Daniel glared at the huge bird, but knew better than to overreact. He tried to focus back on his search, but the bird's damnation of all humanity pecked at him like a demented sparrow. He twisted back. "Where do you get off calling us misfits?"

"It is the basic flaw of your kind. You value individualism at the cost of the general good. The result is a race of the maladjusted. In contrast, the Garuda are ordered, disciplined, and purposeful."

Daniel struggled to come back with something equally insulting, but he had no ammo, since he didn't know anything about Chegta's race. It occurred to him he was pretty sure they didn't call themselves Garuda. "Why do you keep referring to yourself using our word, Garuda."

"You could not pronounce the true name, and I find this demigod of yours a fitting choice."

Daniel rolled his eyes. Holding his annoyance in check, he thought about what he'd gleaned so far. "Okay, if I understand you, each of you is born with a predestined place in Garuda society. Does anyone ever challenge it?"

"To undermine unity is not tolerated."

"Wow. Glad I'm not part of your utopia. Freedom of choice is one of the things humans value most."

"As I said . . . misfits."

Daniel smiled now, no longer insulted by the term. "So tell me, what are these predestined social classes of yours?"

Chegta remained silent, probably debating the wisdom of educating a human on Garuda society. Finally, he spoke again. "There are five castes. The Intellect Caste plans for our future, teaches the young, and administers the laws. Warrior Caste protects and enforces. Those who build and repair are Laborer Caste." The bird fell silent again.

"That's only three," Daniel prompted.

"The fourth are *Kejiiikariiiiitaaii*," he sang.

The sound made Daniel's ears ring.

"Translation is difficult. Dream-keepers may be closest, but insufficient. Their domain is that of the historical and creative imagination—again, insufficient."

Daniel looked up from his task, intrigued. "A single class has charge of imagination? Guess that explains your obvious lack of it."

The bird tilted his head at close to a ninety-degree angle.

Daniel knew the gesture indicated puzzlement among Garuda, too. "By Dream-keepers, you mean creative types, right? Like artists and story-tellers?"

The great beaked head tilted until nearly inverted.

"Well then, what do they do?"

The head flipped upright again. "They care for the sacred ones—a duty and privilege your kind neither comprehend nor appreciate."

"Maybe if you tried explaining things for once. All I ever get are cryptic half-answers."

"The answers are complete. It is your comprehension that fails."

Disgusted, Daniel turned his back on Chegta and returned to his search, but soon stopped again. "Wait, you said five castes. Are these sacred ones the fifth?"

"No. The fifth are those who do not belong among the four. The majority are disposed of, but there are some exceptions."

Daniel scowled, not sure he understood at first. As Chegta's meaning sank in, a slow smile spread across Daniel's face. "You mean misfits, don't you?"

The bird turned his head away and didn't answer.

Tired of playing twenty-questions, Daniel went back to his search. For a long while, the only sounds in the room were his own verbal instructions to his computer.

"Explain!" Chegta suddenly demanded.

Startled, Daniel's eyes flicked from the display to Chegta and back. "I'm just running the same search program, like I told you."

"Choose not this," the bird said and trilled loudly.

"What the hell is your problem?"

"He's talking to me, Daniel." The words were not spoken by Chegta.

Daniel gasped and spun around, elated, only to see the golden eyes of a blue Nereid.

"I remember now, Daniel," it said, impossibly. "I remember everything."

The timbre of the voice, its inflection, the way his name fell off at the end. "Serena?" he asked.

"And Aurora, and more."

"I don't understand."

She looked at Chegta and bowed her head. "Forgive this offense."

"A form revered can never offend," Chegta replied. "Only the wearer."

"What does that mean?" Daniel asked.

"There's no time." She ran to Daniel and pulled him up.

Her golden eyes held flecks of green and her claws were sharp and glassy instead of the dull-edged Nereid black. Questions flooded his brain. *How did she get here? Why does she look like that? And why the hell didn't security sound the alarm?* None of which he had a chance to voice.

"We have to end this," she said tugging him forward. Chegta started to rise. "No, Chegta, you would just confuse and frighten them. Please, wait here."

Chegta clicked in acknowledgement as she dragged Daniel out the door.

"Them who?" Daniel asked, as they trotted down the corridor.

"The Nereids."

Urgency poured from her, filling him with its need. He broke into a run.

***

Sanchez's voice came over the com requesting permission to dock his shuttle. Captain Kowalski grudgingly granted it. Before Premier Bromberg demanded Sanchez and his crew members round up a herd of runaway Nereids, rumors of the chief's moonlighting activities had been mere speculation. No longer. Turned out, Sanchez owned and operated the infamous MLS Trading Company. That revelation spelled the end of Sanchez's military career, which pleased Kowalski no end, but Sanchez would be filthy rich. And that pissed Kowalski off.

He stood now in the cargobay watching his people unload caged Nerieds from a barge. The huge bay door stood open to the vista of starry space, its cold vacuum held back by an energy shield ballooning around the barge and his personnel. Heavy cranes hummed, lowering their powerful electro-magnets to lock onto the

cages one at a time, lifting them into the air and swinging them overhead onto robotic forklifts, which then moved the cages into long,
even rows. The cavernous bay echoed with metallic clangs and the
Nereids' mewling cries. Kowalski thought they sounded like a strange
orchestra of cats and a dolphins trying to find common pitch. The dis-
cordance scraped at his nerves. He wanted this over with.

*Sanchez's better keep his promise that he'll get them out of
here quick.*

"I'll be in and out faster than a two-minute fuck," Sanchez had
told him, ignoring the fact that he was speaking to a superior officer.

Kowalski let the crudeness pass, hoping it was true—and that
he'd never have to deal with Sanchez again. It occurred to him that
the security chief should have reported in by now, but he was nowhere in sight. Farley came walking up. His newly sunburned face
looked grim as he stopped and saluted Kowalski.

"Captain, may I speak with you?" he asked.

Kowalski nodded permission. Farley looked around as if he expected someone to stop him. "I need a transfer, sir. I can't work with
him anymore. I don't like what I'm turning into."

Kowalski didn't have to ask what he meant. "Try holding on a
little while longer."

Farley shook his head. "I'm sorry, sir. I can't do his sh—dirty
work anymore. I just can't."

"Sanchez won't be an issue much longer. His military career's
over."

The muscles in Farley's face relaxed. "That's all I needed to
hear."

"Maybe not all," Kowalski said, remembering that Farley was
on duty that day. "If I find out anyone else knew about this moonlighting operation of his, they won't get off so easy."

"I didn't know, sir," Farley said.

"I'm not sure I believe you, especially since you helped him
cover up what he did to Carrie in that detention cell."

The muscles in Farley's face tightened again.

Kowalski inclined his head and pressed his lips into a line. "One
of those infamous training sessions, I take it?"

Farley swallowed. "Yes, sir."

"So how did he do it?"

"Sir?" Farley.

Kowalski pressed harder. "I want to know how he restrained her."

"He used E.M. manacles."

Kowalski smiled, recognizing the value of what he'd just learned. *Huh, a simple electro-magnet had done what diamond reinforced steel and high-powered energy-fields could not.* Farley scowled at the captain's smile, misinterpreting it, but Kowalski didn't bother justifying himself. "Thank you. You're dismissed," he said, then left to find Sanchez.

He approached a couple of crewmembers unloading the transport. "Have you seen Chief Sanchez?" One waved toward the cages lined up in rows. Kowalski headed in that direction and spotted Sanchez going from cage to cage, reaching through the bars at the wide-eyed Nereids, making them squeal.

"Chief!" he called out, but Sanchez ignored him. Kowalski's patience was gone. "Chief Manuel Sanchez, get your ass over here on the double!"

At that Sanchez stopped, turned his head, and squinted at him just as Daniel ran up with an uncaged Nereid by his side.

"What the hell are you doing?" Kowalski demanded.

"It's Aurora," Daniel answered, placing a hand on the Nereid's shoulder. "She's back."

Kowalski's lips turned down. "Riiight."

"I'm in disguise. Get over it," she said.

A talking Nereid? Could this really be her? "Guess it's a good thing no one used electromagnetic restraints on you this time," he said and watched for a reaction.

The Nereid before him stiffened perceptibly, but offered no response, so he looked at Daniel and explained. "I found out that's what Sanchez used. E.M. manacles."

"You should have told me," Daniel said to the Nereid.

"Why? So that someone else could harm me?" She turned to Kowalski. "We have to stop Sanchez from selling these Nereids."

Kowalski snorted. "I'd like to see you tell him that."

"I will," she replied. "Where is he?"

"Right over—" Kowalski gestured to where Sanchez had stood, but he was no longer there. "Sanchez!"

The overhead lights flickered and motors rumbled to life. Workers in the middle of moving cages through the open hangar cried out as the cargobay door came crashing down on them. Metal shards flew. Blue fur and human flesh splattered the walls. And the Nereids' whimpers turned to high-pitched screams.

Chapter 43

Green-lit energy scattered across the cargobay's door and its control panel, and the sharp smell of ozone filled the air. Crewmembers tried to get to the door controls, but the sparking green energy threw them back. Daniel knew the exterior force field sealing in a protective air supply had a thirty-second delay, but then it would vanish, and anyone caught on the wrong side would be exposed to the frigid vacuum of space. Daniel ran up to the sparking green energy and imagined a shield around his hand and arm. He tried to push through the field, but it resisted and soon biting fire stopped him. He shook off the pain, laid his palm on the floor to send his nanobots past the flickering energy. For a moment, he thought it was working, until searing heat shot up his arms and threw him back.

"Aurora!" he cried out, hoping she would have better luck. Searching for her, he was shocked to see her lying on the ground, doubled in half. Sanchez stood over her. Daniel sprinted toward them only to crash into an invisible wall, nearly knocking himself senseless.

"What the hell?" He rubbed his head.

Aurora and Sanchez were just five feet in front of him. He banged on the force field that shouldn't be there. "That's not a Nereid. That's Aurora . . . I mean, Carrie."

Sanchez didn't even glance at him.

"Leave her alone!" *This doesn't make sense. How is he doing this?* "Sanchez!"

The Chief of Security finally looked at him but instead of seeing beady black eyes, Daniel saw ones of cold, blue ice.

"Well, well, Dr. Walker. It seems you're more resourceful than I thought." The words began with Sanchez's rough tone and ended with the smooth, melodious voice of the Supreme Father.

Cold talons of fear gripped Daniel like a vise. *No, I'm not ready.* His nanobots swarmed inside him, awaiting instruction. *Prepare for battle*, he told them, but beyond that he had no idea what orders to give.

Sanchez's face and body were changing noticeably now.

Kowalski came running up. "Christ! What's happening to him?"

"That's not Sanchez. It's Cadmon Dhyre, aka the Supreme Father Morden Chayd," Daniel said. "Your screening system didn't work."

"Do something."

"Like what?" Daniel banged on the wall again.

"Chayd, stop this!" Kowalski yelled. "Our people are trapped out there."

The cool blue gaze moved to the captain. "Yes, most unfortunate." Cadmon's sigh was so sweet and sad, one might almost believe he cared. "I was forced to seal off the area quickly. This one is very adept at slipping away." His gaze moved to Aurora lying curled at his feet.

The operation lights on the hangar bay door blinked to red, which meant the bubble of breathable air outside had vanished. Someone screamed, and then all went silent. Kowalski put a hand to his forehead. Daniel looked down, overwhelmed with shame.

I should have seen this coming, found a way to stop it.

"Progress often demands sacrifice," Cadmon said.

"You mean like my uncle, Dr. McCormack?" Daniel asked, looking back at him with hate-filled eyes.

"Ah yes, the good doctor. Unfortunately, he was determined to expose my creation. You see my dilemma." He spread his still Sanchez-thick hands apart as if to say, what else could I do?

Why is he bothering to explain? And why is it taking him so long to change back? When he revealed his true face to me before, the nanomorphosis took mere seconds. Maybe all this is stretching him thin—altering his body, controlling the entire cargo bay, battling Aurora—it must be taking a toll. His powers aren't limitless.

Daniel moved sideways, searching for an end point or opening in the invisible wall.

"Don't be stupid," Cadmon said, and raised a sparking hand in Daniel's direction. "Trust me, this time there will be no heroic rescues."

Distract him. The thought came to Daniel as if from somewhere else.

"Is this all your nanogen was meant for? To give yourself a movie idol face, torture people into serving you and kill anyone in your way?" Daniel asked.

Cadmon's smirk faltered ever so slightly.

Was that anger, or maybe even a trace of guilt?

"Hardly. Its purpose should be obvious. It's a cure for the T-nanogen plague. I dedicated my life to rectifying a great wrong and succeeded despite the short-sighted interference of people like yourself."

"Guess that explains why you lost your tenure at the Tokyo Institute."

"They were cowards. The private sector proved even worse, all of them entrenched in self-interest and corporate greed, just like every other so-called normal."

"So you blew up Fabri-Tech's lab to get back at them?"

"It wasn't revenge, it was necessity. Cedric Fredrickson and his board left me no choice. They preferred the status quo, no matter how despicable it might be."

"That was over ten years ago. Doesn't seem like the status quo has changed any. The carrier camps are still full."

"Great change requires great patience. I refuse to expose humanity to my nanogen until I fully understand its ramifications. Unlike the creators of the T-Nanogen I won't allow another plague to develop." He frowned at Aurora lying helpless at his feet. "That's why I'm here. To make sure she doesn't contaminate anyone else. You have no idea how dangerous she is."

Cadmon was shedding more and more of his Sanchez-like characteristics—his hair lightening, his face narrowing, his torso slimming. Sanchez's uniform now hung loose and ill-fitting on a streamlined physique.

"Morden Chayd, Cadmon Dhyre—anagrams—same letters, different order. Guess you wanted someone to eventually make the connection, give you credit," Daniel said.

Good, keep him talking.

"As is my due. Why shouldn't history record that the greatest leap in human evolution was brought about by someone the world despised?"

"I guess that would be satisfying . . . if you actually had the good of your fellow man in mind."

"Oh, but I do. Curing the T-nanogen plague is only the beginning. These nanobots have made me instantly adaptable, and virtually indestructible. It's conceivable I could survive anywhere in any environment. My hope is that my creation will make it so humanity no longer needs to waste precious resources trying to find a Goldilocks planet. Instead, people will live anywhere they want."

"Except you don't seem too keen on sharing. How is it going to help anyone else if you keep it all to yourself?"

"In its current form, I cannot in good conscience distribute it. I must find a way to limit its capabilities. Can you imagine a world filled with ill-prepared people suddenly wielding this kind of power? The wars and interpersonal violence of our past would pale in comparison. To simply loose this on humanity would be unconscionable."

Daniel could see Kowalski listening, drawn in by the apparent reasonableness of Cadmon's argument. *He wants our approval, hungers for it even. He still cares what others think of him.*

Good, use it as a weapon.

Daniel laughed short and bitter. "You've painted yourself as quite the humanitarian, though I doubt all those people on the other side of that door would agree." He pointed at the closed cargobay door and thought of the bodies that must be floating outside. "They were innocent of any of this, but you left them to die. I assume you killed Sanchez as well."

Chayd's features twitched. "As I said, sometimes sacrifice is necessary. Think of them as casualties for the greater good."

"A noble sentiment, but it seems all your good intentions fall apart when it comes to practical application." Daniel felt no sorrow for Sanchez, but Chayd's pattern of both mass and one-on-one murder didn't bode well for anyone. If Chayd had any conscience remaining, it was thoroughly twisted. However, his attempts to justify his actions proved he could still feel something. Daniel pushed harder. "I'm trying to understand what this greater good is you're talking about when it seems like your nanogen hasn't helped anyone but you. Makes me wonder if you've forgotten all about your suffering brethren."

Cadmon smiled and shook his head. "Baiting me is a waste of breath."

"You're probably right. You must be immune to emotion by now, what with all that machinery inside you. Maybe I'm not talking to a human being at all, just a nanogenic puppet."

Cadmon's eyes narrowed and Kowalski put a restraining hand on Daniel's arm. He shook it off and went in hard for Cadmon's mental jugular.

"You're not fooling anyone. We can all see past your posturing and that mask you wear. All your self-righteous justifications are just a cover for wonton destruction and premeditated murder. Everything you've said is either an outright lie or self-delusion. Your superiors had good reason to reject your ideas. They saw what you really are, and you've fulfilled their worst fears, committing cold, calculated murder for the sole purpose of furthering your personal ambition."

"You know nothing of my—"

"You actually believe you're some kind of savior, don't you? The truth is you're just another petty dictator."

"This isn't going to work. I won't allow you to distract me. Her defenses are crumbling as we speak."

Daniel could see Aurora was in serious trouble, pinned to the floor by an invisible weight.

"Yes, you definitely enjoy hurting women, don't you? Like in that holovid Lester sent me. That poor girl had no idea what kind of monster she was dealing with."

Cadmon's self-satisfied smile flattened.

Daniel pressed on. "Now that I think about it, I was wrong to blame nanobots for turning you into something inhuman. You haven't changed a bit. You're still the same sadistic narcissist I saw in that holovid. A pathological killer with the face of a toad!"

Cadmon came at him, bursting through the energy field, eyes blazing in cold fury, hands reaching. Daniel danced back inches from Cadmon's fingertips and sent forth his own army of nanobots.

Cadmon stopped suddenly. His eyes and mouth opened wide. "You liar! You hypocrite! You're using my creation. Mine!"

It took all of Daniel's concentration to fend off Cadmon's attack and sweat beaded on his forehead, but he saw Aurora uncurling from her fetal ball.

It's working!

Aurora struggled to her hands and knees, but could seem to get no farther. This new battle front was helping divide Cadmon's attention, but it wasn't enough.

Daniel yelled at Kowalski. "I need a little help here!"

Kowalski grabbed a long pole hook from the wall and raised it into the air aiming at Cadmon's head, but before he could bring it crashing down, Cadmon shot a bolt of green energy at him. Kowalski dropped the pole and fell to the ground next to Daniel, clutching his wounded arm.

Damn it! Daniel pressed his foot against Kowalski's leg, sending in nanobots with pain suppressants and an urgent message.

Chegta! Get Chegta!

Kowalski crawled away on all fours, pushed to his feet and ran for the exit, but Cadmon's green energy sparked across the exit door blocking him.

"I can't get through!" Kowalski yelled.

Cadmon had them cut off from the rest of the ship. While Cadmon stood tall and strong, Aurora crouched on the floor and Daniel wavered on his feet like a drunkard.

THINK, WALKER, THINK! His gaze searched the bay and stopped on the towering crane with its huge magnet poised in the air.

E.M. manacles had restrained Aurora.

It made sense. Strong electro-magnetic fields scrambled radio signals. In the cab of the crane, a female crewman looked down at him, confusion writ large on her face. From her perspective, two men stood in a staring contest, while a loose Nereid crouched nearby, and the captain and crew were running around trying to open doors without success—a confusing and alarming tableau.

Daniel looked over to Kowalski, who stood at the control panel out of Cadmon's view. Meeting the captain's gaze, Daniel flicked his eyes up at the magnet. The captain nodded in understanding and waved at the crane operator to get her attention. He pointed from the magnet back at Cadmon.

This might put the woman's life in danger, but if Cadmon won this battle they might all be dead soon. She turned to her controls. The crane swung over their heads, smooth and silent. Daniel was careful not to let his eyes track it. Kowalski cranked his good arm in a circle, signaling the crane operator to turn the power up full.

Cadmon staggered. His hands reached for his head and the sparking energy all around the cargo bay went out.

Unfortunately, Daniel fared no better. As if a balloon had popped, weakness overcame him leaving him deflated and empty. He dropped to his knees.

Cadmon remained standing, but his face twisted in pure rage. Snarling, he leaped on Daniel and punched him furiously, landing one blow after another. Daniel tried to protect his face and head, hoping for rescue from Kowalski or the crew. He heard footfalls hurrying his way, but they weren't the captain's or the crew's.

Chegta had beat them to it.

Chapter 44

The giant bird charged into the cargobay, his heavy, splayed feet pounding the metal deck like hammer-falls. Cadmon looked up, sucked in a wide-eyed gasp, and ran.

Daniel uncurled, dropping his arms from his head. Above him, the crane operator lay slumped over her controls—the powerful magnet powered down. With the magnetic field gone, communication with his nanobots returned and his internal army regrouped. Daniel rolled to his hands and knees. Cadmon stood back, watching as Chegta tugged Daniel to his feet, and Aurora grabbed his other arm to steady him. Daniel clutched at his bruised ribs, but felt his strength returning.

"I'm okay, I'm okay," he told them.

"Join us now!" she said.

He felt their minds reaching for his and instinctively his mental wall went up, but he saw Cadmon walking toward them with a Cheshire-cat grin, and the control panels glimmering with interfering green sparks again. It was their only chance.

Daniel dropped his defenses and staggered at the shock of two other minds slamming into his. With their internal armies united, the three turned as one to face the enemy.

Cadmon's grin froze into uncertainty and he hesitated, narrowing his eyes at them. The Nereids mewling ceased, and they watched in silence as if they, too, knew everything depended on what happened next.

"Surrender," Chegta trilled, one voice representing three.

Cadmon barked a surprised laugh. "An English-speaking Garuda. My nanogen at work once again. You can thank me for including your alien DNA in its original design. Otherwise, it would have killed you rather than interfacing."

"I thank you for nothing," Chegta answered, his mind taking the forefront. His gaze focused past Cadmon to the rows of caged Nereids. Daniel felt the dark pupils of Chegta's fist-sized eyes enlarge.

The Nereids stared back, fear and hope mixed equally in their wide-eyed faces.

Chegta looked at Aurora still wearing the same blue-fur as those in the cages. The feathers on Chegta's neck lifted, and he seemed to swell in size as he regarded her with one staring eye, while the other remained trained on the cages beyond.

Daniel felt Chegta's outrage as if it were his own.

This will not be tolerated, the bird threatened in their linked thoughts.

I'm trying to help them, Chegta. They sang for me, Aurora answered.

Impossible. Chegta's disbelief cut through their minds like a knife. *You lie! Humans hear not.*

I heard them, I swear. Look deeper. You know I'm not lying. No one else ever heard them because they've always been kept apart. That's why no one understood.

Chegta looked back at the individual cages, each holding a single Nereid. His anger eased and his mind turned thoughtful. *Humans are even stupider than we imagined.*

Though not privy to the trio's mental communications, Cadmon followed the bird's stare. "I take it these Nereids interest you?"

"Priceless treasures," Chegta replied. "Humans steal what is not theirs, yet know not the value of what they take."

"Then allow me to return them. I want no quarrel with your kind.. Take them and this ship and go home. A gesture of my good will."

Chegta tilted his head as if considering Cadmon's proposal.

Daniel reacted. *Don't listen to him. He's just trying to separate us.*

"You insult me," Chegta said, and Daniel wondered which of them Chegta was addressing, but the rest of his answer was clear. "They are not yours to give and I have no home. You have made me outcaste."

"Because of my nanogen." Cadmon offered a sad smile. "I sympathize. I too have been an outcast on my world. But you're right, the fault is clearly mine. The three of you are unhappy accidents, unintended fall-out from my experiment, mistakes for which I must take full responsibility." He paused to look about the cargobay and all the people trapped in it—some standing, some lying unconscious, some dead. He frowned and shook his head. "Now it appears there may be any number of carriers here. I'll have to sterilize the entire ship."

"What do you mean sterilize?" Daniel asked, his alarm overwhelming their three-way link, pulling his personality to the fore.

"Disassembling the engine core should do it. Worked well with the Fabri-Tech lab, but don't worry, I doubt you'll feel a thing." Cadmon turned to walk away.

"Wait!" Daniel called to him. "The three of us are the only ones infected. You don't have to hurt anyone else."

Cadmon stopped and looked back. "I'm hardly going to take your word for it. I've been fooled before. I didn't recognize you were infected, and now here's a third carrier, a Garuda, no less. No, I can't risk it. Sterilization is the only choice."

"We won't let you." Daniel stepped forward, and the other two moved with him.

Together, they launched their combined armies at Cadmon in an invisible wave. Cadmon flinched and grimaced, but only that. Their attack crashed against his defenses, splattering, dying.

Cadmon sighed deeply. "Face it, even combined you're no match for me. The three of you are mere infants—the result of a few months of experimentation compared to years of my own."

Cadmon waved a hand toward the hangar door and its motors thrummed. The outer door lifted to reveal the dark vista of starry space, with the blue and white Earth below silhouetting the transport parked outside. Human bodies floated in the distance, blown into space when the protective atmospheric balloon had popped. A new bubble existed now, guarding a path for Cadmon's exit. He turned back and smiled sadly at Aurora.

"I did so enjoy our tryst, my dear. Though I don't care much for this latest look of yours, it does demonstrate considerable talent. You would have made an interesting subject, but it appears you're more trouble than you're worth. Pity." He turned away.

Aurora accessed Daniel's mind. *Talk to him, slow him down. I have an idea.*

"If we're infants like you say, then teach us, guide us," Daniel said.

Cadmon paused and turned back with a look of genuine surprise. "You want to learn? From me?" His eyes narrowed as if considering the idea, but then he smiled and shook his head. "I fear you would be ungrateful students."

"You don't know that. Give us a chance," Daniel argued, trying to keep Cadmon's attention. Meanwhile his internal army was working with Chegta's, building a wall to protect Aurora. "I think we might surprise you."

"Doubtful. And certainly not worth the risk."

Cadmon turned away again, but their wall was complete and they were ready. He and Chegta released Aurora from their mental link. *Go!*

Aurora darted away, running for the caged Nereids. Bolts slid aside as she ran past, and the cage doors sprang open. The Nereids scurried free, this way and that, in seeming pandemonium.

Cadmon lifted a hand as if to put an end to such nonsense, but then merely shook his head, turned and walked toward the open cargobay door. A dozen fleeing Nereids crossed his path. A casual wave of his arm sent them sprawling. More ran ahead of him, slowing him, then more and more. What at first had looked like disordered panic now revealed itself to be an organized pattern, lines dashing in front of Cadmon, behind, and alongside. With each gesture of his hand, dozens more fell, but more rushed in, leaping over the fallen, keeping the pattern unbroken. Like well-trained dancers, the Nereids wove together.

Daniel, Aurora and Chegta redirected their armies to protect the Nereids, and attack Cadmon with everything they had, but the Nereids' speed and numbers served even better. Cadmon couldn't zero in on any one of them. There were simply too many, moving too quickly, and their combined nanobot armies kept pummeling Cadmon, keeping his attention divided. He had to simultaneously maintain control of the Niña, defend against their armies, and clear a path through the Nereids. It all proved too much, even for him.

The weaving, darting circle of blue drew ever tighter, enclosing Cadmon as his arms whipped furiously and he screamed angry curses. Soon, all Daniel could see was a spinning circle of crisscrossing Nereids. Above Cadmon's curses, a high-pitched keening rang out, like dolphin or whale song, but more melodious and rhythmical. The song grew in volume, filling the cavernous bay, echoing full and resonant, humming through ship and flesh.

The sparking green energy died, and Chegta's mental link with Daniel broke, releasing him. Daniel spun and waved, yelling to be heard above the alien chorus. "Close the hangar. Shut down the core!"

Crewmen ran to join Kowalski at the control panels, and Daniel hurried to join them.

The hangar door thundered alive again, and closed the cargo-bay off from the dark vista of space.

The voice of Drummond, second in command, boomed over the intercom, finally, able to make contact. "Intruder Alert! All hands to their sta—"

"Drummond!" Kowalski interrupted.

"Captain, what's going on down—"

"Activate emergency shutdown of the reactor core!" Kowalski barked.

"Yes, sir." There was a brief pause. "Emergency shutdown in progress. Are you all right, sir?"

"I am now." Kowalski let out a breath, looked over, and saw Daniel beside him. "Why are you here? Go keep an eye on that lunatic."

Daniel frowned, but trotted back toward the Nereids encircling Cadmon.

Aurora dashed past him and ran to the Captain's side. He turned to see why but with their mental link broken, he had no clue what she was up to. The Nereid song caught his attention again, changing in rhythm. They had stopped weaving in and out. As if finding their places, they now pressed together into a shrinking circle, and their wild song softened into deep soothing tones. Daniel looked back at Aurora for an explanation, but she was gone and Kowalski was coming toward him.

"I've called security," Kowalski said, and looked at the layered Nereid circle. "What are they doing to him?"

"No idea. We need to ask Aurora or Chegta. They seem to know something about them."

Aurora was nowhere to be seen so they turned toward the gigantic bird. Chegta stood facing the Nereid circle, swaying, eyes closed, head bowed. The two men shared a guarded look.

"Maybe later," Kowalski said.

Crewmen raced in, some wearing the navy blue of security with resonators at the ready, others in white, carrying emergency first-aid bags. The medical personnel sprinted to the fallen, both human and Nereid, while security lined up in front of Daniel and the captain.

"Give me your weapon," Daniel told the soldier nearest him.

The woman glanced sideways at her captain, then handed over her pistol.

Daniel hefted the black resonator, determined to end this. Then he noticed Aurora wheeling in a heavy stasis pod, heading toward the circled Nereids.

"She can't be serious." Recovering from his momentary disbelief, Daniel sprinted after her. "Aurora, wait!" Kowalski and the security team followed.

The humming circle of Nereids parted to accommodate Aurora and the stasis pod, then closed ranks again, linking their arms and legs into an impenetrable blue wall. Daniel skidded to a halt with the others.

"Hey!" Daniel tried to squeeze through. "Move!"

The Nereids didn't budge.

Hot with frustration, Daniel gripped his black pistol, but when he saw his own blood lust reflected in the eyes of the soldiers beside him, he took a deep breath, and shook his head.

"We'll wait," he said.

After a long while, and with no apparent signal, the Nereids ended their song on a single note and parted like waves. Daniel hurried forward, dodging the Nereids until he reached Aurora and the pod. He peered through the pod's window, and saw what he expected—the face of his nemesis in quiet repose. The pod's temperature display read absolute zero.

Daniel stared with a black hate at the serene expression on Cadmon's handsome face. It was all he could do not to rip the pod apart with his bare hands. In his peripheral vision he saw Aurora watching him and felt waves of disapproval flooding off her. He wasn't sure he cared. The pistol in his hand hummed on full power, and the tight muscles in his face twitched as rage and conscience warred within him.

Kowalski and the soldiers waited, looking back and forth between Daniel and Aurora.

After several tense seconds, Daniel flipped the power off on his pistol.

"Stand down," he ordered through clenched teeth.

The soldiers lowered their weapons, and Daniel walked away.

Chapter 45

Six days after the showdown with Cadmon Dhyre under the guise of Morden Chayd, Daniel's nerves still sang like taut guitar strings. Sleep was elusive but each night he kept trying. Just as he started to doze off near midnight, his door whisked open. Startled, he leaped from his bed, adrenaline surging. Aurora entered unannounced and uninvited, still looking like a 'Blue Fuzzy.'

"Try knocking for once!" he yelled.

"Calm down," she replied, coming toward him. She folded her overlong arms and leaned back against his desk to face him.

Her manner of speech and body language now resembled Serena's far too much for his comfort, especially exhibited in this Nereid form. The big gold eyes and round face with small furry ears on either side, reminded him of a lemur. If it were blue. And human-sized. And swam like a seal.

"Did you order more pods yet?" she asked.

"I was almost asleep."

"Sleep later. What is the Nereid count?"

"Augh." He rubbed his face and sat down on his mattress. She wasn't going to leave until he answered. "Six thousand forty-three."

"Records show over ten thousand Nereids have been imported to Earth. We need to recover them all."

"Not all of them are still alive. You saw Chayd kill a hundred of them right in front of us," he said, remembering the strange scenario of the Nereids surrounding Chayd—incapacitating him somehow. The mystery of it haunted Daniel and he hadn't slept well since. "I just wish you'd explain why the Garuda value them so much."

"The dreamers are sacred to them."

"Yes, you told me, but why? And how did they stop Chayd?"

"They made him dream the dream of the dreamers."

Daniel sighed. Every conversation he had with Chegta and Aurora about the Nereids went in frustrating circles.

"We must return all of them if we are to make peace," Aurora stated.

"I understand what's at stake. And thanks to Lester's campaign, everyone else does too. Strange having the UCE on our side now."

"Your cousin is grateful to you."

Daniel nodded. When he'd told Lester that Chayd wouldn't be back to bother him, his cousin had spent a full five minutes thanking him. For now, Lester was running the Church in the absent Supreme Father's name, issuing edicts about the danger of owning Nereids and deluging the UN with demands to enact laws against it. People were turning in their pets by the hundreds.

"Is he sending us the contents of Chayd's laboratory as requested?" she asked.

"It should all be here in the morning," Daniel kept his gaze averted since he found her blue-furred face and body disturbing. "Including one lab rat named Sweetheart."

"Interesting person, this cousin of yours. Perhaps he will become the next Supreme Father."

That gave Daniel pause. "Geez, let's hope not. You wouldn't believe all the rotten things he's done to save his own skin."

"I am aware. He participated in covering up the murder of a young woman, profited from the destruction of Fabri-Tech's orbiting laboratory, failed to warn you of Chayd's ill intentions and ran away to save himself when you asked for his help. And yet you've chosen not to implicate him."

Daniel bristled, glaring at her. "Did you steal all that out of my head?"

"Does it matter? It appears you protect him out of family loyalty. Am I correct?"

"No," he snapped, then thought about it. "I don't know. Maybe. I turned over that holovid to the authorities, but it only showed Dhyre and he's listed as deceased, so they closed the case."

"Ah." She nodded, pursing her thin blue-black lips. "You were able to preserve your sense of ethics without personal cost. Well done."

He frowned hard at her. "Why don't you go bug Chegta for a while."

"I am not done here yet. Have you ordered sufficient food supplies for the Nereids?"

Daniel squeezed his irritation into a manageable dot. "We'll have another two hundred thousand pounds by week's end. If we need more, I'll get more." He rubbed his forehead, wishing he were asleep. "Now if you don't mind—"

"I do mind. Are you aware Lauren Chambers was offered a job at UN Headquarters? Senior Resident Expert on the Native Tau Medean Humanoids."

"What? There's no such thing."

"Nevertheless, she accepted the position."

Daniel shook his head.

Aurora stared at him for a long moment. "Why do you not celebrate your accomplishments? You proved Tau Medea is an earth-like planet suitable for human settlement and have ended the Nereid trade by revealing it as the root cause of the Garuda dispute with humanity. This is everything you wanted, is it not?"

"I guess so." He leaned forward, resting his elbows on his knees. As he stared at his bare feet, he wondered if he'd ever need to cut his toenails again. *What about shaving? Can I stop doing that, too?*

"I am sad for Chegta. He expects to be ostracized from his home world," she said.

He blew a raspberry sound. "Breaks my heart."

"Did you know Garuda equate humans with their fifth societal class?"

"Misfits. Yeah, I kind of figured that out." Daniel pinched the bridge of his nose and squeezed his eyes shut. "Look, I really need to get some sleep."

"The exact definition is uncertain. Chegta is reluctant to discuss the subject. Perhaps he does not wish to offend," she said.

"Yeah, well, he offends me plenty."

"Perhaps because you also feel like an outcast and his use of the term 'misfit' causes you emotional injury."

He groaned and closed his eyes again. "Would you please go play junior psychiatrist somewhere else?"

She leaned forward and clapped her hands an inch in front of his face. "Wake up! I would know what you are thinking."

Startled, he flinched backwards. Angry now, he raised his voice. "You want to know what I think? I think you just ruined the first chance I've had at a good night's sleep in days. I think you're a royal pain in the ass, and if humans are misfits, then you and I must be the misfits of all misfits. What I really think is that if either of us had any guts, we'd shove ourselves out an airlock."

Aurora leaned back against the desk again and perused her claws. "You are over-reacting, as usual. But do not worry, I will keep you out of trouble as always."

"Stop pretending like we have a history together. Just because you recovered a few lost memories doesn't make you Serena."

"I could adopt her physical appearance if it would make you more comfortable."

"No. This is weird enough already. Doesn't matter what you look like on the outside anyway. I know what's on the inside. You're just a sack of mechanical bugs. And now, Lord help me, so am I." He put his hands to either side of his head. "Sometimes, I feel like running through the corridors screaming, to get away from all the voices inside me. No wonder Dhyre turned into a lunatic."

"He was already a lunatic. His nanogen merely enabled him to act on pre-existing tendencies resulting from early childhood trauma. Our others don't alter personalities—they enhance them."

"You say that like it's a good thing." He dropped his hands. "Who among us has no dark, unsavory aspects hidden away? That kind of enhancement's a lousy idea for anybody."

"A challenge perhaps," she admitted, "but you possess a well-developed sense of right and wrong. I am not worried."

"I don't know how the hell you can be so complacent. We have no idea what we're turning into. And we've still got that madman on board because you insisted on keeping him alive. Does he still attract you? You still want him? Is that it?"

She folded her furry arms over her flat torso and leaned back. "Yes, I do want him, and so should you. He is our best source of information. The experiment he began is ongoing."

"And we're the lab rats." His voice dripped bitterness.

"An unflattering analogy, but essentially correct. We have an obligation to explore how this nanogen may be of benefit. It could give new meaning to the term human."

He looked at her Nereid face. "I can't argue with that." Suddenly, incongruously, it all seemed like a monstrous joke. He laughed aloud and threw his arms out wide. "So it's all up to us then. You, me, Chegta, and our mad-scientist popsicle—the four 'Misfiteers'— off on some wild adventure of self-discovery as we mutate into God knows what."

"Essentially," she said with a shrug.

He shook his head, no longer amused, and turned away, aching to go somewhere and do something, but he didn't know where or what. He had no idea what he should be doing, even though he'd been doing it full speed.

He sank back on his bed, defeated.

"You are unhappy," she said, peering down at him.

He covered his eyes. "Please, just go away. I can't look at you like that."

"I remain in this form to reassure the Nereids. This experience has left them deeply distressed."

"I can empathize. I'm sure they'll get over it," Daniel mumbled, hands over his face.

"I hope so. I am also hoping to convince them to sing to you."

"I already heard them sing, remember?"

"That was not meant for you. You must hear that which is yours."

He groaned and dropped his arms to his sides. "You sound just like Chegta, talking in cryptic. Maybe your nanobots are short-circuiting."

She laughed, a high-pitched Nereid sound.

"This isn't funny." He sat up, determined now to get the seriousness of the situation through to her. "Don't you get it? These nanobots could be eating away at our minds. What makes us any better or stronger than Cadmon Dhyre and he invented this thing? What happens if we go nuts like he did? Who's going to stick us in stasis pods?"

"This self-pity of yours must cease," she stated. Without warning, she pounced on him, pushed him flat and, straddled him. "Kiss me."

"What? No!" he answered in disgust, but he was pinned down and before he could stop her, she pressed her thin blue mouth against his and their tongues connected. His mouth flamed red hot, the sensation shooting through his nasal cavities up into his brain.

He felt a moment of blind, floundering panic, then splashed into her waiting mind, into the memory of a deep blue ocean filled with alien voices opening her up to a lifetime of memories lost. As he relived her experience of being reborn in a blue ocean dream, the dam in his own mind cracked open and collapsed along with hers.

He felt the warm hugs of his mother, saw the glint of humor in the conspiratorial winks of his father, heard their words of pride, and knew the easy security of unconditional love. He saw his Uncle Charlie, a middle-aged bachelor, welcoming him, struggling to learn how to be both parent and friend. He rejoiced even as he mourned. Other faces flew past—central and bit players in the scenes of his life. Finally, Serena appeared, taking center stage, first as a dedicated scientist with a will of iron, later as his lover, helper, and confidante, then reborn as a red-furred, monkey-like creature on a distant world, later turning into the womanly manifestation of his erotic fantasies, and finally, becoming this wide-eyed blue Nereid sitting on him, determined to connect him to both her and himself.

Daniel no longer saw her manifestations as separate beings, but as Serena—unwavering at the center. From the beginning, she had remained loyal, loving him despite the meagerness with which he shared himself. Cloistered in a shroud of suspicion, keeping a determined distance from her and everyone else, he'd kept defending his choices as a healthy independence, but in reality he'd lived in a self-made prison created by paralyzing fear and self-doubt.

The memories existed in his mind, but their colors changed as he saw them through the clarifying lens of another mind—the mind of a woman who had loved him in a previous life, loved him still, and would continue to love and accept him—whatever form he might take. That profound conviction came not from empty-worded promises, but from the depths of their combined inner selves, hearts and minds joined without disguise or deceit. He felt that love and bond as if it were an extension of his own being, strengthening and surrounding him, amplified by the Nereid song replaying in her mind, and it shook him to his core.

I am not lost. I am not alone.

Tears tracked his cheeks. Slowly, Aurora withdrew until his thoughts were solely his own again.

"I'm sorry," he finally managed to say. "I'm so sorry."

"For what?"

"For being stupid."

"No. Just human."

He tried to laugh, but it came out choked. He took a long, shaky breath and opened his eyes again. He found himself looking into the green eyes of the exotic woman he'd been trying so hard to resist. Having been fur-covered before, she now wore nothing but naked skin. His raw physical attraction to her hit him anew.

"Is it Aurora or Serena?" he asked cautiously.

"I prefer Aurora now, but Serena is still here."

He pushed back the crystal clear strands of hair and felt her smooth skin under his fingertips. He let his hand run down her neck to her breast, then pulled her close to kiss her long and deep. Divesting himself of his pajamas, he pulled her onto the bed with him, running his hands over her, tasting her, until she pressed him back to look in his face.

"I would know what you are experiencing," she said.

"Um . . . okay. What I'm experiencing is terrific."

"No, join with me." Her pupils widened and tiny sparks flickered in her crystal hair.

"Oh." The old fears returned. "That mind-meld stuff's pretty overwhelming."

"We'll go slow."

"What if I don't like it? "

"We'll stop."

Daniel looked into her green cat eyes and took a deep breath. He felt her tingling energy extending toward him, her mind reaching for his again, but gently this time, asking permission. Gradually, he lowered his guard, letting his awareness join with hers. As he made love to her, he felt the delicious friction she experienced as he filled her, the tingle in her nipples as his chest slid over her breasts, the warmth of his breath on her neck, the taste of himself in her mouth. He shared the silk of her skin under his hands, the flavor of her tongue against his, and best of all, the tight hot massage she provided him as he rocked inside her. With exquisite mutual understanding, they pushed each other higher and higher, to the tipping point where they teetered together, prolonging the intense torrent of sensation as long as possible, until they fell as one, riding the wave downward in a combined sweetness reflected endlessly in the mirrors of each other's minds.

For a long while, they lay wrapped in each other's arms and minds, half-dreaming together in the warm glow of their shared awareness, weightless and free without time or place, peaceful and complete with no sense of loneliness or isolation left. He wanted to stay there forever, but even as the thought formed, he grew restless, wanting his individuality back. She withdrew, leaving him with his own thoughts.

Immediately, an old guilt returned to nag at him. "There's something I need to say. About what happened on Mars. It was my fault that you—"

She covered his mouth. "It was not anyone's fault. We each did what was expected of us. Take comfort in knowing that I am now exactly what I choose to be."

"Okay," he said, but knew he couldn't just leave it at that. "You say this is what you've chosen, but I get that this is my hot, secret fantasy, not necessarily yours, so don't feel obligated. Whatever you choose to look like will be perfectly fine with me."

"Doubtful. When I was in the form of a Nereid, it was not fine with you. Besides, I very much enjoy the way this body affects you, not to mention every other human male I encounter."

"Um, yeah . . . about that. I'm a one-on-one kind of guy. Let's not mess around with other people. Agreed?"

"Agreed." After a quiet moment, she added, "It will be interesting to see what form we choose for you."

Taken aback, he almost objected, but quickly recognized his double standard. "Guess we'll have to figure it out together."

"In shared quarters?" she asked.

He laughed, remembering their old argument. "Yes, definitely, in shared quarters."

EPILOGUE

Kowalski and Daniel sat in the captain's quarters, sharing a bottle of well-aged whiskey. After naming and toasting each member of the crew who'd been lost, they drank together in contemplative silence. Kowalski sat in one of his own visitor chairs, Daniel in the other, a gesture Daniel took as establishing them as equals. As usual the captain's quarters were pristine, the desktop empty. The fact that not so much as a digipad or stylus interrupted its surface still amazed Daniel, knowing just now much work Kowalksi did daily. His own desk was nearly always buried under stacks of whatever he was currently working on.

"You and Aurora . . . how's that going?" Kowalski asked.

Daniel's instinct was to downplay their new relationship, but he couldn't quite stop his sheepish grin. "No complaints."

Kowalski squinted at him. "I noticed your scar's gone."

Daniel rubbed his face, embarrassed. "Aurora saw it as a reminder of something painful in my past, so . . ." He shrugged.

"Remodeled anything else?"

"Nothing I'm about to show you."

Kowalski chuckled. "I can only imagine . . . looks like she finally got what she wanted, even though for a long time you made it pretty damn clear it wasn't what you wanted, and yet . . . here you are."

Daniel hesitated to share what all it took to make that happen. "Maybe I didn't really know what I wanted."

"Guess she explained it to you. And now you're like some nauseating romantic cliché, all goopy in love."

"Fuck off." Daniel wanted this conversation over. He was happy and everyone else would just have to deal with it.

Kowalski laughed. "Women. Why do they always have such a compulsion to change us? Guess that's easy enough for you to do now, but not for the rest of us. That's why I'm determined to stay a bachelor."

Only then did Daniel notice the missing wedding ring. The indentation in Kowalski's third finger still showed a line of white. "What happened?"

"Didn't I tell you? Instead of going into stasis like we agreed, my wife decided to divorce me."

"Oh. I'm sorry. I guess with all the drama, we never got around to talking about personal stuff much. Must be rough."

"Eh, just as well," the Captain said with a dismissive shrug and wave of his hand. "We were growing apart anyway. And turns out, being single and famous has its perks. I'm very popular among the ladies these days."

"You're not talking about ship groupies?" Daniel asked, making a face.

"Look, I'm an old fart with a bull-dog face. I can use all the help I can get."

"Okay, okay." Daniel raised his hands, suppressing a laugh. "Well, enjoy it while you can."

"I will, and with no apology. We'll be gone some thirty years this next time and who knows what kind of reception we'll get when we come home, assuming we come back at all. People are already questioning if what we're doing's worth it. I hear complaints about the cost, the risk, blah, blah, blah." Kowalski frowned and the lines on his face deepened, aging him beyond his fifty years. "Not much of the old pioneering spirit left. Especially, when you can play the hero in a virtual mock-up of any adventure you can imagine."

"Maybe they're the smart ones."

"No maybe about it. So who all did you get to sign up for this crazy peace mission of ours?"

"Nakiro's staying on."

"Good. Lauren?"

"No, she got a better offer."

"Too bad, she was easy on the eyes."

"This bachelor stuff is really going to your head."

"Shut up. And who's replacing Dr. McCormack?"

There was no replacing his murdered uncle, but Daniel said, "I picked his chief of surgery, Dr. Veena Patel."

"Patel?"

"You sent her running out of his office not too long ago."

Kowalski puzzled for a moment. "Oh, you mean the one with the weird butterfly tattoo on her forehead. What's that about anyway?"

"It's a cultural thing."

"And you think she's up to running the whole medical department?"

"She was Uncle Charlie's first pick, so yes."

"Patel it is then. Not that you seem to need doctoring anymore. Must be great being able to heal instantly and alter yourself any way you want."

"Sure, as long as you don't mind a few billion artificially intelligent machines taking up residence inside you for the rest of your life."

"I don't know, might be worth it."

"You're right—you don't know. These nanobots may be programmed to serve and protect, but they also have opinions about how to do that and they don't always agree. It's like overseeing a gigantic army with no officers in sight."

"Does sound a little chaotic."

"More than a little. I'm struggling to get a handle on it. Aurora's ahead of me on the learning curve, but she has plenty of trouble with it, too. That's why she's so insistent on keeping Cadmon Dhyre alive. He seemed to be in control. She's hoping he can teach us, but first we'll have to figure out how to keep him from trying to take us apart. Until then, he stays on ice and we're on our own."

"And if you find a way to work with him, you'd be okay with that? After everything he did?"

"I'll never be okay with it, but just because I despise someone doesn't mean I'm not willing to use them."

"That's cold."

"Not as cold as he is right now."

"Got that right." Kowalski lifted his glass, grinning back at Daniel. They clinked their glasses and drank.

"So, do you really believe returning the Nereids to the Garuda will end this war?" Kowalski asked.

"Chegta says it will," Daniel said, but remembered his confusion in trying to understand the images the Garuda warrior shared in their last mind-link. In those flashes of an alien world, he understood it to be dominated by loyalty and obligation combined with a sharp disapproval of humans, none of which he found reassuring. "Though it's hard to know what he's really thinking."

"Most of the time I'm pretty sure he's thinking about decapitating me," Kowalski said. "I hate that we'll have to rely on him to speak for us."

"And that's assuming he even gets the chance. They may attack us on sight."

"But we're broadcasting images of the Nereids on board with us," Kowalski countered. "If they want them back unharmed, they won't risk it. Right?"

"That's the idea. Their safety should ensure ours, at least long enough to surrender."

Kowalski froze. "Wait, did I hear you right? You want us to throw ourselves on their mercy? They hate us!"

"Yes," Daniel replied, "which is precisely why we need to. According to Chegta, it's the only way to convince them we're serious about the greater good.

"But you're not even sure you can trust him. We could all end up dead."

Daniel nodded. "A definite possibility."

Kowalski blew out a deep breath. "Now I understand why you insisted on a skeleton crew." He took another deep swallow.

Daniel set his glass down on the desk. "Devon, you don't need to go."

Kowalski smirked, set his glass beside Daniel's and leaned forward onto his elbows. "You sound like my parents. Know what I told them? I have a burning desire to explore the unknown. I was pretty full of myself, still am I suppose. I've always wanted to see things for myself, so yes, I have to go. I'm not about to give up a chance to look those Garuda bastards in the eye and demand an explanation. If these Nereids are so god damned sacred to them, why the hell didn't they just say so?"

Daniel almost laughed but restrained himself. "Have you ever asked Chegta that?"

"You bet I have."

"And his answer made no sense, right?"

Kowalski's nodded. "The son of a bitch. I think he's being obtuse on purpose."

"Maybe. Maybe not. Communication's a big challenge, even mind-to-mind. I'm working on it."

"Good luck." Kowalski smirked disdainfully and chugged the last of his whiskey.

Daniel recognized Kowalski's distrustful anger, reminded how long his own need for revenge drove him, until his intimate mental connection with Chegta turned that searing hate into an insatiable curiosity.

Aurora and I need to understand Chegta and his race far better than we do now, so we don't get blindsided. And it looks like I'll also need to keep a lid on Kowalski. I can't let him screw up this chance to make peace. Somehow, I need to get us all aligned.

"If this mission of ours has any chance of success, we'll have to work together." Daniel grabbed his glass and swallowed the rest of the whiskey in one gulp, hissing in appreciation as he set it down again. "Especially if we want to live to tell about it."

ACKNOWLEDGEMENTS

This book would not have happened without the support of:

My husband and children who put up with my late-night writing bouts till two in the morning.

San Diego Writers and Alpine Writers Guild whose members provided guidance, support and inspiration.

My editor, Shirley Clukey, who amazed me with her insight and editing expertise.

Alexander Von Ness and Ryan P. Anderson for cover art and design.

Marijke McCandless, my publisher at Wolfheart Press and fellow author.

1899

RECEIVED FEB - 4 2019